Photographs in Time

Terry Segan

ISBN-13: 978-1-7312-0207-9

DEDICATION

For the people in my life that have supported, encouraged, tolerated, endured, and, at times, even loved me, this book is for you:

Paul, Amber, Bree and Greg

ACKNOWLEDGMENTS

A special thanks to a wonderful group of writers, editors and friends:

Brenda, Glory, Jessica, Logo, and Taylor

Cover art by Bree Dagdagan

PHOTOGRAPHS IN TIME

Terry Segan

Chapter 1

Trying to reason with the distraught woman before me, I attempted a brief explanation of the process that led her to this time. "Amanda, somehow the Collector got this one wrong. All of the men are supposed to be thoroughly checked out and cleared as Suitors."

Amanda snapped her head back and glared at me. "Collector? What Collector? You're not making any sense."

"Please, we've only got minutes left. The Collector interviews and researches the history of the men for a match then I, as the Photographer, match a Betrothed with an appropriate Suitor. Somehow, the photographs got switched. I didn't know he was an imposter. Amanda, we can talk about this later. There's too much to explain. Trust me. You're in danger, Ronald isn't the man he seems to be." *Why couldn't I have found her sooner? I don't blame her for not wanting to believe me. I needed more time.*

"Amanda, honey, you have to come back with me now," I implored the young woman.

"But you said I belong here. Ronald is my perfect match. Sami, you can't dangle that in front of me then snatch it away. You just can't!"

Taking Amanda's hands in mine, I tried again, "Look at me, honey. You *must* believe me. I was wrong about Ronald. He isn't who we think he is at all. Please, we're running out of time. I had twenty-four hours to find you and time is almost up. We only have eleven more minutes."

"How could you be wrong? Ronald is a sweet and loving soul. I knew from the moment I gazed into his eyes. All I saw there was love—for me! Nobody has ever looked at me the way *he* looks at me."

"We have to leave now. I will explain more when we get back."

"Back!? Sami, I'm not going back." Panic crossed her features, and she yanked her hands out of mine. Eyes widening, she looked around as if surrounded by wild animals poised to pounce. "No. I won't lose everything."

A lock of silver hair drifted across my cheek as I risked a glance at my Timex. Tucking the strand behind my ear, I see my window slipping away. Only eight minutes left. It had to be enough.

Closing my eyes a moment, I searched for the right words to get Amanda to listen to reason—a tough sell in this already bizarre situation. I had to try. I wouldn't lose another one!

Gently, I reached out and took Amanda's hands again. I wasn't completely sure this would work, but if we stayed firmly connected, we should both be transported. Theoretically, my Collector said this would work. He himself had never done it before, but he knew of another who had tried. Unfortunately, that Collector loosened his grip at the moment of departure and only a portion of the other traveler returned with him.

Even if Amanda didn't believe me, I could keep talking and hope she wouldn't realize my plan. Suddenly the clock slowed. A moment ago, time moved swiftly, yet now when I needed it to expire, the minutes lagged. I mentally willed Amanda, *Just stay connected*.

The younger woman looked lost—the effect exaggerated with her short, oversized dress cinched in at the waist, engulfing her petite frame.

Luck had been on my side. I found Amanda at the bed and breakfast she set up residence in while being courted by Ronald. We always required the Suitor to offer a safe living space for the Betrothed for three to six months during their courtship.

Getting her alone without drawing the attention of the

innkeeper came easily. I wore an outfit befitting the time period and blended in well. We found Amanda nestled on a couch, paging through a copy of Good Housekeeping Magazine dated June 1963, the current month. It featured a picture of a woman wearing a bathing cap that looked like a head of lettuce.

Since she obviously recognized me, the proprietor had discreetly allowed us privacy and left the room.

The moments ticked down. "Honey," I played for time, "I know you had your hopes up, and this can all be set right." Only seconds remained. All I had to do was hold tight and keep her attention focused on me.

The younger woman's breathing slowed as my sense of forced serenity washed over her. The tense crinkles on Amanda's forehead smoothed.

Risking a glance at my watch, I saw the second-hand pass nine and then ten. Ten seconds to go.

"Amanda! Who is this woman?" demanded a stern looking man from the study door, his six-foot two-inch stature filling the frame. "What is she doing to you?"

Whipping her head around, Amanda snapped her hands from my grasp. "No," I screamed, as I stared into those now familiar, icy blue eyes.

A menacing smile spread across his face, looking even more demonic beneath his red hair. He mouthed the words, "You lose again."

I lunged forward in a desperate effort to grab the younger woman back to me. Despite my sixty-two years, I was as agile as I had been at forty-two. But it didn't matter. Time was up.

Chapter 2

I opened my eyes and found myself lying face down on the floor of the photography studio—alone. Engraved in my mind I saw Ronald's face, or at least Ronald was who he called himself this time. And he was right. I had lost again.

Turning my head and glancing up at the row of portraits along the wall, the same face from moments ago stared back, impassive, in the third picture from the right. For the first time, I noticed the slight cocky tilt of the subject's head and the almost wink of his left eye. If only Jimmy had looked at the photograph sooner, I never would have sent Amanda back. While the portraits on either side of Ronald's contained happy, smiling couples, his arms remained empty, as I knew they would.

Tears escaped the corners of my eyes and rolled down my cheeks. Resting my forehead on the floor, I pounded a fist on the carpet. The fullness of its fibers absorbed and muted the blow. Maybe it *was* time to retire. The risks had become too dear. These women trusted me with their lives, and now for a third time, I failed.

I sensed someone walking across the carpet toward me. Recognizing the scent of Jimmy's aftershave, I breathed it in like a healing elixir. It failed to soothe me in my present state.

"It didn't work," he said flatly.

"I had her. Jimmy, I had her! Amanda's hands were firmly in

4

mine." I sobbed and struck the floor again.

He knew when to be quiet and let me collect my thoughts. With them scattered across the universe, this could take a while. As I rolled over and sat up on the floor, I watched him cross the room and sit on the overstuffed couch against the wall. He quietly waited for me to go on. My lord, that man had the patience of a saint!

"She wasn't convinced," I finally said.

"You didn't think she would give in easily, did you?"

"I didn't care if she did or not. All I had to do was hang on to her until time was up! With only seconds to spare, Ronald appeared."

Jimmy reminded me, "You mean Carney. Ronald is the persona he stepped into for that meeting."

"Did you ever find out what happened to the *real* Ronald Hauptman?"

"Not a trace. With no immediate family, there wasn't anybody to go looking either. Carney may have set up the man's exit before leaving that time period. Even in the sixties, records weren't always accurate."

Slowly rising to my feet, I went over to sit beside him. He wrapped his arm around my shoulders and kissed the top of my head as I rested against his chest. Once again, I breathed in his aftershave. It had a fresh scent that reminded me of clean ocean air, though I couldn't remember the name of it right now.

Jimmy's hand massaged my shoulder, trying to loosen the stiffness. I leaned heavier into him and tried to let his warmth comfort me. Like the scent of his aftershave, however, it wouldn't work. I couldn't escape the thoughts in my head that I sent another woman to her death. "I feel like I'm as much of a predator as Carney. Different methods with the same result."

"Sami, don't even think that. What we do has apparently been around for decades. Maybe even centuries. How can those in charge allow it to continue if it were wrong?"

"Those in charge? How can you say that?" I asked, sitting back and meeting his gaze. "We don't even know *who* is in charge. We don't know how this whole process came into being. For all we know, it was created to spread evil."

"I don't believe that," Jimmy told me. "You don't believe that either, otherwise you would never have agreed to be a part of this process."

Had I ever really agreed? Or was I so infatuated with the man sitting beside me that I would have done anything to remain at his side? After he told me his fantastic story of how he became a Collector and needed a partner, I leapt and never looked back. While my dreams of love were fulfilled, did I have the right to meddle with the lives of others thinking I knew best for them too?

Returning to the present, I asked Jimmy, "Were you able to find anything about Amanda in the archives?"

"No. But now that you're back, we'll have to look again since...". He drifted off mid-sentence, rubbing my shoulders.

I finished it for him, "...since I had the chance to save her, but didn't."

"That wasn't what I was going to say!" His furrowed brows showed disappointment.

"Not quite that way," I looked into his vibrant blue eyes. Their color and oval shape had always intrigued me as his heritage was a mix of Chinese and Cherokee Indian. Jimmy broke the gaze and looked down. No matter how kindly he could have worded it, it meant the same. I had the chance to change her fate and failed. "You never told me how you know Carney."

He put both hands on his knees and fidgeted with the fabric of his trousers before replying. "I told you, Sami, he's just another Collector like me. He got recruited by the same Frenchman." Despite his nonchalant attitude, I felt there was more to this than he would admit. He didn't usually hold things back from me.

"That much you told me," I pushed, "but there's more, isn't there?"

"Please, Sami, I feel bad enough we couldn't help Amanda."

"*Save* Amanda. You mean *save* Amanda. She wouldn't have needed help if we'd never meddled in her life."

"Honey, this is what we do. We've helped many couples find love and happiness."

"Yes, but this is not a *business*. We don't calculate the wins, then chalk it up to an occasional corporate loss when it means the loss of a life, especially when the life of a vibrant, living being is snuffed out simply because we thought we could help her find love."

"Don't you think I know that?" Jimmy stared at me again as I heard the escalation in his voice—the hurt obvious on his taut face.

"I'm sorry. I do believe you know that. It just hurts that this is the third time a woman has died. We should have stopped after the second one. After we knew it wasn't a fluke, but the deliberate intention of Carney to kill them. Do you think it's only *our* matches he's targeting?"

Again, Jimmy answered me while staring down at the ground. "I don't know." He wanted to say more yet wouldn't release the words. We'd been together too long for me to misread his attempts at sheltering me from something bad.

We sat in silence for a while. Both of us knew our next step but didn't want to take it. Not able to sit idle any longer, I got up and headed for the door.

"Where are you going?"

I turned for a moment but decided words weren't necessary. My feet moved toward the office again.

"Let me do it," he said as he stood to follow.

"Jimmy, whether I look up what happened to Amanda or you, the result will still be the same. You can't shelter me from this one."

"Can't I spare you the details of…"

My determined glare stopped him cold.

"All right," he acquiesced. "My laptop is at my townhouse anyway. Go pull up the news from that week in 1963."

Despite knowing the result, I couldn't stop myself. It would be horrible, but I needed to see the full scope of my failure. I owed it to Amanda, the one who endured it—the kind soul who entrusted me with her future. By sending her to the past, I had led her to her death.

Heading into my office, I noticed the message light flashing on my answering machine. I saw there were two messages. Deciding to put off my research by a few more moments, I hit the playback button.

The first message was left yesterday, only an hour after I traveled back to find Amanda. The chilling voice on the machine numbed me to the bone. "Hello, my sweet Samantha. Lost again, did you? Well, that's ancient history now, isn't it?" I heard a brief chuckle. "Don't concern yourself with Amanda. I took *really* good

7

care with her. But if you must torture yourself, as I know you will, I suggest you check out the following week of your visit. There you will find a good read in the San Francisco Chronicle. Au revoir for now, dear. Oh, and give Jimmy my regards, will you?"

I froze, not sure I wanted to power up my laptop after all. As the debate raged in my head, the second message, from only forty-five minutes ago, played.

This time I heard a woman's voice. "Hi, Sami. It's Dede. We met on the beach a couple of mornings ago? Well, I've thought a lot about what we talked about and you're right. I do need a bit of fun. I was thinking of coming to your studio tomorrow afternoon as we discussed. Say about two o'clock? Really looking forward to it! I checked out your website and your photographs look like fun. Okay, if I don't hear from you otherwise, I'll see you then!"

Chapter 3

An hour after I shut down my computer, Jimmy found me sitting on the front porch in one of the big wicker chairs. Carrying two glasses of Malbec, he handed me one, then sat down. He had left me alone while I did my research on Amanda.

Sitting in the weakening rays of the late afternoon sun, we gazed out towards the ocean for a few minutes. My house sat up on a hill in Palos Verdes with a fantastic view, yet I didn't see a thing. My eyes refused to focus.

"Did you find her?"

"Yes. The authorities found her floating in the harbor near Pier 39." The monotone of my voice echoed feelings of sorrow and defeat. "She was reported missing by her fiancé, Ronald Hauptman, two days prior."

"Sami, it isn't your fault," he said quietly, placing his hand over mine.

"I'm not up for this argument again." My voice didn't rise above a whisper. "It's all our fault."

We sat in silence as the scent of the ocean encompassed us. Several hundred feet below the waves slapped the beach in a steady rhythm. I loved being close to the ocean. Every night, through the open windows of my bedroom, the sound of the surf lulled me to sleep. I knew it wouldn't tonight.

Bracing myself for the rest of what I discovered in the office, I broke the silence. "He was on the answering machine."

"What? Who?"

"Carney. He's taunting us." My voice got higher and shrill. "Why would he do that? Why would he do any of this?" I sipped my wine and rested my head against the back of the chair. Glancing over, I looked at him as my pulse raced.

Taking a sip himself, Jimmy closed his eyes and leaned back also. I knew this burden weighed on him. There was more to Carney he hadn't shared.

"Tell me. The time for sheltering is over." My gaze hardened. "We're in this together and I can't continue without knowing the truth." Leaning closer to him, I demanded, "You owe me an explanation."

His eyes widened, and he turned my way. "I'm the one that brought you into this. It's my burden, not yours."

"No. It's too late for that. It's *ours*."

"Sweetie, you don't understand how hard this is for me."

Placing my hand on his arm, I said, "And you don't understand how hard it is for me not knowing." The warmth of his tan skin radiated through me. "You have to tell me. It's no longer only yours to bear. I can't begin to figure this out if I don't know all the facts. Please." His gaze met mine, and I saw resolution in it.

"You're right. It's time you know everything. I'd hoped to spare you the history and the horror, but I see that's no longer an option." His fingers wrapped tighter around my hand.

I squeezed back in encouragement.

Withdrawing his hand and wrapping it around the bowl of the wine glass with the other, he began. "Remember the story I told you of how I became a Collector?"

"Yes. The Frenchman came into your grandfather's antique shop where you worked sometimes. He's the Collector that passed this on to you."

"Correct. But that isn't entirely true."

"Which part?" I sat up removing my hand from his arm. A gusty breeze swept across the porch rattling the window screens as if to emphasize my feelings of betrayal that Jimmy had lied to me.

"How I met him. The Frenchman, that is. He'd come into my grandfather's shop, not in search of me, but to see my father. He had been chosen to become a Collector. My father refused. It was right around the time he met my mother."

"So, you weren't even born yet?"

"Will you let me tell this, please? No interruptions. It's hard enough."

I softened a little, yet the hurt of his misleading me lingered. He sensed it even before I spoke. "Okay, honey, go on." We'd been together too long not to read each other's moods.

"Thank you." Narrowing the lids of his eyes, he took a deep breath then continued to speak quietly. "My father wasn't interested in being a Collector, but agreed to stock the film slides needed to make the matches possible."

Jumping in, risking another interruption, I said, "I just have to ask," Jimmy hesitated, yet nodded for me to go on. "How did you know this? You said your father died when you were a teenager."

"I'll get to that. It's part of the history I'm about to reveal. Let me tell it in order. This happened so long ago, and I need to keep it straight in my own head. Maybe we'll discover an overlooked detail that can help us now."

As I settled back into the wicker chair, it creaked like the sound of breaking twigs as I shifted my weight. With a quiet sigh and a gulp of wine, I waited for Jimmy to continue. Maybe he should have brought the bottle out.

"I did meet the Frenchman myself years later while stationed in Viet Nam." He hesitated a moment, "With Carney."

"What? How could you keep that secret?"

"Please. You promised."

I didn't know whether to be angry or sad that he hadn't told me. It didn't matter. Jimmy no longer had the luxury of withholding information, good or bad. I needed the entire truth.

He took a ragged breath. I could tell the guilt raked at his soul by the way he wouldn't look me in the eye.

"Carney and I were friends. We grew up in the same neighborhood in San Francisco but didn't know each other until boot camp, when all this began."

He paused.

I waited.

"In boot camp, we were bunk mates. What are the odds? Most of the guys in our unit were from all over this United States. Carney and I grew up a few blocks apart. Went to the same high school but didn't really know each other. When you grow up in a big city, the world stops at the end of your block—at least when you're a kid.

"But drastic times and all that rot. You know how it goes. A year after my father died, my grandfather told me about the film plates. Being young and knowing *everything,* I thought he was crazy—but he knew. He knew I would get mixed up in it eventually. I used to think a warning would have been nice as to what else it would entail, but it probably wouldn't have mattered." A smile flickered across his face. He always had a soft spot for his grandfather. The death of Jimmy's father had taken its toll on them both.

Jimmy sipped at his wine. "Carney and I became inseparable friends. Oh, the trouble we got into on leave! This one time…" He smiled as he remembered the incident he was about to recount, then stopped. A stony look covered his face as he set his jaw in a scowl. "It doesn't matter. Not important."

"Yes, it is important," I insisted. "Tell me about the good times too."

"Doesn't matter. Not given what's happened. We were friends. Leave it at that."

"Okay. Tell me what I need to know." I reached out and rubbed his arm in encouragement.

"We ended up in Nam—just like every other guy in the Army at that time. We saw our share of action. Lost friends. Same old story that's been told before."

"Why do you do that? It mattered. Don't belittle that. It *is* one of the many accomplishments in your life."

"Sorry, you're right. I get so jaded about the whole time. Not so much about the politics, but what happened to us personally. Carney and me. You know how he got the name Carney?"

"No. Tell me."

"He loved carnivals and the circus. Animals, zoos, the whole bit. That came out in boot camp. We started calling him Carney, and it stuck. His real name was Todd. Todd Merchant. But everyone knew him as Carney.

"Anyway, it happened after another white-knuckle day. We thought we'd see fighting, but thankfully, were wrong. After the first couple of skirmishes, nobody was keen on seeing action. The blood and gore got old fast." Jimmy grimaced as if he'd tasted something sour. "He and I got separated from the unit and stumbled across an old stone temple. Not unusual in the Asian jungles. This one had elephants carved all over the outside. It was astounding! We dubbed it Carney's Temple. Walking around it, we found the entrance and cleared enough of the overgrowth to squeeze through.

"The jungle had mostly reclaimed it. Looked as if nobody ventured inside for decades. Vines and foliage grew all over the open entry and most of the outside. Honestly, we probably wouldn't have noticed it at all had I not tripped. Trying to catch my fall, I grabbed a vine that pulled away to reveal the stonework. The structure stood about twenty feet high and a hundred square feet around. We thought maybe it was a mausoleum or shrine.

"We went inside to explore. We should have been searching for our unit, but at times like that, you took any distraction you could get. No matter the risk."

I leaned forward and touched his arm. "It was an abandoned temple. How much risk could there be?"

"There could have been enemy soldiers inside or a hidden trap. Ancient relics or human life meant nothing to those bastards! They would blow anything up in a heartbeat if it meant killing a few Americans. Instead, we got a surprise that changed our lives forever." Jimmy paused took a sip of wine, then covered my hand with his. "*All* of our lives."

Chapter 4

Jimmy continued, "Luck was on our side that day—or so we thought. Finding the entrance empty, we ventured further inside. Elephant carvings and figures of men covered the walls of the small shrine. They meant nothing to us. A tunnel on the far side of the chamber spiraled downward to a gallery with doorways off each side. We passed them, choosing to see where this passage ended first.

"We inched our way along the walls as the daylight from above faded. Being cautious, we didn't want to light a match.

"As we rounded a bend in the tunnel, a glow of light seeped into the darkness. Shadows danced on the wall ahead. Wary of a possible second entryway, our weapons came up at the ready as we neared the next turn.

"We heard the crackle of a fire echoing off the walls of the cavern. In the silence of the darkness, the noise sounded louder than it should have. The smell of burning twigs grew stronger as we approached.

"Peering in carefully, we discovered an old man sitting beside a low-burning campfire. We knew he couldn't be a local; he was white. Didn't eliminate the possibility of a threat. He wore a pair of khakis and a worn, denim shirt with the sleeves rolled up to the elbows. His leather boots looked as if he'd marched hundreds of miles in them. Maybe he had since he was sitting in the middle of a jungle.

"You could tell this guy had some years on him as his face looked as leathery and worn as his boots, yet his hair was mostly black with just a touch of silver. Even more bizarre, he was drinking tea. Can you believe it? He sat in a camp chair holding a steaming cup, as if at a café on the Champs Elysees."

"You found the Frenchman," I said.

"Yes. He looked at us, smiled and said 'You're late. My 24 hours is almost up and we have a lot of information to cover.' Carney and I looked at each other, then back at the stranger. That's when Carney pinched me. The bastard pinched me! I jumped and asked him why. He said he needed to make sure this was real." Jimmy chuckled.

By the tone in his voice, I could tell Jimmy would remember that life-changing moment until the end of time.

"The man spoke English with a soft French accent, the lilt of his voice almost mesmerizing.

"'Are you for real?' Carney asked him.

"The Frenchman responded with a nod. 'Sit. Share some tea. Quickly though. As I said, you are late, and my time is nearly spent.'

"The whole scene threw us both off balance, so we did as we were told, despite our building curiosity. The Frenchman filled two more tin cups with tea from the pot on the fire and handed us each one. Cupping my hand around the metal, it felt almost too hot to hold.

"It struck me—maybe he *was* waiting for us. Most guys only carried one spare while camping alone. How could he know he'd need two? For all we knew, it could have been laced with arsenic. Carney just shrugged, tipped his cup in a toast, as if to say, 'what the hell' and we drank.

"Carney acted this way in most situations; dive in and see what happens. Me? I followed. Blindly at times, but I always knew it would be a fun ride with him. At least that's what I hoped. Didn't always turn out that way…"

Jimmy's voice drifted off. He sat quietly lost in thought. After several moments he raked his hand through his hair, turned and looked at me. It was as if he suddenly realized I still sat next to him on a porch in Southern California, not a cave in Viet Nam. As

Jimmy's eyes re-focused, he continued his story.

"'Listen,' the man said, 'for this is your time. It wasn't clear whether I would receive one or two. You are both here, so that is how it shall be.' Carney and I looked at each other, then back at the Frenchman. He didn't offer a name. He didn't ask ours. 'I am a Collector. It is time to pass the job to another. You are friends, yes?' We nodded. Maybe the tea made us submit, or perhaps the need for any distraction in that nightmare country. Either way, we both welcomed his words with open arms.

"The Frenchman continued. 'I am leaving the arena, and it is your turn to take over. Only one of you may choose to do this or neither. You always have the choice. However, if you decide to embrace the role of Collector, you must follow through with all your duties. Fulfill your quota of thirty couples, regardless of how long it may take. Leaving the matches unfinished could have serious consequences. Going beyond your quota is allowed, but never be short. Using the tools inappropriately could also have a dire effect.'

"He paused to take a sip of tea. From the deep creases in his face, I thought the conversation might be a strain on him. Carney looked at me, then back at the old man. 'What the *hell* are you talking about? Collector? Quota? Tools? Have you been dabbling a bit too much with the weed, old man?'"

Jimmy chuckled again. "Leave it to Carney to state the obvious. We were both thinking it. As usual, he took the initiative to voice it out loud."

"'Well put, young man. I wondered when one of you would find his voice again. Wasn't sure if I was getting through. Thank you for the confirmation! I believe you may be familiar with some of this?' He must have known my grandfather had tried to tell me about his role in the process, but I wasn't buying into it. Carney glanced my way.

"He continued, 'When this war is over, you will go to New York City. In case you were wondering, the answer is yes, you will both survive the ordeal here. In Chinatown you will find two old antique shops much like your grandfather's in San Francisco,' he said looking at me again. 'They are The Golden Dragon and The Purple Lotus. Ask the proprietor for the set of sepia plates left by the last Collector. Phrase it exactly that way—left by the last

Collector. They will give them to you at no charge and instruct you in their use. Listen carefully and don't stray from the rules."

I nodded. "So, he passed the baton to you and Carney." I knew the sequence as he'd told me about it when we'd first met. The previous Collector chose a new protégé then the new Collector found his own Photographer. Most times the process only passed on to one. Very rarely were two new Collectors chosen when one retired. Nobody knew how many other Collectors were out there working. With jumping back and forth through time and on seven continents, there could be several. Or there could only be one, or two in this case.

Jimmy set his empty wine glass on the table. "Yes. I embraced the idea completely, realizing Grandfather knew the path. I thought maybe he was preparing me to be a keeper of the film plates like my father. Now I believe he aided my becoming a Collector since my father turned it down. He never told me how he knew. Actually, he never told me much of anything, just hinted. That was his way. Drop a few clues then leave you to figure things out on your own. So, Carney and I listened to the rest of what the Frenchman had to say. I sensed Carney wasn't quite buying into it, but the Frenchman knew I believed. He told us of how the sepias worked to connect couples over the decades."

Gently squeezing his hand, I said, "You told me how it worked when we first met. Maybe you should go through it all anyway, to be sure we both have all the details."

"Good idea. As I originally explained, the first step involved a set of thirty, brown-framed sepias for the Collector to go back in time and interview the Suitor, the husband to be. The Suitors were already chosen; he didn't explain by whom. The sepia slide allows the Collector to go back for twenty-four hours, one time only.

"The next set belonged to the Photographer: three for each Suitor—two used by the Betrothed, or bride to be, and one emergency slide if needed by the Photographer. Each frame is color-coded, designating it's use. The Photographer finds an appropriate woman for a union and matches her with a Suitor based on the information gathered by the Collector. Only the Collector and Photographer were to know how the time travel really worked."

I placed my hands in my lap, reviewing what Jimmy said.

"Okay, so far everything is the same as the first time you explained it to me." Tucking a stray hair behind my ear, I couldn't help but smile at the thought of the first time I heard this explanation. How young we both were.

"The yellow-framed slide sends the Betrothed back for one day. The second, which is blue, enables her final journey back into the past for a life with the Suitor. No returning to the present once she went back to the same time twice. Arriving within a thirty-day window either before or after the original date leaves a person permanently in the past.

"The red-framed sepia slide remained for emergency only. If the Photographer needed to go back in case anything came up, she would use it for a twenty-four-hour period of her choosing, within the second to fourth week after the Betrothed's arrival. Rarely were these slides used." Jimmy stood up and walked to the edge of the porch, looking out to the bay below.

He needed to go through the whole thing for his own sanity. After thirty years together, I knew how his thought process worked. He needed to say the details out loud.

Moments later when he returned, the chair creaked as he settled into it. Reaching his hand out to me, we intertwined our fingers, and he gave a squeeze before continuing. "Occasionally, the Betrothed chose not to go back on a second journey. That still counted as a match, despite it not being successful. Neither the Suitor nor the Betrothed get a second chance. It's all or nothing. One time only.

"One caveat applied to the Photographer and Collector as well. They could only go back to a certain time for a single journey. If they traveled back to the same time twice, they would be trapped permanently in that era with no possibility of returning to their original time frame.

"The Frenchman stressed the importance of it all then vanished—mid-sentence!"

"His twenty-four hours was up, wasn't it?" I already knew the answer, but still asked.

"Yes," said Jimmy. "At that point, Carney started to think there might be a kernel of truth in his story. The guy vanished before our eyes. We both agreed he couldn't fake that. We decided to tell no one in our unit; they'd think we smoked too much weed.

Maybe we should've been smoking instead." He squeezed my hand again, "Despite all this, the process led me to you. It was all worth it."

Jimmy gazed into my eyes then leaned over and kissed my lips.

My face flushed with warmth, the way it always did at his touch. *Damn I loved that man!* He saw past the tragedy and mystery surrounding us and the lives we'd touched, only to focus on how it brought us together. I couldn't fault him for that. I treasured our love and life together, yet guilt gnawed at the edges of my happiness. How could I be so selfish when lives had been lost because of us? I struggled with that moral question. No acceptable answer came to mind.

"What happened next?"

"Nothing."

"Nothing?"

"Well, nothing worthwhile. Carney and I chose to not talk about what happened. We instinctively knew to steer clear of a conversation on that subject while still in Nam. The war went on. Our time there ended, with both of us still alive, as predicted."

"Maybe it would have been better if he hadn't survived," I stated angrily, rising to stare out at the ocean.

The oaken boards creaked as he came up behind me, wrapping his arms around my waist. "Don't fall into his trap, Sami. Even your wishing him dead is wrong."

Wrapping my arms over his, I settled back into his embrace. "Carney deserves to die. He's evil. He killed innocent women."

"Yes," he said, "but still…" His voice trailed off.

One point of the story nagged at me. Turning in his arms to face him, I wrapped my arms around his neck. "Jimmy, did the Frenchman ever tell you what he meant by consequences for not fulfilling your quota or using the tools inappropriately?"

He whispered, "We never asked."

"Something else is disturbing about Carney. How can he pass for a man in his mid-forties? He's about the same age as you but doesn't look to be in his sixties. You don't quite look your age either," I stared into his blue eyes, "but I wouldn't think forties. Sorry, hon."

"No worries," he smiled then pulled me in closer. "I don't

know the answer to that one. I've known for a while I'm not aging at a normal rate. I can't explain why."

Chapter 5

Sleep eluded me as Jimmy's revelations swirled in my memory. While he wanted to stay, I told him I needed to be alone. After revealing his story to me, it had been well past dark. He returned to his townhouse in Santa Monica.

Knowing he and Carney had been friends complicated things for me.

As much as I wanted to push my sweet man for more information, I knew by the tired creases around his eyes he was spent for the evening. His story had us sitting on the porch well past dinner time. Telling me the truth about the Frenchman took its toll. The rest would have to hold off until this evening when he came back here for dinner. I asked him to come earlier, but he said he needed to look into a few things. Again, I didn't push. I knew he would tell me when he was ready.

My mind refused to shut down as I skated through the mundane chores of laundry and cleaning the house. Taking a teacup from the cupboard, I dropped a bag into it, leaving the string hanging over the side. As I sat it on the kitchen table, the gears in my head kept spinning. I knew we needed to stop. I also knew we hadn't completed our quota of thirty couples. Three more to go. What if we don't finish? Had Carney quit before fulfilling his quota? Was that why he'd turned against us?

The ringing of the doorbell dragged me out of the turmoil in my mind. It suddenly hit me Dede was coming for a photo session. Time had escaped me. Despite offering to confirm, she didn't leave a return number. I would have called and canceled the session or at least postponed it. After hearing both messages yesterday, I had hit delete without thinking and erased her number from the memory.

Opening the door, I was glad I hadn't canceled. Dede stood on the porch with a huge smile on her face. "Hi, Sami! I hope this is a good time?"

Doing my best to shake off the current worries, I replied, "Of course, it is! I'm so glad you decided to come over."

I stood back while opening the door wider for her to come in. She had the same reaction most people did walking into my house for the first time—wide-eyed, trying to take in everything at once. I lived in a large, Victorian-style home and did my best to furnish it that way to a point. A mix of both modern and old-style furnishings blended well together.

"Did you have any trouble finding me?" I asked.

"Not at all. I checked out your website like you suggested, and the directions were easy as pie. This place is amazing! Did you furnish it yourself or hire a decorator?" I could see the awe in her eyes.

"Actually, it's always a work in progress. I've been decorating it for the last 35 years," I laughed. "Never seems to be finished." I viewed my place with new eyes, trying to see it as this young woman might. Sometimes it took someone else to wake you up and put a different angle on things.

Dede wore blue jeans and a pink t-shirt. Her long black hair, which had been flowing wildly when I last saw her, was tamed into a long braid resting down her back. While not a heavy woman, she was a little plump, yet carried it with ease. What really struck me was the absolute glow in her gray eyes. She had a thirst for life.

The whistle of the kettle let me know it had reached boiling. "I was about to have a cup of tea. Would you like one before we get started?"

"That sounds delightful. My mom and I used to enjoy a cup of Earl Grey together."

"What a coincidence. That's my favorite."

Dede smiled and followed me to the kitchen. I grabbed another cup and dropped a bag of Earl Grey into it. While I poured the hot water, she said, "I already feel at home here."

"Then my work is more than half done. I'm glad you're enjoying yourself."

"Very much so, thank you!" She cast her eyes downward, "Honestly, I don't have many friends."

"A beautiful and outgoing woman like yourself? I find that hard to believe."

Raising her chin back up, she said, "Thank you. It's just that I prefer the solitude of my studio to company most times. Don't get me wrong; I love spending time with friends. Most women have so much drama or babble incessantly, that I get bored. That's kinda snobbish, isn't it?"

"Not at all. I prefer well-grounded people to flighty ones myself."

Dede smiled appreciatively. I guessed she didn't come across many people that embraced her candor. In a comfortable silence we dunked our tea bags up and down to extract the flavor.

With my hands wrapped around my cup, I asked, "So what do you like to do with your free time? I know you said you worked as a manager in a florist shop. Is that your passion?"

"Flowers? No, but I do like creating artistic bouquets. It's the closest I come to my real passion—sculpting and pottery. I love working with clay. Actually, I'm quite good at it! Just not in a position to open my own shop and haven't found a job even close to using my skills."

"That truly is a talent. What's holding you back from opening your own place?"

"Well, Sami, I'm not independently wealthy."

We both laughed.

"It does take a bit of saving. I had to do that with this place."

"Then you understand what I mean," she said.

"Absolutely. Starting your own business is quite risky, but it can also be very rewarding when you're able to make a living of it. You'll get there."

"I believe I will," Dede replied.

After a few moments, I ventured into the line of questioning to evaluate her as a Betrothed. "So, tell me, Dede, what is it you want out of your life? It's obvious your artwork is important to you. What else?"

She stared into her teacup, as if for guidance. Slowly she looked up at me, with her eyes almost watering. "Family," she said. "I want to start a family if ever I could find the right man—one that understands my passion for creating as well as being a mother. I've always thought I would be a great mom."

There it was. The reason why I'd been drawn to Dede down on the beach. She craved a way to continue with her craft while living life as a wife and mother. It was within my power to help her with that. Would I be able to do that successfully without hindrance?

"Dede," I proceeded cautiously. This was always the critical moment I dreaded—running the risk of having a potential Betrothed bolt away screaming. "What would you say if I could give you what you wanted?"

She hesitated a moment, then responded, "I would say I'm confused—but intrigued. What are you talking about? Do you have a nephew you want to set me up with?"

I loved her candor. "Something like that. Want to know more?" I left that thought dangling.

Dede raised her teacup to her lips and took a long sip. Holding the cup a moment, she looked at me then set it back down on the table. "Okay, I'll bite. Tell me more."

That simple statement conveyed skepticism and hope. I pressed, like usual, when trying to persuade a potential Betrothed to have an open mind. It didn't seem I would have too far to push with this one.

When the tea was done and the dirty cups put in the sink, I said, "Let's take a stroll through my studio. There are a couple of things I'd like to show you."

Chapter 6

Dede followed me down the hall to my studio. Once inside, she stopped to examine the portraits of couples lining the walls. "These people look very happy. Are they customers of yours?"

"Yes, in a way."

She glanced at me with her brows arched in an inquisitive look.

"Actually, the women were."

"It's usually the women that like this sort of stuff. The men just go along with it."

"Well," I hesitated, "not always. I'd say the women were customers because I knew them better than the men. Most times I didn't really meet the men, but they were part of this."

"Okay, is it me, or have you started talking in riddles? You're beginning to sound like a fortune cookie with vague suggestions. Give it to me straight, Sami."

I decided she would either take what I said at face value or leave. Either way, the opportunity was hers to embrace or walk away. "I appreciate your directness. So, I'll treat you with the same respect. I'm a Photographer." Dede opened her mouth to reply, but I put up my hand. "Yes, you already know that. But you don't. I have a special job. Not just to take pictures, but to help match women with men who are looking for the same thing. I guess you could say I'm a match-maker."

"You mean like a Yenta?" she laughed.

"In a way. But I'm not Jewish." Now we both giggled. "I do help couples to meet, and there is a man I think would be a good match for you, if you're interested. His portrait is over here."

She followed me across the room to a line-up of three portraits. I pointed to one of a man with long blond hair pulled back in a pony-tail and dressed in a light blue denim shirt and jeans. The top three buttons were undone revealing a silver necklace in the shape of a blazing sun with a turquoise stone set in the center. He looked to be about forty years old.

Pointing at his open shirt, Dede said, "That's a beautiful necklace he's wearing. Turquoise is my favorite. And his eyes. They have a very caring look to them. What's his name?"

I was sure she hadn't missed his good looks. One of the first comments she made were about his eyes. I've always believed you could tell a lot about a person by that one facial feature. It made me more confident in this match.

"His name is Milton Freeman."

"Milton." She mulled the name over. "He strikes me as someone who would never shorten it to Milty or Milt."

Once more she jibed with him perfectly. When Jimmy interviewed the man, one of the questions he asked Milton was if he went by a nick name. His response had been "never."

"No," I responded. "Like you, he's an artist—a painter. He recreates extraordinary desert landscapes."

"Does he live in Southern California?"

"No, he's close to Albuquerque, New Mexico. Milton has a large plot of land in the desert. I guess you could say he lives on a homestead. His studio is a huge barn-type structure. He takes inspiration from the land around him, capturing numerous slopes and buttes on canvas."

Dede inhaled deeply, focused on the image. "I can easily picture a paint brush in his hand. The deep tan on his face tells me he's spent quite a bit of time outside." She stepped closer to the frame and put her hand up to the portrait. Stopping just short of touching it, she turned to me, "May I?"

"Of course, dear. It's a picture. It's not fragile."

Turning back to the portrait, she touched Milton's arm then traced down it. With her fingertips poised against his knuckle, she closed her eyes, as if willing his hand to come to life.

Opening her eyes and taking a step back Dede said, "Sorry. I was just..." Her face flushed lightly as if embarrassed.

"Never be afraid to follow your instincts. You were imagining the possibilities. I do that quite often myself."

I had to help this woman realize her dreams. It was worth the risk. This match, without a doubt, had to happen.

"Would you like to meet him?"

"Yes, I believe I would," she said, never taking her eyes off the portrait. "Is he in town?"

"Tell you what. Come back here tomorrow, say about 10:00, and we'll go from there."

Giving me a sideways look, she said, "You didn't really answer my question."

"Oh, but I did. Now don't get all fancied up or anything. Come just as you are, and I believe you will be quite pleased."

"If I'm going to meet Milton, I wouldn't dream of dressing any other way. I believe we accomplished the goal of this meeting, didn't we?"

I nodded.

"Thank you, Sami."

"You're welcome. I'll walk you out."

Down the hall and out the door, the smile never left Dede's face. Even though I didn't explain much of the meeting process, I knew we'd covered enough.

As I retraced my steps down the hallway, I glanced into my office. The answering machine sat innocently on the desk. While no blinking light indicated a message, the one from last night replayed in my mind. Carney's words haunted me. It wasn't only what he said but the menacing tone in his voice, the way he spoke my name and Jimmy's.

Several hours remained before Jimmy returned. With so much to talk about, I knew it would be an emotional evening. My stomach churned as I braced for the night's conversation.

For right now I forced myself to dwell on happy thoughts of Dede and Milton. Their potential meeting felt right, and I knew it would be a success. At least I hoped it would be.

Chapter 7

"Mmmmm, that smells delicious!" Jimmy said as he came into the kitchen. "One of my favorites *and* a bottle of Zin. Thank you, sweetie."

As I put the finishing touches on a pot of jambalaya, he rewarded me with a kiss on the cheek.

"I thought we could use a break. Open the wine; dinner is almost done."

Throughout the meal, we avoided talking about the problems. We didn't talk much at all, just enjoyed each other's company. Jimmy suggested a walk after savoring his last sip of wine.

Hand in hand we sauntered down the hill to the strand that ran along the beach. I braced myself to bring up the subject. Anxiety pulsed through me.

I squeezed his hand. "What do you think happened to turn Carney against you? Or into what he is now?"

A few moments elapsed before Jimmy answered. "He broke the rules. He used the slides for personal gain."

"How?" I asked, stopping to turn towards him.

With the slightest of tugs on Jimmy's part, we began walking again. "He used it to secure his Photographer."

That seemed odd. The way he phrased it. "What do you mean by *secure*? Did he send her back in time so they would meet in an earlier year? That doesn't seem like a misuse of the slides. How is it any different than us sending Betrotheds back in time to meet their mates?"

"It's the way he went about it."

"What do you mean?"

"*He* traveled back. Carney went through time for April. That was her name."

"So, you've met her?"

"Yes. Carney and I were still friends. Actually, the three of us became quite close." As we strolled, the waves lapping against the sand echoed softly in the background. I noticed a soft smile on Jimmy's face. "I have many happy memories of that time."

"Tell me about her."

"There's so much to tell. April was an amazing woman. Such a beautiful soul. You rarely find that in people." Stopping and facing me, he leaned down and placed a tender kiss on my lips. "A soul as beautiful as yours."

Despite our years together, he could still take my breath away. I felt a blush rise on my cheeks. "Are they still together?"

His smile slipped away. In a flat voice, he said, "No. She's dead." Still holding my hand, Jimmy turned back to the path to continue our walk.

Such a powerful memory had to be the key to everything. Maybe Jimmy tried to make things right, yet it remained beyond his reach.

"What does all this have to do with Carney's misusing the slides? Was April supposed to be a Betrothed?"

"No. For all I know, she should never have been part of the process. It happened about a year after we each secured our box of slides in New York City. Carney went to the Golden Dragon, while I retrieved mine from the Purple Lotus. Our respective shop owners explained how to go back in time and interview the pre-chosen Suitors. We were told there was no rush to find a Photographer until we got to know all thirty. Without getting a sense of each man first, we were advised that we should hold off on making matches."

"You didn't meet me until four years later," I interjected. "By then your interviews had been finished for over a year."

He spoke as if in a fog—his thoughts far away. "I know."

"So, Carney met April a year after the two of you began? He

didn't waste much time. Were his interviews complete?"

"No. He wasn't even a third of the way through them. Carney and I shared an apartment in San Francisco. I was going to law school and working as a waiter. Carney worked in a men's clothing store while studying for a psychology degree."

Their sharing an apartment hit me hard. I should be over his hiding the great friendship between the two men. Still, every time I learned a new nugget of information, it felt like a punch to the stomach.

Jimmy sighed and raked a hand through his hair. "I'm sorry— more secrets. I'm asking for your patience."

"I know. I'm trying," I said, looking out at the ocean.

"The memory of their meeting is so clear in my mind. Carney and I were out at one of those trendy bars in downtown San Francisco called Liquid Stylings. April came in alone and sat down at the bar. With a smile and a nod, the bartender placed a glass of red wine in front of her. April looked to be about twenty-five, with blond hair and pale skin. We moved right in and began talking to her. Both of us found the young lady attractive, yet she acted like she didn't notice or care."

Jimmy's lips curved up. I could see he had been quite smitten with April. It must have been a hard blow when she chose Carney over him.

"So, she chose Carney."

Jimmy raked a free hand through his hair again. "Not exactly. You see, while we all hit it off, she and the bartender, Tony, were engaged. That's why she sat alone at the bar."

"She broke her engagement to be with Carney?" I continued to guess.

The smile flitted away again. "No. We sat at that bar talking with her. She was intriguing to listen to. She attended classes in archeology at the local college. Not to become an archeologist, but because it fascinated her. When Tony got off at midnight, he joined us for a round before the two of them left. They were very much in love."

A smile came to my face as I knew that emotion quite well.

"On the nights he worked, she came to the bar after her shift ended at the cosmetics counter in Macy's. Carney convinced them to tell us how they met. It seemed odd to me as he was never sentimental. I figured he wanted to prolong the evening and keep her talking. Turns out she had gone into the bar six months prior with a date. April and the man got into an argument because he accused her of flirting with other men. He didn't understand her friendly, outgoing nature. When Tony suggested the man lighten up, he responded by telling Tony to mind his own business. April told her date not to talk to people that way. Her date raised his hand to smack her across the face. Tony dove across the bar and knocked him over. After a few blows were exchanged, the man stormed out and said Tony could keep the whore."

"I'm getting a bit lost here, honey." I stopped walking. "If April loved Tony, how did she end up with Carney?"

"He met her at Macy's a few days later." Another sweep of his hand through his hair. We came to a bench and sat down. I listened to the raucous call of the seagulls while waiting for him to go on.

Finally, taking a deep breath, he continued. "That Saturday I worked the lunch shift. When I got home, I found a note from Carney telling me to meet him at Liquid Stylings at nine o'clock. It seemed a little odd, but I went.

"I arrived first. A different bartender brought me my beer while Tony chatted with a couple of patrons at the other end of the bar. Carney walked in escorting April. Before I could greet her by name, he introduced us as if she and I were strangers. She didn't appear to know me. He explained how he met her at Macy's while buying perfume for his mom's birthday and had invited April to dinner. They were rounding off the night with drinks. Carney led the conversation as if we just happened to run into each other, so I played along thinking it was a joke.

"Tony came over, tossing out a casual greeting, then asked for their drink orders. April ordered a glass of red wine, and he asked her Cabernet or Pinot Noir."

I did a double take and looked at Jimmy. "What do you mean he asked for her drink order? Didn't he have it ready?"

"No. They didn't know each other."

"How could they not? Unless…" It hit me—unless they hadn't met! That's what Jimmy meant. "What did Carney do?"

"At first he wouldn't tell me. Obviously, whatever he'd done was a result of the time-travel slides."

Barely able to contain myself, I opened my mouth to guess

again. Jimmy held up his hand. When I acquiesced with a nod, he caressed my cheek.

It struck me as odd that this was difficult for him since we were very much in love. He'd said many times how we made the perfect couple. It couldn't be he was angry at having lost out to Carney, but the way Carney won April seemed wrong as I suspected what he'd done.

Lowering his hand, he placed it on my knee and squeezed gently. "Carney went back in time. He went back and made sure he was the one to stop April's date. Only there for twenty-four hours, he couldn't strike up a friendship with her. Not unless he wanted to return a second time and be trapped. This meant she never met Tony. Not in a way that would make her become involved with him. When April saw Carney at work that day, he brought up the incident with her angry date. Of course, she remembered him and agreed to dinner."

"He misused the slides."

Jimmy nodded.

Carney's actions made me angry. "He used them for personal gain. He broke one of the cardinal rules the Frenchman warned you against."

"I can't tell you how many times I tried to reason with myself that it couldn't be considered personal gain since she ended up his Photographer. With her gregarious personality, she was a natural at bringing in Betrotheds. I stopped thinking of how they met and focused on their success together."

"It was still wrong, honey. You know that."

"I know, sweetie. But after it was done, what choice did I have? They were so happy."

"Yes, but what about Tony? Didn't he deserve to be happy too?" I found this hard to swallow. He accepted the events and did nothing to stop them. But then there would be the paradox of his meddling in timelines he shouldn't have been involved in either. There was always the possibility that even if he prevented Carney from meeting April, it wouldn't have assured Tony would still be with her. Once you started messing with timelines, you weren't guaranteed the original results.

I looked up to see Jimmy watching me carefully, as I worked out the ramifications. He knew I was going through a list of "what ifs" in my head, yet none of the conclusions were good.

"You get there yet?"

I sank back against the bench and nodded. "I do have a question."

"Yes?"

"I know that we're aware of both timelines when time is changed during this process. Did April remember her life with Tony once she became a Photographer?"

"No. I guess since it happened before she worked with Carney, she didn't know events that happened prior."

After a long silence, I asked, "What happened to April?"

Not getting an immediate response, I watched the activity around us. A mother and her small son walked along the beach where the waves tickled their toes. Each time the cold water touched the little boy, he squealed with delight. The bliss of his innocence made me envious. I often wondered what it would have been like to raise a child. I had relinquished that option when I chose this life.

Jimmy's cell phone beeped and he retrieved it from his pocket. Glancing at the screen a grimace crossed his face. "One of my clients," he said. "She just got served with papers. An unexpected turn in the case. I'm sorry."

"We need to get to the bottom of this," I said, surprised he would leave in the middle.

"I know, but this won't be solved in an hour. I have to attend to my legal obligations. Sorry."

I hesitated a beat, then nodded. "I know. Call me later."

As Jimmy walked away, an inconsistency struck me. How did Carney go back only six months prior? None of the slides we had allowed such a short hop.

Chapter 8

I didn't hear from Jimmy until after ten o'clock. He'd stayed later than planned due to his distraught client and decided to go to bed at his townhouse. He was due in court this morning, so the story of April would have to wait.

Sitting at my kitchen table, I robotically brought a coffee mug to my lips, focusing on Dede's upcoming journey later this morning. This match between her and Milton felt right, yet Carney's reckless actions intruded on my thoughts. His total disregard for the rules was disturbing enough—his murderous acts unforgivable.

A few minutes before nine o'clock, I went into my office to retrieve the box of film slides from the large safe in the corner of the room. From the three-pack labeled "Milton Freeman," I withdrew the yellow-framed one that would send Dede back for twenty-four hours and its holder needed to facilitate the time travel. If things went well, she would also use the blue slide that sends her back permanently.

Returning the remaining two slides to the safe, I thought about the red-framed one good for a single emergency twenty-four-hour trip. The memory of going back for Amanda sent a shiver of horror and guilt through me; her fate continued to haunt me.

Grabbing a few hundred dollars from the cash box, I locked the safe and carried all the items to my studio. The money was for the Betrothed to take with her. All the bills were produced before the mid-seventies.

Placing the time portal device next to the cash on the table, I secured the slide and pressed the button on the back. It would take an hour to power up. This set-up was intentionally placed behind the subject. The process didn't really involve a camera at all, but one was put in front of the Betrothed for effect. Once Dede was seated on the bench, one press of the timer started the thirty-second count down.

I envisioned Dede and Milton with arms around each other, smiling out from his picture on the wall. While fearing Carney's continued interference with our matches, I also reminded myself this was what I agreed to do. I didn't want to find out what the consequences were if Jimmy and I quit before fulfilling our quota.

When the doorbell rang at ten o'clock, the familiar hum of adrenaline flowed through my veins. My next Betrothed was here!

As I opened the door, Dede gave me a big hug. "Hi, Sami!" She glowed with excitement—judging by her huge smile.

Such a warm and loving person. More and more I knew this match was meant to be. Jimmy had described Milton as having a caring temperament.

Stepping away from the doorway for her to enter, I noticed she dressed as if it were just another day: a light blue t-shirt and faded denim jeans. The pants were well-worn, but not those fancy designer ones.

"I'm so glad you're here. You look perfect!"

"I know you told me not to fuss, but I had to a bit."

She looked no different than yesterday.

"Look," she said, "mascara!" We burst out laughing.

"Then I guess you're ready to meet Milton!"

"I don't feel anxious about this meeting. Strange, huh?"

"No, not really. You seemed very comfortable with the idea of him. Maybe that's why I suggested the two of you meet."

She looked around with wide eyes and an expectant smile. "Is he here yet?"

"You'll be going to see him. I hope you're okay with that."

Dede thought for a moment, the shine never leaving her face. "That's okay. Will you be going with me?"

"No, you'll be meeting him alone."

"Of course. Milton and I are adults. We shouldn't need a chaperone!" I wished we'd met under different circumstances. Dede's friendship would've been enjoyable.

The whistle of the kettle reminded me I had put the water on to boil before she arrived. "Let's have a quick cup of tea while I fill you in on the details."

She followed me to the kitchen where two mugs with a bag of Earl Grey in each waited. "Have a seat."

After pouring the water into the cups, I sat down.

As I inhaled the subtle aroma in the steam, she asked, "So how does this work?"

Not wanting to delay, I dove right in with the details. "It requires a leap of faith on your part."

"There you go with the fortune cookie language again. Just give it to me straight."

"You got it. I knew beating around the bush wasn't your style."

"Never has been."

"That portrait you saw of Milton was taken at his ranch in New Mexico. The year was 1975."

Her face screwed up. "You're hooking me up with a senior citizen?" Uncertainty marred her pretty features.

"No." I dunked my teabag a few times then set it on a small dish. When I raised my head, she looked directly into my eyes waiting for answers.

"As I said, it requires a leap of faith. In that portrait, Milton is thirty-eight years old. Only about five years older than yourself, I'm guessing?"

"You're good."

"Years of practice, dear." I ran my finger around the rim of the cup. "So...you'll be going back to the year 1975. How do you feel about that?"

She sipped her tea, then set the mug down a little harder than expected. It clunked as it hit the wooden table. She searched my face as if looking for a clue as to where I was going with this.

"You haven't run out of the house screaming, so I guess you're willing to hear more."

She inclined her head in a gesture to continue.

"I'm a Photographer. Not in the typical sense of a person who takes pictures. I'm involved in a process that allows me to match women with potential Suitors so that they can make a life together. Rarely do I meet those Suitors as I work with a Collector who interviews the men."

"This Collector, you have confidence in his judgment?" Again, that trusting intuition kicked in with her. Most women, at this point, started firing off questions trying to poke holes in my explanation.

"Implicitly."

"The Collector met with Milton in 1975?"

"Yes, he went back to that year."

"Went back?"

I nodded. "As will you." There, it was out.

Dede took another drink, this time setting the mug down gently.

"All of the women in those portraits in my studio were women I've met over the last thirty years. The Suitors they ended up with were born many years before them. They all began their lives together in the decade the men were from. One went as far back as the 1920's, but most traveled only three or four decades. As you will, to meet Milton."

"And how, exactly…"

"I'll take your picture with my sepia camera. When the flash goes off, you'll be transported through time to New Mexico. The year will be 1975. Milton will be there to greet you."

"How long has he been waiting for me?" Raising her eyebrows, she added, "If you're pulling my leg, at least this makes for an interesting story. Right?"

I nodded. "At the very least. To answer your question, he's been waiting all his life, just as you have. Though technically, it's only been a week since the Collector interviewed him in his time."

"Strangely, this is making sense in a science fiction sort of way. What happens if I don't like him? How will I get back? Or is it all or nothing?"

"You go for twenty-four hours the first time."

"I'll be making more than one trip? Is that how he courts me?" she laughed. "Every time we have a date I'll time travel?"

"Not exactly. You can only go back twice. The second time is permanent." I remained silent a few minutes, allowing her time to digest my last statement.

"If I take the second trip, I won't be coming back to the present?"

"Correct. I liken it to getting a tattoo—it's permanent."

A smile spread across Dede's face again. "So…once I get there, do I get older?"

"Of course! You'll continue to age from that point and live out a natural life-time—just starting from the time you arrive. Once you return to the present after your visit, you'll have a week to wrap up your exit from this time period. In order for me to continue my work, it's best for you not to leave anything suspicious for people to question. Most women quit their job and release their living space, claiming a sick relative or such. Am I correct in guessing you haven't any close relatives and very few friends?"

Her forehead wrinkled, and she frowned. "Sami, how did you know about all that? It's true. All of it. But how could you know?"

"Well, this is where a bit more mysticism comes in. All the men, which we call Suitors, come to us pre-chosen. We only interview, never select. The same with you, or a Betrothed, as we like to call you. The women who cross my path have all been…well…mostly alone. And lonely."

Dede's eyes watered as she raised the cup, then put it down. Picking up the mug again, she took a sip. Gazing at me over the edge of it, she said, "That's how you knew I'd take the bait and show up today. Isn't it?"

"Yes. But it's not a bad thing. How do you know this isn't the way your life is supposed to be? Not everyone is a good fit for the time they currently live in. How do you know you aren't better suited for the past? It opens up your road to happiness. Love and family, isn't that what you said you wanted?"

"It is."

"Both you and Milton are artists. You already share a common love for creating things, just with different mediums. He paints. You sculpt."

We sat in silence for a few minutes. "Explain to me again how this works. Is it painful when I travel back? Who will Milton tell people I am? Do I keep my name?" Her hands shook, and she had to hold onto her cup with both hands.

Her reaction was normal. Usually I explained the process before Betrotheds showed up for the first journey. It hadn't seemed necessary yesterday, but maybe I had misjudged. What had I been thinking? Easy for me. I work with this all the time. Pulling myself from my thoughts, I responded, "No, it isn't painful at all."

"Have you ever traveled back?" Anxiety etched itself in the lines of her face. She had doubts. Not about meeting the Suitor, it seemed, but about the process to get there.

"Yes, a couple of times. It's quite smooth traveling." I tried to keep my voice steady and light—so she could hear the confidence in it. Maybe it would help calm her nervousness. "For this first trip, you won't need anything in the way of identification. In fact, you need to leave everything here, so you don't take things back that don't belong in that time period. Like your driver's license and credit cards."

This last thought seemed to spook her more as she got up from the table and went to the kitchen window. Knowing she would be virtually stranded for twenty-four hours, this wasn't an easy choice.

Turning around, she asked, "Won't I need those things when I get there? What if Milton isn't there like he's supposed to be?"

"Not to worry," I assured her, "he'll be there. Our Suitors have never missed a date." I cleared the table and placed the dishes in the sink. "If you choose to go back a final time, that week will also give my Collector the opportunity to create the proper identification for that period. Luckily, computer systems weren't as advanced in the 1970's as they are now."

"I see," was all she said with a wrinkled forehead trying to puzzle this out. Dede started to slowly pace back and forth.

"We stick as close to your current history as possible. That way it will be easier for you to remember. You'll just need to be careful about dates and timelines when interacting with other people besides Milton. This enables him to give a plausible background for you also."

Coming to a standstill, she looked over at me with a confident grin. She'd made her decision. "Okay, Sami. Let's do this!"

Dede followed me to the studio and I gestured for her to enter first. At the doorway, she hesitated and took a couple of deep breaths, then entered the room. From the door frame, I watched her stroll past the portraits on the wall, studying each one. I knew she was viewing them in a new light.

"Is this a new Suitor waiting for a bride?" Dede asked, pointing at one. "I don't remember seeing that one yesterday."

I stepped into the room and froze. The portrait of Carney posing as Ronald Hauptman hung on the wall again.

Chapter 9

Not wanting to stare into those menacing eyes, I looked away and sat down on the couch. I'd removed that portrait from the wall the day after I failed to convince Amanda to return with me. Yet here it hung back in its original spot. There was only one explanation for it being there. The thought of Carney in my home sent chills through my body.

This threw a new light on the situation. Not wanting to divulge too much, I needed to let Dede know this journey wasn't without risks.

"Actually," I started, "that was one of my failures."

"The woman, the Betrothed as you say, didn't go back a second time?"

"No, she did. It's just that she didn't appear in the portrait." My eyes lost focus for a moment. "I didn't find her in time."

Dede turned and looked at me. "What does that mean, exactly?"

Trying to pull it together, I realized I couldn't tell her what really happened. I hated to lie. She deserved the truth, but I remained hopeful she would get the life she wanted.

There was also a healthy dose of selfishness involved. I didn't want to experience the consequences of falling short of fulfilling our quota. If Carney was an example, it seemed to turn your soul black—though it could be different for each person. "I don't know what happened to her. She never got the life she hoped for. You need to realize there are risks to all this. It's up to you to decide if they're worth it."

Dede walked to the end of the gallery and sat on the bench in front of the camera. From the concerned expression on her face, I knew she was weighing the odds of whether to walk away or give it her all. There wasn't any halfway in this business—not for the Betrotheds.

"What do you think happened to her?"

"I couldn't say." Lord, how I hated lying.

I sensed she knew that wasn't entirely accurate. Or was it just my guilt?

"Do you ever know what happens with the women you send back? How it all works out for them? Does the marriage turn sour? Are they stuck?" Her face visually softened as if realizing she was firing off questions in an accusatory manner.

"No," that much I could be honest about, "not really. Beyond seeing the Betrotheds appear in the portrait after the second journey, I don't really know. I know the marriage took place when they end up beside their Suitor, but nothing beyond that. Maybe a part of me doesn't want to know. It pains me to think of them winding up in a loveless marriage. I could try looking them up on the internet, but it wouldn't truly give me a sense of what their life was like."

"I guess not," she answered. "That's where that leap of faith really kicks in, huh?"

"Probably. So, what are your instincts telling you, Dede?"

She sat for a long moment looking at the portraits. Rising, she walked over to Milton's. Staring at it, she reached her fingers up to his and closed her eyes as she had done yesterday. Placing her hand on the picture, I saw her curl it as if trying to grab hold.

From where I sat on the couch, I saw her face scrunch in concentration. Her eyes popped open.

"Send me back," she said quietly. "Send me back."

Getting up, I took her by the hand and led her to the cushioned bench in front of the old-time camera. Grabbing the bills from the table, I handed them to her. She looked confused for a moment.

"This is in case you need money for any reason. Can't send you back penniless, can I?"

She stuck the bills into a front pocket. As she sat down, she looked up at me. Taking both her hands in mine, I gave them a squeeze, "Good luck."

Dede nodded and placed her hands in her lap. Sitting up straight, as if she were truly posing for a portrait, she faced the camera. I stepped behind her to confirm the mechanism was at full power and pressed the timing button. It started at thirty and counted down. Immediately, I stepped behind my camera and grabbed the dangling cord with the cushioned button that Dede believed would take her picture and send her back to 1975.

"Breathe, dear," I finally said.

She looked shocked as she expelled air. I guess she hadn't realized she was holding her breath. Looking at me, she winked. Suddenly, a light flashed from behind her, and the bench was empty.

All I could do now was go about my day. This time tomorrow I would return to my studio to greet Dede as she returned to this decade. I hoped she'd be anxious to go back to Milton and begin her new life. Only time would tell.

Summoning my courage, I walked over to the portrait of Carney, my steps hesitant. I tried to picture him in a different light, as the friend Jimmy had known. Having met the monster he'd become, it was impossible to envision him any other way.

Stepping closer, I grabbed hold of the frame and removed the portrait from the wall. The weight of it threw me off balance, and it dropped. With a muffled thump, it landed on the carpet then crashed against the wall. The frame leaned at an angle. In a fit of rage. I raised my foot and stomped through the picture. The photo crumpled and tore, yet most of the face still looked up at me as if to inflict more torment. His eyes burned into mine.

"Is that any way to treat fine art?" The voice came from the doorway. It was *his* voice—the one from the answering machine. Except now it was live and echoing through my studio.

I whipped around to face Carney. Wearing beach shorts, a t-shirt, and sneakers, he looked like any other inhabitant of the Southern California beach area. But I knew better.

"Tsk, tsk. That portrait was part of your process. Aren't you concerned about such rash actions?"

Controlling my voice, I asked, "What do you want?"

He studied me a moment. It almost felt dirty the way he scrutinized me up and down. The stench of a musky cologne permeated the room. "I thought I would pop in and say hello." He nodded toward his portrait. "Obviously, you're less than pleased with my decorating attempts."

I tried to remain calm. "What is it you want? With Jimmy? And me? Why are you interfering with innocent lives?"

"Innocent?" His voice escalated. "*Innocent?* Ask your Collector about being innocent!"

I wasn't sure where he was going with this. Being alone with him was dangerous. Maybe if I kept him talking, I could figure out an escape.

"Please, Carney, tell me what you want. Why are you doing this?" Reaching down deep to reel in every ounce of control I could muster, my hands curled into fists digging the nails into my palms in frustration. The pain helped keep me sharp. I didn't want him to fluster me. The question was could I hold on to that?

"Jimmy knows. Ask him."

"He doesn't. So, I'm asking you. Why would you interfere with our work? Those women didn't deserve to die. What we do here is good. Tell me what you really want."

Carney stared back, his face a stony façade that gave nothing away. "I want Jimmy to pay for taking away my April. I want to destroy everything he holds dear."

Revenge? Carney wanted revenge? Somehow, he was blaming Jimmy for April's death. I wished Jimmy had finished telling me about her.

"So, you blame Jimmy. Tell me why?"

"No."

"Why not?"

"He needs to admit what he did! Until he does, I will continue to...*persuade* him."

Another shiver ran through me. The way he phrased that— persuade him. I knew what that meant. We needed to stop Carney. But how? And at what cost until we figured it out? I began to fear for Dede's life. He obviously knew I had just sent back another Betrothed.

Suddenly, Carney lifted his hand to his forehead pretending to grab a hat and tip it as he gave a slight bow. "Au revoir for now, my *sweet* Sami. And tell Jimmy to give my regards to…Daddy. He was most helpful."

I stood paralyzed as he turned on his heel and left. His footsteps echoed down the hall, and the front door slammed shut. I ran to slide the deadbolt home and leaned with my back against the door.

Tremors coursed through my body. Wrapping my arms around myself, I stood for several minutes. As soon as I trusted my legs to hold my weight, I secured every window and door in the house.

Questions tumbled around in my head like waves pummeling the shore. From what Carney had said, I knew there was more to April. How did Jimmy's father tie into all of this? He was a keeper of the slides but had died long before Jimmy and Carney had become Collectors.

Chapter 10

I jumped on the computer to research what I could. Jimmy never told me April's last name, so that ruled out looking up anything on her. I searched for information on the death of Jimmy's father, Jason. He was stabbed while working in their shop when Jimmy was a teenager. With cash still in the register, the police chalked it up to a botched robbery.

Either the theft got interrupted, or it wasn't money the assailant wanted. Unfortunately, the death of a Chinese man in the sixties wasn't big news—a sad reality of our country in that era. It might have been part of a spree. Two blocks away the body of a young Caucasian man was found stabbed to death in an alley. The police never identified the victim.

I spent the rest of the afternoon trying to find anything else but came up empty. When Jimmy arrived that evening, he found me in the office. As he poked his head through the door, I looked up and was sure my expression hid nothing. His forehead creased, and the concern on his face mirrored mine.

"Should I ask how your day went?"

Logging off from the computer, I got up and walked toward him. Snuggling up to him and brushing a quick kiss across his lips, I said, "I sent Dede back on her first journey."

"Dede? A new Betrothed?"

With everything going on, Jimmy didn't know about her

46

message on the answering machine. I passed him in the doorway and strode toward the living room. "Yes. I sent her back to meet Milton."

"Milton?" He wasn't connecting the dots. We sat down on the couch.

"Milton Freeman, the painter. Dede is into clay and sculpting. They should be a good match."

"Oh, right. The artist in New Mexico. From the mid-70's, right?"

"Yes. She returns tomorrow morning around ten o'clock."

Jimmy threw his arm around me and gave a squeeze. "Good. He was a well-grounded individual. Matching him with a creative-type woman seems fitting. Are you anxious about the meeting?"

"Only for her safety."

"Honey, we can't stop. The work we do is good."

"I know." I didn't know how to tell him what happened, so I simply blurted it out. "He was here."

Pulling away from me, he turned. "Who? Milton?"

"No! Carney. Carney was here. In my house. In my studio!"

Jimmy rake a hand through his hair. "What? Did he hurt you? What did he say?"

"No, he didn't touch me."

"Did he see you send Dede back?"

"Yes, I'm sure he did. I don't think he was here for our Betrothed this time. At least I hope not, for her sake. He hung his picture back on the wall, the one where he posed as Ronald Hauptman. I discovered it right before Dede travelled back."

"You sent her anyway?" He put a hand on my leg.

"Yes. I told Dede the journey wasn't without risks. She still chose to go."

"You didn't tell her about the others?"

"No." I leaned into him to gain strength from his warmth. "What would be the point?"

"It probably wouldn't have mattered. Carney hasn't interfered with all the matches. So, you didn't actually see him before her trip?"

"No. He made himself known right after she disappeared."

Jimmy raked his hand through his hair again. "What did he want?"

"Revenge. He blames you for April's death. Why would he say that?"

Leaning against the cushion, he closed his eyes. "I don't know." Sitting up he opened his eyes and added, "Carney killed her. I don't think he intended to, but he did. I tried to save her."

"He believes you're to blame. And there's more." Knowing there was no way to soften this next blow distressed me. I got up and walked to the fireplace. Placing my hands on the rough bricks, the cuts on my palms stung with irritation. I bowed my head.

"Tell me, sweetie."

"I don't know what this means." I turned around. "He said for you to give your regards to…"

"To who?" Alarm registered on his face.

"He said…to give your regards…he said to give your regards to Daddy. He was 'most helpful.' That's exactly what he said." I walked back over to the couch and sat beside him.

All the color drained from his face. God only knew the thoughts flashing through his mind. I was sure he felt his life as a Collector contributed to his father's death, despite not taking on his role until years after the murder. Yet his dad had agreed to be a keeper of the slides. Jimmy couldn't take the blame. Jason chose that role before his son was ever born.

"What else did Carney say to you?"

"That's all. I'm sorry, sweetie. Do you think he had something to do with your father's murder?"

He stood, thrusting his hands into his pockets, and walked out of the room. I heard the front door open, then close gently.

Assuming he stopped on the porch, I walked through the dining room, grabbed a bottle of merlot off the wine rack and continued into the kitchen to open it. My mind churned; Carney might have murdered Jimmy's father. Why else would he have brought it up? Was it a ploy to cause more turmoil?

Retrieving two glasses from the cupboard, I joined Jimmy on the front porch. He sat slumped forward with his head in his hands. When he looked up to take his wine glass, his pallor frightened me. I sat in the chair beside him. The wicker creaked loudly in the silence of the evening. I asked, "What do you know about your father's death?"

"That he was stabbed. And it wasn't a robbery like the police claimed."

Jimmy hadn't talked about his father's death beyond the fact that it happened. I never felt the need to push him for details until now. "Why do you say that?"

"My grandfather seemed to know but would never speak of it. Now I wish I'd forced him to tell me."

"He wasn't very talkative. He always conveyed politeness, but never any warmth."

"Something in him died with my father's passing. If it hadn't been for having to help my mother raise me, I think he would have crawled into that coffin with his son."

"I always got the feeling your grandfather knew way more about this whole process than he let on. Did you think so?"

Jimmy sat his glass on the table, stood up and walked to the end of the porch. "Yes. His way was to allow people to figure things out on their own. Once I got involved with the slides, he became even more tight-lipped about the process, as if he feared sharing too much."

I stared out at the ocean, waiting for him to pull his thoughts together. The more information we pieced together, the more questions we had.

A light breeze, damp from the evening air, tickled my face.

Turning to face me, Jimmy said, "I think Grandfather felt somewhat responsible for Dad's death. He was the reason my father became involved in this match-making mess."

"But it was your father's choice to participate. He had the opportunity to turn it down, just like turning down the role of Collector."

"I believe Dad became a keeper of the slides to appease Grandfather. I don't think he wanted anything to do with it. My mother never talked about it, but I could tell she wasn't happy."

"I wish we could talk to your Grandfather, maybe get him to tell us more."

"Sami, don't even think about it. Going back to talk to him is a bad idea."

I stood up and walked toward him. "Why?" My determination echoed in my footsteps across the boards. "I could use one of the emergency slides to travel back to a time after your father's death. He has to know more."

"Maybe he doesn't. It wouldn't be right using the slides that way."

Desperation laced my voice. "It's not for personal gain. It's to stop a monster. I can't sit here and do nothing." I searched his eyes for a sign of agreement. There wasn't any.

He wrapped his arms around me and rested his chin on the top of my head. Burying my face in his chest, I breathed in the scent of his cologne.

Jimmy pondered, "The thing is, I don't know if Carney could have been directly involved in the murder. I only remember one timeline for my father. If Carney had gone back and been the one to kill him, there would be two timelines. Since we became Collectors at the same time, I would be aware of anything he might have done to change history."

I pulled my head away from his chest and looked up. "You're right. He couldn't have been the murderer. He must be using the incident to hurt you."

Reaching up, I gently placed my hand on his cheek. "Tell me more about April."

Chapter 11

"Let's go back inside," Jimmy said. "With Carney having been here, I feel exposed sitting on the porch."

"Okay. I'm still a bit shaken too."

We grabbed our glasses, and Jimmy picked up the bottle. Inside, we sat side by side on the couch in front of the unlit fireplace. The room still smelled faintly of the wood fire we'd had there last week.

Jimmy asked, "Where did I leave off?"

"You told me how Carney prevented April from meeting Tony and she became his Photographer."

"Right. Well, within four months Carney and April found a house together. Carney enlightened her on our job as Collectors. She was absolutely entranced with the process and thrilled to become his Photographer."

With a grin, I recalled Jimmy asking me to be his Photographer. "If he was as persuasive as you were, I can't imagine her saying no."

"It didn't take much convincing. They set up a small photo studio in the study of their house, something like yours but on a smaller scale. They didn't quite follow the rules though. Both the Frenchman and the shopkeeper who dispensed the slides told us the interviews must be completed *before* making matches—all the interviews. As I said earlier, Carney had only completed a third of his Suitor meetings."

"Something has been nagging at me ever since you told me about Carney going back and being the one to save April from her abusive date. How did he go back only six months and meet her? All of the slides send you back to Suitors much earlier. At least a couple of decades."

Jimmy raked a hand through his hair. "At first Carney wouldn't tell me. I asked him for weeks how he'd gone back on such a short jump through time. He just said his slides were different than mine. Finally, giving up, I simply rejoiced in the fact that my friend and April were happy. After they completed their first match, the three of us drove out to a small winery north of San Francisco. It became a favorite of ours. After each special occasion, we drank a bottle from that vineyard.

"As much as we both loved Carney, sometimes his rambunctious personality overwhelmed us. Sitting and having a quiet conversation didn't make it onto the agenda. More and more April and I met for lunch while Carney was in class or at work. Finding new places to have afternoon tea was also something we shared."

Astounded by this I asked, "You had an affair with her?"

"What?" He broke out of his reverie and looked at me with confusion in his eyes. I thought it was a reasonable assumption, despite being out of character. This man wasn't the type to dally with another man's woman. "Oh, no. Nothing like that. It was more like a brother and sister thing. We had a great relationship, but not on a romantic level. We both knew our boundaries and never crossed them. Besides, she loved Carney."

Relieved, I waited for him to continue. Not that I was jealous. We both had relationships with other people before we met.

"Carney had known about us spending time together. It never seemed to bother him. At first."

"Did they continue to place Betrotheds?"

"Yes. They placed four. When I asked him how the rest of the Suitor interviews were going, he said he hadn't completed any more."

Placing a hand on my cheek in surprise, I asked, "He didn't finish? But he knew the requirements. They shouldn't have continued with matches until all the Suitors were interviewed."

"I told him that several times. It seems he hadn't told April all the rules to this business. The role of helping lonely women find true love exhilarated her, and she had no idea there could be consequences involved."

"I can understand her excitement. Every time we help a woman go back, it gives me a rush. But we follow the guidelines of this whole process. No matches were made until all the Suitors had been interviewed."

"I know. But no amount of talking would get Carney to change."

"Were there any significant repercussions you could see?"

Jimmy placed a hand on my knee. "Not immediately." His voice coarsened as he tried to hold his emotions at bay. "The changes in Carney were so subtle, neither of us noticed until it was too late."

"What changed?" Jimmy's foreboding tone scared me.

"He started dropping innuendos about our relationship— April's and mine. Like he didn't trust our *innocent* friendship, as he put it."

He was jealous. Knowing Carney as he is now, it's hard to picture him the way Jimmy first knew him. A bit of a troublemaker, but an upstanding guy. Had he ever been good though? Jimmy always looked for the best in people. Is it possible his loving nature didn't acknowledge Carney's twisted ways until it was too late? Maybe that compounded his guilt. The thought that maybe he could have stopped all this before it began must be eating away at him.

On the other hand, would that have meant we'd never met? He would never give up the opportunity to meet me. He said as much many times. Could I ever make the choice to forgo our meeting to undo all the evil Carney wrought? Would I, given the chance?

Lost in my own thoughts, I didn't realize Jimmy started speaking again until he spoke my name and gently shook my shoulder. "Sorry, honey. My thoughts were drifting."

He raised my hand to his lips then placed it on his knee, covering it with his own. "It's all right. These last several months have taken their toll on both of us."

I rested my head on his shoulder. We cuddled, both of us lost in our own thoughts. The lingering wood fire scent played lightly about the room.

"Shall I go on?" he finally asked.

Lifting my head up off his shoulder, I nodded.

"April tried to brush away Carney's off-handed accusations. Most times, he seemed appeased. We did back off on our private lunches and get-togethers. Neither of us wanted to ruin the friendship the three of us shared. I missed her company. She was a great sounding board while I struggled to balance work and law school. April kept hoping I would meet my Photographer—so we could become a foursome.

"I even introduced her to my grandfather. She enjoyed meeting him, but my grandfather's comment afterward will always echo through my mind."

"What did he say?"

"He said, she was *wrong*."

"What did he mean by that?"

"He wouldn't tell me. Just repeated that she was *wrong*."

"Wrong about what? Something she said?"

"The way Grandfather said the word it didn't seem like he was referring to their conversation. I think it was something about her. As if he knew how Carney and April met."

I thought about this a moment. Jimmy was at least the third generation to be involved with the process. Maybe it went back farther than three generations, and his grandfather really did know more than he let on. Perhaps I should go back and talk to him about his son's murder and meeting April. It technically wouldn't be considered misusing the slides if it would stop Carney's killing spree. Few matches used the third slide, good for one 24-hour trip. I could use one to go back in time to any date after his grandfather met April, as long as the location was close enough to San Francisco. Since Jimmy opposed the idea, this would have to be a secret journey. It bothered me to do something behind his back, but this might be the only way to learn more.

Shaking off my current line of thinking, I forced myself back to the present conversation. "Tell me more about April and Carney."

"Like I said, he started to change. After April and I backed off a bit, he seemed to relax. For a little while anyway. Then his jealousy came back full force. He started acting irrationally.

Carney forced April to hurry through the next two matches, even though she was doubtful of both unions. We talked about them before the women were sent back. It was like Carney wanted to be in control of everything."

"Did they have enough Suitors to make compatible matches?"

He frowned. "That was April's hesitation too. She tried to hold off making any further matches between Suitors and Betrotheds she wasn't sure of. She took her responsibility seriously. Carney wouldn't have any of her hesitations. He told her the women would be better off going back than staying in their present situations. She gave in and moved forward. The first woman went back for the twenty-four-hour period, but refused to return to her Suitor permanently."

"It wasn't the right match," I said, stating the obvious.

"No. Everyone saw it but Carney."

"So, the woman walked away, and the poor Suitor was left alone as his slides were spent. How sad for both." I patted his hand. "It must have bothered you too."

"Yes, honey. It bothered both of us, but April loved Carney and did as he asked. The second woman returned anxious to go back to her Suitor. When she went back to the past for the second and final journey, she never appeared in the photo. We never found out what happened. After that, April started to resist Carney's pushing. She held her ground and said both happened because he hadn't finished the interviews. Her refusal to cultivate any additional Betrotheds angered him. During one of their arguments, he told her she wouldn't even be involved if he hadn't saved her from an otherwise mundane future."

"Did Carney tell her how he manipulated their meeting?" I imagined the turmoil April would have been in at that revelation.

"No. He refused to explain, so she came to me. I danced around the truth and wouldn't tell her specifics. What would be the point? She was already in an awful state with Carney. Knowing about Tony wouldn't have helped."

I was torn about what would have been the right thing to do. Jimmy had a point, though. What good would it have done since there was no going back and changing her past?

"Accusations and arguments weren't the only things. Carney became physically violent. It started with grabbing her roughly from time to time, then he began hitting her. He was always apologetic afterward, but it didn't erase the bruises or the emotional scars."

He got up off the couch and paced from one end of the room to the other. I could see Carney's brutality still upset him. These events happened over thirty years ago but were obviously imprinted in his mind, as if they took place yesterday.

"Honey, come sit down." I patted the cushion beside me.

Jimmy stopped pacing and looked at me. "Sorry. It's just that...". His voice trailed off.

"I know. This isn't easy for you. Please, come sit back down. Finish it."

Chapter 12

Jimmy sat on the couch beside me, leaning forward with his elbows on his knees and his palms against his forehead.

"April knew Carney would never willingly let her go but she knew she had to get away from him when he became more violent. We both feared for her life. He even took a swing at me a couple of times."

"The misuse of the slides sent him to a dark place."

"I guess you could say that. The fun-loving man I knew from the army was long gone and April, the jewel of his life, was no longer safe."

"You helped her get away, didn't you?" I asked.

"I tried. But it went horribly wrong." Jimmy grabbed his wine glass and leaned back into the cushions. He took a long drink then closed his eyes.

How I wished I could erase the pained expression on his face. Putting my hand on his arm, I gently squeezed. "Finish it, honey. Tell me what happened."

He looked at me and set the glass on the coffee table. "Both April and I knew she needed to get far away. It wouldn't be as simple as leaving town. She needed to go where he would never think of looking. To another place...and time."

"April used the slides to hide, didn't she?"

"Yes. She thought Carney would never know since he hadn't

completed his part of the process. She took a set of slides for a Suitor he hadn't interviewed. They were for New York City in the year 1948. World War II was over and she could easily disappear. Her plan was to go to New York and secure passage to Egypt."

"Why Egypt?"

"Two reasons. First, she'd taken archeology classes because she was fascinated with the Egyptian tombs. It would be easy to get lost in Cairo, maybe even get involved in some of the digs going on. The second was if Carney ever did track her to that time, he could never find her if she left the country."

"That meant you would never see her again either." I bit my lip with concern. Knowing how much he loved her, even as a friend, the thought of losing her forever must have tortured him.

He winced as if in pain. "It was the only way to ensure her safety."

I nodded, and he continued. "Since the slides were for a Suitor who hadn't been interviewed, nobody waited for her in that time. A contact of mine created the necessary credentials. April went back for the twenty-four-hour period to secure passage on a ship headed for Africa, using part of the twenty thousand dollars in cash we had amassed from that era. She checked into a hotel to leave the belongings she'd bought."

"What a brilliant plan!"

"It seemed flawless. I was nervous about her using a set of slides from their own stash, but she refused to use one of mine. She feared a misuse like that would work against me. I didn't care. I wanted her safe."

My phone in the office rang. We both froze, and I decided to let the answering machine get it. Fearing who it might be, I didn't want to be interrupted. I needed to know what happened.

Jimmy asked, "Did you want to get that?"

"No. Keep going. How was April able to leave for twenty-four hours without Carney suspecting anything?"

"She pretended to go on a trip to Napa with a girlfriend. She'd done that before, so it went unnoticed—or so we thought. The first journey went smoothly. When April came back, she was flush with excitement and couldn't wait to tell me all she'd accomplished. I was glad for her.

"On her second and final journey, I used the third slide to meet her there. Since it allowed me to set a date between one and four weeks after her final arrival, I could time it just right to see her set sail—or so I thought. She insisted on doing this by herself, but I knew she wanted me there.

"When it was time, my slide landed me in a discreet corner of Central Park beside a duck pond. I arrived in time to see Carney holding her."

"What! How did he find out? How could he be there if you used the third slide? His interview slide would have been a week before her first journey, and that only had a twenty-four-hour time frame."

"I don't know how he did it, but he was there. I arrived close enough to see the fear in April's eyes." Jimmy's tone became louder. "As he gripped both her hands, his face was contorted with rage. She screamed and begged him to let her go. I saw her feet digging into the ground as she tried to pull away from him. He said he was taking her back."

The agony in his voice raised goosebumps on my body. I rubbed my arms for warmth.

"At the last second April pulled one hand free and tugged to release her other arm. That's when Carney disappeared—taking her right arm and shoulder with him."

"What!" I gripped the edges of the couch cushions, imagining what Jimmy just told me.

Tears shone in Jimmy's eyes. "He didn't have a close enough grip. It was horrible. Like her arm and shoulder were sheared off by cut glass. And the blood." He bent forward with his head in his hands. "There was so much blood. I reached her as she crumpled to the ground writhing in agony." He raised his eyes to meet mine. "Sami, it was awful! This beautiful woman turned to carnage.

"Her face turned white. Blood gushed out, turning the grass around her a muddy brown. Her eyes were wide open. I saw her light go out." Jimmy raked his hands through his hair and lowered his head. Tears streamed down his face.

I wrapped my arms around him, tasting salt on my lips as our tears mingled.

No words of comfort could ease the pain or erase the vivid images of April's death. I held onto Jimmy, rocking him as I would a hurt child. How many times had he replayed that scene in his head, beating himself up knowing that if he'd arrived a few moments sooner, he might have saved her? Maybe that was April's penalty for misusing the slides. If it was, it seemed unjust considering the way she was dragged into this life.

His voice muffled in my shoulder; he continued in a monotone. "I held her as long as I could. A crowd gathered. There were police. My hands were sticky as the blood dried on them. The rest was a blur. I held her until they pulled me away. I couldn't bear to let go, but they made me."

"Who, honey?"

"I don't know. The crowd. The police. The ambulance crew. It doesn't matter. They took her. When the police questioned me, I couldn't speak. Down at the station, they tried for hours to get me to tell them what happened. How could I explain it?

"Several hours later, I found myself back in my apartment. I don't remember how long I sat there. I woke up on the floor the next day, my clothes covered in blood—April's blood."

"You went to Carney's place, didn't you?"

Jimmy withdrew from my arms with a gentle squeeze. "I wanted to kill him."

"But you couldn't do it."

"I would have! But the house was empty except for April's belongings. He had taken everything of his including all the slides and the holder. I haven't seen him since. Or at least until he switched his photograph for Amanda's Suitor."

"Did you ever try to get more information out of your Grandfather? Did you tell him what happened?"

Sitting back, he wiped the tears from his face. "No. The man lost enough when he lost his son. I couldn't go to him with this. Besides, what would it matter? April was dead."

"But, honey, he's got to know more than he told you. How many generations has your family really been involved? I find it hard to believe there aren't more. Three of you took this on—that you know of. And what about Carney? Was his family involved? Is it simply passed on from generation to generation?" I stopped, realizing I was assaulting him with questions.

"I can't deny that I haven't thought of all this too, but Grandfather is dead and whatever knowledge he had is gone."

"You know that isn't true."

"No, Sami! I can't allow it!"

I sat straight and stared at him. The lash of his words stung. He'd never spoken to me like that before.

Shock replaced the vehemence on his face. Softening his voice, he said, "I'm sorry, honey. I don't know where that came from."

I put my hand on his cheek, still damp from tears. "I do. What happened to April *is not* your fault. You know that. Whether you have a family history and Carney doesn't, it's the Frenchman that brought both of you into this at the same time. It was Carney who pulled April in. Not you. You need to let go of the guilt and focus on stopping him now, in the present."

"Why do you say that?"

"Because I know you. You thought about going back again to save April, even if it meant you'd be trapped. What stopped you?"

"I didn't have any slides that would get me back at the right time. How do you always know?" he asked, taking both my hands in his.

"Because I love you, and after thirty plus years of dancing beside you, I know your nature."

With a firmer grip, he said, "And I know yours." The set of his jaw told me he knew what I was planning.

Despite his protesting, I mentally reviewed the emergency slides sitting in the safe that could take me to the right time in San Francisco. With or without Jimmy's blessing, I was going to visit his Grandfather. It appeared to be the only way to stop Carney.

Chapter 13

Neither Jimmy nor I felt like eating dinner. We drained the rest of the wine bottle and opened another. My next step loomed before me; it was one I would take alone. I had to speak to Jimmy's grandfather. I saw no other way.

We talked about Dede and Milton and how we hoped their meeting was going well. I still had a good feeling about the match and hoped Carney wouldn't interfere. His popping up while Dede traveled back worried me. Thoughts of him haunted my sleep after Jimmy and I went to bed.

When Jimmy left for work before nine in the morning, I jumped into action before I could second guess myself.

Going directly to my safe in the office, I retrieved the left-over emergency slides with the red frame. I needed to find a location in or close to San Francisco with a date after Jimmy's grandfather met April. A pang of guilt engulfed me knowing this journey was without Jimmy's blessing.

Jimmy's grandfather died in 1992. The remaining slide for Blanche when she met Randy from Napa Valley in the year 1979 would be close enough. If a second trip became necessary, I also had a slide for 1984 that would land me in Monterey. Selecting the slide, holder and small box full of cash from the mid-twentieth century, I took a thousand dollars. It would be enough to cover any emergency expenses. I returned the cash box and remaining slides to the safe and locked it.

Upstairs in my bedroom I secured the red frame in the holder and dialed the date at the bottom. The time of day always matched the current time in the present. These emergency slides were the only ones that allowed me to set a specific day which was one to four weeks after the Betrothed's second journey.

I hesitated a moment as a thought struck me as odd. Jimmy said Carney's explanation of being able to go back only six months was that his slides were different than Jimmy's. What if that wasn't a lie? Had he been given slides allowing a time frame to be set for other than the three-week span of a Betrothed's journey as well as a location? Another question Jimmy's grandfather might be able to answer.

With renewed determination, I pressed the button to power up the device. An hour would give me just enough time to welcome Dede back to this decade then be on my way.

I stashed the currency in my purse, set it on the dresser, and returned to my studio to await the Betrothed's return.

Sitting on the couch in my studio, excitement filled me. Despite this being a fact-finding mission that might not go well, the thought of time-traveling gave me a rush. It always did. The minutes ticked down. To the second, Dede materialized in front of the bench with a hand extended in front of her. It was as if she'd been reaching for something—or someone. Looking around confused, she focused on me.

When I stood up to greet here, Dede took me by surprise by throwing her arms around my shoulders and holding on tight. Releasing her embrace, she laughed. "Sorry, but I don't know how to thank you enough!"

"Well,…your welcome!" No need to ask how the meeting went. The glow of joy emanating from her made my heart glad.

She looked down and grabbed the pendant around her neck. "Look! Milton said I was his night time sky." Suspended from a delicate chain, a crescent moon made of turquoise lay against her fair skin. Five delicate stars surrounded the moon, spraying out on silver rays.

"It's exquisite. Did he buy that for you?"

"Actually," she said with a blush rising on her cheeks, "he had it made the same time as his sun necklace. He knew when he found the woman of his dreams, she would fit this necklace. It was like Milton knew I would be the one! Can you imagine that? He got it for me before we ever met. He said my dark hair was the complement to his sun colored locks. Sami, I can't tell you how perfect the man is. Do I really have to wait a week to go back?"

I couldn't hold back my joyful laughter, a welcome release from the stress of the past few days and a reminder of why I became a Photographer. The sparkle in Dede's eyes made it all worthwhile.

Placing my hand on her arm, I said, "Yes, unfortunately. You need time to wrap up your life here and for us to create your credentials. If there's anything you want to take with you, it's best to fit it into a backpack. Remember, nothing that is obviously outside of your new time frame. I guess there's no need to ask how your 'date' went?"

"Oh, Sami. Milton is all I've ever wanted. And he was thrilled that I'm an artist too! He started clearing part of his studio, which is *huge*, to make room for my sculpting." She was babbling. I'd seen that euphoria with most matches. Witnessing it again enhanced my joy from helping these couples.

"Dede, I can't tell you how happy I am for you. It thrills me you've found a good match."

She took a deep breath, as if composing herself. "I can't begin to tell you how grateful I am. But it does make me wonder."

"What?" I asked, with a hand to my chest.

"Oh, not about Milton and me." I was sure she could see the relief on my face.

"About what, dear?"

"You do so much to help…well…women like me, I guess you would say. But what about you?"

"Me?" I wasn't sure where this was leading. "What do you mean?"

"What about you? I mean…well…don't you get a match?"

Now I understood. This woman was beside herself with glee, yet concerned about me. Her compassion would have made her a good Photographer. "You're so sweet to be concerned. But, you see, my match is the one that brought me into this business."

"Your Collector."

I smiled and felt my cheeks flush. "Yes. My Collector is my

match. With this business or not, I love that man with all my heart. So yes, I've found mine," I said placing both hands over my heart. "I wish you and I had met under different circumstances."

"Why?" Dede asked.

"Because I would've enjoyed having you as a friend. We're very much alike. On the other hand, it makes me ecstatic you'll go on to an amazing life with a man you truly love. Not to worry, so will I."

"Good. So, I come back here in a week?"

"Yup! Go wrap up your life in this time line. You have a new one to begin!"

I walked her to the front door and waved as she drove away. I prayed everything would go smoothly with her return to Milton.

Back in the house I thought about turning off the slide holder and waiting a day, but didn't want to talk myself out of the journey. No sense in trying to hide my trip from Jimmy either. He already knew my mindset. It was now or never.

Going to my bedroom closet, I put on a pair of Levi jeans with a plain white t-shirt. Putting on a denim jacket, I was ready to blend into the landscape. Knowing Jimmy would come here tonight after work, I decided to leave him a note as to when I'd be back. No sense in causing him any more worry than necessary—especially, since Carney had been here.

I wrote that this was something I needed to do for both of us, and that I loved him. With the note propped up on the kitchen counter against a bottle of his favorite merlot, I ran back to my bedroom. The holder had reached full power. Without another thought, I slung my purse over my shoulder, depressed the thirty-second timer, and waited for the flash.

I appeared beside a small diner in Napa Valley. The year was 1979. Being three weeks after Blanche had gone back for her final journey to be with Randy, I hoped not to run into her on my walk to the bus station. The next coach to San Francisco would depart in ninety minutes. I purchased my ticket.

It was amusing to me to see the bell-bottomed jeans and tie-dyed shirts of the era. Not everyone was consumed by the current fashions, yet the braids and long hair on both the women *and* men were amusing. Watching the local populace kept me entertained while waiting for my bus.

Reaching the bus station in San Francisco, I jumped on a cable car and made my way to Chinatown. Less than five hours after arriving in this bygone era, I stood in front of the Jade Pagoda. Taking a deep breath, I went inside.

Chapter 14

Ding-a-ling jingled the bell over the door as I entered. The scent of sandalwood incense hit me immediately. I surveyed the old shop, watching dust motes swirl in the sunlight as rays peeked through the windows.

The store was just as I remembered it when Jimmy first brought me here in 1983 to meet his grandfather.

I meandered over to a glass case displaying necklaces and bracelets. On closer examination, a few items were unidentifiable.

"You see something you like, lady? I make you good deal." The young Chinese man shuffled toward me. He wore the stereotypical black pants with a white tunic and black slippers. His face reflected a mixed-race heritage, but Asian features dominated, except for those amazing blue eyes. The only things missing were a cap and long braid to look like he stepped out of China a hundred years ago.

I thought it best to test the waters before asking to speak with the proprietor, Mr. Chang. "How much for that one, with the red jewel?" I asked, pointing at a necklace in the case.

"Ohhhh, that one very special, very dear," the young man pined.

"Does that mean you think I can't afford it?"

"Oh, no! I not mean disrespect. It special piece of jewelry. It belong to very special lady. My family bring it here when we come from China. But I make you good deal. Po always make good deal. Especially for pretty lady."

I pressed my fingers on the glass and leaned in. "It seems quite dusty. How can I tell what it really looks like? Perhaps I should look elsewhere?"

"No. Po will shine it up for you. You see. It very pretty necklace. Bring luck for person that wear it."

Grabbing a set of keys from his pocket he went to unlock the case.

"How lucky can it be for the last owner if it ended up for sale in a junk shop?"

"Last lady that own necklace live very, very long life. Very lucky. Very rich. You try it on?"

Looking him in the eye, I said, "Cut the crap, Jimmy. You're not fresh off the boat, so you can drop the accent."

Po looked devastated for a brief moment. Letting out a long sigh, he straightened up and asked, "Okay, what precinct are you from and what are you looking for today? We only sell cheap trinkets to the tourists, so whatever you're after, you won't find it here in my grandfather's shop. And yes, he did come from China, as you probably already know."

With a huge smile, I extended my hand. "Let's start over. I'm Sami, and I'm not from any of your local precincts, however, I'm dead sure what I'm looking for can be found in this shop."

"So, who sent you, Sami?" Jimmy ignored my hand, giving up any pretense of being a meek Chinaman peddling his wares.

I thought it all right to fabricate just a bit to speed things up, "As a matter of fact, Jimmy, you did!"

He warily looked me in the eye.

Tilting my head back I gave him a wink.

"So, you're from the future?"

"Yes."

"Are you a Betrothed?" I knew at that point Jimmy was in the midst of interviewing his Suitors. He had told me he liked working in his grandfather's shop to perfect his acting skills as a lawyer. It would be handy in crafting his actions for opening and closing arguments once he began working in court.

"Not exactly. I'm here to talk to your grandfather. Will you get him, please?"

He hesitated a minute and looked at me with distrust. It was almost comical knowing what we would become to each other. I had hoped to catch the grandfather alone and not run into Jimmy. Now he would know both timelines since I'd meddled. It couldn't be helped. This trip was necessary.

"What do you want with him?"

Telling him the true reason wasn't an option. Not knowing what damage was already being done to the timeline, my contact needed to be as limited as possible. "He'll know." I believed that to be a lie, but maybe not.

"He's not here."

"When will he return?"

"Maybe tomorrow." Jimmy looked down at the counter then turned away.

He was a bad liar. Even in the present, he wouldn't look me in the eye when he didn't want to tell me something. His aversion disturbed me. By the time he'd met me his demeanor had softened. Losing April only a couple years earlier must have hardened him during this time.

The beads hanging over the doorway to the back room clacked together as I saw Mr. Chang pushing them aside to pass through. "It is okay, Jimmy. I will speak with her." Slim with silver hair, he wasn't quite as tall as his grandson. The man would be somewhere in his seventies at this time. He appeared more comfortable in the traditional garb.

Jimmy looked a little put off at having his authority overruled but nodded in respect to the old man. Mr. Chang said to his grandson, "Leave us, please."

Not wanting to break eye contact with the grandfather, I didn't look Jimmy's way but knew there must have been shock and disappointment on his face. Respect for his elders ran deep and I heard him go through the doorway to the back room. Probably not far, but I couldn't see beyond the white beads.

"You don't belong here," the grandfather said.

"Do you know why I'm here, Mr. Chang?"

Staring at me with a stony expression, he repeated, "You don't belong here. You should not have come."

"Well, I'm here now. And I need your help." Then I lowered my voice, "Jimmy and I need your help."

His expression never changed. "He would never have given you permission to come here."

"You're right. So, I didn't ask. Please, Mr. Chang, you may be the only one with the answers we need."

"Why do you need these answers?"

"To stop a monster. You already know this though, don't you?"

"I know many things. What makes you think if I answer your questions, things can be changed?" He wasn't making this easy. Asking the right questions would be the only way to get the information I required. Mr. Chang wasn't going to volunteer anything. I had to convince him.

The bell over the door jangled and a couple with two young boys came in. The children looked to be around nine and ten. "Mom, look at this cool dragon!"

"Yes, honey. Please don't touch anything. I'm sure it'll break easily."

We both watched the family for a moment, then heard the clacking of beads. Young Jimmy walked past his grandfather to greet the new patrons. I noticed he didn't make any pretense of using a fake accent this time. "Good afternoon. There are a lot of treasures to see here. It's okay to touch things, just be gentle. After all, this isn't a museum!"

The mother smiled appreciatively. The father remained passive. Probably wondering how much this little venture was about to cost him.

I turned my attention back to the grandfather. "Is there some place we can talk? I promise not to take up too much of your time. It *is* important. You know I wouldn't have come if it wasn't."

He scrutinized me a moment longer, then walked over to the beaded doorway. Pushing the strings aside, he stepped out of the way and held them while looking back in my direction. I took this as an invitation and crossed the threshold.

Stacks of boxes lined one wall. A desk stood at the back of the room with piles of papers on one corner, a telephone, and an adding machine. The room looked much as I had envisioned it. I had never seen it the times I visited; his grandfather had been very guarded about his space beyond.

Mr. Chang followed me then shuffled to a door off to the

right. Opening it revealed a stairway going up. This time he went on ahead. I followed, closing the door behind me.

At the top of the stairs, we turned left into a large living room. The area was immaculate with two overstuffed red couches in the far corner. Tossed about the room were beautiful brocade pillows made of black velvet fabric and embroidered in golds and red. The ones on the floor, large enough to sit on, matched smaller versions on the couches. A black lacquer coffee table with ivory insets depicting a dragon sat in front of them.

He led the way toward the back and we entered a spacious kitchen where he gestured for me to take a seat at the table. Two small Chinese teacups had been set out beside a steaming pot of Oolong, judging from the fragrance. As I sat down, I wondered again how much he really knew.

After pouring tea into both cups, Mr. Chang finally made eye contact. And waited. We both sipped. It was up to me to get this going.

"Thank you for the tea." Not receiving a response, I continued. "I need you to tell me how to stop a monster. Tell me how to stop Carney."

Chapter 15

"His soul has turned black. I cannot help you," Mr. Chang said. I knew English was his second language but detected only a hint of an accent.

"So, you know what he's doing. How?"

"All I know is his Photographer was wrong."

"What do you mean by *wrong*?" Jimmy told me his grandfather said that and wouldn't explain.

"She did not belong in the timeline he forced her into. He was supposed to have another Photographer."

If this man already knew, why hadn't he done something about it? "She was never supposed to be a Photographer?"

"I did not say that."

"Then what are you saying?" I was trying hard to keep the frustration out of my voice.

"She was never supposed to be *his* Photographer."

The shock on my face must have been obvious as I sat back in my chair. My mind spun. This changed things. Jimmy assumed April was never supposed to be part of this process at all. Now it seems she had been destined to be involved, but with another Collector. When Carney dragged her into his life, he interfered with someone else's life, not just Tony's. It also meant all the potential matches she should've made with her Collector might have been destroyed as well. The ramifications were overwhelming.

"So Jimmy already told you what happened with Carney and April?"

"He did not need to. I could see her soul when we met. It was clouded. She was not right. And his was black. There was no mistaking it."

"What do you mean you could see her soul?"

"I cannot explain it. This does not concern you. You should leave."

I sat there a moment. "If you really wanted me to leave, then why are we in your home having tea? You knew I was coming, didn't you?"

Again, my questions went unanswered as he continued to sip from his cup.

"You know I won't leave until you tell me."

"Or I could wait until you go back to your own time. How many of your twenty-four hours have you used up already?" he asked smiling for the first time. There wasn't any joy in his expression as he settled back in his chair challenging me.

"You're right. You could wait for me to simply disappear, but do you think I would have come, if it wasn't crucial? I need your help. *We* need your help. Carney is taking innocent lives. He has to be stopped."

"He is not my problem. I dispense the slides, nothing more. That is my role!"

This was getting me nowhere fast. As much as it broke my heart, I had to touch his inner being. Only then might he feel compelled to share what he knew. God forgive me! "He may have been involved in your son's death as well."

The old man slammed his teacup on the table and sat up straight in his chair. This was either new information, or he was shocked I would use such a tactic. I didn't care. One way or another he needed to talk to me.

"Get out!" His booming voice felt like a slap in the face. Almost regretting what I did, I knew I had found the chink in his armor.

"We can't change that past," I said, "but you can help me change the future. Please, Mr. Chang," I pleaded, "tell me how to stop Carney."

It was a standoff. One I hoped to win. The struggle on his face as he crinkled his forehead and set his jaw was clear. He knew more, much more. *But why wouldn't he share what he knew?*

"You must trap him in time."

"How?"

"There is another I need to speak with first. It will be breaking more rules, but you don't seem averse to doing that," he said in a condescending voice.

For the first time, I found myself smiling at the old man. While his tone was harsh, he seemed to be softening. Sensing an opening, I pressed on.

"Fair enough. Do whatever you need to help us stop that man. You must know how Carney was able to hop through time six months prior, when he first interfered with April's life. How was that possible?"

"I believe you already know."

"Perhaps. My suspicions suggest he got hold of a special slide that allowed him to set the date and location to whenever he wanted."

"See? You do not need me for answers."

"How did he know such a thing existed? Are his slides different from the ones given to Jimmy?"

He fell silent as if evaluating how much to tell me. With a sigh, he said, "The proprietor of the Golden Dragon overstepped his bounds. He has been relieved of his role—too late to prevent this chain of events."

"What did he do?"

"He allowed Carney to have one of the emergency slides that enabled him to set any time and place in history he chose. These slides are rare and only entrusted to worthy distributors. The character of that proprietor was misjudged."

"Are there more of those slides?"

"Why do you need to know?"

"Isn't it obvious? Carney must have found a supply of them. He had to have more than one to be wreaking this kind of devastation. He seems to be jumping through time at will. That would require more than one slide."

"It would not be a breach to tell you there are special proprietors selected to distribute such slides. They are to give no more than two to any one Collector, and only in special circumstances."

"Do you think Carney found out which proprietors have them and has been collecting them?"

"No, I do not."

"What do you mean?" I asked again, frustrated at the tiny bits of information he chose to dole out.

"Enough. I have already told you too much. You need to leave."

I sat there deciding whether all my leverage was used up. There was still more to know. The shadows outside the kitchen window grew as dusk began to fall.

"You haven't told me how to trap Carney in time. Or what that even means."

"You will go now," he said firmly.

"I'll show you to the door." We both looked over to see Jimmy standing in the doorway. Not knowing how long he'd been listening, I hoped he hadn't overheard too much. "I closed up the shop, Grandfather," he added.

Mr. Chang nodded as he stood, waiting for me to do the same. Our meeting seemed to be over for today.

Rising as well, I nudged him one more time. "How will I know what to do? You haven't told me."

"Come back tomorrow morning," was all he said. He turned around and walked out the other door leading from the kitchen.

"This way," Jimmy said, his voice firm. "You've upset my grandfather enough."

I strode past him toward the stairway in the living room with him behind me. It hurt to hear such hostility from the man who would later share my life. Going through the store room and the shop, I stopped at the front door and waited for Jimmy to unlock it. He reached over and slid open the bolt. I didn't wait for him to open the door for me.

Outside, I turned to him, "I'll be at the Hyatt by Fisherman's Wharf if your grandfather is willing to discuss more tonight." His response was the door slamming in my face. Turning and setting off at a brisk pace to a busy intersection, I flagged down a taxi to take me to the hotel. The Wharf was always a favorite of mine in San Francisco. With the calm lapping of the ocean, it would be a good place to review everything Mr. Chang had divulged.

Chapter 16

As I checked into the room, my stomach grumbled. Going a whole day with only coffee and toast wasn't cutting it for me. I found a small café near the Wharf serving delicious clam chowder and a decent chardonnay.

Seated at a window overlooking the harbor, I sifted through everything Mr. Chang told me. The questions he answered led to more questions. By the time I paid the bill, my mind had drifted to the present time, too. Jimmy would be at my house by now and have found the note. He would also be aware of the new timeline since his younger self was present when I spoke with his grandfather today, in 1979. Hoping Jimmy wasn't too angry, I wandered back to the hotel.

Fatigue overcame me in my hotel room. Even my apprehension about tomorrow and whether Mr. Chang would divulge anything useful disappeared as soon as I lay my head on the pillow.

A loud ringing jolted me out of a deep sleep. It took a few seconds for me to realize it was the phone on the night stand. The bedside clock read 2:13 a.m.

"Hello," I stuttered, still a bit groggy.

"This is the front desk. I'm sorry to disturb you at such a late hour, ma'am. There is a Jimmy Chang down here *insisting* he see you. He says it's an emergency. If you would like, we can have security escort him out..."

"No!" I yelled into the phone. Forcing myself to calm down, I controlled my voice, "No, that won't be necessary. Please tell Mr. Chang I'll be right down."

"Yes, ma'am. Thank you, ma'am. Have a good evening."

Which Jimmy was it? Past or present? Possibly my current Jimmy had secured a special slide and travelled here. I didn't think the Jimmy from this era would do me harm, but I felt safer meeting downstairs.

My stomach twisted into knots fearing I might get off the elevator to be greeted by the Jimmy from my own time. Would he be angry? Concerned? Not to mention the huge risk if he came back to San Francisco now. Running into yourself was never a good idea.

Dressing quickly, I ran a comb through my hair and brushed my teeth then grabbed my purse on the way out the door.

I stepped into the elevator and hit the Lobby button. The metal frame creaked in a symphony of moans as it inched downward. While the floor indicator dinged with every passing level, almost deafening in the confined space, I took deep breaths and thought about what to say if it was my present Jimmy.

The doors slid open to reveal young Jimmy with his arms crossed and tapping his foot. His glare bored into me. Wearing denim jeans and a gray, long-sleeved t-shirt, he looked more like the young man I would meet in about four years. I hoped that meeting would still happen after this encounter.

"Grandfather is missing," he spat. "What did you say to him?"

I stood motionless not knowing how to respond. The elevator doors started to close, and I shot my hand out to stop them, then stepped into the lobby. "What do you mean he's missing?"

"After you went out the front door of the shop, I went back upstairs to his apartment. He was gone."

"Gone?"

"Yes, gone. As in not home!"

Obviously, the apartment had a private entrance. Mr. Chang must've used it while Jimmy had gone downstairs. Finding my voice again, "I have no idea where he went."

Looking up, the clerk behind the front desk watched us. A wandering security guard kept glancing our way. His steady footsteps, echoing through the cavernous entryway, hesitated each time Jimmy spoke. Deciding this conversation was best held somewhere more private, I walked to a grouping of couches and chairs in a far corner of the lobby. Jimmy followed.

"Tell me what you talked about. I heard you mention Carney's name. Do you know where that bastard is? Are you his new Photographer?"

The shock on my face must have startled him. He was obviously about to fire off more questions, but simply closed his mouth. It occurred to me that this might have been the turning point for Jimmy. My interacting with him here in 1979 may have been what happened before. Because of this visit, he didn't tell me the truth about the Frenchman and his friendship with Carney. It may have been an attempt to change the future after he met me and realized I was his Photographer. History repeated itself anyway; I came back and met him in this decade.

My next words might change our future. They needed to be chosen carefully. "No, I'm not Carney's Photographer."

He ran his fingers through his hair. "I'm sorry. I didn't mean to accuse you of anything, but my grandfather went missing right after you left. Please, tell me what you talked about."

"Jimmy, you've already begun your interviews with the Suitors. You aren't naïve to this process. You also know I can't tell you why I'm here. It could make things worse."

"What if it could make things better? It's obvious you're here to change something. How do you know I'm not the one that can do it? My grandfather didn't provide enough answers to satisfy you, did he? Maybe *I'm* really the one you've come to see."

That never occurred to me. This time period was after Carney inadvertently killed April. That couldn't be changed. But what if the Jimmy now was able to find Carney and stop him before he started his killing spree?

This line of thought didn't feel right. Giving Jimmy information from the future could put him at risk. Not a chance worth taking. I needed to find out from Mr. Chang how to trap Carney in time. It was up to me to stop him. I felt it in my heart.

"The only thing I can tell you is your grandfather said he would have to consult with someone else. Maybe that's where he is now."

Jimmy mulled that over. "I don't know who that would be. In the years since Grandfather told me about his role, he's never mentioned anyone else he was involved with."

"Do you think he meant another distributor? He knew of the ones at the Purple Lotus and the Golden Dragon in New York. Perhaps he knows one locally?" It wasn't much to go on, but I couldn't tell him anything of future events. It was too risky. Since he'd already lost track of Carney, there was no need to involve him further.

"It seems we've both reached a dead end." The young man sank down onto one of the couches and expelled an exasperated sigh.

I gently perched on the cushion next to him. He was right. If Mr. Chang was missing, then I wouldn't get any more information. A thought struck me, "Does he ever use the slides? I mean, how does he get a new supply when needed?"

"He's never told me. Every time I've asked, he says I don't need to know. Grandfather also said it's safer for me to stick with my role and not involve myself further."

I put my hand gently on his shoulder. "When he said that, do you think he was referring to your father's murder?"

This took him by surprise as he whipped his head around to look at me. "Why would you say that? He was murdered in an attempted robbery. For whatever reason, the burglar was startled or interrupted and took off before stealing anything. Do you know more?"

"No." That was the truth and my attempt at putting together more pieces of this puzzle. "You're right it's probably unrelated."

His eyes narrowed. I knew he didn't believe me. I wasn't sure I believed it myself. No use pursuing that point with nothing else to go on.

"I'm sorry to have woken you." More of the Jimmy I would come to love was showing through. Right now, he remained a tormented young man trying to make sense of the family business.

"Don't worry about it. I hope your grandfather is all right. Can I come by in the morning? There are more questions only he would have answers to."

Thinking this over, Jimmy asked, "Would it stop you if my answer was no?"

I gave him a lopsided smile.

"I didn't think so. When are your twenty-four hours up?"

"At 10:45 tomorrow morning." No sense hiding that point.

"Come by when the shop opens." With a slight nod, he stood and walked away.

I watched as he strode through the front door of the lobby before I walked over to the elevator.

Back in my room, I lay down thinking sleep would elude me. Despite being consumed with thoughts of whether Mr. Chang would reappear and share any additional information, I drifted off. I woke to the ringing of the bedside phone at 7:00 a.m.—my wake-up call.

After a quick shower, I got dressed and sat on the balcony drinking my morning coffee. The misty ocean air felt good; it's dampness on my skin refreshing. Since the Jade Pagoda didn't open until 9:00 a.m., I checked out of the hotel and walked down to the Wharf. I sat on a bench by the pier, munching on a freshly baked croissant from a nearby bakery and enjoyed the harbor life.

Seagulls drifted over the white-capped water and landed with grace on the pylons. Their raucous calls echoed across the harbor. Boats with their sails securely tied down for the night, bobbed up and down as waves slapped the sides. What would it be like to sail away without a thought of anything beyond the present day?

At 8:45 a.m., I wandered back to the street and caught a cab to the Jade Pagoda. It was fifteen minutes past opening time. The door was locked, and the Closed sign still displayed in the window. I knocked gently, then louder. Minutes passed. Nobody answered. I peered through the dirty windows the best I could. The lights were out. I couldn't see anyone.

I thought of finding the private entry to the apartment. Assuming it was located on the side or back, I tried to go around the building. A locked iron gate blocked the narrow alleyway between the Jade Pagoda and the building next door. I jiggled the gate, scaring a gray cat. It jumped off a trash can, sending the lid to clatter on the ground.

Frustrated, I went back to the front door and peered in. Still no movement. I knocked again with no luck. My time here was almost up.

Since Mr. Chang had been missing last night, I hoped he was

checking with his other source and would tell me what I needed to know this morning. Those possibilities faded as my precious minutes ticked away.

Across the street, I grabbed a cup of tea at a small counter service cafe and sat outside watching the shop. My frustration mounted as I grasped the paper cup too tightly and splashed hot tea on my fingers. At 10:40 a.m. the light from the back room came on in the Jade Pagoda. Abandoning my tea, I bolted across the street. I pounded on the door and looked through the glass. Five minutes. Only five minutes before I had to return to my present.

Mr. Chang walked towards me. My hands balled into anxious fists at his lack of urgency. Then he turned as someone came through the beaded doorway from the store-room. I couldn't clearly see who. It wasn't Jimmy. The person appeared shorter than Mr. Chang. The dimness of the shop hindered my vision. A flash of white shirt was all I could see.

Frantically, I knocked again. He had to let me in. One more minute! Mr. Chang looked at me again, then behind him. Turning away, he walked toward the stranger.

My fist swung to knock against a glass door that was no longer there. I almost fell over. Catching the top of the dresser to steady myself, I put both hands flat on the surface and leaned over.

"Welcome back, Mademoiselle," said a voice behind me.

Chapter 17

My body tensed as panic filled me. I spun around; a stranger sat on my bed. I looked toward the door.

"Do not be alarmed, Mademoiselle. I will not harm you."

Though he spoke perfect English, his voice had a slight foreign accent. Looking to be about a decade older than myself, he wore khaki pants. The crispness of his white long-sleeved shirt suggested he wasn't some common hoodlum.

Leaning back against the dresser, I asked the obvious question. "Who are you?"

He chuckled as if surprised. "I believe your Collector refers to me as 'The Frenchman.' You may call me, Francois."

I remained standing. Though I sensed no malice in this man, his presence in my bedroom unnerved me. *How had he come to be here?* A tingle of excitement replaced my apprehension. If anyone could provide information, it was The Frenchman.

"Please," he said, "but I've frightened you. That was not my intention. The kettle is at a boil. Perhaps we can adjourn to your kitchen for some tea and conversation?"

"Oh, yes. Tea. Yes, tea would be good." I sounded like a moron. Where was Jimmy? Surely, he would have read my note last night. Maybe it angered him, and now I was on my own to sort this out. No, he wouldn't do that, no matter how angry he may have gotten. He would know the only way to get help was for me to take this journey. We were out of options.

Francois stood and gestured for me to precede him through the door. Mustering a modicum of composure, I set down my purse and went downstairs to the kitchen. On the table sat two mugs with Earl Gray tea bags in them. Shades of my last meeting with Dede washed over me. I now felt the same confusion she must have when I told her how she would go about meeting Milton.

The tea kettle quietly whistled as it simmered over a low flame. How long had he been waiting for me in my house?

"Please," he said, "allow me." The Frenchman gestured for me to sit while he poured water into both mugs. "I do enjoy a good cup of tea. Do you not?"

"Uh, yes." I waited as he placed the kettle on the stove then sat opposite me at the table.

"I'm sorry to have startled you, Mademoiselle. I did not mean to frighten you upon your return."

Looking over to where I'd left the note for Jimmy, I saw it was gone. His eyes followed my gaze.

"Again, I am sorry, but I removed the note you left for your Collector. I need to speak to you alone first."

Anger overtook me as I placed my hands flat on the table. "Why would you do that? What can you say to me and not Jimmy?"

"Ah, you have regained your composure. Good." He sat back as if proud of this accomplishment.

"If that's meant to soothe me, it doesn't."

I watched as he removed his teabag and placed it on the small dish beside the mug. Resigning myself to participate in his ritual, I did the same. We both drank. It struck me how he introduced himself to Jimmy and Carney the same way—over tea.

"How did you know I would be returning from a journey?"

"Did you not see me when you were at the door in San Francisco?"

Thinking for a moment about my last minutes in front of Mr. Chang's shop, I remembered the glimpse of a white shirt, but nothing more.

"You were at the Jade Pagoda right before I returned here. It was you coming out of the back room, wasn't it?"

"See? You know more than you realize."

"You were the one Mr. Chang had to consult with?" It was a rhetorical question. I already knew the answer.

"Yes. He told me why you visited him. You know, Mademoiselle, you need to be careful how you use the slides. You came close to using them for personal gain."

My voice rose in anger. It seemed he was trying to make me mad. "How is it personal gain when I'm trying to stop a lunatic?"

"Carney is a problem. I'd had high hopes for that one. He is special."

"Special? In what way?"

"He is from one of the four original bloodlines. The Four Families, if you will. But that is not your concern."

"He's murdering my Betrotheds! I'd say anything having to do with him is my concern. Wouldn't you?"

The Frenchman put his hands up in front of him in a gesture of surrender. "Some things have no bearing here—but you are right. We need to solve this. And quickly."

"How do I trap him in time?"

"Chang told you about that? He should not have. I am not sure you should be the one."

"Why not?" My eyes widened. He was here for a reason. If it wasn't to help me stop Carney, then why?

"Trapping someone in time is dangerous. I do not think you should attempt this."

Shoving my chair away from the table, I walked across the kitchen. Fury engulfed me. He had the knowledge to help but wasn't willing to share it. My tennis shoes squeaked on the tile as I whipped back around to face him again. "If not me, then who?" I spat.

"Mademoiselle, please, sit down."

"I've had a stressful twenty-four hours. I'm tired, frustrated, and angry. I need answers. Now you're telling me you know how to stop Carney, but don't think I should be the one to do it. I'm not going to sit across a table from you having a pleasant conversation when a murderer is out there with a vendetta against Jimmy and me. Who knows how many more will die before he is stopped? This has gone way beyond polite conversation! Are you going to tell me what I need to know or not?"

We'd come to an impasse with me standing in front of him

glaring, while he sat sipping his tea, his features calm.

"It seems you have a bit of a stubborn streak, no?" He smiled for the first time.

Unable to help myself, my lips returned the gesture. "Well, I've heard its part of my charm."

This exacted a hearty laugh from Francois. "Now I see why you were chosen for this job. Having the ability to 'roll with the punches' as you Americans say, is a desirable trait. Do you not agree?"

"Yes, I guess I would. Not only with us Americans. You seem to have endured this game quite a while. When Jimmy told me about you, I thought he said you were…ah…what was the phrase he used? Oh yeah, *leaving the arena*. So why are you still here?"

"It has been a while since I have walked on a beach. May we continue our conversation out on your Strand?"

I saw no reason not to. Removing my denim jacket and hanging it on the back of the chair, Francois followed me to the front door.

We headed down the hill to the beach in silence. Exaggerating a deep breath, he seemed to relish the ocean air.

When we reached the Strand and level ground I asked "How long have you been in this game?"

"Why do you ask?"

"Humor me."

"I never could resist a beautiful lady. I have been in this business for over 80 years."

I did a double take. "How is that possible? You don't look a day over 70."

"You are too kind, Mademoiselle." He bowed his head. "I am 112 years old."

Stopping in shock, I stared, waiting for him to crack and say he was kidding. That admission never came. "How is that possible?"

"I am sure you suspected. Traveling through time seems to hinder the aging process. I guess you could say it is a happy side effect. The more jumps you make, the more years are erased."

"That's why Carney was able to pass himself off as a 42-year-old man, even though he is 65. He's jumped many times, hasn't he?"

"Yes."

A flash of orange caught my eye as a plastic disc flew by, almost hitting Francois in the head. He instinctively ducked, then we both laughed. "What is that?" he asked.

"It's called a frisbee. Haven't you seen them before? They're very popular at the beach."

"No. It looks quite fun."

A young boy of about six raced past us, kicking up sand as he retrieved the disc. We watched as the child grabbed it and raced back the way he came, curling his arm in then out as he threw the frisbee toward an older boy. Overshooting his target, the boy watched as his playmate chased the toy down the beach. Both were giggling.

Pulling myself back to our conversation, I asked, "So you've made quite a few jumps through time, haven't you?"

"Yes."

"How have you been able to do this? Like timing precisely when I would return today? Can emergency slides do that?"

He didn't answer. A cloud seemed to overshadow him as he clasped his hands behind his back, looking down at the pavement. I got the feeling information was not going to flow like it had.

"Sami. Sami!"

We both turned to see Jimmy striding along the Strand. From the flush of his face and furrowed brow, I could tell he was more than a little angry.

Chapter 18

As Jimmy hurried to us, he froze at the sight of Francois. "You! What are *you* doing here?"

"A pleasure to see you again, Monsieur."

Jimmy's body stiffened. "It's been forty years. Why are you here now?" His face grew redder.

"Jimmy, please. He's here to help us."

As if suddenly remembering it was me he chased, Jimmy shifted his focus to my face. "I've been worried sick about you. With Carney on the loose, you should have left me a note that you went back."

"Forgive me, sir. The note was in place when she traveled. I removed it. It seems my efforts to speak to the lady alone were for naught," Francois said.

Placing my hand on Jimmy's arm, a pang of guilt resonated through me. "You knew I went back. Now you know the two timelines."

Taking a steadying breath, Jimmy shook his head. "No. There is only one timeline."

"How can that be? I ran into your younger self at the Jade Pagoda."

"That was how history went the first time. Of course, I didn't realize who you were until we met a few years later."

"Then why did you try to stop me from going back?"

His taut face softened as he looked into my eyes, "To keep you safe. With that monster on the loose, I had no way of knowing if he might follow you back."

The frisbee flying in our direction distracted us. This time, the Frenchman reached out and grabbed the disc before it sailed into my shoulder. The young boy ran up and retrieved his toy with a mumbled thanks.

Francois said, "Perhaps we should wander out of the combat zone. Oui?" He gestured back the way we'd come.

Walking up the hill to my house, Jimmy took my hand, twining his fingers with mine. Even though he knew where, or rather when, I had gone, I sensed the worry within him. He hadn't needed the note to know the time I would be returning; he remembered our encounter from 1979. The concern must stem from his not knowing exactly what date I departed this decade to go back.

"How did you know where to find me, honey? I mean down at the beach."

"I didn't. Pulling into your driveway, I saw you and a stranger heading down the hill."

When we arrived back at the house, Francois settled into one of the wicker chairs.

"I very much like your front porch, Mademoiselle. Very peaceful."

His casual attitude grated on my nerves. He behaved as if he were a friend dropping by for a visit.

Jimmy and I took seats next to each other, both looking expectantly at Francois. He didn't take his cue to speak, so I turned to Jimmy. "Your grandfather was hesitant to help me."

"I knew he would be. Did he, in the end?"

"Somewhat. He told me the only way to stop Carney is to trap him in time."

Jimmy swiped his hand through his hair. "Trap him in time? What does that mean?"

"I don't know." I shifted my attention to Francois, "But I think you do."

"I told you, Mademoiselle, it is not a task for you."

I slapped both hands down on the arms of my chair. "Dammit, why not?"

"If you do not execute it just right, you could be trapped in time as well."

"Tell us how to do this. We'll weigh the risks," I looked to Jimmy for support.

He chimed in, "Tell us what we need to do. We'll handle it."

The chair creaked as the Frenchman leaned back. He seemed to be debating the best course. His reluctance to share his knowledge struck me as strange since he came specifically to talk to me. What did he have to say that would require privacy?

"Well, isn't *this* a cozy little reunion?"

We all swiveled our heads as one toward the voice coming from the far end of the porch.

"Carney," Jimmy seethed as he stood up. The color rose in his face.

"Good to see you, Jimmy. It's been too many years." He wore the same shorts and t-shirt from the other day in my studio. The stench of his musky cologne wafted across the porch. I grimaced as the odor conjured up the horrid memory of his last visit.

Carney casually leaned against the house with his arms crossed and focused his attention on the Frenchman. "And aren't you a blast from the past, old man. Long time no see. Glad you made it out of the jungles of Nam. I'm happy to say you were right about the two of us surviving. Any more predictions to share with us today?"

Francois quietly stood up, but Carney wasn't done speaking. "Tell me, what do I call you? The Frenchman feels so...what's the word...clandestine? I could call you Francois. Or would you prefer...Grandpa?"

"What!" I jumped to my feet. I couldn't believe what I was hearing.

"So, you know," replied Francois calmly, looking at our intruder.

My voice escalated to a hysterical level. "He's your grandson? This man is actually your flesh and blood? When were you going to tell us? Or was *that* information we didn't need to know, Francois?"

"Mademoiselle, please. It will be all right."

"Your grandson is a murderer. How can that be all right?"

Gesturing with his hands, palms down, Jimmy said "Sami,

calm down. We need to sort this out."

"Yes, Jimmy," Carney mocked, "let's *calmly* sort this out. You always were a problem solver."

"So, Todd, tell me how you discovered I am your grandfather." Francois appeared unruffled by this scene as if he expected Carney to show up.

"Don't call me that! My name is Carney."

"As you wish...Carney. Tell me."

"While looking through old family photographs years ago, after we'd met in Viet Nam. Mom told me you were her father. She never knew you because you abandoned Grandma before she was born. Guess you weren't exactly a role model, were you?"

Francois said, "Perhaps that is a story for another time."

Carney continued, ignoring Francois' attempt to interject. "I also had an interesting conversation with an Italian chap. He was very helpful. Too bad his usefulness ended. I hear the authorities never identified his body, the poor soul. He had done a *bad* thing anyway, so I guess it was really justice in the end. Or I should say, for his end." He smirked as he reminisced.

"Right now, shall we talk about your inappropriate behavior? It needs to end." Francois remained matter-of-fact.

Carney pushed off from the wall of the house. "Hmmmm...inappropriate. That's an interesting way to phrase it." As he walked to the outer edge of the porch, Carney's sneakers scuffed across the boards. He stopped and leaned against a post. "I would rather discuss what this little meeting is about. You're talking about me, aren't you? Please, do share! What clever plan have you come up with to stop my diabolical ways?"

"This isn't a game. You're killing innocent women." My fists clenched. Anger won out over the fear pulsing through me.

His voice escalated. "Just like my April was innocent. And Jimmy killed her!"

Jimmy stomped down on the floor with one foot. "You were the one that tried to take her back against her will! It was you she had to run from!"

I placed my hand on Jimmy's arm. This distracted him enough to look at me and take a deep breath. He visibly calmed down, though his shaking hands told me his anger festered below the surface. We had no idea where Carney was going with this conversation or why he was even here. Loss of control could only aggravate the situation.

"You shouldn't have meddled," he said still looking at Jimmy. "My April was just fine. It was *you* who caused all our problems with your *friendship*. I know you were trying to take her from me. You were always jealous. It's because of you she's dead!"

Carney pulled a hand gun out of his pocket and aimed it at me. I froze as fear radiated through my body. "Maybe you need to know what it feels like to lose someone so dear. Perhaps life without your sweet Sami is something you should experience."

Jimmy reached to pull me behind him. A shot blasted out. I heard a thud on the boards behind us.

Turning around, Francois laid face down on the porch.

My gaze flew back toward Carney and his weapon. I was afraid to move.

"Dang," he said, "I guess I missed...this time." A satanic grin spread across his face as he disappeared.

I ran to the Frenchman and knelt down. Jimmy helped me roll him over. Blood oozed from his chest.

"Hold on, Francois. We'll get you help." I pressed my hand over the wound and applied as much pressure as I could, but it didn't staunch the flow. I felt helpless.

Blood seeped from the corner of his mouth. "You must..." His voice faded to a harsh whisper.

"Don't try to talk," Jimmy said, pulling his cell phone out of his back pocket. "Save your strength. We'll get you help."

He whispered. "You must listen." He put his hand on mine.

I looked at Jimmy and shook my head. Though I didn't have any medical training, I knew the wound was fatal. "Francois, please." I pleaded, not sure if I wanted him to be still or tell us what he could before time ran out.

He struggled for breath. "Please...," his voice weak, yet he persisted. "You must...you must stop him. Set them...same date...same location...same..." His voice gurgled, but he continued to try.

Knowing he wouldn't last much longer, I was desperate to extract whatever information he could manage. "How do we set more than one date and location?"

"Both...set them...same date...same location...zero time."

"What do you mean *them*?" I asked quietly. Mr. Chang had referred to slides allowing someone to set a specific date and place; I assumed he was referring to one of those.

Jimmy didn't know about them yet. He asked, "What are you talking about? We don't have any control over the dates or places. Francois, you're not making sense."

I took over the conversation. "I know about the special slides. How do we find them? I know only special distributors have them."

"No...those are...wrong. Family...Slides." His pale face bore testimony to the toll the effort was taking. "Only...four...you need...get...them."

Sitting back on his heels, Jimmy looked at me in disbelief. Everything swirled about us. I felt betrayal at having knowledge he didn't. There hadn't been time to fill him in on the part of my journey he hadn't witnessed as a young man.

I returned my attention to Francois. His head had fallen back at an odd angle. His eyes closed.

"Francois. Francois! Tell me where we can find these Family Slides. Please!"

His eyes remained closed. I released the pressure on his wound and sat back. Suddenly his eyes shot open, but it was too late. He vanished. Time was up.

Chapter 19

I sat on the porch staring at the spot Francois occupied moments ago. A pool of his blood stained the oak boards as it seeped through the cracks.

Jimmy knelt beside me with an arm wrapped around my shoulders. The late afternoon sun beat down on us, but I couldn't feel its warmth. My body shook, and he pulled me closer. Burying my face in his chest, I cried. I cried for Francois, for the women whose lives Carney had taken, and for the part we unwittingly played in all this tragedy.

"Shhhh, sweetie."

His shirt became damp from the tears I couldn't turn off. I wasn't sure I could handle any more. Part of me wanted to walk away from it all. The consequences be damned!

Jimmy helped me to my feet and into the house. Everything was a blur. He guided me to the living room couch and pulled me down next to him. My throat tightened at the thoughts of Francois.

After several minutes, I struggled to form words. "Jimmy," I pushed out in a hoarse whisper, "we need to finish this. Whatever it takes."

"I know," he muttered, hugging me tighter.

Pulling away, my voice gained strength. "We need to find the Family Slides, but I don't see how you can set more than one location on one slide, even if it's the same place."

"He said 'them.' Maybe we need all four."

"We don't even know how to find *one*. Maybe we need to only find two. He said *both* locations."

"Please, let me handle this. I'm responsible."

I was appalled he would take the blame for all this. Jimmy had to know Carney's actions were beyond his control. "How do you figure?"

"Carney was my friend."

"And the Frenchman brought both of you into this. Carney's grandfather, for God's sake." My tone escalated, and I couldn't control it. "That is *not* your doing."

"Maybe it is. Think about it, Sami. The Four Families. One of them has to be mine, for three generations, maybe more. Francois' and Carney's must be another one."

"We have no clue who the other two might be."

"Then that's why…"

"Don't you dare!" I cut him off. "Don't give me that lineage crap. Regardless of who belongs to the Four Families, we're in this together. Whether it be by genetics or selection, we are *both* part of this, and we *both* need to work on solving this mess. Even if it means destroying everything in the end. Maybe it's time the process stopped."

Jimmy sat back into the couch cushions, his brow furrowed. I'm sure the thought to end everything, not just Carney's rampage never crossed his mind. It was ever-present in my head. This might be the only way to stop the evil.

"What are you suggesting?" he asked.

I took a deep breath. He wasn't going to like my proposal. "We have another slide that will take me back to talk to your grandfather. The emergency slide from Christy and Jackson would land me in Monterey, California in 1984."

"No," he blurted.

"What do you mean 'no?' The only way to get more information is to talk to your grandfather. There's no other option. Without it, we're at Carney's mercy. I'm not waiting to see what he does next. We have to do this. *I* have to do this."

Jimmy swiped a hand through his hair in frustration and looked down at the floor. After a moment, he straightened up and turned toward me. "You were right the first time."

The confusion on my face must have been obvious. "What?"

"The part where you said *we* have to do this. *We* will go back and talk to my grandfather."

"How do you propose that?" What he suggested sent shivers of apprehension down my spine. I knew what he meant, and it terrified me after hearing about April's demise.

"Honey, you know it can be done."

"In theory, yes."

"Not in theory. We just have to go about it the right way."

I gripped my knees. "Jimmy, please, let me go alone. Besides, what if you run into your young self?"

"I won't. By 1984 I lived in this area, nowhere near San Francisco. If we both go, Grandfather will know the need is dire. He might be more willing to share what he knows."

I sank back into the couch and placed my hands over my eyes to relieve the pressure building behind them. It was incredibly risky yet I, too, believed it could work. "Okay. It still makes me nervous, but we'll both go. First, the preparations need to be made for Dede's journey back to Milton. If we're going to do this, we must keep moving forward with our matches. Being so close to finishing our quota, it would be senseless to quit now." Despite saying the words, I didn't really believe it in my heart, but I felt we needed to try.

Jimmy looked at me for a moment, then nodded. "Tomorrow I'll get her credentials started. Do you have Dede's information sheet filled out, so Daniel can create a plausible background she can remember?"

"Yes, it's in my desk. I'll get it." Having a plan of action gave me a new sense of purpose.

Glad for an excuse to focus on something other than Francois' brutal murder, I got up and walked to the office. Upon entering, I noticed the light blinking on my answering machine. I'd forgotten the phone rang the other day while Jimmy told me about April's attempt to leave Carney. With trepidation, I hit the play back button.

"Hel…Hello? Hi. Sami? I'm not really good at these things. Okay, hi. My name is, Stella. I work with Dede. Well, sometimes I do. At the flower shop, I mean. Oh, sorry. Um…anyway…she told me she was coming to see you. Well, that you did old time photographs. Dress up and take a picture I guess. Um...well...it sounds like fun. And...um...oh darn. Sorry. Okay, I would like to have my picture taken too. You know, dress up and do a photo shoot, I guess? I need some fun in my life. So...anyway, please call me so I can set up an appointment. Okay, bye. Oh! My number is 310-555-0210. Okay, thanks! Hope to hear from you soon. Bye!"

I mulled over the message. Stella seemed to be another lost soul in need of help. If things went well, she would be number 29. Damn! Even with thoughts of abandoning the whole match-making thing, it apparently wasn't willing to go away. My work loomed before me.

Remembering the reason for being in the office, I opened the right-hand drawer of my desk and grabbed the form with Dede's information. Hers was the only one in there. Once a Betrothed went back on her second journey, the sheet was destroyed. Didn't want a paper trail on any of the women.

As I walked back into the living room, Jimmy spoke on the phone. He was ordering Pad Thai Noodles with a side of shrimp shumai from a local Thai restaurant. I loved shumai. By the time it was delivered, I might be able to eat.

The Frenchman being shot in front of us nagged at me. Not even the delicate aroma of the take-out filling the kitchen sparked our appetites. As we picked at the food, we talked about our upcoming journey.

"So, we go tomorrow?" I asked Jimmy as he pushed his noodles around the plate with his fork.

"Yes. I'll go see Daniel in the morning to get Dede's credentials started. Now, tell me what you and Grandfather talked about."

It struck me he wasn't present for most of our discussion in the past. I filled him in on everything Mr. Chang told me, as well as the questions I asked that weren't answered.

After my visit to 1979, young Jimmy had grilled his grandfather about my visit, to no avail. The old man told him nothing.

Hearing April was supposed to be involved in the process shocked my Jimmy. He kept going back to that point. "You're sure Grandfather said April was supposed to be a Photographer?"

"Yes, just not Carney's Photographer."

"That makes sense. She possessed great compassion and tried to make good matches. Sadly, she didn't have full access to all the Suitors. Tony wasn't involved in the process, and she wouldn't have stayed with him."

"How do you know that, honey?"

"I have to admit to checking up on his history years later." He gave me a sheepish grin. "It always bothered me how Tony lost out on a life with April. Turns out he did get married—to another man. Guess he and April wouldn't have worked out anyway."

Funny how life takes such twists and turns, even without the slides. At least Tony had love in his life. I wondered who the other Collector was that April should have spent her life with as a Photographer.

Chapter 20

The next morning, I woke to find myself alone. Heading downstairs, the aroma of coffee lured me into the kitchen. After pouring myself a mug, I wandered through the house looking for Jimmy.

Hearing scraping noises from the front porch, I stepped outside. The smell of bleach assaulted me. Jimmy knelt on his hands and knees scrubbing the boards where Francois had lain. He turned as I sat down in a nearby chair.

"You really are my hero."

"I know," he said. Turning back around, he continued working at the blood stains with a wire brush. The scratching of his strokes echoed across the boards. Some discoloration remained, but most was gone. With time, all the signs would be erased—at least visually.

"How'd you sleep?" he asked, still fussing with the scrub brush.

Thinking back to the twisted sheets and blankets I left curled over the bed, lying was out of the question. "Not well. You?"

"Like I'd been in a wrestling match." He turned, gave me a wink, then returned to his task.

"Sorry." My restlessness had robbed both of us of sleep—me waking on and off from pieces of scattered dreams, him trying to win back some of the covers. "When are you going over to

Daniel's?"

"Around 11:00."

The time on the coffee maker had been 10:15. He must have been out here a good hour or two to have removed all those stains before I got up.

"So, by the time I'm back," he continued, "we should be able to go at about 2:00."

"Sounds like a plan."

"And, Sami," he said without turning around, "please wait for me to go with you."

"Honey, I wasn't..."

Turning, he chastised, "Don't tell me you didn't think about it. I know you too well." His tone softened. "Promise you'll wait."

Looking down at my coffee, I mumbled, "I will."

"No. Look me in the eye and say the words."

Taking a deep breath, I raised my head and looked directly at him. "I promise. No going alone."

"Thank you. You may resume your caffeine intake now." He grinned and stood up.

Returning the smile, I shifted my gaze to the vast ocean below. It promised to be another beautiful day on the Southern California coast. Thoughts of what lay ahead of us, darkened my mood. It wasn't going to be easy, but this journey had to be taken.

While Jimmy showered and changed clothes, I remained on the porch sipping coffee. Nervous tension rippled through my body as I thought about our impending trip.

Jimmy kissed my cheek then gave me a stern look on his way out. His meaning was unmistakable. I would wait until he returned for us to go together to speak with his grandfather. I kept my promises.

After a second cup of coffee, I hopped in the shower. Standing there, reveling in the warm water cascading over my skin, I didn't want to step out and prepare for our journey. I allowed myself several more minutes before turning off the water.

Unlike the last time I went back to speak with Mr. Chang, a chill of foreboding coursed down my spine. If we failed to get all the information we needed, there would be no second chance. We would be out of slides that could put us close enough to San Francisco in the right time period.

This made me think about the Betrotheds I sent back. Is this how they felt if they had the slightest bit of doubt about the life they were throwing themselves into? The second journey was always the most critical, as it was permanent. While this trip wouldn't forever strand us in that time period, the journey still had a finality about it. With the slides we had, there would be no third attempt. Our only chance lay in discovering the location of special slides that allow the operator to select a date and place. I hoped we wouldn't need one.

Since I had my doubts about Mr. Chang disclosing all the information we needed to stop Carney, I also wondered about his willingness to share the location of those slides. Hopefully, Jimmy would know how to get to his grandfather.

About 1:00 p.m. I went into my office and unlocked the safe. Removing the red-framed slide from Christy's union with Jackson in Monterey, I hesitated. Thoughts of this journey sent shivers down my body. Maybe it was a good thing Jimmy insisted we go together. Despite my determination to stop Carney, I wasn't sure if I was up to going back alone.

Taking enough money from the cash box to cover any emergency, I grabbed the slide holder. After locking the safe, I carried the items to my studio.

Setting the holder on the table and slipping the frame securely in place, I depressed the power button. We would leave in one hour.

I moved the bench out of the way to allow room for both of us.

"It'll be all right," Jimmy said from the doorway.

He startled me as I didn't hear him come in. "I hope so. This journey makes me more nervous than my first time going back to talk with your grandfather."

"He's really a warm and fuzzy guy, once you get to know him."

We looked at each other for a second, then burst out laughing—more from relief than humor.

"Thanks," I said, "I needed that."

Jimmy walked over and wrapped his arms around me. I buried my face in his chest and breathed in the clean musky scent of his aftershave. Kissing the top of my head, he pulled back and said, "Come on, Sami. Let's get all 1980's-like."

"Okay, but if you start talking like a Valley Girl, I'm going alone. I mean it!"

"Like fur-sure."

With a playful scowl, I narrowed eyes my eyes at him.

He changed his tune. "I mean, okay."

"Better." With a quick kiss on his lips, I slipped from his embrace and headed upstairs.

He followed me as far as the hallway.

In the bedroom I grabbed my denim jacket to go with the jeans and t-shirt I wore.

Returning down the steps, I heard the metal clunk of the safe door closing in my office. He walked out and handed me a driver's license from the decade we were going to with a current picture. He removed his current identification and credit cards from his wallet, and slipped a similar driver's license in their place. He also took some bills out of his pocket and stuffed them in his wallet. I was going to tell him I already had cash, but we had to be prepared in case we were separated for any reason.

When I went back the first time, I forgot to bring my valid ID. Luckily, at the hotel, when I pretended to have lost my license, they didn't press me for anything else since I had enough cash to cover the room for the night.

Carrying my jacket, I walked into the studio and deposited it on the bench before returning to the kitchen. We still had half an hour until the holder would be at full power. We should eat a quick lunch, but my stomach was so full of knots that food wasn't an option. Jimmy, however, made himself a turkey sandwich.

I sat opposite him at the table with a bottle of water, silently reviewing all the questions we needed Mr. Chang to answer.

"Stop it, Sami."

"Stop what?"

"You know." He reached out and covered my hand with his. "Quit making yourself crazy trying to second guess everything we need to ask Grandfather."

"Honey, I just want to make sure we don't forget anything."

"We won't. Try to relax," he implored me. "You keep riling yourself up and you'll get me all worked up too. We need to stay focused."

Pulling my hand away and carrying my water, I walked out of

the kitchen toward the front door. I needed fresh air. Out on the porch I glanced to the right at the discolored boards. With a shudder, I turned left and went to the chair at the far end.

All I could do was breathe deeply for a few moments. The plastic container crinkled as I tensed and released my grip.

I reached over to set my water on the small round table next to my chair and misjudged the distance. The bottle hit the edge, and I lost my grip. With a loud splat, it landed on the boards and rolled toward the end of the porch.

Jumping out of my chair, I bent down and retrieved it, mere inches from the edge. As I stood and turned toward the front door, a card on the floor caught my eye. A California driver's license sat on the back of the porch against the house. I picked it up to look at the name and picture. Made of unfinished card stock, not the plastic ones I was used to seeing, it belonged to a man named Paolo Fortuno. The license was issued in 1965, and the man had been born in 1941.

How on earth could it have gotten here? Maybe it blew up from the beach, though why someone would be carrying a driver's license from 1965 was beyond me. The picture was grainy, yet familiar.

As I turned to take it into the house to show Jimmy, my eyes focused on the spot where Francois had lain, his blood seeping out of him. In a flash, something Carney casually mentioned came back to me. Something about a young Italian man being most helpful.

Did Carney accidentally drop the license here? Or did he leave it intentionally? Why would he leave clues? Unless, it was an attempt to throw us off balance. I tucked the card into my back pocket and decided not to mention it to Jimmy just yet. Something nagged at me, and I couldn't quite place it. Maybe this was one more thing we needed to ask Mr. Chang. Perhaps he would know the young man.

Chapter 21

With renewed determination, I entered the house ready to take the next step. I found Jimmy washing up his lunch plate and glass, as if it were a day like any other. His composure unnerved me. He reminded me of calm waters amidst a storm.

"Ready to take a blast through time?" I asked him.

"Almost," he said, finishing his task. He set the wet dishes in the rack, dried his hands, and hung the towel back on the hook near the sink. Finally, he turned. "Okay, I'm ready. Let's go."

As he walked past me toward the kitchen door, he grasped my hand. Stopping at the hall closet, he grabbed his blue windbreaker and slipped it on. Walking into the studio I looked around for my jacket. I was sure I'd left it draped across the bench.

"What's wrong?" Jimmy asked.

"I thought I left my jacket in here."

"The denim one?"

"Yes, over there," I pointed to the bench.

"I think I saw it hanging over your chair in the kitchen." He squeezed my hand, then let go. "Better grab it. That part of the coast can be chilly."

"Okay, I'll only be a moment."

Going back down the hallway, I entered the kitchen. My jacket was nowhere in sight. I was sure I'd left it in the studio. Suddenly, I realized Jimmy's plan.

Turning on my heels, I ran back the way I'd come. As I hurried through the doorway, I caught him just in time.

Jimmy looked at me with sadness in his eyes. He knew I felt betrayed. "I'm sorry, sweetie. I just couldn't take the risk. Please understa…". With a flash from behind him, he disappeared.

"Dammit!" I yelled across the empty studio. He made such a big deal of my promising not to go alone, it never crossed my mind to doubt *him*. That was probably intentional.

I felt torn between anger and disappointment.

He knew I'd be upset. What was he thinking? Why did he do it? I knew thoughts of April were fresh in his mind. The fear he felt about my surviving the journey must have worried him more than dealing with me upon his return. It would be an agonizing twenty-four hours for me.

I felt helpless, robbed of the opportunity to get the answers we wanted from Mr. Chang. Would Jimmy remember everything we needed to discuss? At this point it was out of my hands.

Walking over to the couch against the wall, I threw myself down onto the cushions and expelled a breath in exasperation. Teetering on the edge of anger and acceptance, I remembered the license in my back pocket.

I looked again at the ID of Paolo Fortuno. Surely, I could dig up something on the internet about him. At least it would keep me occupied. Whether Carney left it intentionally or accidentally on my porch, it could be beneficial to discover this young man's identity and his connection.

Sitting in front of my laptop in the office, I typed in the man's name. Five matches came up. Two of them were teenagers at this point in time, so they would be too young. One was born in 1932. Again, not the right age. The final two were born in 1957 and 1978. None of them matched the birth year of 1941.

Years aren't always relative in my business. I decided to see if either of the last two had pictures. Bingo! The photo of the man born in 1957 was a bit grainy, but still recognizable as the Paolo on the driver's license from 1967. Out of curiosity, I pulled up one of the man born in 1978. No surprise. It matched.

I compared those of the other three. The one from 1932, a plain black and white picture, was clearly not the right guy. The two teenagers were, as I suspected, not him.

Going back to the two matches, I tried to find current information. It turned out the Paolo born in 1978 lived nearby in Laguna Beach. Wondering if there was anything on the man born in 1957, I pulled up my browsing history to find it again.

As I was about to select the correct one, my eye wandered down to the searches of the other day. On the list was the information I tried to find on the death of Jimmy's father. Anger and regret at missing out on questioning Mr. Chang washed over me again. His refusal to answer any of Jimmy's questions at the time, made him seem guilty of withholding information.

Moving on to find the Paolo I was searching for, it struck me where I'd seen his face before. I looked through my list of newspaper articles and pulled up the one with a picture of Jimmy's father. It also showed a picture of the unidentified victim found stabbed in an alleyway a few blocks from the shop.

I enlarged the picture and compared it to the driver's license— an exact match, identical down to the shirt and gold cross necklace. Paolo Fortuno must have been a Collector. It could explain why he would've travelled back in time. The driver's license was obviously a fake that had been created the same time as his journey.

I looked down at the address in Laguna Beach I'd written on a note pad. Now the question remained, *when* did he travel back? Could he still be alive now? Only one way to find out.

Standing abruptly, my chair rolled back and slammed into the wall. The noise made me jump. This moment of fear caused me to reconsider what I was about to do. While it seemed the best course of action, what would I find at the house in Laguna? What if he was a Collector turned evil like Carney? Then again, he may have been another one of Carney's victims.

My mind replayed our conversation on the porch yesterday. Carney all but admitted to murdering the Italian man, but also stated the young man had gotten what he deserved. I had to risk it. While Jimmy was doing what he could to extract information from his grandfather, I needed to explore every possible avenue.

Grabbing my purse and car keys from the kitchen counter, I ran out the door to the garage. Backing down the driveway, my foot hit the brakes and the tires squealed on the pavement. Shifting my car into park, I hesitated. Maybe I should wait for Jimmy to return and we could do this together. This was a complete unknown that could end badly.

No, we couldn't afford to waste any more time. I slipped my car back into reverse and continued down the driveway to the street. Having punched the address into the GPS in my phone, I turned the car south.

Traffic already filled the roads for the late afternoon rush hour. Freeways in Los Angeles were notorious for being several lanes of cars crawling along at a glacial pace. It took over ninety minutes to reach Paolo's neighborhood.

Following the directions spouted by my phone, I found myself traveling down neatly hedged streets of large estates, probably built on old money by the looks of the stately residences.

I arrived at a gated driveway with a large Tudor style house set back from the road. I rolled down the car window and pressed a large button at the bottom of the keypad mounted on a post.

Several moments passed with no response. Pressing the button again, I silently prayed there would be someone home.

"What do you want?" boomed a voice from the speaker.

Not knowing how the person answering would take this request, I bolstered my voice with confidence. "I'm here to see Paolo Fortuno."

Receiving no answer, I wondered if the transmitter was broken. My hand reached out to press the call button again. Before making contact, the sound of creaking iron filled the silence. The gates slowly swung open. It seemed I was being invited in. What else would be included with my entrance ticket?

Chapter 22

The expanse of the Tudor-style mansion intimidated me as I pulled up. The timber and brick exterior belonged somewhere in the British countryside, rather than a Southern California community. As I rolled to a stop on the tiled driveway, I saw no sign of life. Getting out of my SUV, I walked up the front steps.

Before I could knock, the door opened. A tall, distinguished looking gentleman with a neatly manicured goatee and mustache filled the frame. With his thinning gray hair trimmed close on the sides, a guess would put him in his late seventies. It was a familiar face.

The man demanded, "What do you want?"

The hostility in his tone tongue-tied me for a few seconds, then I spoke in a calm voice, "I would like to speak to Paolo Fortuno. Is he home?"

Glaring at me, he responded in clear English, despite his Italian accent, "I am Paolo Fortuno."

Speech eluded me as I stared in confusion.

"It appears I am not whom you expected."

"Well…no." My mind raced. "It's just, well, you seem older than…"

"Ah. You must be looking for my son, Paolo, Jr."

Of course, I should have realized. Thinking back to my internet search, the man in front of me could be the Paolo born in

1932, but that would make him closer to 90 years old. Not out of the question if he was part of the process and had travelled several times. "Yes, is he here?"

He searched my face as if evaluating me before asking, "What do you want with my son?"

I couldn't tell him the truth. Honestly, I wasn't quite sure what I would ask Paolo, Jr, until I had a better grasp of his involvement with Carney. "Forgive me, but it's a personal matter. You understand, don't you?"

"No, I do not. It is obvious you have never met him. Why are you here?"

Paolo, Sr., shifted uncomfortably as if irritated. If the situation wasn't defused quickly, I would get no information at all.

Rather than giving him a direct answer, I tried another tactic. "When was the last time you saw your son, sir?"

"You are not with the authorities, are you?" It seemed more of a statement than a question.

"No."

"Then I ask again, why are you here?" His face began to redden.

Trying to gain his trust, I withdrew the driver's license from my purse. Hesitating a moment, I handed it to the old man. "Because of this."

Despite his agitation, his long fingers gently took the card. As Paolo studied it, his eyes watered. Brushing the moisture away with the back of his hand, in a softened voice he said, "Perhaps you should come in."

As he stepped back from the doorway, I went inside. The entryway of the house exuded elegance with its soft shades of rose and gray woven throughout the wallpaper and accent pieces.

"Please, this way." Paolo gestured toward a sitting room off to the right.

I perched on the edge of a sage colored couch under the front window. He sat opposite me in a matching love seat. From a dish of potpourri on the end table, lavender scented the air.

"I haven't seen Junior in two years. He never returned from his last journey." His jaw tensed.

Since the old man was bringing me into his confidence, with no pretense of not knowing about the process, I asked the question burning at the front of my brain. "So, he was a Collector?"

"Yes. And it is obvious you are somehow involved. Are you of the French or British family?"

I learned more in that one question than I'd expected from this conversation. "I'm only a Photographer. Forgive me, I know your name, but didn't introduce myself. I'm Sami. My Collector is Jimmy Chang." If I was to get anywhere fast, I needed to speak plainly and share what I knew. Just maybe, Paolo would do the same.

"Ahh, Chang's grandson." He looked pensive for a moment then returned his focus to me. "How did you get this driver's license?"

How could I tell this man his son was killed? Not sure how much to reveal right now, I tried to get a little more information before answering. "Allow me a moment first. Was your son's last journey to interview a Suitor?"

"No, his interviews were complete. He had not found his Photographer. His instructions were to retrieve her from an earlier decade, but she was not there."

"Can you tell me how he knew that?"

"His box included an extra slide and a biography of his Photographer, a young woman. The slide would be used to bring her forward in time."

It surprised me his Photographer would come from a prior decade. That meant he would have to go back himself and bring her to the future with him. This added a new twist. It also assured me Jimmy's fears were unfounded. If Paolo was expected to bring his Photographer with him, it would have been safe for Jimmy and me to travel back together.

"What do you mean? She wasn't at the designated location?"

"Correct. His instructions were to locate her in San Francisco in the year 1976. Despite being engaged to another man the marriage would not happen. After meeting Paolo, she would agree to travel forward in time to work with him."

The similarity was too great. I already knew who his Photographer should have been. I asked the question anyway. "What was her name?"

"It was April. April Finch."

Speechless, I tilted my head back. My hands covered my

closed eyes as I processed what he'd just told me. A whiff of lavender calmed me.

Snapping out of my thoughts, I looked back at Paolo. "So why was he going back to San Francisco in 1966?"

The old man slumped forward. "He was misusing the slides."

"How?"

"I told him he should not travel back for personal gain. If this was how life played out and his time as a Collector ended without a Photographer, it meant the process should end. Being young and foolish, he would not listen."

"What did he do, Mr. Fortuno?"

"Please, call me Paolo."

"All right, Paolo."

He stared up at the ceiling as his hands balled into fists in his lap.

"He insisted on setting things right, so he could retrieve his Photographer. I am sure that man was the cause of all this!"

"What man?"

"Carney. My son had invited him to the house before he realized Carney was the one who stole his Photographer. And, we believe he took our Family Slide."

So, as I'd suspected, Carney had been involved with the younger Paolo. Maybe there was a reason I missed out on this second trip to speak with Jimmy's grandfather. I stumbled on another source that may be able to help us.

"What exactly is a Family Slide?"

"I am not sure I should be telling you this, but now, what does it matter? Our lineage is done. The Family Slides have been entrusted to the Four Families for generations—one for each family. They have been passed on to a child or grandchild when they were old enough to be involved. Sometimes, not until they were in their thirties or forties, depending on the elder's involvement in the process."

As I waited for him to continue, I knew I was obligated to tell him what I think happened to Paolo, Jr. He deserved closure.

He temples his fingers. "As I said, there were four of them." That much I knew from Francois. "The slide allows the traveler to set any date, time and place he wants, as well as how long he wishes to stay. It can also be reused."

A major difference from the special slides that only allowed a single 24-hour journey to a date and place of the users choosing. These slides opened a whole new realm of travel, because they could be used as often as needed. Obviously, Carney had gotten hold of one but not his family's; Francois had still been using it, up until yesterday.

"What makes you think Carney stole yours?"

"Too many coincidences to not be true. You don't need details. I know it happened."

I shifted on the couch and crossed my legs. "So why did your son go to 1966?"

"To get the Chang's Family Slide. He travelled back with a one-time use slide he secured from his distributor. This was already a misuse of the process. He begged Chang to let him use their family slide. The old man refused so, he went back again, using a second emergency slide. He wanted to ask Jason Chang, your Collector's father, to lend him the device."

"Why didn't he just do that to begin with?"

"It was my doing. I suggested going to the elder Chang would be more appropriate." His voice cracked. "I was wrong.

"History showed Jason Chang was the victim of a murder during a robbery. My son thought if he went back and asked Jason for the slide and the man refused, he would return later that day to avert the crime. He believed Jason would be grateful enough to allow him use of the Family Slide. Only he never returned."

I sighed with sadness for his son's doomed quest. "Didn't you think he might have gotten trapped in that decade? Maybe got the timing wrong and returned too close to a time he'd gone to before?"

"No. That is not possible," he said, his voice back under control. "He was of the blood lines from one of the Four Families."

"I don't understand."

"We cannot be trapped back in time by repeating a location."

Another nugget of information that took me completely by surprise. I wondered if Jimmy knew this. With a Family Slide and his heritage, Carney was virtually unstoppable.

I asked, "So why wouldn't Paolo have returned?"

"The only way he would not, is if he was dead. Since he departed from his studio here in the house, there is no other explanation." The old man sat up straight with tears rolling down his cheeks. Retrieving a handkerchief from his pocket, he dabbed at his eyes. "You have not told me how you came into possession of his identification."

He deserved answers too. "I found it on my porch. I believe it was left there...by Carney."

"So you know this man? Is he a friend?"

"No. He murdered three of my Betrotheds." There was no avoiding it now. "And I believe he murdered your son. I'm so sorry, Paolo."

Chapter 23

Paolo remained seated. He made no effort to wipe away the tears. "How do you know?"

"Carney hinted at it. Whether he's the murderer or not, your son died back in 1966—the same day Mr. Chang's son was murdered."

The old man recovered quicker than expected. "Tell me what happened. Were you there?"

The question took me by surprise. "No. We've been trying to piece things together—my Collector and I, that is. While searching the internet for details on the murder of Jimmy's father, we found a newspaper article mentioning a man found dead a few blocks from the Jade Pagoda. He was never identified, but the picture is identical to the one on the license. I'm sorry, Paolo. It's your son.

"Since my Collector only knows the one timeline, it seems Jason Chang was murdered regardless of your son being there or Carney's interference."

"I see," he said and stared at the ceiling, his hands trembling.

Nothing I could say would soothe Paolo. But maybe I could gain information that might help stop Carney. "Would you be willing to answer a few questions about the process?"

His forehead wrinkled, then he shrugged and nodded for me to continue.

"How would Paolo, Jr., have brought his Photographer

forward? Exactly how could he insure they both arrived safely through time?"

"Your Collector should have received this information from his grandfather. Did he not?"

"No. It seems Mr. Chang was reluctant to share much. We didn't know about the four family bloodlines until recently. Francois gave us quite a bit of information."

"Ah, Francois is a good man. Very honorable. I haven't seen him for years. How is he?"

"Another victim of Carney's, I'm afraid. Did you know he's Francois' grandson?"

"What? How can that be?" he asked, jumping to his feet. He paced the room. "It is not possible someone so sinister could be related to that family."

"It's true. Please tell me. How can travel be done safely with two people?" I felt a twinge of guilt pushing him unfairly.

The lines on his face deepened. "As you wish. I don't see the point, but will share what I know. So long as both travelers have their hands firmly gripped together, the journey is successful. This is critical. If the hold is loosened at all, or only one hand each, then the passenger, as you could call her, does not make it."

Thoughts of April's horrible death flashed through my head. Jimmy's description had been so vivid. The visions I'd conjured up could never be erased.

The old man stood by the other window with his back to me. I walked over to him and placed my hand on his shoulder. "Thank you. I know this is difficult for you."

He turned to look at me, eyes still brimming with moisture.

"Would you like me to leave?" I didn't want to, but felt every question inflicted more misery on this grieving man.

"Sami, you are a compassionate woman. Your Collector is a lucky man."

I answered with a nod of thanks. He returned a sad smile. Having not been a parent, I could only imagine the harsh grief of losing a child, even one already grown.

Straightening his shoulders and regaining his composure, Paolo asked, "What else would you like to know? I wish to help you stop that demon from harming others."

"Thank you."

"Please, I need some fresh air. Shall we sit on the back patio and sip a bit of Cabernet? I could use some right now."

"Sounds good to me," I said, grateful as my throat felt parched.

He gestured for me to accompany him through the house to the kitchen at the back. Exiting out onto a beautiful, slate-tiled patio that overlooked an expanse of newly-mowed lawn, I inhaled the smell of fresh cut grass and sat on a cushioned chair beneath a green canopy.

Paolo disappeared into the house and returned a few minutes later carrying a wine decanter and two glasses. He set them down on the small table between the two chairs, and poured a full glass for each of us. He handed me one and took the other for himself.

"To resolution," he said, tapping his glass to mine.

"To resolution." That seemed a fitting toast, and one I hoped we could all live up to in the near future.

Taking a seat, he asked, "What else would you like to know?"

"From what I've pieced together, you're saying there are Four Family bloodlines involved in this process."

He nodded.

"Including yours, I have met three of the families. For lack of a better description, they are the Chinese, French and Italian lineages. According to you the fourth one is English."

"Yes, the British line has ended."

"What do you mean ended?"

Twirling his wine glass he answered. "Years back, there was a horrible fire in the family home in Surrey. All perished except for their young toddler, whom the nanny was able to rescue before the house became completely engulfed in flames. Two generations were wiped out, along with all the tools their family possessed for the process. The Family Slide was also destroyed in the blaze."

"How sad. What happened to the child?"

"I believe she was sent to a distant relative here in the States, unaware of the process. Despite calling ourselves part of the Four Families, there are really only three now."

That meant only three Family Slides remained. Carney possessed one, Chang had another, but where was the one Francois had? I hoped we only needed two slides to trap Carney in time. Otherwise, there was no way to accomplish this task. Francois couldn't have survived the gunshot wound which meant, wherever he departed from, the slide had either been retrieved or stolen. Since he wore the same outfit in 1979 as he had upon my return to the present, I guessed he left it somewhere in that year.

I couldn't count on Jimmy getting all the necessary information from his grandfather. Hopefully Paolo possessed knowledge of everything Chang and Francois did. "I traveled back to the year 1979 to speak with Mr. Chang. He told me the only way to stop Carney is to trap him in time. Francois said it could only be done with the Family Slides. We need to set the same date, time and location, but no time span. What does that mean exactly?"

"The length of time the traveler would stay. You must set it to zero."

"You're saying these slides allow you to set a time span longer or shorter than twenty-four hours?"

A fire glowed in Paolo's eyes. "Yes." He touched my hand. "Carney must be stopped."

I now knew he would freely give me any information he had. "How do we set two locations on one? Does the slide allow that?"

"Not one slide. You need two. Two family slides need to be used. You must set the same date and time on both, the allotted time set to zero, and the same location on each one. That is the only way he will be trapped at the time and location of your choosing."

"So, you believe this process will stop him from returning?"

"It has been said that is the only way to trap someone from the four bloodlines. Never have I heard of it being necessary, until now."

I leaned back into the cushion of my chair with an exasperated sigh. "You don't know if it will work?"

"As I said, it has never been tried. That is simply the information passed down to each new generation. Obviously, those who created all this believed it would be needed at some point."

"Who did create this whole process?"

"That has never been disclosed to any of us. It is an advanced creation which outdates the technology we know today and a mystery that, I am afraid, will never be answered."

I sipped my wine, staring across the lawn at its beautiful border of neatly trimmed hedges. Sprawls of flower beds scattered throughout the yard in splashes of color. Knowing what lay ahead of us, I couldn't enjoy the peaceful setting. A bush of crimson roses reminded me of Francois' blood seeping across my porch.

"What happens to someone when this process is carried out?"

Paolo was nearly to the bottom of his glass and reached to pour another. He tilted the bottle toward me first. I declined, having drank little of mine. His hand slipped and the decanter clinked against my glass, but didn't break it.

After refilling his glass, he answered. "It is said he is trapped forever and cannot return."

"I see. So, first Jimmy and I have to acquire two family slides."

The man studied me for a moment. I crinkled my face wondering what he found fascinating.

"Yes. You were hoping for a more, how shall I say, final solution?"

He read me well. "You mean I was hoping it would kill him?"

He nodded. "Performing murder by your own hand does not seem like something you are capable of doing."

The thought of shooting Carney the way he had his own grandfather, made me believe I could. In the end, if I didn't possess the ability to take a life, this horror would never be finished. Trapping him in time was a solution I *could* follow through on. Where would I find two of the remaining three slides? That seemed to be the biggest hurdle before us. The next would be to locate Carney.

The fear of his having stolen the Chang Family Slide from Paolo, Jr., haunted me. I clung to the hope that Jason Chang had not been willing to part with it. If he did surrender the device to Paolo, it could mean that Carney possessed two of the remaining three. If that were the case, we might need to locate the one used by Francois.

Glancing at my host, I noticed his glass was already half empty. Despite putting forth a noble effort, his stamina waned. His face had paled and bore a worn-out expression. I knew this conversation had drained him more than he would admit.

Setting my glass on the table, I stood. "I believe I've taken up enough of your time, Paolo. Thank you for the information."

He graciously took my extended hand and brushed the back of

it with his lips in the old-world style. "It has been a pleasure meeting you, Sami. Thank you for the details about Junior. I pray you and your Collector are able to stop that evil man."

"I hope so. Wish me luck on finding the slides. If you have any suggestions, please let me know." I reached into the purse still slung across my shoulder, and retrieved a business card. Handing it to him, I said, "Here's my number. I'll show myself out."

He studied it. "Your last name is Manchester?" He asked it as if the name meant something to him.

"Yes." I waited for him to go on.

Staring at the card a moment longer, his mouth puckered as if to ask another question. Instead, he leaned back in his chair, his gaze shifting to the yard as he raised the wine glass toward his lips. After taking a sip he said, "Good luck, Sami."

Chapter 24

The entire night and following morning dragged. I tried my best to fill the minutes before Jimmy returned from 1984. Anxious to hear what his grandfather might have told him, I also couldn't wait to share what Paolo knew.

As the seconds ticked down, I waited on the couch in my studio. Jimmy materialized, looking worn out and clutching something wrapped in green silk. His gaze settled on my face. I was sure he tried to assess whether I was furious or relieved.

He walked over and sat beside me. Without a word I took his cheeks in my hands and kissed him on the lips. "Welcome home, honey."

"Sami, I'm sorry…"

"Shhhh. You've already said that."

"I know, but please understand I…"

"No," I said holding up my hand. "You did what you felt best. As usual, it involved taking care of me. How can I fault you for that?"

Caressing my cheek, he said, "You still amaze me. Just when I think I have it all figured out, you add another twist on things." He chuckled, "Thank you for not removing my head."

"You're welcome," I brushed his lips with mine. "Now, tell me everything."

"Well, Grandfather was none too pleased that I'd misused the slides. He tried to blame you and I wouldn't have it."

I laughed. "You're my hero."

"It took several hours to get any information out of him. He told me all this meddling in time could lead to more tragedy."

"Did he know what happened to Francois?"

"Yes," he said grasping both my hands. "As we suspected, he died shortly after returning. When Grandfather didn't hear from him after his journey to see you, he went to Francois' house in a suburb north of San Francisco, using a spare key to gain entry.

"His body lay sprawled in the studio. From the blood stains across the carpet, it appeared Francois had dragged himself over to the fireplace. Beside him were the remains of his holder and slide. He must have used the last of his strength to smash them with a poker."

"It was one of the Family Slides, wasn't it?"

He released my hands. "Yes."

"That only leaves two. And Carney has one of them."

His eyes widened with surprise. "How could you know that?"

"We'll get to that after. I did quite a bit of research on my own. What's that?" I asked, pointing at the bundle resting in his lap.

"Grandfather was reluctant to part with this. Finally, he agreed we needed to end this horror. He planned to put a stop to everything, and never intended to give me this before he died. That's why he never passed on the history of our family and the others either."

As Jimmy spoke, he slowly unwrapped the scarf to reveal a slide permanently secured in a dark wooden holder. He pointed to the three spinning dials at the bottom. "These knobs allow you to pick the month, day and year for the date you want to land; the hours and minutes for the time; and allotted hours and minutes for the duration you want to be gone."

"It's your family slide."

"Yes."

"How do you set the location?"

"You have to press the button in front of the space that shows the location and speak it, then the name of the location will be displayed."

I nodded, fascinated that this antiquated looking device

possessed such an advanced technology. Made me wonder again who really created these things.

"To trap Carney, Grandfather told me we must set the time and place, leaving the length of time at zero. That would leave him back in time, never to return. But only if we did it with two slides. He said Carney has been using a family slide that is not his own. We need to secure that one too for this to work."

I picked up the device to examine it, turning the frame around and sideways. It appeared no different from the slides we used for the Betrotheds, except for the permanent holder. I assumed the two components together were the catalyst for allowing the traveler unlimited jumps. With the information Paolo gave me about the four bloodlines not getting stuck in a time they visited more than once, it left Carney with limitless options. "We finally have the means to put a stop to his murderous spree—if we can find Carney and his slide, then use it against him."

"Yes. Now tell me what you've been up to and how is it you suddenly know there are only two?"

We sat in the studio while I filled him in on everything from finding Paolo's driver's license to my conversation with the senior Fortuno. Most of it was new information to Jimmy, so it seemed Mr. Chang had remained tight-lipped about the whole process and what had already happened in the past.

"Sami, you took a big risk going to that man's house. What if he had turned as evil as Carney?"

"No more of a risk than your going back to talk to your grandfather," I said stubbornly.

"How can you compare the two? The Fortuno family is a complete unknown. Please promise you won't do anything like that again."

"Guess we're even," I said with a playful smirk.

He acquiesced. "Touché. No more solo journeys without the other's permission. Agreed?"

"I love you," I said, kissing him again.

Putting his hand under my chin and tilting my face, he returned the gentle kiss. I wrapped my arms around his waist, laid my head on his shoulder and savored his familiar smell.

When we parted, he stood up. "Let's secure this."

I followed him into the office where he placed the slide inside the safe and locked it. Before leaving, I played Stella's message from the other day on the answering machine.

"What do you think?" I asked. "Could she be number twenty-nine?"

"As much as I want to quit, we needed to fulfill our obligation. Give her a call tomorrow and feel her out. With only two Suitors left, let's hope she's a match for one. It's a bit out of the ordinary though, having someone connected to a previous Betrothed. Do you think Dede told her the real story?"

"No, she couldn't have," I said. "The call came in during Dede's first meeting with Milton. When Dede told Stella about my studio services, she wouldn't have known about the process yet."

"What are your instincts saying?"

"I'll call her tomorrow."

He turned to me. "Okay. You know, I keep thinking..."

"What?"

Jimmy swiped his hand through his hair. "Paolo told you my lineage allows me to visit the same place as many times as I want without getting stuck?"

"That's what he said. Why?"

"Nothing concrete. Right now, we need to figure out how to find Carney. None of this can work unless we have his slide too."

Jimmy went up to the bedroom to change clothes. Even though we chose to live apart, we both had clothes at each other's homes. With all the love he and I felt for each other, we were too independent for a common home and neither had an interest in marriage. This arrangement worked for us.

Returning downstairs, wearing slacks and a white button-down shirt, Jimmy found me in the kitchen putting on the tea kettle. His car keys jangled in his hand.

I looked up. "Going somewhere?"

Holding up his cell phone, he said, "Unfortunately, I need to attend to my day job. I'm going into the office for a few hours."

"Coming back for dinner?" I asked, putting the second mug back into the cupboard.

"Probably not. I'm really beat. We both had a busy twenty-four hours, and I need time to sort through all this new information."

"Okay. I'll let you know how things go with Stella. When do

you pick up Dede's credentials?"

"Daniel will have them ready tomorrow," he said, pulling me close.

I enjoyed his embrace.

With a quick peck on my cheek, Jimmy went down the hall and out the front door. I needed time to figure things out too. Despite Mr. Chang not sharing much information, what he did say spoke volumes. Apparently, he felt ours should be the last generation to carry on the process. Even though he wasn't directly involved in some of the events, I think the demise began when the British family perished in the fire. Strange, it never occurred to me to ask Paolo their name.

With the death of Junior, and both Jimmy and Carney being childless, there wasn't anyone to carry on the inheritance. Ours truly was the final generation. Maybe the time had come to close this chapter. While it served a purpose for the Betrotheds and Suitors, the cost continued to escalate at a horrific rate for those that died. After fulfilling our obligation, there would be no more matches.

Rather than putting any more of our Betrotheds at risk, I decided to hold off meeting Stella until Dede travelled safely back to Milton. I would call her tomorrow, but not schedule a session until after that final journey.

Chapter 25

I opened the front door to find Dede bouncing with excitement and holding a loaded down backpack. Around her neck she wore the half-moon necklace the Suitor gave her on the first journey back.

"Well, I can see you're not excited at all!" We both laughed. "Please, come in. Are those all the treasures you chose to take with you?"

Dede stepped in, and I closed the door behind her.

"Yes. It wasn't hard to decide. A couple pictures of my parents and a few special pieces of jewelry. Other than that, the rest is sculpting tools. Nothing else I really needed."

"I'm glad you feel that way. So many of the Betrotheds find it hard to part with their belongings."

"Not me. I donated my car to a local charity, gave up my apartment and told my employer I had a sick aunt back in Des Moines. She didn't even blink. I believe I'm ready to exit the decade!" The energy emanating from her could have lit a city block. I couldn't wait for Dede to begin life with Milton.

I nodded toward the necklace. "I see you're wearing your *new* jewelry as well."

"Oh, Sami, I haven't taken it off. It helped keep me focused on getting everything done. I've hardly slept a wink all week!"

"No second thoughts then?" I already knew the answer, but asked anyway.

"None at all." Her smile was infectious, and I couldn't help but return it.

"Then follow me," I said leading her to my studio.

On a side table sat a small manila envelope with credentials. It held a driver's license with Dede's name issued in 1972, along with a birth certificate claiming she was born in Chicago in the year 1947. An information sheet gave a brief synopsis of her life, including schools attended, and how she came to be in New Mexico. Nothing too detailed, as that was always best. The envelope contained a couple thousand dollars from the appropriate period as an emergency fund.

After reviewing the contents, I handed the envelope to her. She tucked it away in a side pocket of her backpack.

"Oh, by the way, I spoke to your friend, Stella. She has an appointment at the end of the week for a photo session."

"Well, she's really just a co-worker. We aren't exactly friends. I hope you don't mind. After coming here, before I knew how you *really* helped women with matches, I suggested she call. Don't worry, I haven't told her a thing. Besides, at the time, I thought you were a matchmaker, but here in the present."

It was good Dede hadn't shared what really happens here, just in case Stella didn't fit one of the remaining Suitors.

"I simply suggested it would be fun to do a photo session. She went through a horrible divorce about a year ago and has been a terrible shut-in, other than work. In the last week or so, she suddenly started begging me to go out and do things with her. I think she's lonely. So...well...maybe you could help her?"

"She comes here the end of the week. We'll go from there. Meanwhile, you have a date to keep. Or should I say a life!" We laughed like little girls. "Study your credentials, and use whatever is comfortable for you. Remember, less is more. Don't offer anything unless you need to. After a while, people will simply accept you as Milton's wife and move on."

"I love the sound of that—Milton's wife. So, I guess this is it?"

I nodded, and she threw her arms around me. No words were necessary; I knew how she felt. Releasing me, Dede secured her backpack in place and took a seat on the cushioned bench one last time.

Stepping behind her, I depressed the timer and the thirty second count down began.

"I wish you the long and happy life you deserve. May it be filled with love and family."

Dede sat there beaming. With a flash of light, she was gone.

"Please, let her get everything she deserves." I stared at the empty bench.

Jimmy and I had yet to figure out a way to confront Carney. We decided there needed to be a reason for him to come to us, something he couldn't live without. To stop his reign of terror, we must find out where he kept the stolen Family Slide, and if he possessed any of the one-time slides. If he had any of the latter, we couldn't risk allowing him to remain in the present.

Looking over at Milton's portrait, Dede now stood beside him. His arm curled around her while they gazed into each other's eyes. True perfection—the thing they both deserved.

A half hour after Dede's departure, my doorbell rang. A man dressed in a courier service uniform held a medium-sized package wrapped in brown butcher paper.

"I have a package for Sami Manchester," he said.

"That's me." I'd never received a package via private courier. It piqued my curiosity.

He extended the electronic clipboard and a plastic stylus. "Sign here please."

I scribbled my name, handed the stylus back and received the package. "Thank you," I mumbled as I noticed the return address boasted Albuquerque, New Mexico, but no name.

As I sat in a wicker chair on the patio, my pulse quickened. This could be good news or another sick aspect of Carney's demented mind. Unable to stand the suspense any longer, I ripped off the paper. It contained two brownish-red items wrapped in bubble wrap.

With great care, I unwrapped one to reveal a beautifully crafted ceramic mug with a clear glaze that preserved the earthen color of the clay. An engraved sun blazed on the side. Setting it on the table beside me, I grabbed the other one from the box and removed the tape and bubble wrap.

The second cup was identical, except for one detail. Instead of the blazing sun, it bore a crescent moon with five shooting stars emanating out from it.

Glancing down inside the box, something rested flat on the bottom. Placing the second mug beside the first, I picked up a narrow manila envelope. I recognized it as the same type I used for credentials. It contained a picture of a large, extended family consisting of an older couple, three middle-aged couples, and eight children of varying ages from toddler to young adults. The elderly couple looked familiar.

Flipping the picture over, I found a single sentence written across the back: *Thanks for all the years of happiness.*

My heart soared with glee at the wonderful life Dede and Milton had achieved. Settling back against the wicker, I looked up smiling—except there stood Carney. My face chilled as I felt the color drain from it.

"Presents! How exciting. Is it your birthday? Don't tell me I've missed it!"

I dropped the picture and it fluttered to the floorboards, landing face up at his feet. Carney glanced down and studied it a moment.

"What a handsome family," he said looking back in my direction. "I always wondered what it would be like to have children and grandchildren. I guess neither one of us had that pleasure. Such a shame."

Gaining courage, I spat out, "The world should be glad you never procreated. Lord only knows what kind of abominations you would've produced." The fire in my belly helped to quell the fear. His presence unnerved me. I hoped he wasn't here to do me harm. If he'd wanted to, he would have killed me that first day he showed up in my studio.

"Ouch, that hurt. You should be grateful I allowed this Betrothed to have her perfect life. That's my gift to you. In exchange, I expect something back."

"What could I possibly offer you? And why would I give you anything?"

"It's just a small item," he said almost making his comment seem inconsequential as he looked down and studied his finger nails. "I want the Chang Family Slide." He looked back up and stared at me as if judging my reaction.

I leaned back into my chair, with the wicker creaking, and

mimicked his facial expressions. Attempting to sound just as casual, I purred, "What makes you think I have it?"

"Don't play with me, sweet Sami. I know the old man gave it to Jimmy."

"You're mistaken. It was never passed on to him." That wasn't a lie. Jimmy had to go back in time to retrieve it. "Besides, you have the Fortuno's Family Slide. Why would you need another?"

"Oh, so you've met the doddering old fool, have you? He fill your head with stories of how I stole his son's future?"

"Didn't you?"

"That depends on what you're referring to," he said with a bit of color rising into his cheeks.

Obviously, I'd hit a nerve. Good—time to press my advantage. "April was never meant to be yours. You destroyed Paolo's happiness and all his matches."

"April *was* mine! The process be damned!" He seethed. This apparently wasn't the subject he'd come to discuss. Time to press further.

"You've taken many things that aren't yours. Your birthright was intact, yet it wasn't enough. You knew you were destined to play a bigger role with Francois being your grandfather. Why wasn't it enough for you?"

His face visibly relaxed as he composed himself. "Like every entitled generation, I want more. I want control. Not be some puppet on a string doing the bidding of whoever created this mess."

I should have realized it sooner. It was a basic human instinct in some—the need to dominate. After tasting great power with time-traveling, he wasn't willing to relinquish anything. His delusions blossomed to epic proportions.

Glancing down at the picture of the happy family staring up at me, I set the box next to the mugs. Instinctively, I reached down to pick up the photo.

"Allow me," Carney said scooping it up before I could get to it. He held it out, his glare daring me to take it.

I reached for the photo. Before I could stop him, he dropped it and grabbed my outstretched hand. Dragging me to my feet, he seized my other hand and yanked me closer.

"Let's go for a spin, shall we?"
The world around me changed.

Chapter 26

Carney still held my hands. I ripped them free with such force, I almost fell backward before regaining my balance.

"Welcome to my humble abode," he said.

From the looks of my surroundings, we were in a study or converted bedroom. "Where am I?"

"Don't you mean *when* are you?"

His words slammed into me like a freight train. *When* had he taken me to? Location wasn't as important. Since I was basically luggage on this journey, I wouldn't be returning to where we started in 24 hours. Carney had dragged me with him on his return trip.

"You look confused, my dear. Maybe you should lie down." The tight smile on his lips oozed with malice as he savored my discomfort.

Backing farther away, I looked about for clues that might point to where and when he had taken me. The room was sparsely decorated. There were two portraits hanging on the wall with smiling couples. Could those be the only successful matches he and April made? Bumping into something behind me, I glanced back over my shoulder and saw an oak sideboard table. On it sat the twin of what Jimmy brought back—a Family Slide. So close, yet it might as well have been miles away.

"Come," he said.

My focus returned to my abductor as he reached for me. I visibly recoiled at the thought of his callous touch again and dropped my hands to my sides.

"As you wish," he nodded. Turning and walking to the door, he retrieved a key from his pocket and unlocked it. Seems he wasn't taking any chances while off on a journey. Opening the door, he stood aside and gestured for me to go through.

With no other option, I walked into the hallway. Obviously, we were inside a house—quite a large one from the number of doors off the walkway. I made sure to keep Carney in my sight. As he followed me, closing the door behind him, he turned and locked it again.

"Can't be too careful these days. You never know who might wander in while I'm out and about. Hmmm?" He rambled casually as he dropped the key back into his pocket.

"Why did you bring me here?" I asked, amazed at the steadiness in my voice.

"Just trying to teach your Collector a little lesson."

"Which is?"

"I will continue to take things away from him until he gives me what I want!" The anger in his voice scared me. His constant swirl of emotions broiling under the surface was disturbing. Trying to figure out an escape would be even harder since I never knew what to expect. One moment he chatted reasonably, and the next his ire soared out of control. All the more reason for me to maintain a calm exterior.

Looking at him, I asked, "Where to from here?"

"Up."

"Up?"

He walked past me to the next door on the left, which had a dead bolt on the outside. As he swung it open, the hinges creaked in protest. Glancing behind me I saw the staircase going down. Before I could act on my next thought, Carney grabbed my arm and yanked me toward the open door.

"Your visit isn't over yet, my dear. This way please."

My body tensed with his touch. Knowing he was stronger than me, I didn't resist. I saw a narrow flight of stairs. He forced me ahead of him and onto the first step.

With a loud bang, the door slammed behind me and I heard

the bolt slide home.

"No," I involuntarily cried, whipping around. Even as I grabbed the knob and turned it, I knew it would be no use. The door wouldn't budge.

"Enjoy the view, my dear," he yelled. Chuckling as he went, I heard his footsteps retreating down the hallway.

With a deep breath, I turned back toward the staircase and hesitantly went up. No use standing by a locked door. Fear raced through my mind, not knowing what to expect once I reached the top. The wooden steps creaked from my weight. It felt like wandering through a carnival maze, waiting for something to jump out at every turn.

Approaching the top of the stairs, the space was awash with sunlight. I walked up on the side of a room and found myself in a large square tower. Huge picture windows covered all four sides from floor to ceiling. The house sat on a hilltop looking out on the neighborhoods below. Turning around I saw a large expanse of ocean.

Running to the window, I put my hands flat against the cool glass and stared in horror. It was the same bay visible from my front porch. Looking off to the right and down the hill, I spied my house. There was a clear view of the front lawn, part of the porch and driveway. In it sat Jimmy's car. I struggled for breath as shock set in.

I sank to my knees on the plush blue carpet. Once down I turned around and sat leaning against the window gasping. How long had he lived here? How many hours had he spent watching Jimmy and me? The room started to spin. Putting my face in my hands I tried to shut out the questions in my head. The ramifications were deafening.

After a few moments my breathing returned to normal. I leaned my head back against the glass. Looking around my prison cell, there was no furniture—simply a carpeted room with windows. I heard a car start below and saw a silver sedan backing out of the driveway three stories down. A hand reached out the window and waved in my direction. The bastard! He was leaving me trapped here.

Once the sun went down, people might be able to see me better through the lit windows, as most of the immediate neighbors were blocked by foliage. Then I noticed there were no light fixtures in this tower. Without light on the inside, I would be in complete darkness and not visible to the outside world.

The only mode of escape might be to throw my body against the door in hopes the hinges would give way. Not being very strong, I had my doubts but needed to try. Simply awaiting my fate didn't sit well with me. I had to do something, even if it seemed futile.

Glancing back at the street below, I saw the sedan working its way down the hill. Rising on shaky legs, I managed to get to the stairs. Gaining strength as I went, I proceeded down to the locked door.

Trying the handle once again, the door pushed opened easily. I hesitated. He must have come back and slid open the bolt. I'd given up trying to figure out his logic.

Cautiously, I stuck my head out the doorway, expecting to see Carney standing there ready to taunt me more. The hall remained empty. Hoping he hadn't turned the car around, I raced for the stairs and flew down them. At the bottom I saw the front door and angled toward it.

Turning my head, I stopped dead. The house was completely empty. Absolutely no furniture in sight. Heavy white drapes on all the windows were the only touch. Just enough to let light through, but too dense for outsiders to see in.

He doesn't really live here? Risking precious time, I wandered through the living room, into the empty dining area and back to a cavernous kitchen. It too was devoid of decoration or furnishings except for curtains covering the windows.

Realizing my curiosity put me in needless peril, I ran back through the bottom floor to the front of the house. I'd spent enough time exploring and bolted through the door.

Once out on the porch, I tripped over a newspaper on the floorboards. Seeing no sign of the silver car, I stooped and picked up the daily. The date read two days from when he took me. Only two days! I prayed this wasn't another ploy of his. If Carney didn't actually live here, there was no reason for a regular newspaper delivery.

Not wasting a moment longer, I dropped the paper as I tore for the driveway and out onto the street. I quickly found one of the public stairways that would take me down towards the beach, but more importantly, to my own street.

Partway down I sat on the steps out of breath. After resting a few moments, I got up and continued the descent at a slower pace until I reached my street. The stairway emptied onto the road only five houses from my own.

Arriving at my front door, I tore through it. Just as quickly, I slammed the door closed and locked it behind me.

Jimmy rushed out of the office. "Where were you? Or *when* were you?"

Chapter 27

Jimmy's furrowed brow and droopy eyes displayed the panic he endured.

Throwing my arms around his neck, he pulled me close. I melted into the embrace. "He took...he...he took me," I stuttered out. "I didn't know how far forward or back in time we went. He has a house here. Please, tell me it's only been two days. Tell me!"

"Who? Carney?"

"Yes!"

Jimmy held me closer. We stood there a moment clinging to each other.

When he eased his hold, I pulled back. Keeping one arm over my shoulders, Jimmy led me to the couch in the living room. Once I calmed down, and he confirmed I'd only been gone two days, I told him what happened.

His shock mirrored mine when I told him how close Carney had been to us at times.

"But the house was empty?" This concerned him almost as much as its location. "That means he's still playing games. And he said he wants my Family Slide?"

"Yes. I didn't let on that you got it after going back. Not sure if he believed me when I told him your grandfather held onto it."

"I don't understand why he would want both. If they're reusable, there should be no need." Jimmy looked down, lost in

136

thought.

"Do you think he knows there's only two left?"

Jimmy looked back at me. "I doubt it. My grandfather would be the only one to know that Francois destroyed his own."

"Carney wants to be in control. Maybe he wants to be the only one with the power to jump randomly. Unless...," I hesitated, grasping Jimmy's hand. Another horrible thought struck me as it drained the warmth from my face.

"What, honey?" He gave my hand an encouraging squeeze.

"What if he knows about trapping someone in time? And that *someone* is you. What if he wants to permanently send you back like we plan to do to him?"

Jimmy sat back against the couch cushions raking his hand through his hair. "This is becoming too complicated. Now that we know how to stop him, we need to find a way to execute it quickly. I can't see him trying to trap me. If he wants me gone, why not just shoot me like he did his grandfather?"

"No suffering that way. He's talked about you living without me. If he wanted to kill you or me, he would have by now. Instead, I believe he wants us both to suffer by living apart."

"You may be right. All the more reason to get the Fortuno's Family Slide away from him and set up a trap," Jimmy said.

We sat quietly for a moment, lost in our own thoughts.

"How do you feel about breaking and entering?" I asked with a sidewise glance.

"No, Sami. You're not going back to that house."

"This time I won't be alone. Let's go now, before he's back."

"Do you really think he left the Family Slide there knowing you could get out of the tower room? Don't kid yourself. He took it with him when he left."

Pulling my hand from his and turning to face him, I asked, "Isn't it worth the look?"

"No. I have a better idea," he said with a sly grin. "Two can play this game."

"You're starting to scare me. What've you got in mind?" I didn't know whether to be hopeful or afraid of his plan.

"Tell me exactly how long ago you appeared inside Carney's house."

"I would say it's only been about thirty minutes, maybe forty at the most." His plan started to become clear to me. "No, absolutely not. You can't risk it. What if you miscalculate on the exact time? What if Carney has a gun?"

"Sweetie, we may not have an opportunity like this again. Right now we know exactly where that family slide is, or at least was about half an hour ago. We need to chance it."

He was right. It could take us days or even weeks to find another opportunity like this again. We needed to take the risk.

"Do you think you can request a location that specific? Since the room was locked, you need to land inside. The timing has to be just right in order to get there after he left and before he returned with me. I don't know how long he set the timer for when he grabbed me from the front porch."

"Grandfather said the location can be intricately detailed. All we need is the address of the house. What street were you on?"

"Crandall Avenue."

"Ok, a few minutes on the computer can get us the house number. The homes are all unique around here, so it shouldn't be hard to find."

"Jimmy, you're a genius! All you have to do is time it for only a few minutes, so you can appear while he's here with me, and be gone before we get back. You shouldn't need more than a minute to grab the slide and vanish."

He stood up and slowly walked to the fireplace, then turned around. "That wasn't precisely my intention."

"You can't get there too long before since he probably brought the slide with him."

"Yes, honey, I'm sure you're right. I'll arrive only a few minutes before he comes back with you."

"That's timing it rather close, isn't it?" I got off the couch and stepped over to him. He needed to be gone before Carney arrived with me in tow.

"It's the whole point of it. I intend to be there when he arrives with you. Then you'll be traveling back here with me."

I should've known he'd never leave me there alone with what happened. Since the scene would be different, Carney might not release me after finding his mode of transportation missing. Whether he would suspect Jimmy of getting in and stealing it or not, he wouldn't be willing to lose what leverage he had to bargain with. And that leverage was me.

"I guess you're right," I said hesitantly. "This is the best shot we've got. Does the Family Slide need an hour to power up, like the other holder?"

"Yes, in that aspect it's the same. No sense wasting any more time," he said heading for the office. "You hop on the computer and get that address. Then I'll power up our transportation."

It amazed me how events could turn so quickly from abject fear to having a sense of purpose. We finally had a real chance at stopping the monster. Once in possession of the slides, it would only be a matter of getting him to come to us. That shouldn't be difficult given we'd have exactly what he wanted—two family slides. I hoped we could pull this scheme off. Timing would be crucial.

Finding the address of Carney's house, I gave it to Jimmy.

He depressed the button on the front and spoke clearly, "Twenty-three seventy-five Crandall Avenue, Palos Verdes, CA, first upstairs bedroom on the left."

The location appeared in writing on the screen at the bottom of the frame.

"Maybe we can take a hint from that mad man. You should leave from the bedroom," I suggested. "We'll lock the door from inside. Just in case we have any unwanted visitors, the Family Slide will be safe."

"Good idea. You'll be safer too. When I return, I expect you to be with me instead of waiting. That's another thing Grandfather told me. When you go forward in time, there is only one of you, no duplicates."

"That'll be weird."

"Better than having two of you," he smirked. "I can barely handle one!"

"Understandable," I laughed.

As Jimmy carried the slide upstairs, it dawned on me I never showed him the package from Dede. Going out to the front porch, I retrieved the two mugs, still sitting on the small table. The photo had probably blown away, but it wasn't important, the message got conveyed. I put the mugs on top of the bubble wrap in the box and carried the bundle into the house.

I found Jimmy in the kitchen and showed him what Dede sent,

while explaining the significance of the sun and moon markings. The gesture tickled him as much as me, knowing the couple got their long and happy life together. Nice to see the good in all this mess.

The thought also made me a bit sad. Dede and Milton would be one of the very last couples brought together. After we completed our twenty-ninth and thirtieth matches, the process would be done forever. There wasn't anyone to continue— probably best, given the evil twist it had taken.

Soon all the journeys would cease. The only question left was what to do with the Family Slides once we'd trapped Carney in time. Destruction seemed the logical option, yet what if something came up and they were needed? Guess we'd jump off that bridge when we came to it.

Chapter 28

The frame reached full power. Jimmy and I stood in the bedroom holding each other's hands. "Now remember," I told him, "Paolo said for us to make the trip safely, we need to be holding firmly with *both* hands. That's how he…I mean…that's how Carney took me." I found myself gripping Jimmy's hands harder than intended.

"Relax, Sami." Jimmy shook my hands, getting me to loosen my hold. "You've told me three times in the last hour."

"I'm sorry, honey. It just makes me nervous that something might go wrong. We still don't know if Carney is armed."

"Won't matter. I'm only there for a few minutes, and in the last minute is when you and he will appear. We can do this."

"What if I was a bit off on the time?"

"Then I take the trip again. Remember, repeating a location doesn't trap me. We'll have more than one shot if it doesn't work on the first try."

"Hopefully, I won't be too startled to do the right thing when I appear with Carney and see you." My mind raced over all the things that could go wrong. It was out of my control since I wouldn't have any knowledge of what would take place. More importantly, Carney wouldn't know either.

"Okay. Time for me to go." Jimmy released my hands, adjusted the satchel strapped over his shoulder, and depressed the thirty-second timer. I backed across the room.

"I love you," I said.

Jimmy smiled. With a flash from behind him, I stood alone in the bedroom. Now I had five minutes to endure—better than the twenty-four hours the last time he travelled. Sitting down on my bed, I anxiously stared at the spot where he would reappear, hopefully with me.

The minutes ticked down. Suddenly Jimmy was back, and we were holding hands in front of the dresser. Dried blood stained his shirt. The second timeline hit me immediately—as did the third.

The images appeared in my mind. When I materialized in Carney's house, as before, I ripped my hands out of his and backed away. That's when Jimmy plowed into him, knocking Carney over.

Stunning Carney, Jimmy turned to take a step toward me.

"Jimmy, look out!"

He whipped around only to have Carney slam into him and the two went down. He was pinned, but not for long. Before Carney could back off, Jimmy banged his forehead into Carney's nose. Blood sprayed over them both. Jimmy managed to roll him over and gain the advantage. This time Carney remained too dazed to react.

Jimmy jumped up and raced toward me with his hands out, yelling, "Sami, hands!"

I reached out, but he disappeared.

Still hazy in the present, as multiple memories filled my brain at once, I found my voice. "Did you get it?" I asked, looking hopeful. Then I realized he no longer had the satchel over his shoulder.

"Yes, it's over there," he said pointing toward the dresser. He reached over and grabbed the bag. Opening it, he removed the Fortuno's Family Slide and sat it next to his own. They looked identical. "I didn't get you the first time. When I returned here, you were gone. So, I reset the timer and left the satchel behind. This time I didn't want another encounter with Carney that might put you at risk. What happened after I disappeared?"

The memories continued to flood over me. "Carney became enraged." I reached my hand up to my cheek as I remembered him slapping me.

"I'm sorry I missed you the first time." Jimmy said. He walked over and gently rested his hand on my tender skin. "He hit you, didn't he?"

"Yes, but it was barely a graze. His bloody nose kept him preoccupied. As he held onto his face with one hand, he unlocked the door and shoved me out into the hallway. He still forced me up the stairs and secured the bolt."

"I hoped that's how it would go. It seemed best to retrieve you from up in the tower. Carney might have been prepared for me to reappear had I tried to get you from the same room. He knew I would come back."

"Good thinking, honey."

After going to the top of the stairs and discovering the location of the house, I had just sunk down with my back against the window when Jimmy appeared again. He grabbed both my hands and pulled me up into an embrace. Hesitant to let go, I knew we needed to hold hands to make sure the connection was firm. It's possible that as long as we were holding each other, it might work, but I didn't want to chance it. A moment later we stood back in my bedroom safe and together.

Jimmy put his hand on my cheek. "This can be erased."

"No. We're both here and have the slide. That's all that matters."

He paced furiously. I knew it angered him that Carney hurt me, but the wound would heal. Looking at my face in the mirror, I barely detected a mark.

"Jimmy, it's okay. Let it go. You did enough damage to him, as well as taking a big risk going back a second time. He might have changed his original plan and not put me in the tower. Let's move forward. We have the slides."

"Okay," he said quietly. "Let the games begin." We both stared at the two slides secured permanently in their holders.

"What now?" I asked.

"We find a way to lure Carney to us. Then we send that bastard permanently back in time where he can't do any more harm."

"Let's lock both devices in the safe until we figure out a next step."

"Until this gets wrapped up, I'm staying here. With Carney stuck in the present, we need to be prepared for anything."

"We also don't know if he has any special, one-time use

slides," I said. Since nothing he did followed any sense of reason, we had to be constantly on our toes.

"I know, and he might try using one of those to steal this back. Right now, the advantage is ours since he won't know *when* I left to retrieve you and the slide. Let's see how long we can keep the edge and trap him."

"We need to keep moving forward with the process too," I said. "Stella comes tomorrow. I'll see if she might be a good match for one of our two remaining Suitors."

"What time is that?" he asked, while removing his shirt and walking toward the bathroom to clean up the blood.

"She'll be here after she gets off work from the flower shop at 2:00."

"Good enough. I'll go into the office in the morning to wrap some things up, so I can be available over the next few days. Let's see if our opportunity presents itself. Meanwhile, when I'm not here, you keep this house locked up tight. Agreed?" He looked into my eyes with concern.

"I know the drill. Believe me, I don't want Carney wandering in here again uninvited."

I heard the water running for a few minutes before he returned to retrieve another shirt from the closet.

"Right now, I need to go to my place and gather a few extra things. Come with me?"

"As long as we can stop by the grocery store on the way back. We're out of coffee, and that could be tragic," I play-punched him in the shoulder and grinned.

"Consider me your personal chauffeur." He bowed from the waist, then grabbed the two slides off the dresser and carried them downstairs to the safe.

Chapter 29

The next day, Stella arrived right on time. With Jimmy still at the office, my house remained locked up. Opening the door, after checking the peep hole, I found her to be a petite little thing, with dull brown hair and a high squeaky voice. My guess put her age at late twenties or early thirties.

"It's a pleasure to meet you Stella." I extended my hand and she shook it gently. My thumb brushed across a jagged scar on the back of her hand. Looking out toward the street, I didn't see a car. "Did you drive here?"

She quickly pulled her hand back. "Oh, no, I don't drive. The traffic here is too crazy. I came on the bus," she said nervously. "I hope that's okay?"

Stunned for a moment, I thought, *why wouldn't it be okay?* "Of course, that's fine. Let's have some tea in the kitchen, and chat about what type of photos you're looking for."

"I'm not sure about this, but Dede said she had fun."

"Yes, she enjoyed her session. How is she?" I had to play along, so she didn't suspect I knew more than I should.

"Oh, I guess you wouldn't know, would you?"

"Know what?" I acted concerned, with my eyes wide.

"She quit the flower shop," Stella went on.

"No, no I didn't. Did she get another job?"

"I'm not sure. Her aunt back in Iowa is sick. No other

relatives, I guess. Dede moved there to take care of her. Probably a long-term illness since she pretty much gave up her life here. I'm really going to miss her. She was my only friend."

That seemed a bit strange, since Dede had said she and Stella were just co-workers, not necessarily close. Maybe this woman felt so lonely she made up friendships. I hoped she would be a good fit for one of the two remaining Suitors.

"Surely, you have more than one friend," I said with a light laugh, as I led her down the hallway to the kitchen. The aroma of fresh baked banana bread swirled through the air as the loaf sat cooling on a rack beside the stove. Steam spouted from the kettle while it simmered on low.

"Well, there's Maggie. She's my neighbor, but is in her 90's. Not much of a friend. We have dinner occasionally at her apartment or mine at the complex we live in. Most of my friends disappeared when Gerald left me for *that woman*."

I gestured for her to have a seat at the table. "I'm sorry to hear that. Tell me about Maggie." Sometimes listening to how a potential Betrothed viewed others, gave me a better sense of what they were like themselves. Obviously, the bitterness of her divorce still ran deep, so it might be too soon for her to venture into a new relationship.

She took a seat at the table, as I poured the hot water into our two cups. As I sat one in front of Stella, she wrapped her hands around the hot cup. Once again I noticed the puckered skin across her left hand. She looked down at the tea. "Well, there isn't much to tell—except she was a young woman in the 1940's. Such a romantic era, don't you think?" Stella looked up at me, her eyes now had a little sparkle in them. "With World War II going on, the big band music, soldiers in uniform, how could it not be romantic? Don't you think so?"

"Well, it was a bit before my time, dear."

"Oh, no, I didn't mean to say you were that old. Sorry, I didn't mean..." Stella bit her lip and looked nervously down at her cup again.

This poor woman had no self-confidence. Doing the best thing to break her out of her shell—I laughed. She looked up and saw I took no offense at all, but found it amusing. She joined in, a little nervously at first, until we were both enjoying the moment.

"Now, Stella, that's better. Lighten up. This visit is all about fun. That's all. Just relax and enjoy it."

"Dede told me you were very vibrant. I definitely agree."

"Well, thank you. Now tell me what else you like about the 1940's. You seem very enamored of the era." What I didn't say, was one of the remaining Suitors whose portrait hung in the gallery, lived in 1945. Perhaps Stella would be number twenty-nine after all.

"Well, my neighbor Maggie can't say enough about the era. She described it as magical! That's why I'd like to wear an outfit from that period for my photo session."

"Magical. What a great word to describe the forties. I guess in a way that's true. The expectations in life were so different then," I mused. "Tell me more about why you're so enthralled with that period."

"Family life seemed more important than today. Well, maybe not more important... perhaps genuine. Couples worked things out, rather than cutting and running. They didn't just file and be done with it." She hesitated, lost in her own thoughts.

"Is that what happened to you? With Gerald I mean?" I needed to know more about her history. Stella opened that door.

After taking a couple sips, she nervously clattered the mug as she sat it back on the table. "Yes. Twelve years erased by simply signing a few papers and paying a fee. He felt we'd grown apart. I wanted to try saving our marriage, but he wasn't interested. Begging to go to counseling annoyed him. In fact, everything I did annoyed Gerald over the last few years. You see, he'd met Ruth, and they were very much in love." She stopped and stared into her tea. Tears welled up in the corners of her eyes, until she managed to gain control of her emotions once again.

Looking up into my eyes, she said, "I'm sorry, Sami. Maybe I shouldn't have come."

The heartbreaking pain on the woman's face made me want to help her. I reached out and grasped her hand, once more feeling the nasty scar. "You don't have to go on if you don't want to."

She pulled her hand away. "I guess you're wondering how I got this?" Stella nodded toward her damaged hand.

"No. You don't have to talk about it."

"There's not much to say. It was a kitchen accident. Gerald

said he was sorry. He didn't mean to do it."

This concerned me, that Gerald might have gotten violent. There may be a lot more healing needed than I first suspected. From the look of the white, furrowed skin, the wound happened at least a few years ago. "Are you sure you're all right, honey? We don't have to talk about any of this if you don't want to."

Wiping her eyes with the back of her hand, she smiled. "It's okay. Actually, feels good to talk about it. That is if you don't mind listening. Maggie is the only one I can talk too, and even she seems tired of hearing my story. I'm sorry."

"Oh, don't be. So, it sounds like Gerald has moved on to another marriage."

"Yes," she went on more composed, "he felt Ruth was a better fit for him—closer to his own age. Gerald is eighteen years older than me. I never really saw the age difference, but I guess he did. When we first got married, we'd talked about having children. But then he changed and lost interest in being a father. Ruth is past that age with children of her own. I'm 32 and could still have babies, but now I guess I've missed my chance."

My heart ached for this young woman. A full life of love and family could still be possible. Despite her being a bit raw from the divorce, I believed the sweet, mild-mannered Archie from 1945 would be a good fit. Our conversation needed to steer away from the bitterness.

"Tell me more about Maggie. You met her when you moved into your apartment?"

"Huh? Oh, no. Maggie is the reason I found the apartment. You see, she lived next door to Gerald's mother in San Diego. They had been friends and she watched him grow up. Guess you could say she remained the only friend that stuck with me after the split."

"Well, it sounds like she's been a great influence on you. It's nice to have steady friends like Maggie." Another coincidence. Archie lived in San Diego.

"Yes, I suppose," she said looking down at the table.

Making up my mind, I stood and cleared our empty mugs. "Stella," I said, "would you like to see my studio?"

Her face brightened. "Oh, yes," she spouted a little too loudly. Toning down her voice, she said, "I thought you'd decided not to do my session."

"Not at all. Why would you think that?"

"Never mind. It's silly. Please, let's go to your studio."

Quickly standing as well, she followed me out of the kitchen and down the hall. As Stella stepped in, she immediately caught sight of Dede's and Milton's portrait.

"Wow! Dede looks great! And happy. Who's the man that posed with her? They look so good together."

"Another customer that had the same artistic flair she did. He agreed to pose with her in a couple pictures."

"What's his name? Do you think he would pose with me? I'd love to have a session like that."

"Well," I began cautiously, "I can't tell you his name. Since he's a customer, I feel that's confidential information. You understand, don't you?"

"Oh, right. Guess I didn't think about that."

"Besides, it sounds like you're looking for a different era. Not his style. Perhaps I could convince a past customer to return and pose with you. Like this gentleman over here," I gestured toward Archie's portrait. He wore an army uniform that identified him as being in the military during World War II. The pants and shirt were khaki colored, with a brown tie and he wore a cloth garrison cap.

"Oh, my," she uttered. After staring at the picture for a long moment, she turned and asked, "Do you think he would agree to sit with me? I mean do a session?"

"Actually, he asked to do a joint session if ever I found a lady interested. His name I can tell you, since he gave me permission. It's Archie Blake."

"Archie Blake," Stella repeated the name. "Even his name seems to fit, doesn't it?" She gave out a slight giggle. I witnessed an amazing transformation in this young woman's whole demeanor.

"There it is!"

"What?" She had a confused look on her face.

"That smile you'll be needing. Can't do a photo session without it!"

Her cheeks reddened as she blushed, and her smile grew wider.

"How does tomorrow sound?"

"Perfect! I'm actually off work, so will come back whatever time Mr. Blake can make it."

"I'm sure he'd prefer you called him Archie."

"Archie," she repeated.

"Ten o'clock sound good?"

"I'll be here. I can't wait. Thank you, Sami. Thank you so much!"

"You're welcome. Come, I'll show you out." I indicated the hallway in which we'd entered, then walked with her to the door. "Just bring the outfit you want to wear, and we'll have some fun. Okay?"

"Okay," she said as she walked out and across the porch, practically bounding down the one step. I watched as she hurried to the end of the driveway. Stella seemed off in her own world already as she purposefully strode down the sidewalk.

Chapter 30

The savory aroma of meatloaf filled the kitchen. We sat at the table eating dinner when Jimmy asked, "So you think Stella would be a good fit for Archie?"

"Yes, I believe so," I answered. "From the sounds of her life, the ex-husband treated her like excess baggage. He's eighteen years older. She desperately wanted to have children, but after they were married, he changed his mind about being a parent. Stella is 32-years old and Archie is 38. Both still young enough to have children."

"Sounds like we'll only be one match away from completing our quota. After that we can be done with the process."

"You really think we can finish this, honey?" I asked him, lifting my glass for a sip of wine.

"We're so close. Now that we have Carney's Family Slide, he can't interfere with our matches."

"Providing he doesn't have more special slides," I reminded him.

"Try to stay positive, Sami. We can end this. And send him someplace he'll no longer be a menace."

"I'm trying, honey, I'm really trying. It's just..."

"We'll get him," he said, placing his hand over mine for a moment. "Keep moving forward. Did you tell Stella how she'll really meet Archie?"

"No. I wanted to talk to you about it first. She's still trying to get over the divorce. I'm not completely sure Stella is ready for another relationship. There might not have been enough healing time."

"Look at how everything fits." Jimmy said, sweeping his hand through the air. "These women come across your path because they're right for one of our Suitors. Stella is one of them. What are the odds a potential Betrothed, who loves the 40's, would randomly find her way to your door? With only two men left, that's hard to come by."

"I find it too coincidental, don't you think? She's such a perfect match that it almost seems…well…planned." I put my fork down and looked him in the eye.

"How could anyone plan this? Least of all Carney? I know that's what you're thinking."

"Of course, that's what I'm thinking. You do have a point though. How could he possibly know what Suitors we have left?"

"See? You've squelched your own fears," said Jimmy, reaching across the dinner table and covering my hand again. The warmth of his touch radiated up my arm.

"All right," I managed a smile. "With everything that's gone on, I'm looking for demons where there aren't any. Stella would be a great Betrothed for Archie. I'll present the process to her when she comes tomorrow and hopefully she'll be willing to take a chance."

"That's my girl," Jimmy patted my hand then resumed eating. "Sounds like a perfect match to me," he said in between mouthfuls of meatloaf and mashed potatoes. "Don't worry, honey, it'll be fine. You'll see."

Picking up my own fork, I scooped up some potatoes. Despite his confidence, it made my mind spin in several directions. It came down to me just wanting to place number twenty-nine. Thirty loomed around the corner.

The next morning I still had reservations about sending Stella back. Something seemed off. Not able to pinpoint it, I focused on her journey. Retrieving Archie's yellow-framed slide from the safe, I placed it into the holder and pressed the activation button.

At 10:00 on the dot, my doorbell rang. Despite being in the house, Jimmy agreed to make himself scarce. Because Stella had such a skittish personality, I thought a stranger being here might make her nervous.

When I opened the door, she wore a basic beige dress, matching pumps, and a red pillbox hat with a bit of netting over the front. She personified a woman of the 1940's.

"You look perfect," I exclaimed. "That's a great outfit. Wherever did you find it?"

"Do you really like it?" she touched the hat with nervous fingers.

"Of course, I do! You definitely fit the era."

"I have to admit I've had the clothes for months. Found the dress and hat in a thrift store. I wanted to wear it last Halloween, but didn't have anywhere to go." Recovering quickly, she asked, "Is Archie here?" The clothes transformed the young woman, building her confidence.

"No, he isn't. "

Stella looked close to tears. "He wasn't interested in me, was he?"

"No, not at all," I treaded cautiously. "You're actually going to meet him somewhere else."

She tilted her head to the side. "I'm confused. Don't all your sessions take place here?"

As we spoke, I led her to my studio. Time for the blatant truth. "Stella, I'm going to do more than just take your picture."

"Oh?"

"I want you to keep an open mind." I gestured to the room around us with a sweep of my arm. "Look around at the portraits in this room."

Stella squinted, then looking around, she started to examine the pictures.

"What do you see in them?"

"People. People whose pictures you've taken, I'd imagine."

"That's a start. Notice anything else?"

Stella looked back at me, a little perturbed, starting to form the word *no* with her lips. Then she stopped, and took another look.

"They're all couples," she stated. "Except for those two over there." She pointed at Archie's picture and the one next to it.

I nodded. "I introduced all those couples."

"When you say *couples*," Stella asked, "do you mean two

people that ended up together? Like in a relationship…or even…*marriage*?"

"Now you're catching on." Smiling at Stella, I allowed her a few moments to let my words sink in.

Just like Dede, she started looking at the portraits in a new light—with renewed hope. I'd planted the seed of potential happiness, and it started blooming.

"Dede is in one of those portraits. She really didn't go back to Iowa to take care of a sick aunt." Finally, she made the connection.

Time for me to believe in the process and take a risk. "No, she didn't. You see that man she's pictured with?"

"Yes." Stella said, as she stepped closer to look at Dede's and Milton's picture.

"She's with him now. In Albuquerque, New Mexico."

"Dede moved to New Mexico?" Stella turned to look at me.

"Yes," I hesitated. "She went back to be with him in Albuquerque—in the year 1975."

"What! Are you nuts?" Stella looked doubtful.

When I didn't respond, the puzzled look on her face slid off. "You're serious, aren't you?"

"Yes."

"How is that possible? How did she go *back?*"

I extended my hand and asked, "Are you ready to take a leap of faith?"

The question hung in the air for a couple moments, like an elephant in the room. It wouldn't be ignored, and it deserved some serious consideration. She looked over at Archie's portrait.

Turning back my way, she reached out and grasped my hand. "Yes. I want to believe."

Feeling the puckered skin of her scar, this time she didn't pull away. "Do you have any plans for the next 24 hours?"

"Just work at 10:00 tomorrow."

"Can you be a little late?"

She thought a minute, then slowly nodded.

"Want to meet Archie? Like your friend, Maggie, he lived in San Diego."

"You're sending me back to the 1940's, aren't you?"

"Nineteen-forty-five to be exact. Wanna go?"

She nodded once.

"Okay. Details. You will pose for my camera. When it flashes, you'll be sent back to 1945 for exactly 24 hours. Archie will be there to greet you. If you two decide this is the life you both want, then you will have one week to wrap up your life in the present. You'll be photographed one more time and go back permanently. Questions?"

While talking, I led Stella over to the cushioned bench. She glanced at the bench, the camera, then back at me.

She bit her lower lip. "I should have many."

"But you don't, do you?"

Stella shook her head. "No. I want to be *happy*. I want to be *loved*."

"You just might get your wish." I raised my brow at her. "Ready to give it a whirl?"

Again, she nodded once.

I really expected more resistance. It's not everyday someone offers you a trip back in time. Yet Stella was ready to trust me and go. She must be a very lonely soul.

"So, what do I do?" she asked, eyes open wide.

"Sit there, smile, and I'll do the rest. Ready?"

She sat on the bench staring down at the floor for a moment. Finally lifting her chin, she looked me in the eye and in a breathy declaration said, "Yes."

Stepping behind her, I pressed the button and the thirty-second countdown began. With my hand on her shoulder, I gave a reassuring squeeze. Keeping up the farce of using my sepia camera, I grabbed the cushioned button.

A sly smile spread across Stella's face. It was out of character and confirmed my earlier fears that something wasn't right. My mind immediately flashed to Carney.

Chapter 31

The digital clock on the corner table glowed 10:22. I stood rooted to the floor, unsure what to do next. At exactly 10:19 Stella had returned. Instead of the glowing young woman I expected, there sat a deranged wraith.

Tears streamed down her cheeks as she laughed hysterically. Stella's disheveled hair poked out from under the pillbox hat and swirled around her face like tendrils. Gripped tightly in her hand was a bloody kitchen knife. The beige dress, drenched with blood, clung to her body like a stocking. Over and over she repeated the phrase, *"you will never be."* She chanted it like a prayer, as if a repentant sinner working her way through a rosary.

I swallowed hard and cautiously approached, stopping a few feet away. "Stella, honey, what happened?"

She continued to laugh. I wasn't sure she heard me. "Stella…Stella…" No response. Trying again, louder, "STELLA!"

She snapped out of her private world. The laughter stopped. Staring directly into my eyes, I thought she might come after me with the knife. She looked down at her hand and screamed, as if seeing the bloody weapon for the first time, and loosened her grip. It fell to the floor. Watching it drop, I felt like it moved in slow motion, making a soft thud on the carpet as it bounced twice and landed at her feet.

Looking back up at me Stella said, "I had to do it. You see, don't you? He caused such pain. Being back there, I couldn't allow it to happen again. I just couldn't, could I? I did the right thing. Tell me I did the right thing!" she pleaded, her voice growing shrill.

"Tell me exactly what you did. Are you hurt? Did you hurt Archie? Did he hurt you?"

"Archie? Why would I hurt Archie? He's a sweet man. He wants to marry me. Archie said he would do anything for me. Can you imagine? Anything I asked!"

"Are you bleeding?"

"Bleeding?" She looked down at her dress. "Oh, no, it's not mine," Stella said with a chuckle. "You thought I was bleeding? No, no, I'm fine. This is from Caitlin."

"Honey, who's Caitlin?" It took all my strength to remain calm.

I heard Jimmy's footsteps pad on the carpet as he ran through the door, but didn't take my eyes off the woman. He came to a stop behind me, gently putting his hand on my hip. Relief surged through my body, as I felt his warm breath on the back of my neck. Stella didn't appear to notice him as she gave no acknowledgement of his entrance.

Fearing she might snap and pick up the knife, my uncertainty of whether I could talk her down from this manic state continued to fester. Inside my head I screamed in fear, yet outside managed to stay in control.

My mind raced, trying to remember Archie's history and if there was a woman named Caitlin. I kept coming up blank. Both his mother and sister were in his life at the time Stella went back, but neither had that name.

Standing there, I quietly waited for her to continue. She remained seated as a smile spread across her face. Tracks of drying tears marred her cheeks. In a casual voice, as if we were two girlfriends having a gab session, Stella said, "His mother, of course." She acted as if this explained everything.

"No, Stella, Archie's mother is Roberta. It isn't Caitlin."

"Archie's mother? Oh, don't be silly. I would never cause Archie pain like that. He loves his mother dearly. There was no time for me to meet her, but I'm sure I will love her too."

She was now quite at ease with herself. With a grin on her face and a vague look in her eyes, I knew Stella's thoughts weren't on the present moment.

Reeling her back in, "Stella." No response. "Stella, honey, please look at me."

Focus came back into her eyes anew. "Yes? Can I go now? I've a million things to do before I return to Archie."

"Please, tell me who Caitlin is. Whose mother is she?"

"Can't you see?" she asked, holding up her left hand. The skin was smooth and unblemished. "I've erased him completely!"

My fear grew. "Who did you erase?"

"Why Gerald, of course. Who else would be affected by Caitlin being gone?"

Terror seeped further into my soul as I realized the scenario playing out here. I felt Jimmy's hand tighten on my hip.

"What do you mean by *gone*, Stella?"

"What do you think *gone* means? Dead! Gone! No more!"

"You killed her, didn't you?"

"I had too," Stella started to get annoyed. "Well, actually, *we* had to. When I told Archie about Gerald, he had to help me. He *wanted* to help me. I told you, he would do anything I asked. Now Gerald is no more. Or never will be. However, that works. I won't be hurt by him. Carney was right. He's such a brilliant man!" Stella sat there, smiling, off in her own universe again.

"Who did you say was right?" My instincts had been on target—too late.

"Carney, your Collector that took pictures of the men. With such an odd name, there can't be more than one."

I felt my face pale from the shock. That mad man still meddled with our matches. It never occurred to me he could send in an imposter with sinister intentions. He helped this woman take revenge on her ex-husband. Stella didn't seem the type, yet what did I really know about her. This was worse than I ever dreamed. She killed an innocent woman—her ex-husband's mother.

As if reading my mind, Jimmy said, "There's no fixing this."

Noticing him for the first time, Stella screamed, "Who's that?"

"He's my Collector. The one who photographed Archie and the other men we match with women like you." I spoke evenly, hoping to calm her down.

"I don't understand. Carney said *he* was your Collector. Do you have two?"

"Carney isn't my Collector. He lied to you. What exactly did he tell you, sweetie?"

She sat on the bench with a look of horror on her face. For the first time Stella seemed to realize what she'd done. Whether she felt remorse or fear, it didn't matter. The situation finally sank in.

With my mind spinning, we now faced a moral dilemma. If Stella went back, she'd be arrested. Would that be wrong? She was a murderer. To do nothing would be the same as if we harbored a fugitive. My sense of morality went askew. Does that mean I'm just as guilty for sending her back? Yet how could I know this would happen? That this *could* happen? The lines between right and wrong blurred.

Extending my hand, I beckoned, "Come, Stella, let's get you cleaned up."

She looked at me a moment, then slowly rose. Thankfully leaving the knife where it lay, she extended her hand and took mine.

Glancing at Jimmy I said, "I'm taking her upstairs to get showered off. We'll decide what to do afterward." Gesturing with my head toward the knife, I asked, "Can you…". I didn't complete the request.

Jimmy nodded and said, "I'll take care of it. You deal with Stella."

She allowed me to lead her upstairs and into my bathroom. I helped her take off her hat, shoes and dress, then gave her privacy to remove the rest. Before leaving, I placed a towel on the counter and turned on the shower to get warm.

I took out a pair of sweatpants, sweatshirt and slip-on canvas shoes from my closet. We were close in size, except my foot looked a bit larger. It would have to do. Laying the clothes out on the bed with some undergarments, I left the room, closing the door behind me.

Back downstairs, I found Jimmy in the kitchen washing off the knife. When finished, he dropped it in the trash.

As I sat down on a chair at the dining table, I asked, "What now?"

"I don't know. I just don't know. Carney has escalated to a whole new level of evil."

"How could he have known about Archie?"

Jimmy came over and sat opposite me. "His uniform is pretty explicit for the World War II era. Carney probably saw the pictures when he was in your studio."

"I never thought of that. But how would he know the name or location?" I asked.

"He didn't need the name, just the location. The background gave it away. He's standing in front of the Mission Beach Roller Coaster. It's an icon in the city. Been there since the 1920's. Anyone recognizing that would know the location was near San Diego."

My wooden chair creaked as I leaned against the backrest. "Now the question is, what do we do about Stella?"

Chapter 32

"Maybe we should send her back," he said, "to answer for her actions. She killed a woman in cold blood."

As Jimmy and I sat at the kitchen table, we could hear the shower running upstairs. It would take more than hot water to wash away the blood on Stella's hands.

"Where do we go from here?" I asked him.

"Isn't it obvious? We have to do what's right."

"Which is?" I wrinkled my brow.

"Sami, with or without Carney's interference, Stella murdered someone. Her psyche may have been fragile and easily influenced, but she still took the life of an innocent woman. The act was premeditated. And now one of our Suitor's is left holding the bag, even though he's just as guilty for assisting. I'm sure if we looked up Archie's history on the internet, he'll have spent the rest of his life in a military jail. Being in the army meant no civilian prison for him."

"Stella would end up in a cell too."

"Which is where she belongs," he said quietly.

I knew he was right, but didn't think I could send Stella back knowing the life she would lead. It would be worse than being dead. Damn Carney!

"Jimmy, let's start by getting Stella to spend the night. She should have people around her right now."

"And what if she decides to remove any witnesses?" He swiped a hand through his hair.

"She wouldn't do that," I started getting upset.

Jimmy let out a long breath. "Just like she wouldn't commit murder?"

We sat there in silence for a few moments.

"Thank you for the clothes," said Stella from the kitchen doorway.

I hadn't realized the shower upstairs stopped. Not sure how long she'd been standing there, I didn't know what she overheard.

"Stella, honey, come sit with us." I stood up and gestured to the chair next to me.

She hesitated. Then her shoes emitted tiny squeaks on the tiled floor as she walked over to take a seat. Delicately perching on the edge of the chair, she stared down at the table.

Jimmy took the reins of the conversation. Reaching out his hand, he gently said, "Hello, Stella, my name is Jimmy."

Slowly looking up and staring at his outstretched hand, she gingerly grasped his fingers and gave a little pressure. Not really a handshake, but it would do. She released Jimmy's hand and looked back down.

"Tell us," Jimmy said, "how did you meet Carney?"

"So, you do know him?" Her eyes shot up and looked from Jimmy to me.

"Yes, honey," I said. "He was a Collector. He performed interviews of Suitors while working with a different Photographer. She had been a friend of Jimmy's," I added in the hopes of making her feel comfortable enough to tell us how she landed in this situation.

"She *was* a friend? His Photographer? She isn't any more?"

I took a deep breath. Maybe that wasn't the best information to share.

"She passed away years ago," Jimmy offered, trying to down play it.

I gave him a quick smile of thanks. Looking back to Stella, I reiterated the question. "How did you meet Carney?"

"He came into the flower shop to buy flowers for his girlfriend, April."

Jimmy and I exchanged a brief glance then focused back on

Stella. "Was he with her?" Jimmy treaded carefully.

"Oh, no, he said he wanted to surprise her. Such a sweet man. He asked how long I'd been with my boyfriend. Can you imagine? He thought I had a boyfriend." Her face lit up as she looked off into space.

When she didn't continue, I nudged her a bit. "What did you talk about, honey?"

Turning my way, she answered, "Oh, just chit chat. And then he left."

"He didn't say anything else to you?"

"That time, no. But then he came back the next day and said he couldn't get me out of his head. That sweet man thought about *me*."

"What did he say?" I squeeze her shoulder in encouragement.

"Well, he started telling me about the *process*. You know, the one you're all involved in? That happened right after Dede told me about going to you for her photo session. He suggested I try to spend some time with her and maybe she would share her experience. But Carney said not to let on that I knew about it. It had to remain our secret, so I wouldn't scare Dede off."

"Did Dede tell you about Milton?" I asked.

"Oh, no. She always did the right thing. She once ran down the street after a customer because he'd overpaid."

I didn't think Dede would have let on what I really did in my photo sessions. "So how did he come to tell you about this process?"

"Well, I have to admit, it didn't feel completely right, his having a girlfriend and all, but we went out for coffee. I told him about Gerald. Carney was appalled at how he treated me. He said he might be able to help me fix what happened." She absent-mindedly began rubbing the back of her left hand with her right.

"Of course, at first I didn't believe him. His amazing stories about jumping through time finally convinced me." She started getting excited. I knew how intoxicating the process could be.

"Do you know how he found out about Archie?" Jimmy asked.

"Of course. Carney interviewed him as a Suitor. How could you not know that? He wouldn't tell me the man's name because the Photographer always filled in those details." She looked pensive a moment before continuing. "There were actually two men—one in San Diego during World War II and another Suitor from New York City in the 1950's. After I explained about my ex-husband being from San Diego, he didn't mention the other gentleman again. Guess he thought Archie fit me best. He was right, wasn't he?" She looked at me for encouragement.

Fear raced through me as I thought about Doug Pendry, our final Suitor. I looked at Jimmy. His brow wrinkled with concern as well. The same thought might be going through his mind. How can we trust the next Betrothed that would finish our quota?

Stella put her hand lightly on my arm. When I looked over at her, she said, "I'm very tired now and would like to go home. There's so much to do before going back to Archie."

"Stella?" Jimmy asked as she broke her focus with me and looked to him. "Do you mind if I ask you a couple more questions? It won't take long. Sami, I think it would be best if you didn't hear this," he added to me.

Feeling confused, I nodded. "I'll just leave you two for a moment."

"No, we'll go into the studio. It involves the portraits."

Strange, I thought. What could he possibly need to ask her privately? Surely, he would fill me in afterwards. Maybe he thought Stella might feel overwhelmed with two of us present.

"Would you mind coming with me, Stella?" While asking, he stood up, walked to our side of the table and held out his hand. Gingerly she grasped his fingers and allowed Jimmy to lead her out of the kitchen.

At the doorway she looked nervously back at me. I nodded encouragement. After a moment's hesitation, she allowed Jimmy to escort her out.

Consumed with curiosity, I sat waiting. After a few minutes Jimmy came back into the kitchen. Stella wasn't with him. "Did you let her leave? I didn't hear the front door."

His face stretched taut and expressionless. "I'm sorry, Sami. She's gone."

Realization washed over me as I bolted out of my chair and raced for the studio. On the table behind the bench sat a spent slide with a blue frame. Moving in close to look at the name on the bottom, I already knew it had to be the second one for Archie.

Jimmy must have set it while I helped Stella upstairs. "No!" I screamed.

Jimmy came up from behind and wrapped his strong arms around me. "I'm sorry, honey," he whispered in my ear. "You know it had to be done. I wasn't sure you would've allowed me to follow through. I'm so sorry."

I turned in the embrace, wrapped my arms around Jimmy's waist while nestling my head against his shoulder. After a few moments I pulled my head back. With teary eyes, I told him, "You did the right thing."

"We could find out what happened to her and Archie," he suggested.

"I don't want to know," I placed my head against his shoulder again. "I don't want to know." This time my words were muffled, but it didn't matter.

Chapter 33

After another restless night's sleep, I gave up about 6:00. For once Jimmy weathered the storm of my tossing and turning, as he still slept. Quietly slipping out of the bedroom, I went downstairs to make coffee.

While it brewed, I found clean shorts and t-shirt in the laundry room and changed. Stella's dress, hat and shoes were neatly piled on the dryer. The clothes had the innocent scent of a spring day left by the detergent. Jimmy had been busy after I went to bed last night. I don't know what his intentions were with Stella's things, but we needed to get rid of them. Probably the trash was best.

Once the coffee finished, I poured myself a cup. Slipping into a pair of flip flops and throwing on a sweatshirt by the front door, I went outside to savor the early morning quiet. Receiving no peace, my mind churned with thoughts of how to trap Carney in time.

A car door slammed, breaking me out of my reverie. I saw a black Lincoln Continental parked at the curb. Not something you find every day, especially in the beach areas. Paolo stood beside the car returning my gaze. So wrapped up in my own thoughts, I hadn't noticed if he just pulled up or if the car had been parked already.

After retrieving something from the passenger seat, he slowly came up my driveway. He carried a small wooden box. Recognizing it as the same type that sat locked away in my safe, I knew he held Paolo, Jr.'s, set of slides.

"Forgive the intrusion, Sami, but I needed to talk with you." He stood on the edge of the porch waiting. His formal upbringing wouldn't allow him to proceed further without an invitation.

Standing up I gestured to a chair next to mine. "Please, come join me. It's no intrusion at all. Would you like some coffee?"

Slowly he stepped up onto the porch, gave a formal nod and took a seat, settling the box on his lap. "Coffee would be most welcome, thank you. I drink it with cream, if it's not too much trouble."

Nodding back, I went into the house with my own cup in tow. In the kitchen I retrieved a mug from the cupboard, added cream and poured in coffee. Giving a warm-up to my own black brew, I carried them out the front door.

Paolo sat there staring out to sea. He didn't turn when I set the mug down on the table beside him. A moment later he looked at me in surprise, as if he had been so lost in thought, he hadn't heard me come back outside.

"You are most kind, Sami. Thank you."

"You're quite welcome. I see you've brought your son's slides," I continued as I retook my seat. "Why?"

"I thought perhaps…well…those Suitors and potential Betrotheds deserve a chance. Maybe you and your Collector…" He trailed off, not able to finish the request.

"I'm sorry, sir, but after our last match, we're done," Jimmy said from the front doorway.

I hadn't heard Jimmy come outside. Carrying his own coffee, he walked up to Paolo and extended his free hand. "Jimmy Chang, Mr. Fortuno. It's a pleasure to meet you. Sorry about the circumstances."

Without standing, Paolo reached out and shook Jimmy's hand. "The pleasure is mine," he said formally. "Please call me Paolo. So, you're Chang's grandson?"

"Yes," Jimmy said as he released the old man's hand and took the seat on my other side. "I don't mean to sound rude, but we're one match away from completing our quota. Once we've satisfied the thirtieth match, we're done. You'll need to find someone else to complete your son's work. That is if you feel it's worth finishing. With all the tragedy that's befallen the process, it seems to me you would be as anxious as we are to see it end."

Paolo sat back in the wicker chair. It groaned in protest as he shifted his weight. With the quiet of the morning, the noise sounded exceedingly loud. "I did not mean to offend. It just seemed that perhaps a small piece of Junior could be at rest knowing his job was accomplished. Obviously, I have overstepped my bounds. My apologies. I will go," he said as he began to stand up.

Looking to Jimmy, then putting my hand on Paolo's arm, I gave it a gentle squeeze. "Please, Paolo, wait. It's a noble gesture. We appreciate the opportunity, don't we, Jimmy?" I nodded toward him to speak up.

"Yes, Sami's right. I didn't mean to sound harsh. Carney has done a world of damage to all of us. I understand how you feel about your son's work. It doesn't need to end, but we're just not the ones to complete the job. Maybe you can find a couple more fitting to fulfill this goal for you. Right now, we need to focus our efforts on trapping Carney. You know of the process to trap him in time? So he can't come back?"

Paolo settled back into his seat and again focused his gaze seaward. "Of course, that information is passed on with the Family Slide. My father instructed me in the act, yet had never known it to be used. It is only for the most dire of circumstances."

"I believe we're to that point," I said. "There's no other way to stop Carney's murderous spree. He's destroyed too many lives already, including our last Betrothed. This can't go on."

"Yes, I agree," Paolo said. "But to do that, you will need two Family Slides. One is not enough. You must have two."

We never thought to notify Paolo of our latest development. I looked at Jimmy and he seemed to know what I was thinking. He nodded his head firmly, as if encouraging me to tell Paolo.

"Paolo, due to recent developments, we have two slides." It never occurred to me the old man may want his slide back. Perhaps he wanted to hatch a plan to save his son.

"So, you've obtained the Frenchman's slide?" Paolo would have no way of knowing that Francois' was destroyed.

"No. Mr. Chang confirmed that after his last journey, suffering from a fatal gunshot wound delivered by his grandson, Francois smashed his Family Slide before expiring."

"He destroyed it with his own hand? He must have had powerful reasons to choose that path," the elder Fortuno said. "By simple deduction, that means you have acquired my family's slide as well as your own, have you not?"

"Yes," Jimmy replied. "I guess it's for us to ask permission. May we keep yours to stop Carney?"

Both of us sat there holding our breath staring at the old man. I felt Jimmy grab my hand. If he said he wanted the slide back, would we be obligated to give it to him?

After several painful moments, we could see the resolve and determination come over Paolo's face. He held his head up, set his jaw firmly and answered, "It would be my honor to have even a small part in stopping that mad man. Please use whatever means necessary, including the Fortuno slide. You have my blessing and permission to keep it."

Reaching over with my free hand, I grasped Paolo's. "Thank you. We promise to do whatever it takes to stop him. We won't let up until he's trapped."

"Please let me know if there is any further assistance I can render. Whatever means I have is at your disposal." He stood up still holding the box of slides. The parcel remained lovingly grasped within his large hands.

"For now," Jimmy suggested, "the best thing you can do is lock those slides up securely. As long as Carney is on the prowl, he may use any means, including those slides, to continue jumping through time. Right now, he's locked into the present. He may be getting desperate, so please take good care of them."

"Understood. Thank you for the hospitality, Sami. Contact me if you need anything."

He stood there a moment looking lost. Instinctively I stepped up, threw my arms about his neck and gave him an awkward hug, with the box between us. He held tightly to his treasure, yet I felt a light kiss brushed across my cheek as I released him.

"Good luck," he said before turning around and walking down the driveway. He gently placed the box on the passenger seat, closed the car door and walked to the driver's side.

Jimmy came over and put his free arm around my shoulders as we watched him drive away. Instead of feeling sorry for the old man, I had nothing but respect. Even at the loss of his son, he still wanted to see the job completed.

A thought suddenly struck me. Looking up at Jimmy, I said, "I know how to trap Carney."

Jimmy gave me a sidewise glance, and took the bait. "Ok, lovely lady, I'm listening."

Chapter 34

"We pretend to return the Fortuno Family Slide?" asked Jimmy, tilting his head. I could tell he thought this wasn't the best plan.

"Yes." Pulling away from his embrace, I took a sip of coffee, then set it on the small table. Turning back to him, I continued. "Don't you see? He's broken into the Fortuno home and stolen it once before. I believe he's arrogant enough to think he can do it a second time. That's when we have the slides activated and ready to trap him. What do you think?"

Jimmy mulled this over, sipping from his own mug. "It just might work. Do you think Paolo will go along with it?"

"There's no doubt in my mind. Carney killed his son. There's nothing that man won't agree to if it means stopping this monster. It won't bring back Junior, but it will exact justice."

"What's your plan?" Jimmy asked, as he walked over to the wicker chair and sat down.

Sitting myself, I spelled out my idea. "We make a show of giving Paolo back the Family Slide right here on the porch. Hopefully, Carney will be up in his tower watching."

"He's probably keeping closer tabs on us than we'd like to think. I imagine he's panicking now that he can't randomly jump, and it's killing him," said Jimmy.

"That's what I'm thinking too. Even though it makes my skin crawl, I think his vigilance is relentless." It took all my strength not to look up in the direction of Carney's house. "Do you think he even wonders what happened to Stella?"

"I don't know, sweetie." He reached over and placed a hand on my arm. "He may have written her off as another pawn in his game."

At the thoughts of our recent Betrothed, I went into the house, grabbed Stella's clothes and tied them up in a plastic bag. Walking out to the trash can on the side of the house, I dropped the bundle in. Closing the lid seemed so horrific an end to such a fragile life. I couldn't help feeling partly responsible for that sad creature being led astray.

Back on the porch, Jimmy sipped his coffee. So deep in thought, I sat down next to him without saying a word. Staring out at the ocean, I felt his hand gently cover mine and squeeze.

As I turned to face him, we gazed into each other's eyes. He leaned in and kissed me on the lips. "You know what frightens me most?"

"Uh-uh," I shook my head.

"Losing you. I don't think I could go on if you weren't here with me. All these years, we've chosen to live apart. We've always wanted our own space to retreat to. Why do we do that?"

I breathed deeply, savoring the ocean's scent. A gentle breeze rustled the leaves in the trees. Sitting here with my perfect man, I wondered what thoughts churned in his head. I contemplated the question and finally answered."Fear."

"Fear of getting too close and losing. Am I right?"

"Yes." I gazed into his pensive blue eyes.

"Sami, I love you very much."

"I love you, too. You've always known that."

"Yes, I have. That's why I have to say this to you."

Fear coupled with sheer terror filled my head. He was breaking up with me to keep me safe! That had to be it.

"You know," he said, "I love to see the emotion race across your face and your hazel eyes go wide when you think you know what's going on—but this time, you don't."

I crinkled my brow with obvious confusion.

Jimmy laughed and set his mug on the table beside him. Still holding my hand, he got out of his chair and down on one knee. With his other hand, he pulled a small box out of his pocket and flipped it open. Inside rested a ring. A simple band woven of fine silver strands.

I gasped, not expecting anything like this.

He looked into my eyes and said, "Samantha, I love you from the bottom of my heart. Will you marry me?"

"Yes!" My answer was immediate, and much louder than either of us expected.

"Take your time. You don't want to make any hasty decisions." He laughed.

Pulling my hand free, I leaned over and threw both arms around his neck. Kissing him on the lips, I pulled back, "Yes, I will marry you."

Jimmy removed the ring from the box and gently slipped it onto my finger. "When?" he asked.

Bursting out laughing, the two of us stood and he pulled me into his arms. In the midst of all this chaos, joy and love still existed, but now was not the time to plan a wedding.

We went into the house and made breakfast together. Over toast, bacon and eggs, we began plotting our next move to trap Carney. Despite the joy we both felt, business had to take precedence.

"So how do you want to approach Paolo?" I asked.

Jimmy thought about it a moment then said, "We go to his house. It's crucial we're familiar with the location so there are no surprises. But we really need a reason for Carney to go to Paolo. With having to power up the slides for an hour, we can't leave too much to chance."

"What if Paolo invited Carney to his house?"

"Why would he do that?"

"Think about the facts," I said, getting up to refill our coffee mugs. "Carney doesn't know Paolo suspects him of killing Junior. The only truth known to all of us is that Carney stole April, his son's photographer. What if Paolo expected Carney to complete his son's work?"

"That could be a good angle." Jimmy nodded as I handed back his mug.

"Paolo could offer to give him the box of slides suggesting he help the Suitors and Betrotheds that were robbed of a chance at happiness. Carney would jump at the chance of getting the emergency slides. The dates might coincide with something to his advantage. He may think he can use them to get back one of the Family Slides."

"Sami, you're a genius! That could be just the bait we need to get him to the Fortuno house."

"Except, when he arrives, we'll be there waiting."

"We need to warn Paolo that Carney could be armed. As well thought out as this plan may be, there are still factors we can't count on. His having a gun is a strong possibility," Jimmy pointed out.

As we sat finishing our breakfast, I had to ask the question that burned in my mind. "Jimmy, why did you choose now to propose to me?"

He reached across the table and picked up my left hand. Gently, his thumb rubbed the ring. My whole arm tingled with warmth. "Because I always took it for granted you would be in my life. The events over the last few months made me realize that when our time is up, there are no second chances. No going back, no matter how many slides we have. When it finally comes time for me to leave this existence, I want it to be as your husband. It would be the one thing in life I'd regret not following through on."

"You don't think we'll both survive this, do you?"

He raised my hand to his lips and kissed the back. Without a word, he got up and walked out of the kitchen. Tears slid down my cheeks. Regardless of the cost, he intended to stop Carney. No matter what it took. And there was nothing I could do about it.

Chapter 35

While cleaning up our breakfast dishes, I heard Jimmy on the phone with Paolo, asking if we could come over for a talk.

"See you tonight," he said, as he walked back into the kitchen and ended the call. Looking up from his phone, he continued, "We're all set."

"Did you explain our plan?"

"No. I thought it best to discuss it in person. I'm sure he knows why we're asking to come over."

"He's very intuitive. Maybe he'll have something to add to the trap."

"I believe he already has."

"What do you mean?" I asked.

"He had to have known we would turn him down as far as finishing his son's work. Maybe he just wanted to get that box of slides out in the open. For someone else to see."

"That never occurred to me. When I went to see him, it was before Carney snatched me and we knew he had a house nearby. Paolo must have assumed he'd been watching us. How else would he be able to keep interfering with our work?"

This also made me think about our scene on the porch earlier. Carney may have been witness to the proposal. Was it Jimmy's intention to further stir things up? With Carney's anger growing, it might make him reckless in his actions to get at us and the slides.

While I didn't like the idea of Jimmy using our intimate moment to further our plan of trapping Carney, it reinforced the idea that we must use every means possible.

"Why are we going so late?" I asked.

"Paolo has appointments most of the day and won't be home until after 6:30. Besides, that gives us a little bit of time to celebrate our engagement." The mischievous grin on his face, told me the afternoon would go all too quickly.

Pulling open the cupboard, I grabbed two wine glasses. "It may be a little early for libations, but today calls for an exception." Giving him a wink, I asked, "See you upstairs?"

"I'm way ahead of you. I've been saving a cabernet from that quaint little winery we discovered in Santa Ynez. Give me a moment to pop it open, and I'll be right up."

The rest of the day was devoted to nothing but celebrating our happiness. After an early dinner, we were ready to leave.

"Let's go," Jimmy said.

I grabbed my purse from the kitchen counter, and we headed for the front door. Just as a precaution, Jimmy popped into the office and retrieved the Family Slides from the safe. We didn't want to get this far, only to lose the means we needed to finish Carney.

Neither one of us said much on the drive to Laguna Beach. The two slides rode safely in my lap, both wrapped in the green silk scarf and nestled in a canvas bag. I gave Jimmy directions as he guided his silver Jaguar through the neighborhoods leading to the Fortuno mansion. At the gate he pressed the button. A moment later the iron groaned as it swung open. Paolo must be as anxious as we were to end this saga.

When we drove up to the house, the front door stood open. Jimmy came around to my side of the car, opened the door and grabbed the bag. Reaching back in, he helped me out.

I gripped his hand as we walked cautiously up to the entrance and peered inside. The light was on in the entryway, but no movement of any kind. "Hello," I said. No answer.

"Paolo?" Jimmy called. Still nothing.

"I don't like the looks of this," I said. "Something doesn't feel right."

Just then Paolo came hurrying over from somewhere in the

house. He wore a pair of khaki pants and a t-shirt. It seemed out of character as the prior times I'd seen him he dressed more formally in slacks and a button-down shirt.

"My apologies for not being here to greet you when you drove up. As I awaited your arrival, my phone rang and the help has gone home for the evening. Please, come in."

I sighed with relief as we entered the house.

"Thank you for seeing us, Paolo," I said, as we walked past him. He nodded, then gestured toward the sitting room he led me to on my first visit. This time I smelled the delicate scent of roses. The bowl on the end table brimmed with a potpourri of dried petals.

"I trust you have a plan?"

"Yes," Jimmy said. "That's why we're here and hoping you'd be willing to help."

"As I stated earlier, I am at your disposal. Whatever is in my power to do, I will. What did you have in mind?"

Jimmy and I sat together on the couch. Once again, Paolo took the love seat across from us.

"We want you to invite Carney here, to your home. He doesn't know we've told you he murdered your son, does he?"

"As far as I know, he does not. I haven't spoken with him since Junior discovered the loss of his Photographer at that monster's hands. Maybe he doesn't know I suspect his involvement with my son's death."

"Good. Keep it that way," Jimmy said. "Make the same suggestion to him that you made to us. Offer to give him Paolo, Jr.'s, slides in hopes he will complete the matches your son began."

"Do you think he'll take the bait?"

"Absolutely," I said. "Right now he's trapped in the present, with no means of traveling through time. Without your Family Slide, he's out of options, other than the Suitor slides he never completed. Obviously, none of them are for the correct time periods he needs, otherwise he would have used them by now to steal one of the devices."

"I agree," the old man said. "So, if he believes my son's allotment might help him to further his exploits, he will agree to meet with me."

"Yes," Jimmy said. "But you know there's a risk? He murdered his own grandfather in cold blood. He wouldn't hesitate shooting you too."

"I understand," replied Paolo. "It is a chance I am willing to take. What have I got left? My wife is gone these last ten years, and Junior was our only child. If I can help stop this demon, then my life still has purpose."

"Do you know how to reach him?" Jimmy looked concerned as he said this. I knew it didn't sit well with him—this man may be sacrificing his life to help us.

"If his phone is still the same, then yes. I know what to say to entice him here."

"Good. When he comes, we'll also be waiting. It would be best to coerce him into your son's studio. Can you show us the room?" As he said this, Jimmy reached over and took my hand. I felt his thumb caressing my skin.

Paolo hesitated at this suggestion. "Of course," he finally said, "come with me." He led the way out of the sitting room back through the entryway. Instead of going right toward the kitchen, he veered left down another hallway.

Opening a door to the left, the old man stopped so abruptly we almost bumped into him. As my lips pursed to question the delay, his foot crossed the threshold and he entered the room. We followed. Both walls to the left and right were lined with portraits of men from past eras. These were the thirty Suitors interviewed by Paolo, Jr. Lacking a Photographer, none of the men received the bride promised. It broke my heart. The room screamed of loneliness and disappointment. More injustice as a result of Carney's evil.

The sense of longing from the men in the portraits overwhelmed me. "I need some fresh air. Give me a moment, please." I hurried from the room toward the back of the house. Finding a door to the outside, I bolted onto the patio trying to catch my breath.

Warm arms wrapped around me from behind. "You all right?" Jimmy asked.

I allowed him to encircle me in an embrace, but didn't turn around. Instead I focused on the beauty around us while leaning my head back onto his shoulder. Through the dusk I could still make out the neatly trimmed hedges. The fragrant scent of rose bushes and lavender swirled in the air. How could so many fresh signs of life surround a structure full of utter disappointment and heartbreak? This structure wasn't a mansion, but a mausoleum. The thought of Paolo spending his days and hours in a perpetual cloud of loss, wrenched at my heart.

Finally feeling my pulse come down to a steady beat, I turned around. "I'm okay now. It's just...the portraits...the loss..."

"Shhh, honey. It's okay. Maybe when this task is complete, we can help them. Not necessarily ourselves, but perhaps we can find a couple with noble intentions to finish the work."

I nodded. Looking up into his eyes, they still sparkled the way they had when I first met him. I gently kissed his lips. "Okay, let's take a look at the snare we need to set."

Releasing me, he led me back into the house and the studio.

"I'm sorry, Paolo," I tried to explain, "it was just so...so..."

"Do not worry. To be honest I needed a moment alone as well. I have not been in here for over a year. The sadness would not permit me to enter. But now, with your help, this room may heal, and perhaps even breath life again. You understand?"

"We do," said Jimmy.

That's when the lights went out.

Chapter 36

Jimmy gripped my arm. "Sami, stay here," he whispered into my ear. Then he let go.

The room had no windows, so we were in complete darkness.

"Jimmy," I whispered back louder than anticipated, "where are you going?"

"Paolo?" Jimmy's voice came from across the room by the door.

"I'm here. Where are the Family Slides?" he quietly asked.

"Back in the sitting room. Take care of my girl. I need to go get them."

"Jimmy, don't leave. He might have his gun," I said.

"You believe Carney is here," Paolo stated. "She is safe with me. Come," he said as I felt his hand on my arm, guiding me toward the back corner of the room.

To my amazement, he led me through a doorway. I could sense the closeness as we entered. Instinctively, I reached out and felt the edge of the wall as we went inside. Not feeling a door jam, just a smooth flat edge, I assumed we were in a closet or small storage space. Strange, I didn't remember seeing it when we first entered. From the staleness of the air, the room hadn't been used in a while.

I had no doubts about why the lights went out. Could we be smarter than *him* to survive this?

"Stay here," Paolo said. The door closed with a light click. I stood alone.

This didn't sit right with me. I felt infuriated at the way both men tried to shelter me. Putting my hands out in front, I walked toward where I heard the door close. My hands met the wall. I felt the rough, glossy texture of what must be wallpaper. There had to be a handle or doorknob somewhere. Damn, why didn't I have my phone on me? I'd left my purse in the living room, not thinking I would need anything from it while here in the house.

Finally catching my hand on a metal lever, I swiveled it down and pushed forward. The door wouldn't budge. Keeping my grip on the handle, I pulled it toward me and felt a gust of fresh air from the opening. Stepping back into the studio, I tried focusing my eyes, to no avail. Without even a trace of light, I couldn't make out a thing.

Instead of proceeding further, I stood still and enlisted my other senses. Closing my eyes, and concentrating on sounds, I heard breathing. That must be Paolo with his slow, steady rhythm. Straining, I tried to detect anyone else in the room. Nothing.

On the front end, I heard the door from the hallway open, then close.

"Sami, Paolo, where are you?" Jimmy asked in a hushed tone.

"Jimmy, I'm here."

"As am I," said Paolo.

He stood closer to me than I realized.

"Sami, I thought you would remain in the hidden room to keep safe."

"I appreciate your intentions, Paolo, but I am *not* sitting this one out," I stated firmly, but quietly. "Jimmy, did you get the slides?"

"Yes, help me activate them. It seems our timeline has been moved up considerably. This may be the perfect situation to trap Carney when he thinks he has the upper hand."

"Where and when should we set them for?" We'd never talked about the logistics. It would need to be a time and place where he wouldn't have access to slides. Not knowing how far back this process went, that might be difficult. Our best guess would have to do.

"I don't know," Jimmy answered. "Paolo, are there limits on

how far back in time we can send him or locations?"

"This is all new territory for me as well. As explained, I have never heard of anyone using this process to trap someone in time."

"Okay, how about Alaska in the early 1800's? There was life up there. None of us are murderers, so we need to send him somewhere he can survive."

"You are a better man then I, Jimmy Chang," said Paolo. "The Titanic's maiden voyage would be my first choice." Loathing seethed through his voice. He continued, "Even Alaska in the 1800's can allow him to get back to the United States. Perhaps a remote island?"

"Whatever we choose, needs to be quick. We have no idea where he is in the house, and it will take an hour to power up."

"Then let's take a page from history. Send him to Elba, an island in the Mediterranean, in the year 1815," Paolo offered quietly.

"That's where Napoleon spent his exile, didn't he?" I asked, quite impressed with his suggestion.

"Yes. Perhaps he and that despot would have lots to talk about," he said. Even though I couldn't see his face, I knew Paolo smiled at that thought.

"Works for me," Jimmy said. "Sami, come hold my phone so I can see."

I saw the flashlight on his cell phone activate and moved over toward the light. Grabbing his phone and shining the beam on him, he set one on the floor.

Holding the first slide up toward his mouth, he depressed the button underneath the location and quietly spoke, "Elba Island in the Mediterranean." Releasing the button, his words appeared on the frame. Quickly he set the date, June 4, 1815. He swirled the time to read 5:00 a.m. He left the number *zero* underneath the time allotment.

Quickly he handed the frame to Paolo, who had walked over to join us. Picking up the second Family Slide, he repeated the procedure and set up identical instructions.

Time was not on our side right now. We had no idea what Carney was up too, yet we needed to stall him for an hour while the slides powered up.

Once the settings of the second device were completed, Jimmy grabbed his cell phone from me and ran the light around the room. He stopped as it hit a side table toward the back, then flitted the beam across the room and saw its twin on the opposite wall. Since the studio was narrow, the space would be perfect.

"Paolo, hit the activation button, then take the slide and set it on the table to the right." Paolo followed the light and walked to the designated spot.

Jimmy took his slide to the table on the left. Sitting on each table was a large, square urn with silk palm fronds sticking out. The receptacles had just enough room to slip the devices inside behind the plants. They wouldn't be visible until it was time to remove the slides to activate the 30 second countdown. Every possible advantage had to be used right now.

"Paolo, hide it in the urn behind the palm fronds for now," Jimmy said.

I could hear the rustling as Paolo did as requested. Hopefully they would be overlooked by Carney if he were to come into this room.

"When both are powered up," whispered Paolo, "we need to depress the activation buttons at precisely the same time, or it will not send him back permanently."

"I understand," said Jimmy, as he turned off the flashlight on his phone.

"What will we do for an hour?" I asked. "Jimmy, I don't like this. Right now, he has the advantage."

"Does he," Jimmy asked. "Carney has no way of knowing we brought both Family Slides."

"He does if he watched us leave the house. What else could we possibly have in that bag?"

Despite our voices being no louder than a whisper, it still sounded like we were shouting in the stillness of the room. The door to the hallway opened.

"Greetings, my friends," Carney bellowed through the room. "What are you up to now?" There was a moment of silence before he illuminated a flashlight and scanned the floor, just as we were closing the door to the hidden room.

Paolo had the forethought to quickly escort us through the hidden entry when we'd heard Carney open the door. The man may be in his nineties, but his reflexes were that of someone much younger.

"Won't he find the door?" I whispered.

"The entrance is hidden," Paolo answered just as quietly. "There is a hidden lever on the left side of the portrait hanging beside the doorway. I had this room installed after our Family Slide was stolen. My hope of retrieving the slide required a plan to keep it safe. As you know, I never had that opportunity. Now I never will."

"Yes, you will," I said. "Once we trap him, the slide will be yours again."

There was no answer to that, but I could hear Paolo quietly sigh. I assumed he felt there would be no need for it, with his son being gone.

"Sami, quiet. We don't want to give ourselves away," Jimmy whispered in my ear.

Chapter 37

I felt a hand on my arm gently guiding me further away from the door. Hearing a lever being pulled, I felt a waft of fresh air brush across my face. There was another entrance.

Paolo herded us through the other doorway and into a clothes closet. The hangers scratched on the rod as we bumped into whatever was stored there. They scraped once again as I heard them pushed aside so the door could be cracked open. After a moment's hesitation, it was opened wide. This room had a window as a modicum of light seeped in. Just enough for me to see shapes in the tiny refuge.

"This way," he quietly told us. The light dissipated a moment as his tall figure stepped through the doorway. Jimmy nudged me forward into the room. As he followed, I heard the door to the hidden room click shut. We were in a bedroom. From what I could make out in the dim light, probably a guest room, as there didn't appear to be many personal items on the dresser or floor.

"What if Carney tries to get in? He'll see us for sure," I said.

"Not to worry, I keep this room locked. Without a key, the only way to open it is from the inside. We'll be safe in here for a while."

I could feel the warmth of Jimmy's body brush against my arm as he stood close. It seemed like we lingered in there for an eternity, but it could only have been a few minutes.

"We need to come up with a plan to lure him into the studio when the timer is ready," I said.

"No need to lead him on a chase through the house," Jimmy whispered. The light of his phone came on. "It's been twelve minutes since we set the..."

We heard the door knob rattle. It sounded like someone trying to turn it back and forth in an effort to work the door open. I held my breath hoping he wouldn't succeed.

Carney banged on the door and made me jump. Jimmy put his hands on my arms and rested his head on my shoulder from behind to calm me down.

"Come out, come out," Carney shouted. "We're a bit old for Hide and Seek, don't you think?"

Jimmy's grip tensed, but we remained quiet. Hopefully he would think it was simply another empty room and move on. Staying here was probably the best idea to kill the time we needed for the slides to power up.

The knob jiggled again, but the door remained in place. "Damn," Carney said, "they can't be that dumb, I guess."

We heard light footsteps as they padded down the hallway toward the back of the house. For now it seemed Carney believed we weren't hiding in the room. Hopefully he moved on and wasn't looking for a way to pick the lock.

"What now?" I asked Jimmy.

"We wait. Paolo, do you have any more of these secret passage ways?"

"No. I am afraid there is only the one. I created the hideaway solely to keep the Family Slide safe, should it ever be returned."

"Is there anyone else in the house we should be concerned with?" Jimmy asked.

"No. I sent all the servants home for the night, telling them I needed to be alone. They're used to that, as it happens quite often. Especially lately...," he trailed off.

I felt Jimmy squeeze my arms and then release. We both knew the sadness that hovered about Paolo. It amazed me he could still go on with life after all that happened. His grief must be overwhelming sometimes.

"I think we should try to get out of this room and perhaps make a dash for the front door," said Paolo.

"Why would we do that?" I asked. "We're safe in here. He's moved on."

"It's only a matter of time before he figures out this is the only locked room in the house. While there is a lock on the door, it can be broken. We need to move while he is searching elsewhere."

"Paolo's right. We can't stay here. Let's go," said Jimmy.

Light footsteps quietly padded across the room. I heard the deadbolt turn. As the door was pulled open the hinges creaked. He stopped and we all listened. There was no noise outside in the hallway. Slowly Jimmy pulled it open further, so we could all slip out.

The house remained mostly dark, but we could see enough to make our way down the passage to the front entry. As we scurried toward our exit, a flashlight blinded us.

"It's about time, old man," Carney said. "I was beginning to worry you'd gone back on our bargain."

My hands balled into fists as I realized what was happening. "You made a deal with him?" I shouted at Paolo.

"I am sorry, Sami. But it was the only way for me to go on."

Jimmy stepped in front of me as we realized Carney's other hand held a gun.

"Be a good chap and turn on the lights, will you Paolo? This whole charade of traipsing around in the dark is getting old."

"As you wish. Do not do anything rash while I am gone, please."

"Just do it, old man! My patience is wearing thin," spat out Carney. "We'll wait here," he said to Jimmy and me. "And bring our sweet Sami back out where I can see her."

Jimmy hesitated to move out from in front of me.

"Do it now!" Carney's voice had an edge of hysteria in it.

"It's okay, Jimmy. Let me beside you," I said, trying to remain calm. It took all my strength not to give Carney any more reaction than necessary. Moving from behind him, Jimmy put his arm around my shoulders and pulled me close.

When the lights came back on, we were blinded for a moment. I was afraid Jimmy might try to make a move, but Carney must have anticipated that and stood several feet away. No chance of diving at him.

"Now, that's better. We can all see clearly," smiled Carney.

"Shall we retire to the sitting room?"

I knew that was an order, not a request. So did Jimmy. He held on firmly as we made our way into the side room and sat on the couch. Right back where we'd started the evening.

Paolo reappeared in the room, refusing to look at either Jimmy or me. Instead he focused on Carney.

"Stop trying to look remorseful, old man. You're as guilty as I am in all this. We all make our choices. Some of us are just better at living with them."

This struck fire in Paolo's eyes. "My name is Paolo. I would appreciate your addressing me as such," he said with his head held high and his gaze firm.

"As you wish, *Paolo*."

"Thank you. Now tell me what you promised. I've upheld my end of the bargain," Paolo said.

"When this is done," Carney replied.

"No, now!"

He was a different man. Not one we'd met before. His agitation grew by the minute and I began to fear him as much as I feared Carney. Glancing over at Jimmy, I could tell by the steely scowl on his face he was just as confused as I about Paolo's sudden change in loyalties.

Carney released a snicker. "Very well, *Paolo*, I'll give you the information you crave. While I was there, I did not kill your son."

Realization washed over me. He wanted details about his son's death. All this was to find out what happened to Paolo, Jr. Maybe even find a way to prevent his death. This man was no different than the rest of us in wanting to hold dear the ones we loved. Except this time it would cost Jimmy and me our lives, or at least our life together, I feared.

My anger grew. "You sold us out for information?"

Paolo looked at me for the first time since entering the room. "What if it was Jimmy that was murdered? You would do the same!"

"Not at the expense of innocent lives," I replied indignantly.

"Are we really innocent? For good or bad, we all interfere with timelines of others' lives. Who are we to say who gets love and who does not?"

Paolo spewed out hate. Or was it guilt for dragging his son

into a role he really had no control over. If Junior had been given a choice like I had, would he have said no? Maybe that was part of what was driving Paolo. The guilt of putting his son at mortal risk.

I tried to reason with him. "You know this is wrong. Why would you turn against us? You can't change what happened to Junior."

"That's where you're wrong," he whispered. Once again Paolo glared at Carney and refused to relinquish his gaze from the man with all the answers.

"As I said," continued Carney, "I did not kill your son."

Chapter 38

"You were there," Paolo stated.

"Yes, old man, I was there," Carney said. This time Paolo let the *old man* reference slide. "Guess there's no harm in their knowing," he said gesturing at us. "They'll have a lot of time apart to think about it." Again, that evil grin spread across his face.

I gripped Jimmy's leg, as my hand rested just above his knee. He gave me a reassuring hug, but I knew he couldn't be sure if this would really turn out okay.

Carney saw the gesture and snickered.

"As I said, I witnessed the murder. Breaking into your house, knowing Junior would do something stupid, I found his spent slide set for 1966. From the date and location, I knew he believed he could save Jimmy's dear old dad and return with the Chang Family Slide as a reward. So, I went home and set your Family Slide to arrive just before the event and waited outside the shop."

Jimmy's grip on my arm tightened. I could tell it enraged him knowing what would happen next. Since he only remembered one timeline, the young man's attempt to save Jimmy's father never worked.

"Just before Junior arrived, I slipped into the shop with some tourists." Carney continued, "I hid off to the side, with a view of the back register as well as out onto the street through the front window. The other patrons left, and the shop was empty. Two young Chinese men got out of a black sedan and came inside."

I tried to decide whether Carney made all this up, or if it was genuine. It didn't seem like a lie, but he'd gotten so good at deceit, I couldn't tell for sure.

He continued, "The men went up to Chang and were trying to shake him down for protection money. They said they were from some gang, but I don't remember who. It's not important."

"Yes, it is!" Jimmy chimed in.

Carney aimed his gun at me anew. "Another outburst and your beloved will have a hole in her!" His anger mirrored Jimmy's.

Jimmy took a deep breath, but I knew it didn't clam him. Nothing would at this point.

"What happened next?" asked Paolo anxiously. "Tell me about Junior."

Everyone in the room grew more agitated by the moment. I could feel the tension as it thickened and wrapped around me like a blanket. This wasn't going to end well for any of us.

"I'm getting to that," Carney said testily. "One of the Chinese went around the counter and grabbed Chang from behind by the elbows. He forced him in front of the other man. I give your father credit," he said looking at Jimmy. "Your dad had balls. He spit in the head man's face—just hocked out a juicy one. I saw it slide down the guy's cheek," Carney laughed. "Unfortunately, that pissed him off. So, the guy stabbed him."

Jimmy's breathing got faster. I squeezed his leg, trying to lend support. There was no comfort this time. Hearing first-hand about his father's murder must have been torture.

"But where was Junior?" Paolo persisted.

"Calm down, I'm getting to that. Just as Chang got skewered, Junior entered the shop. In that moment I'm sure he realized he'd arrived too late to save the man. Too late to save himself as well. He turned and bolted out the door. Both thugs saw him. The lead guy pulled the knife out of Chang's gut as the other one released him. He fell to the floor.

"The men took off after Junior while I followed at a safe distance. I'm sure you can figure out the rest."

"Tell me," Paolo demanded quietly. From the pallor of his face, you could see the fight drained out of him.

"Very well, it's your dime. They caught up with Junior in an

191

alleyway a few blocks away. No questions asked, they stabbed him and took off. Seeing it was a bad idea for the cops to find a corpse not from the current decade, I removed everything from his pockets. It looked like a robbery."

"How noble of you," Jimmy said sarcastically. "Weren't you just the model time traveler, so concerned for others."

"Give it a rest, Jimmy. I handled the situation in order to preserve *our* way of life."

"You mean to cover your ass," Jimmy's tone escalated.

I rubbed his arm, trying to get him to focus on our current situation. While he didn't look at me, I knew my point was taken as he covered my hand with his. The warmth of it gave me courage for whatever came next.

"So, you see," Carney continued, "I can't take credit for the murder of your son," he said looking at Paolo, "or your father." With that last part he glanced toward Jimmy.

"You could have stopped them," Jimmy glared.

"And why would I put myself at risk? That was ancient history. Not my concern," he swept it away as if it were a mere discrepancy.

We all sat in silence for a few moments, each with our own thoughts. So much was happening here. I wasn't sure which one of us, if any, would survive the next hour.

"Now, Paolo, how many minutes do we have left before the blessed event?" Carney's anticipation of the ensuing proceedings made me ill. The man had no remorse for past crimes or those he was about to commit.

"By my clock, we have eight minutes remaining."

"Gee, kids," he said to Jimmy and me, "it looks as if our time together is almost up. Well," he hesitated, "at least Jimmy's and my time together. You, my sweet Sami, will be around a bit longer. Actually, a lot longer, if I have anything to do with it."

He sat there gleaming. It scared the hell out of me. I knew what he had in store for Jimmy, but not a clue about myself. The unknown frightened me more than knowing for sure my fate.

"Shall we adjourn to the studio, my friends?" Carney wavered the gun in our direction.

We hesitantly rose and preceded him out of the room.

Paolo remained still, but Carney wouldn't allow it. "Come, my friend. You're part of this too."

"I would rather wait here," Paolo said.

"Sorry, that's not the deal. Let's go."

Reluctantly he got up and walked beside Carney. Once inside the studio, Paolo produced a length of rope from his pocket. Taking my arm, he tried to pull me gently away from Jimmy.

"Leave her be," Jimmy said pulling me back toward him.

"Uh, uh," said Carney waggling the gun. "This is a solo journey for you, my friend. Now stand back!"

Jimmy released me and threw up his hands. Paolo grasped my arm once again and led me to a chair.

"How could you go along with him?" I asked. "Despite not killing your son, he stood by and did nothing. You knew, somehow, he took part. How could you do this?"

"I am sorry, but I had to know. I needed to know. Please understand."

"Sorry, Paolo, not this time. Your actions are wrong, and you know it," I replied firmly.

He looked down at the floor as he pushed me gently onto the chair. Walking behind, he grasped my arms and pulled my hands behind the seat back. Using the rope, he bound my wrists loosely. It seemed strange he didn't cinch them tight.

Just before he stood up, I felt him place something small and metallic in my hands. Walking around to the front of the chair, he looked me in the eye. With his back to Carney, he whispered gravely, "This must be," and gave a wink.

I gingerly felt what he'd placed in my grasp—a small knife. More like a miniature dagger to be exact, with a sharp, two-sided blade. I immediately set to work rubbing it against the ropes.

"Hurry up, old man. Let's get this over with." Looking at Jimmy, he said, "Say hello to old Napoleon for me, will you?" To emphasize his point, Carney shoved Jimmy to a spot between the two tables in the studio.

Jimmy glared at Paolo, who shrugged. So, it was Carney's idea to set the slides for Elba.

Pointing toward the side closest to Paolo, Carney demanded, "Get the slide and prepare to press the activation button. Do it exactly right, or you'll meet the same fate as Junior."

Paolo whipped his head around and glared at Carney, then

walked to the table and retrieved the Family Slide from inside the urn. Carney did the same using one hand so he could keep the gun on Jimmy.

Looking up from the frame, Carney said, "This one's ready. How about yours?"

"This one as well," Paolo answered.

"Good. Jimmy, I hate long good-byes, so we won't have one. Sorry, no farewell kiss from your Sami either. I'm just not that sentimental," Carney spewed.

"No, please," I begged.

Giving me a moment's glance, Carney just shook his head, then turned away. "On the count of three, activate the timer."

Chapter 39

"Carney, please don't do this," I continued to plead. "You can't get April back. And Paolo, you can't get Junior back without there being consequences. Please stop this madness!"

"Ohhh, the poor wretched Betrothed, begging for her Suitor. Isn't *this* a tragedy in the making? Don't think I didn't see that heartwarming proposal scene on your porch. It almost brought a tear to my eye." Carney sounded sympathetic, but we all knew better. "Now be quiet or I might not allow you to stay in this timeline either!"

"Please, Carney, just..."

"Enough! Stop wasting your breath. Paolo, on my count— one...two...three!"

With that both Carney and Paolo pressed the buttons at the same time and sat their slides on the respective tables. The timers counted down from 30. Jimmy stood in the middle with his hands at his sides, knowing his time was up. He had lost. *We* had lost.

As Paolo walked over beside Carney, he placed his hands on the table, looking down with remorse.

"Turn around, old man, and witness your handiwork. You're part of this too," chastised Carney.

Paolo slowly raised his hands off the table, then grabbed the urn and slammed it into the back of Carney's head. The man fell down, smacking his hands against the ground and releasing the gun. He laid there stunned as the weapon skittered across the floor.

Jimmy sprang into action and grabbed Carney by the feet, dragging him to the space between the two slides.

I continued working the blade against the last fibers of the rope that bound my hands.

Carney started shaking his head and pushing himself up on his hands and knees. Paolo moved out of the way so as not to get caught by the flash.

"Jimmy," I cried, "get out of there. The 30 seconds is almost up!" Desperate for him to move clear of the flash zone, I felt time slipping away. As the ropes fell from my wrists, I dropped the knife and bolted to my feet.

Pushing himself onto his haunches, Carney began to stand up and stagger away from the space between the slides. Jimmy moved in from behind and grabbed him around the waist. Lifting Carney completely off the floor and backing up, I saw the muscles in his arms bulging from the strain of the other man's weight.

"Sami," he yelled. "I love you!"

"No, Jimmy. Don't!" I ran toward him, but Paolo grabbed me and held fast. I struggled against his grip, trying to get to my heroic man.

My eyes locked with Jimmy's as he held Carney and backed into the center of the area. He mouthed the words, "Good bye."

With a flash, they were both gone.

"Jimmy!" I cried. Paolo released me. Dropping to my knees, I whispered, "No." My fists pounded against the carpet in dull thuds. Tears streamed down my face.

There was no telling how long I sat there before Paolo gently grasped my arms and helped me to my feet. "I'm sorry, Sami. It had to look as if I were in collusion with Carney. I never meant for this to happen. Jimmy was supposed to be out of the way and that villain unconscious. Believe me I didn't want…"

"I know, Paolo. I know," I whispered, taking his hand. "It was a good plan. Only it didn't work. Not completely."

As the tears dried on my face, an idea struck me. "Wait a minute," I said getting excited. "I can go back and rescue Jimmy. Just like he retrieved me from Carney's."

Running over to one of the Family Slides I picked it up and turned to Paolo. "We can reset just one slide. I can go to Elba

Island and bring Jimmy back."

"No," Paolo said quietly.

"What do you mean *no*. I'm not asking permission," I said indignantly. This man didn't have a say in the situation any more. It was up to me now.

"That's not what I meant."

Ignoring him, I held up the device and pressed the location button. Clearly, I spoke, "Elba Island in the Mediterranean." Releasing the button, the words didn't appear. I pressed the button again and repeated the location. Still, the screen remained black.

Tossing it down onto the surface from where it came, I ran to the other table and grabbed that frame and holder. Pressing the button, I clearly pronounced, "Elba Island in the Mediterranean." Nothing appeared on the screen.

Looking to Paolo for guidance, I asked, "Why isn't it working?"

"I told you it wouldn't."

"Why? Do the slides need time to re-charge before we use them again?"

"No, Sami."

The fears swirling in my head started to take shape as I focused on what Paolo was trying to tell me. "How long before we can reset one?" I asked, my voice cracking.

"Sami," the sadness in his eyes bored through my soul.

Warm tears streamed down my face as I began to comprehend what he meant. "No..." My voice faded.

"I am sorry. The Family Slides may only be used once to trap someone in time—and then never again."

Dropping to my knees once more I held my face in my hands. The roughness of the carpet scraped at my legs. My body wracked with grief as reality set in. Jimmy was gone for good with no way of retrieving him. The slides were finished.

Thinking back over the warnings of Mr. Chang and the Frenchman, I now knew the risks they were referring to. Even Paolo hinted about the finality of the Family Slides once they were used in such a manner. We gambled and lost—both Jimmy and me. Regardless of the time period, we would never be together again. My heart slowed, and I wanted to let it stop. There was nothing left for me.

I now knew the desolation Paolo felt. Also, I believed his intentions were honorable. He knew once the slides were used to trap Carney in time, they would be dead. There would be no going back to save his son. He invented a farce to lure Carney to the house. His plans needed to be kept secret from us for them to be believable.

Feeling Paolo's gentle hands on my shoulders, I allowed him to help me to my feet and lead me from the studio. We went into the kitchen, where he sat me on a stool by the counter. Retrieving two small glasses from a cupboard, he poured a healthy amount of whiskey into each, then set the bottle on the counter.

"Here," he said, handing me one of the tumblers. "It won't take away the pain, but may numb it for the moment."

Bringing the glass up to my lips, I tasted the fiery liquid, but couldn't drink. Setting it back on the counter, I looked up. "Thank you, Paolo, but I'd like to go home now."

Hesitating a moment, he asked, "Shall I drive you?"

"No. Thank you," I replied. "I'd like to be alone right now."

"Perhaps you should spend the night here. You can drive home in the morning after you've had some rest."

I reached out and rested my hand on Paolo's arm. Without another word, he nodded. Getting off the stool, we walked to the front sitting room where I retrieved my purse. There was a spare car key on my ring—the original set now irretrievable. At this thought, tears seeped out of my eyes anew. Wiping them away with my fingers, I couldn't turn around to say good-by.

Heading straight for the door, I didn't wait for Paolo to open it. There were no more words to be said. The door gently closed behind me.

Slowly I walked to the driver's side and got in behind the wheel. After adjusting the seat and mirrors, I put the key into the ignition and started the engine. Still devastated, I placed both hands on the wheel and leaned my forehead against it. A few seconds later I took a deep breath, sat up and shifted the car into gear. As I looped around the driveway and back toward the gate, I slowed, waiting for the creaking ironwork to allow my exit.

Chapter 40

How I managed to navigate home, remains a mystery. I woke up and found myself still in Jimmy's parked car on the driveway. The late morning sun was trying to peek through the dark clouds, without much success. Raindrops cascaded onto the windshield.

As I got out of the car, my legs were stiff from sleeping sitting up all night. Spots of water speckled my shirt as I slowly walked to the front of the house. The damp fabric stuck to my skin.

Stepping onto the porch, I couldn't face going inside yet. My body collapsed into the nearest wicker chair, as I set my purse on the table beside it.

I took a few moments to simply breathe, while staring out toward the ocean. The water churned with white caps from the building storm. Raindrops continued to tap dance on the roof and the edges of the porch, as delicate splatters hit my legs. My eyes tracked a seagull as he drifted on the wind. He soared up and down, barely moving his wings, not in the least bit bothered by the shower.

Looking around the porch, I thought of Jimmy, as he went down on one knee before me. He'd proposed only yesterday, yet it felt like a lifetime ago. My head turned to the spot where remnants of Francois' blood stained the wooden planks. My face grimaced as I remembered all the horror we'd witnessed. Did the good outweigh any of it?

I stood up, bracing for my next steps as I grabbed my purse and walked into the house. Jimmy's things needed to be cleared out—eventually. An explanation should be formulated in case someone asked about his disappearance. Somehow, I didn't care what anyone thought.

Going down the hall to the kitchen, out of habit I went to place my bag on the counter. As I walked across the room, a chair scraped on the tile. Whipping my head toward the table, Mr. Chang stood there.

"I pray you do not mind, but I helped myself to a cup of tea."

The shocked look on my face must have spoken volumes.

He immediately followed up with, "Perhaps I can offer you a cup of tea. You look very much like you need one. Please, sit." He gestured to the chair across from him.

Too worn out to protest, or even answer, I sat down. The kettle simmered on the stove with the steam escaping through the spout. He retrieved a cup from the cupboard, dropped in a bag from the canister on the counter and poured hot water into the cup. Once he'd carefully set the hot brew in front of me, he sat down himself.

When the shock wore off and I found my voice, I asked, "Mr. Chang, why are you here? If you came to speak with Jimmy, you're too late. He's..." I couldn't bring myself to say it.

"No, I have come to speak with you."

"What's left to say? Jimmy is gone. The two remaining Family Slides are useless. The only good is we finally stopped Carney. I hope it was worth it."

"I believe so."

I looked at him in utter astonishment. Having just told this man his grandson was basically dead, long gone by now, he believed it was all worth it. The cold-hearted bastard! "I'm sorry I can't share your opinion." Lifting the tea up to my lips, I carefully sipped. Much better than the whiskey Paolo offered me, the warm liquid cascaded down my throat.

"We have all lost much because of this process."

"That, I can agree with, Mr. Chang. So, tell me, why the visit?"

With a crinkled brow, he appeared to be debating his response. Already tough to read, the man acted unsure of himself. That never happened in our last encounter.

"I am misusing the slides."

"Excuse me?" I asked.

"You heard me correctly. I am misusing the slides. And as usual, time is almost up. I expected you home hours ago." His face displayed no emotion with his firmly set jaw and hard eyes. The intentions of his unexpected visit remained unclear to me.

"How did you get here?"

"Why do you waste time with questions you already know the answer to? Isn't it obvious I used one of the special slides?"

"I suppose so. It's been an awful 24 hours, so you'll excuse me if I'm not at the top of my game for this little encounter. After our last meeting, I find it hard to believe you sought me out. You also seem to know what's happened to Jimmy and why he's not here. I don't even want to know how you have that information. Exhaustion is about to consume me, so if you could just cut to the chase, it would be greatly appreciated."

"You had so much fight in you last time we met," Mr. Chang began. "It surprises me to find you so defeated."

"Perhaps you should go back a day and join us in our last escapade. Participating in that experience would explain why I am so *defeated*," I spat out. Instead of depression, fury was taking over.

"Good, now you are focused."

"What...you..." I glared at him a moment, then realized his plan. Mr. Chang was actually pulling me back from the edge and forcing me to think clearly. I thought it wouldn't be possible for a long while, yet he managed that task in a few well-placed sentences. To my surprise, I began to have a smidgen of admiration for this old man.

"Are you ready to listen to me?" he asked.

"I suppose so." While I couldn't muster a smile, he brought me back enough to focus on what he needed to say.

"As the remaining member of your family, it is left to me, an elder in this process, to enlighten you."

"As usual, you're talking in riddles, Mr. Chang. I'm aware no other family members remain. Without siblings or cousins, I'm the last generation of Manchesters. Why is that important here?"

"Because you are the last generation of Manchesters." He sat up straight in his chair and sipped his tea.

I tilted my head and squinted my eyes in confusion. His sly grin told me he enjoyed my discomfort.

"I understand Mr. Fortuno explained to you about the Four Families upon your first meeting."

"Yes. He told me the families were down to three these last couple generations, as the British family and all their equipment for the process perished in a fire. All were lost but the youngest child rescued by a servant and placed with relatives."

"That is correct—except there were no surviving relatives. The governess took it upon herself to raise the child here in America. She adopted the girl and the family name to perpetuate it. Your mother never married the man you called father, is that not true?"

"Yes, she was very progressive for her time. What's that got to do with anything?"

"Did Fortuno tell you the name of the British family?"

"Well...no...I guess he never did. It didn't occur to me to ask either."

"Your mother never married, so her surname is yours as well, correct?"

"Yes," I replied in frustration, as he dragged out his explanation. "Manchester. Our last name is Manchester."

"And so is the British family," Mr. Chang quipped.

Shock washed across my face as I felt the color drain. If I followed accurately, I was a descendant of one of the Four Families—the remaining member of the British family. Recovering, I asked, "Why did you wait all these years to step in? My mother deserved an opportunity to participate in this process. Why did you skip a generation?"

"I did not. Your mother had no interest."

"She knew?" I had a hard time believing my mother never told me about our family history. Being adamant about preserving the family name, why hadn't she become a Photographer?

"Yes," Mr. Chang said. "She politely declined my offer to involve herself. Your mother believed that somehow the process got her family killed."

"Was she right?" I asked indignantly.

"No. Francois went to the aftermath of the tragedy. A servant admitted to knocking over a candle and the fire quickly blazed out of control. Nothing more than an accident. However, your mother didn't believe the story and wanted nothing to do with the process. In honor of her family, she kept the last name intact."

"Mr. Chang, I see where you're going. What does all that matter now? Obviously, you're telling me I'm the only remaining member of the British faction in this whole mess. But it's over. All the Family Slides are destroyed. There are no descendants to carry on the process, even if they wanted to, and my precious Jimmy is gone. He sacrificed himself to stop Carney. And here I sit alone. What was it all for?"

Outside thunder clapped, as if emphasizing my displeasure. The noise made me almost jump out of my seat, while Mr. Chang remained calmly sipping tea. We sat not speaking for a few moments, listening to the rumble of the rain as it pelted the roof and sidewalks outside. The cadence became louder and faster, as the storm let loose its fury.

Turning to the chair next to him, Mr. Chang retrieved a wooden box. Opening it, he lifted out something wrapped in a green silk scarf.

"This belongs to you," he said, handing it across the table.

Chapter 41

Taking the bundle from his outstretched hands, I placed it in front of me. Carefully unwrapping the delicate swath of silk, I revealed a slide secured permanently in its holder.

My jaw dropped in astonishment. I looked from the slide, to Mr. Chang, and back at the slide again.

"I cannot believe *you* are finally speechless, Miss Manchester." A satisfied smile spread across his face. For the first time I detected a note of joy in his expression.

Not being able to stop myself, I jumped up, hurried around the table and threw my arms around the old man. He tensed, not returning the gesture, but then relaxed.

"I can bring Jimmy home."

"While I do not approve of using the slides for personal gain, consider it a wedding gift."

"So Francois didn't really smash his Family Slide?"

"This device is not Francois'. It belongs to your family. While the fire did wipe out everyone but your mother of the Manchesters, the Family Slide was retrieved. It had been kept in a studio in the back of the house where the fire did not reach."

"How did you come to have it?" I asked, sitting back down.

"Francois acquired this legacy before it fell into the wrong hands. He placed it in my care years ago. It has sat in a safe these many years waiting—until now."

I picked up the frame and turned it over, examining every inch. Disbelief swept through me like a hot flash. In my hands rested the ability to bring Jimmy home to the present—back to me.

There was no doubt in my mind of success. If I didn't achieve finding him the first time, the trip could be repeated as many times as needed. Knowing I descended from the British family, revisiting a location wouldn't strand me.

"I need to get ready," I said carrying the slide toward the hallway.

"Miss Manchester," he called.

Turning around I looked back at the old man.

"While I want to see my grandson put back into his own timeline, I must reiterate my warning. Using the slides for personal gain may have consequences. While your actions are based on love for Jimmy, it does not guarantee you will go on to live a happy life. You saw what misusing the slides did to Carney."

Hesitating at the door, Mr. Chang's words resonated through my head. "It's a risk I'm willing to take. Jimmy got dragged back in time stopping a monster. There has to be a reward for such a selfless act."

With a nod, he disappeared. My intuition told me this should be the last time I'd ever see Mr. Chang. Returning my Family Slide must have been an obligation he needed to fulfill. The man had done what he could to help his grandson, and now left the final actions in my hands.

In my studio, I walked to the back and placed the slide on the table. Depressing the button and speaking clearly, the location appeared on the screen—Elba Island in the Mediterranean. Twirling the buttons for the date and stopping on June 4, 1815, I then set the time for fifteen minutes prior to Jimmy's and Carney's arrival. A time span of one half hour should be sufficient. Lastly, I activated the device for the one-hour warm-up period.

Arriving prior to the men gave me an opportunity to check out the area. I hoped by duplicating the exact wording, it would land me in the same spot on the island. If not, and Jimmy couldn't be found in the 15 minutes after he appeared, I would try again. Not knowing what to expect in this archaic land, it seemed safest to make several short trips. If it required additional journeys, I could get more specific on the location.

Nothing in my wardrobe would pass as appropriate for the era, so I opted for comfortable clothing. After changing into a pair of jeans and t-shirt, a zip-hooded sweatshirt was added to my ensemble, along with a pair of sneakers. Going back to my closet, I retrieved the locked box that held a loaded pistol with an extra clip. The key was kept in my jewelry box. Not sure of my capability to use the weapon if it became necessary, I hoped the instance wouldn't arise.

When they arrived on the island, I prayed Carney would still be stunned from the blow Paolo gave him with the urn. That would allow Jimmy and I to go off on our own until time counted down. Now that we knew how to safely travel together, we could get back here without difficulty.

The palms of my hands were damp with sweat. Fifty minutes remained. As I wondered how to endure the wait, the door bell rang. It made me nervous as I wasn't expecting anyone.

Opening the front door, an elderly woman waited, her hair wet and a bit disheveled from the storm. She smiled, not saying a word. Around her neck, she wore a silver and turquoise necklace. The crescent moon with shooting stars was unmistakable.

"Dede!" I exclaimed.

She looked relieved as she threw her arms around me and we embraced.

"What are you doing here?"

"Oh, Sami, I can't begin to tell you what a wonderful life Milton and I have enjoyed together."

"Is he gone?" I asked in dismay.

"Oh, no. He's alive and well. Still painting up a storm." She radiated with pride while talking about her husband. It had been a good match.

I sighed with relief. "Please," I said, realizing we were still standing in the doorway, "come in."

Dede entered the house and looked around. "I can't believe how many years it's been since I first stepped through your entryway. Only about a week for you."

"It does boggle the mind sometimes. Shall we have tea?"

"That's how it all began," she said reflectively.

"Yes." What a relief to have something joyful occupy my time, other than anxious worry.

"I would love some."

We walked to the back of the house and into the kitchen. I relit the burner underneath the kettle, still warm from earlier.

"It's so good to see you," I said. "What brings you to Southern California? Is Milton with you?"

"No, he's back in Albuquerque. He believes I'm visiting a girlfriend."

"I see," I replied, starting to think this was more than a casual visit. "Technically, you are. I would like to think we'd become friends in the short time we had together."

"Me too. This is difficult for me, Sami, as I don't know if this is an option."

I tilted my head quizzically at her. "You've got my attention. Tell me what's going on in your world."

The relief at my welcoming response showed in her bright smile. She was one of the few Betrotheds I'd wished I could have gotten to know better. Dede had a very accepting and compassionate soul.

"Well, did you receive the mugs I sent you with the family picture?"

"Yes, thank you. I can't express my excitement enough at receiving your package. You're pleased with your life?"

"Incredibly," she beamed. "Milton is an amazing man, as well as a loving husband and father. And grandfather too!" She laughed with delight.

Joining in with her, I chuckled also.

"It's my oldest granddaughter, you see," she said.

"What do you mean?" I asked, more than a little bit concerned.

"Well, she's 24-years-old. And divorced."

"Oh, I'm sorry to hear that."

"Actually," Dede continued, "that's a good thing. Her ex-husband was verbally and…well…physically abusive."

"Oh Dede, I'm so sorry."

The tea kettle whistled, and I excused myself to get up and pour the hot water into our cups, each with a bag of Earl Gray. Once I placed them before us, she continued.

"Well, you see, he's…he's stalking her. Her parents, as well as Milton and I, are at our wits' end. There's nothing we can do to keep that man away from her. We've tried legal action, but it doesn't stop him. They've been divorced for two years. We have no other options."

I sat there quietly, realizing what she was about to ask me. Since the ex-husband wasn't part of this process, it would never occur to him to search beyond the present time.

"You want me to hide her in time, don't you?" I asked.

She sat looking into her tea cup, as if for guidance. Finally, looking beseechingly into my eyes, she asked, "Would you?"

I could see the pain in her expression. She knew that by sending her granddaughter to another time, she would never see her again. Yet this would allow the young woman to be safe and happy. I thought about the 30th Suitor we had left.

"What's your granddaughter's name?"

"Cecily. Her name is Cecily, and she's desperate to get away from this man."

"Have you told her how you and Milton met?"

"No. I didn't want to get her hopes up. We're desperate. Sami, there's no other way to keep him away from her. Can you help us? Will you help us?"

I sat there thinking of Doug Pendry in New York City. If he wasn't a good match for Cecily, there weren't any other options. And it wouldn't be fair to Doug to throw a Betrothed at him that wasn't right. Yet, maybe fate played one more hand here. What if she were the one to finish our quota? The only way to know would be to talk to her in person.

"Did Cecily come with you?"

"No," said Dede. "Like I said, I didn't want to get her hopes up if you couldn't do this for us."

"Understandable," I said. "We do have one more Suitor. Now that doesn't mean she would be a good fit. I need to meet and talk with her a bit. That's how it's done. Would you be willing to bring her here, with no expectations?"

"Of course," Dede exclaimed, sounding relieved. "Cecily is so much like me, it's almost like looking in a mirror. Her adventurous spirit is mine. The only exception is her artistry in painting, which she gets from her grandfather. When can we come back?"

I didn't want to give her false hope, in case something went wrong retrieving Jimmy. There were too many variables at play.

"Let's set it for next Wednesday. I have some things that need attending to over the next few days. Would Wednesday work for you?"

"Oh, yes!" The hope shining in her eyes brightened her whole face. Dede apparently loved Cecily very much. If it were in my power to help the young woman, I would.

By the time our tea cups were empty, the storm clouds had rolled away, and the sun shone through the windows. We finished our chat and I sent Dede on her way.

Hurrying into the studio, the slide indicated full power. It probably had been for almost twenty minutes. Time for *my* leap of faith.

Chapter 42

Sitting on the bench in my studio facing the slide, I waited for the flash. It blinded me when it came.

The sound of gently lapping water could be heard as my vision returned. My eyes cleared to reveal a beach. I sat on a boulder of a small jetty. A narrow expanse of white sand ran between a border of blue-green water on one side and sea grass on the other. Early morning dampness swirled about me.

Perhaps fewer occupants of the Italian island would be wandering about this time of day. I didn't see a dock or boat launch area, so any fisherman setting off to work wouldn't leave from here. If my luck held, Jimmy would arrive nearby.

Standing up on my perch, I surveyed the surroundings. The area looked deserted. The land rose up into rocky hills behind me. Scanning the immediate vicinity, it didn't show signs of life such as footprints or beaten down pathways. I patted the bulge in my right front pocket where the pistol was stowed. Once again, I hoped it wouldn't be necessary to take it out, let alone use it.

Looking at the watch on my wrist, five minutes remained until Jimmy and Carney would appear. I thought it best to stay out of sight, hidden amongst the boulders. While there didn't appear to be anybody around, I wanted to avoid encounters with any of the locals. I wasn't anxious to become a part of history.

As the minutes counted down, I scanned the beach. Five

minutes became ten, and still no sign of them. Climbing over the boulder, I scurried to higher rocks. On the other side of the jetty, I spied the men wrestling in the grass.

"Jimmy," I yelled, as he now lay motionless.

Carney stood over him holding a rock. As I scrambled off the jetty, he tossed it back and forth between his hands. Moving closer, I saw Jimmy lying face down in the grass with blood trickling from the back of his head.

"You bastard!"

"Well, look at you," Carney said, as he glanced at Jimmy, then back at me. He continued, "I was just repaying the favor your buddy Paolo extended to me." His hand reached up and rubbed the back of his head. "I think my aim is better though."

Approaching them, the weapon in my pocket weighed against my leg. I wasn't anxious to bring it out for fear of Carney overpowering me. I stopped short.

My love finally stirred. "Jimmy," I called.

He moaned as he rolled over and struggled to sit up. Carney turned toward him, raising the rock as he approached.

"Stop right there!" I drew my pistol and pointed it at him. It took all my concentration to steady my hand. If he knew I was unsure, he might call my bluff.

"I guess all the sweetness just drained out of darling Sami. Is it in your resolve to shoot, my dear? What if I walked toward you, so we can see how determined you really are to protect the man you love?" He took a couple of steps in my direction.

"Don't," I held the gun higher.

Carney stopped walking. "I must say, it's a surprise to see you here. How long do you have? You only get one try at this. Did you allow enough time to swoop in and rescue your *fiancé*?" he sneered.

Finally, something he didn't know. This man wasn't aware of my lineage. There would be other tries if I failed to reach Jimmy in time.

"So, I guess you managed to find dear old Grandpa's Family Slide. That fool Paolo didn't think I knew trapping someone in time would destroy the two devices used. All it would have taken on my part was a bit of sleuthing in San Francisco. With Junior's slides, I could have done it, but maybe now you made it easier."

He took another step in my direction.

He was calling my bluff. Time for action. I fired off a shot just to his left. While I didn't like using a firearm, Jimmy had ensured my skills were honed to hit a target.

Carney froze, then gave me an appreciative nod. Maybe that should be the plan—just shoot him to get Jimmy and myself back to our own time.

Glancing at my watch, two minutes remained.

"You're out of time, aren't you?" Carney gloated, "Failed again. My buddy Jimmy and I will have lots of time to get reacquainted."

"I don't think so," Jimmy said. He had managed to get up and stagger in my direction.

The distance proved too great. As the seconds ticked down, I ran toward Jimmy. Carney launched the rock at Jimmy, forcing him to dive onto the sand. Getting up and stumbling, I knew he wouldn't make it to me in time. With twenty feet between us, we couldn't close the gap fast enough.

"Jimmy, catch!" I hurled the gun his way. It soared for his outstretched hands. "Ten minutes!" I screamed.

Still running, my shin banged on the table against the wall as I appeared back in my studio. My hands instinctively rose to stop my momentum.

I hoped Jimmy knew what I meant when I yelled "ten minutes". His grandfather might have shared my lineage with him. Knowing the old man's reluctance to impart more knowledge than necessary though, he may have kept quiet.

Manipulating the slide, I repeated the process to set up my journey and arrive ten minutes after I left Elba. If Jimmy stayed on the beach, finding him should be easy. Having left behind the only weapon available, I would be defenseless. Since our outlandish garb would give us away immediately, I hoped not to have to wander. It might keep me from getting to him, if I chose the wrong direction.

Waiting another hour was like enduring an eternity. Finally, the minutes ticked down and it was time to activate the 30-second counter. I prayed this journey would be a success and not require another jump.

With my back to the slide this time, I waited for the flash. It illuminated the room. Back on the jetty, the boulder dampened my jeans. Sitting where I had landed the first time, I immediately jumped up and scurried over the rocks to the side where I'd left Jimmy.

Scanning the area, I found him in the grass. He lay prone and not moving. "No!" I screamed.

I jumped down onto the beach and ran through the tall grass to where he lay. Rolling him over, blood stained the ground. I gently slapped him in the face, hoping to awaken him.

No response.

No pulse.

No breathing.

"Jimmy, no," I cried.

His skin felt cool to the touch, the life drained out of him. Looking at where the blood originated from his chest, I saw two gunshot wounds side by side. *Dammit!* Carney must have gotten the gun away from him. My heart wrenched in pain.

I sat there holding him until my time was almost up. Releasing my grasp with seconds to spare, I reappeared alone in the studio. Shock ran through my body leaving me immobile. This time, I didn't hurry to reactivate the slide to get back.

Coming out of my stupor, I tried to figure out the best course of action. The timing had to be just right to stop Carney from killing Jimmy.

I went into the kitchen and grabbed a bottle of cold water from the refrigerator. Taking it out to the porch, my body collapsed into one of the wicker chairs. A cool breeze tickled my face. I knew I could save Jimmy and bring him home, yet Mr. Chang's prophetic words haunted my thoughts. The more times the slides were used for personal gain, the more I put both Jimmy and me at risk for things to go awry. Even though it was my choice, did I have the right to choose for Jimmy? Would he make the same decision if our roles were reversed? Yes. He would.

Lost in a bubble of thought, I jumped, knocking over my water. Paolo approached from the edge of the porch.

"How long have you been there?" I asked, standing to retrieve the bottle.

"Not long. I did not want to intrude. Your thoughts were far away."

I motioned toward a chair. "It's okay. Please, sit down. Would you like something to drink?"

"If it is not too much trouble, water would be refreshing."

I retrieved another bottle from the house, glad for the company. Sorting this out on my own was pushing me over the edge of sanity. I attempted a smile as I handed him the water.

"I wanted to see how you were doing," said Paolo.

Rather than filling him in on the day's events, I decided to get more information. "Did you know I was the sole survivor of the Manchester family—the British family as you referred to them?"

"I suspected. The matching name seemed too much of a coincidence."

"Why didn't you say anything?" I asked.

"It did not seem important at the time. Now, with Jimmy gone, I am sure you are trying to find a way to retrieve him. Correct?"

I looked at him before casting my gaze back out to the ocean. "It seems I was given assistance from an unlikely place."

Chapter 43

"This process is full of many unexpected twists and turns," said Paolo.

"So, it seems," I replied, taking a sip of water. The liquid trickled down my throat, giving me the soothing effect I'd hoped for. It wasn't a cure for my current anxiety, but a much-needed respite.

"How did you find out about your lineage?"

"Mr. Chang was waiting for me when I returned from your house. He offered a gift, as well as some valuable information."

"Can I assume he gave you the means to retrieve his grandson from the 1800's?"

"Yes. Remember how you told me the Manchester Family Slide perished in the fire along with the remaining heirs except the child? Well, the slide managed to survive unscathed."

"This is news. I wonder why Chang felt the need to keep that a secret. Did he retrieve it from Britain?"

"No, Francois had a hand in the acquisition. He entrusted Mr. Chang with it's safe keeping until he could return it to the family. My mother was never interested, so he held it for me."

"Why have you not used it then?"

"I did—twice. The first time I found them too late and didn't make it to Jimmy in time to bring him back. The second time, he was...he..." I found it hard to say the words. A seagull swooped by the porch giving off a raucous call, as if to chastise me for my improper use of the process.

"What is it, Sami? What did you find back there?"

"He was dead. Jimmy was dead. I'm sure Carney shot him."

"How could he have gotten another weapon so quickly? The one he had at my house is still there."

"It was mine. Just before I disappeared, I tossed the gun to Jimmy. Carney must have gotten it away from him and used it."

"Now you have a dilemma. Do you use the slide a third time to prevent his death, not knowing if that is how it was supposed to happen anyway?"

"How did you know?" I looked at Paolo in utter surprise that he suggested the notion, despite its truth.

"It is the same struggle I endured when you told me you acquired the Fortuno Family slide from Carney. Did I have the right to use it and attempt to stop Junior's death? The consequences may not have allowed us to live a happy life, despite his being saved. Perhaps when someone dies due to this process, it's what would have happened anyway, whether it be in the present or the past."

"That's my fear. Maybe Jimmy was supposed to die. But he went back without a weapon. What if my going back to save him changed his timeline? There are too many permeations when we meddle with time, aren't there, Paolo?"

"I wish I had all the answers. The question now is, will *you* go back once more?"

This query hung in the air between us. The seagull hovered nearby again, as if it were looking for answers too. The bird was so close I could see the blemishes in its feather pattern.

Paolo's question seemed almost like a dare. Would I temp fate one more time to make things come out right in my world? Would I be allowed my indulgence? Fate could be as fickle as time. You may get what you want, yet it might not be as imagined.

With resolution I answered him. "How can I not? If there's a chance of saving Jimmy and bringing him back to the present, I have to try." I stood up and walked to the far end of the porch, rolling the water bottle between my fingers. Sunlight reflected off the liquid and danced on the ground. More memories flooded in as I remembered finding Paolo, Jr.'s, license from the 1960's. So much turmoil.

"There is your answer then." As if to punctuate his comment, Paolo set his empty container down on the table next to him with a loud crinkle as the plastic hit the surface. He rose out of his seat.

I turned and looked at him. This man lost much, as we all had. How much was our right to reclaim?

"It seems you have a journey ahead of you," he said as he gave me a nod goodnight. Turning slowly, he walked off the porch toward the driveway.

"Paolo?" I called.

He stopped and turned his head my way.

"Would you've gone back, given the chance?"

After hesitating a moment, he simply shrugged.

I watched him walk down the driveway to his vehicle. My gaze returned to the ocean, while I leaned against the nearest post. It creaked with my weight. The noise of a car engine ignited with a roar, then faded as he drove away. The sound of the surf pounding on the shore echoed up to my ears.

The damp air chilled my skin as I finished my water, so I went inside. Out of recent habit, the front door was secured. After depositing the empty containers beside the kitchen sink, I went about the house making sure all the windows and outside doors were locked.

As anxious as I was to go back and save Jimmy, the stress of the past day took its toll. If I wasn't well rested and primed for action, things might continue to go wrong. I doubted sleep would find me tonight, but I had to try and get some rest. My mind needed to be sharp. With great reluctance, I removed the Family Slide from my studio and locked it up in the office safe.

Despite concerns, sleep consumed me quickly. I awoke to the morning sun peeking through the blinds of my bedroom window, still wearing the same clothes from the night before. My memory failed as I couldn't remember lying down. It must have happened at some point, otherwise how would I have gotten here?

Getting up and wandering downstairs, I set up the coffee maker and selected the strong brew button. While waiting for it to finish, I went back upstairs, showered and changed into fresh clothes.

When the coffee finished dripping and the scent of hazelnut

wafted through the kitchen, I poured myself a cup and went into my studio. Besides getting rest, I needed to prepare myself mentally for this next journey. Reflectively studying each portrait, I wondered how all their lives really turned out—except for the four women that never got the life promised. Sadness overtook me thinking about their fate, but I shook it off. It wouldn't do any good dwelling on the evil that befell them. All had perished at Carney's hands. That notion made me even more certain I was justified in cheating death to save Jimmy. It seemed a fair trade.

I lingered in my studio longer than intended. The doorbell rang and dragged me out of my reverie. Looking at my watch, it was about 10:15.

Cautiously looking through the peephole in the door, there stood a delivery man wearing a beige uniform. As I opened the door, he held a small padded envelope and an electronic clipboard.

"Samantha Manchester?" he inquired.

"Yes," I said, "that's me."

"Sign here, ma'am," the courier pointed as he held out the device then handed me the stylus to scribble my name. Always made me wonder why they bothered as most signatures on those things didn't look legible.

"Thank you, ma'am," he said as he handed me the parcel. "Have a nice day," he added with a cursory smile that was gone in an instant. Turning away he strode off to his truck parked at the curb.

Looking down at the tan and crinkled parcel in my hand, I immediately noticed the return address written in the upper left corner with no name. None was needed. I recognized the Chinatown location in San Francisco immediately—The Jade Pagoda.

The ink appeared faded, as if it had been written long ago. The package itself looked worn. A date stamped on the side read February 23, 1983. Perhaps when the package had been received by the delivery service?

Carefully tearing open the parcel, I found a green, silk scarf wrapped around a yellowed piece of paper. All it said was: February 15, 1983. I didn't recognize the hand writing, but I had a hunch who penned the note.

I was being summoned by the elder Chang. My intuition about

not seeing him again had been misguided. The journey to Elba Island in the year 1815 would have to be put on hold. It distressed me not to go immediately back on a third, and hopefully final journey to retrieve Jimmy. Given his recent willingness to help me, I felt obligated to honor Mr. Chang's request. There must be a reason he chose this day for delivery. Nothing that man did could be construed as mere coincidence.

Since the note didn't specify a time, I assumed a precise hour and minute wasn't necessary. Carrying the paper into my office, I retrieved my Family Slide from the safe.

Taking the device into the studio, I pressed the button and clearly gave the location, "The Jade Pagoda, Chinatown, San Francisco, upstairs living room." No need to alarm any store patrons that may be inside the shop. I spun the date wheels to February 15, 1983, set it for 12:00 noon and selected a time frame of four hours. My index finger poked the power button. In an hour, I would know why my presence was required.

Even though I knew Carney no longer posed a threat in the present time, it was still prudent to be cautious. I double-checked the lock on the front door.

To fill the hour-long wait, I set about doing research. Using the computer, I wanted to make sure Carney hadn't done anything to make himself noteworthy in history. My extensive search on the internet, turned nothing up that would've even referred to Carney. That didn't necessarily comfort me. It still concerned me he might have somehow escaped from that time. I didn't see how, but the fear lingered.

As the hour dragged on, it was finally time to journey back to the Jade Pagoda. Roughly two years prior to the date, Mr. Chang would have passed away.

In the studio, I pressed the thirty-second timer, sat down on the cushioned bench and waited for the flash. This time I kept my eyes closed, so wasn't blinded when it hit.

Appearing in the living room, the place was as I remembered it from my first visit to Mr. Chang in 1979. The two red couches and all the other furnishings were mostly in their places.

Behind me I heard a familiar voice. "So, you got my note."

Chapter 44

"Jimmy!" I whipped around and found him leaning in the doorway to the kitchen. Launching myself, I almost knocked the man over as my arms went around his neck.

He started to return the embrace, then winced with pain. Pulling back, I saw something uneven underneath his shirt. Placing my hand on the spot, I felt a wide bandage wrapped around his chest.

"You were shot," I remembered. "The second time I went back you were…were…" it was difficult for me to say the words.

"I was dead," he filled in for me.

"Yes," I whispered, caressing his cheek.

"Grandfather told me you saw my lifeless body the second time you went back."

"How could he know?" I asked.

Sighing, Jimmy said, "He won't tell me. There's more going on than he'll reveal. But he said you saw me dead, and he couldn't let you try a third time. He stepped in, even though he knew it was wrong."

"He went back to Elba Island and brought you here? But that's personal gain. Why would he suddenly change?"

"Again, he won't say. All I know is Carney wrestled the gun away and shot me twice. Next thing I know Grandfather squatted beside me taking my hands. When I woke up I was in my old room in his apartment with this bandage."

"I have a friend that is a doctor," Mr. Chang said as he entered the living room from the top of the stairs.

We both turned to look at him. I spoke first. "How did you know where and when to go back?"

"Miss Manchester, why do you continually ask questions you know I cannot answer? Can you not just be happy my grandson has been returned to you?"

I stared at him for a moment. Then I kissed Jimmy on the cheek and walked over to Mr. Chang.

"You're going to hug me again aren't you?" he asked cringing.

"Not if it makes you uncomfortable," I said. Then threw my arms around the man and held him close a minute. Like before he was stiff but didn't push me away. As I released him, I saw a brief smile flash across his face.

Returning to Jimmy's side, I asked, "So can I take you back with me?"

"That's why you're here. Grandfather sent for you, so you wouldn't go back a third time," he said hesitantly.

"What happened to Carney?" I had to know.

"After he shot me, he ran off. I started to lose consciousness, until Grandfather came."

"You used one of the one-time use slides to get him? Were you there when I went back the second time? There's no other way you would have known what I found," I said to Mr. Chang.

He gave me a slight nod. That would be all the explanation offered. "You have seen the last of Carney. He will no longer be a threat to any of us."

Jimmy started to sag a bit, so I tucked myself under his arm and helped him to the couch. "How long have you been here?" I asked.

"Grandfather retrieved me a week ago. I'm mostly mended, just makes me a bit tired when I exert myself. Or get the life squeezed out of me," he said with a sly grin.

Sitting next to him, I beamed with joy. Things had finally come around right, and we were rid of Carney's evil ministrations.

"Now you have choices to make," Mr. Chang said. "You have one more match to complete your quota, do you not?" He walked toward us and sank down onto the other couch. The crimson cushions swallowed his thin frame.

"Yes, I guess we do. There *is* a possible Betrothed for our final match in 1952 New York City." Looking at Jimmy I said, "It's Dede's granddaughter. She came to me yesterday asking for help. The young woman's ex-husband has been stalking her, and Dede feels it's the only way to safely get her away from him. That wouldn't be a misuse of the slides, would it?" Looking at the old man, I waited for his reaction.

He was silent a moment. It always seemed to be his way. Finally, he spoke. "There are no coincidences in this business. You should know that by now."

"Well, then," Jimmy said. "It looks like retirement is right around the corner for us." Still having his arm around my shoulders, he pulled me in closer. "You still interested in going through your golden years as Mrs. Chang?"

I held up my left hand for both of us to see the delicate silver strands wrapped around my ring finger. Gazing into his eyes, I asked, "What do you think?"

Kissing me on the lips, he said, "I think we have a wedding to plan."

Mr. Chang quietly, but purposefully, cleared his throat, as if to remind us he was still present. We both turned to look at him then laughed.

His expression turned serious. "You also have another choice to make."

"About what?" I asked.

"There remains one more box of slides, with thirty Suitors waiting for their brides."

"Are you telling us we're expected to fulfill Paolo, Jr.'s, quota as well as our own? That could take years!" I felt Jimmy's pressure on my arm, urging me to calm down.

"Grandfather, how can you lay that obligation on us? Shouldn't that be Paolo's burden?"

"You misunderstand me. I do not expect you to place the Betrothed's yourselves. But I think you will know a way to assist in that task."

As cryptic as always, Mr. Chang simply got up and walked into the kitchen, leaving us to puzzle out what he really meant.

Once again, he'd only given a small portion of what he wanted us to do, without fully explaining his request.

"Jimmy, how can he ask us to keep going? Once we place a bride with our thirtieth Suitor, we should be permitted to focus on our own lives. The slides and process are done as far as we're concerned, right?"

"I'm not sure what Grandfather meant, honey," he said, placing a hand on my cheek. "Since we never had children, there are no more heirs to carry on. How much longer are we here for?"

Looking at my watch, we'd only used a half an hour. "We have three and a half more hours. I set the time span for four. Why? What do you have in mind?"

"Let me talk to Grandfather. Maybe he'll offer up a few more clues about what he means by facilitating the fulfillment of the Fortuno slides."

"Either way it sounds like we won't be off the hook after our quota is fulfilled. It hardly seems fair after everything we've been through," I pouted.

Smiling at me, he placed another soft kiss on my lips. "Don't you worry, my Betrothed. I'll get this sorted out."

I liked the sound of that—Betrothed. Since my mom never married, but loved my father, not tying the knot seemed fine with me. Now that marriage loomed before me, it was exciting, and obviously something I'd always wanted.

Thinking of my mother, I asked, "Did your grandfather tell you how I was able to return more than once?"

"Yes, that much he revealed. Of course, he always holds back some details. Like why he didn't offer your Family Slide when he surrendered the Chang Family Slide to me. It might have eliminated some of what occurred."

"Well," I said, "maybe it was the only way to account for all four of the Family devices. If we hadn't stolen the Fortuno slide, it might have been lost forever. At least in its deactivated state, we know nobody else can use it."

"As Grandfather keeps reminding us, not all of our questions will be answered."

Leaning into him, I knew the pressure from my body caused him to wince slightly, but I needed to be close. The warmth that radiated out from him spread through me and calmed my nerves.

At some point this roller coaster ride needed to end. Until then, we wouldn't be free to focus on our own lives without constant concern for others and the process. It was time for us to *leave the arena*, as Francois would have said.

Chapter 45

With a few hours to kill, we chose to leave Mr. Chang to his own thoughts for a bit. We wandered down the street for lunch and took advantage of the authentic cuisine available there in China Town. Putting the process aside for the next couple hours, we talked of our upcoming nuptials. It was liberating to discuss something normal.

Back in the apartment, we found Jimmy's grandfather enjoying tea in the kitchen—with a guest.

"Jimmy told me you found him dead in his home," I blurted out to Mr. Chang, "and that he smashed his Family Slide."

"A pleasure to see you too, Mademoiselle. Congratulations on your upcoming marriage."

"Francois, how did you survive that wound?" I asked.

"I guess you could say my body is very resilient," he chuckled.

Looking to the other elder, I remained confused, and a little bit angry. "Why did you tell Jimmy that Francois was dead?"

Mr. Chang continued sipping his tea for a moment before answering. Placing his cup on the table, he put his arms up and shrugged. "I lied." The playful grin on his face was out of character.

"That's obvious, but why?"

Francois and Mr. Chang exchanged a silent glance.

"I'm sorry, Mademoiselle, but that is something you do not need to know. Suffice it to say, my *death* was necessary to end all the evil. It was quite uncomfortable, I have to admit. Had it not been for my friend, Chang, I surely would have perished."

"When will you two stop talking in riddles?" I asked. "Every time we meet, I walk away with more questions than answers." My hands involuntarily worked themselves in and out of fists. My feet twitched and wanted to start pacing, but there wasn't enough space in the crowded kitchen.

"Grandfather," Jimmy pleaded, "I can't enter into marriage with this woman having secrets. You must bring her into your trust, like you have shared with me. She has more than proven her worth."

Now I was really confused. Jimmy had shared more than a living space with his grandfather since being retrieved from exile on Elba Island. Just when I thought we were given as much information as we would ever be allowed, there remained more.

Mr. Chang looked to Francois once again, who gave him a slight nod of assent. "Very well," he said, "it seems you have won over our confidence, Miss Manchester. However, what you are about to hear is a tale that is ages old. It is not to be shared with anyone. Do I have your solemn vow, this information will not go beyond your ears?"

The severity of the situation took hold of me. Mr. Chang was about to impart sacred knowledge of the process. The solemnity of the mood struck me that not many involved were taken into this confidence. I felt honored and frightened all at once. Gulping, I said, "I promise."

Both older men nodded, and Mr. Chang continued. "The part you are aware of is that there are four families. All of us in this room belongs to one of three. The fourth one is the Fortuno family."

"Yes, I…"

He held up his hand, "Please, Miss Manchester, no interruptions. Some stories must be allowed to flow in their own rhythm. Do you not agree?"

Not being able to help myself, I smiled then nodded. He was politely telling me to shut up and listen. For once, I had to agree with him.

"Francois let you in on the secret of traveling through time. It erases years. More years than you may realize."

Jimmy put his hand on the small of my back and guided me to a chair at the table. While his grandfather had been talking, he'd prepared tea for both of us. I sat in front of a cup with steam rising. He took his place in the chair across from me with a cup of his own.

"I must again confess, Mademoiselle, that I told you a little white lie," Francois interjected.

"You mean other than faking your death?" I asked with a smirk on my face.

He burst out in a hearty laugh. "You truly do amuse me with your bluntness. If only more women were like you, we men would not always be in a quandary over what you are thinking."

"It's part of her charm," Jimmy chimed in.

"I believe you will have your hands full with your soon-to-be bride."

We all got a laugh out of Francois' observation. How could I take offense when I knew he was right?

"As I was saying," Mr. Chang brought us back to the conversation at hand, "while time travel erases years, there is more at play for us Elders."

This stopped me cold. "Elders? What do you mean by that," I started to feel there was a severe undertone to this conversation.

"While I call myself Jimmy's grandfather, my life began a few generations back. As did Francois'."

My eyes grew wide as I tried to grasp what I was hearing. "You aren't really Jimmy's grandfather? But he *is* of the Four Families. He could repeat a location. Are you saying the two of you aren't related?"

"Not at all. Jimmy is of my lineage. However, I was born in the year 1812. His father was not actually my son, but one of my descendants. The same is true of Francois and Carney. While it seemed he was Carney's grandfather, he too was born a few generations prior."

My chair scraped on the linoleum floor with a loud smudging sound as I pushed back from the table and stood up. Walking to the window as if gasping for air, I found it hard to believe what I was being told. Strange how I accepted the whole match-making process with such ease yet found it odd I couldn't grasp this additional twist without a healthy amount of amazement.

"Please, Miss Manchester," suggested Francois, "Sami, sit down. It is a fantastic tale, yes, but one I know you would want to hear. You have been questing for the truth, and here it is. Come sit back down."

I turned to see all three men looking at me. The anxious expression on Jimmy's face pleaded for me to accept this truth. How could I not? After all these years participating in this bizarre lifestyle, it was merely one more chapter of the process. One I longed to hear. My resistance to believe surprised me more than anyone here.

Jimmy stood up and held his hand out. "I know exactly how you feel, honey. When Grandfather told me, I didn't want to believe him at first. Until I realized it all made sense the way things have happened."

"But, if he really isn't your grandfather, what happened to your real grandfather?" I looked from him to Mr. Chang.

"He was killed in China before Jimmy was born, along with his wife. It broke my heart as he was only 42 years old. Too young to go on and be with the ancestors. There was a riot in the small town we lived in. I do not even remember the cause. Yet that is what happened. Life in China was hard. That is why I took Jimmy's father and moved to California. It seemed a better place."

With that thought he stopped, and I could see his eyes watering. Quickly he looked down and concentrated on his tea. Francois reached across the table and put his hand on the other man's arm. They both must have endured loss and death living as long as they claimed, while their offspring lived a mortal life.

A question popped into my mind. "Did you have a choice?"

This seemed to fluster both men as they contemplated my question. "What do you mean?" Mr. Chang finally asked.

"Did you have a choice to become what you are?" I thought it was a valid notion. While they both seemed sad from the passing of generations, at some point they had chosen this life. The blame would have fallen on themselves.

"That question has many answers," Francois offered. "When offered this life, it seemed we did not have a choice. Ultimately, you are right, it was our own doing."

"Tell me how it began."

Chapter 46

"It was shortly after the First Opium War in China. The British fought the Qing Empire and won in 1842," began Mr. Chang. "The Treaty of Nanjing was signed, and Hong Kong became a British colony."

Trying to calculate the years in my head, I realized he was thirty years old when the treaty had been signed. "Did you live in Hong Kong?"

"Briefly. When the British took over it was hard to find employment beyond servant positions. I worked as a guide to the British families that poured in and wanted adventure beyond the city limits.

"Having grown up in the provinces, I was quite familiar with many of the ancient ruins long abandoned by my people. The foreigners were fascinated with them."

"So, you worked for the British?" I asked, sipping my tea.

"I worked for myself," he stated proudly, almost annoyed at the question.

"Grandfather," Jimmy interjected, "she meant no disrespect. It was simply a question. You've got to admit, this is quite a fantastic tale to believe. Hearing it told a second time, it still throws me off balance."

I looked at Jimmy with an appreciative smile. Reaching across the table I placed my hand over his and left it there. Ever my hero, defending me to the last.

"You are right. I am sorry, Miss Manchester. Much of my life has been spent receiving disdain from those that do not try to understand other cultures. You did not deserve to be categorized with them."

"It's all right, Mr. Chang. No offense taken. Please continue. I want to know the rest."

The old man nodded his head, took a long draw from his tea cup, then gently placed it back on the table. Jimmy had refilled it for him while he talked.

"As I said, I worked as a guide. The day it all began, I was leading a small group of men that wanted to venture further into the wilds of China than most. The leader was from a wealthy British family that had hired my services before. I led him, his wife and two small boys to see some of the surrounding area. Not too far as the boys were quite young and did not settle down for long journeys. The family name was Manchester," he said, directing his gaze at me.

A small gasp escaped my lips, realizing how close to home this immediately became. Obviously, the man was my ancestor.

"Yes, you are his descendant," he smiled, as he knew what was going through my mind without my saying it aloud.

"So, one of his sons was my…"

"Please, Miss Manchester, let me tell it. This time I am sure your questions will be answered. Patience for now."

With a nod and a smile, I remained silent.

"Accompanying Winston Manchester were two European friends—Antonio Fortuno and Francois."

Looking at the man sitting beside me, his expression showed concern. Squinting my eyes and tilting my head, I wasn't sure why he suddenly became serious.

As Francois looked my direction, he understood my concern, "Ah, you see this part disturbs me. I was not, how would you say…as *enlightened* as I am now. Chang is my oldest and most cherished friend. At the time, I was young and arrogant. I did not believe someone of Asian descent could be as sophisticated as those of us from Europe. How misguided we can be in our youth."

He and Chang exchanged a look of understanding. "There has been much water under the bridge, my good friend," Chang said.

"We have all made misguided assumptions at times in our lives. How else could we evolve if we did not continue to learn and appreciate the world around us."

"Well put, my friend. Please continue with the history," said Francois.

He nodded and went on with his tale. "As I said, we were four. The fourth member, Antonio, is not the Fortuno you have come to know. He has long left this earth, but was an important part, as we all were.

"I knew of a tomb not often visited, and a half day's travel from Hong Kong. We had arranged to set up camp nearby and spend three days exploring the place. Once inside, the men were fascinated with the writings on the walls. They were ancient writings, not decipherable by even me. The language was unknown. Having seen it many times, I chose to rest off in a corner, so they could explore. As I slide down the wall to the floor and leaned back, the strangest thing happened."

He stopped to sip his tea. Then set the cup down. I wasn't sure he was going to continue, as he simply stared off into space.

"Grandfather," Jimmy said. There was no response. He tried again, "Grandfather?" Still nothing.

"Chang, my friend," Francois gently shook Chang's arm. This brought him out of his trance. As his eyes focused on his old pal, he looked unsure for a moment

"I am sorry. It was so long ago yet seems like yesterday. The decades have come and gone, but it will always remain fresh in my mind."

I removed my hand from Jimmy's and reached out to the older man. He didn't flinch from my touch this time. As my hand covered his, he gave the briefest of smiles, then rescinded his hand and dropped both into his lap.

There was no insult in the gesture. I could tell by his expression that his thoughts were elsewhere, not on the present.

"Tell us what happened," I prompted him.

"The wall opened," was all he said.

"What do you mean?" I asked.

"I must have triggered a latch as I leaned back. The wall slid out from behind me. As it did, I fell backwards hitting my head on the floor. Immediately jumping to my feet and whipping around, there now revealed a small chamber. It was smaller than the one we were in and contained four pedestals. Atop each one rested what we now call the Family Slides. Of course, at the time, we had no clue what these strange fixtures meant."

"What did your companions think? What did you think?" I couldn't begin to imagine what it must have been like to make such a discovery. Especially in that era, when cameras were in their infancy.

"My friend, Chang, was in awe," Francois stepped in. "I had seen a camera and was familiar with the slides used. In this I was able to identify the objects. Though not why they would be in this ancient tomb."

The other man picked up the story. "We all ventured into the chamber. It was odd that none of us thought to be afraid. The fascination of such *modern* items being here, must have put us at ease. We examined the devices but did not pick them up. Noticing the lights began to activate slowly around the frame should have scared us yet didn't. Scouring the walls, there were writings, but nothing any of us could translate.

"We spent about an hour exploring the chamber, before returning to the pedestals. Each of us gravitated toward one and stood before it. I noticed the lights on my frame were all illuminated. That was when the flash went off."

I sat there a moment trying to visual the scene. All I could focus on was the flash, that I knew all too well. Trying to think back to the first time I travelled with the slides, I still couldn't fathom their shock. When I journeyed, I knew full well what was happening. They didn't. "Where or when did it take you?"

Mr. Chang looked at me and said, "It took me here. To the Jade Pagoda. The proprietor knew I was coming. It turns out he was the man I purchased this store from when we arrived decades later."

"You went forward in time then?" I couldn't stop from asking the question.

"Yes, all of us did."

"All four of you arrived here?" I was bursting with questions but restrained myself to ask just the one.

"No, only me. We each went to a different location. Francois and Fortuno went to the Golden Dragon and the Purple Lotus in

New York City. The very same ones that Carney and you were sent to," he added, looking at Jimmy.

"Manchester was the only one that did not end up in the United States. He found himself in the Lotus Petal on Charing Cross in London.

"The proprietor in each shop was prepared for our arrival. As you can imagine, the shock of being propelled a century into the future had been overwhelming. Most of the twenty-four hours was spent calming us each down. They immediately tried to explain how we arrived at their shops, and the task set out, if we chose to participate. The process was laid out in detail, and we were each given a box of slides to begin matches."

"So, all of you began as Collectors?" I asked.

"Yes," Mr. Chang said. "We were first told how to use the Family Slides, so if we needed guidance, we could travel to our respective proprietors. Many mysteries remain as they would not reveal who created these slides or where they originated. Perhaps it was so old nobody truly knew how they came into existence. Like most ancient information, it had been lost."

There remained much to ask before returning to our current time. Of course, I would journey back without a problem, but Jimmy and I needed to be together for him to return with me. Even though I knew I could come back again, something told me this would be one of our last trips here.

Jimmy saw me glance at the time and I mouthed, "Twenty-two minutes." He nodded and instinctively checked the clock on the wall.

Chapter 47

"That is how it began," Mr. Chang spoke as if he had reached the end of his tale.

"This is where you finished telling me, Grandfather," Jimmy said, "but there's more, isn't there?"

Once again, Francois and Mr. Chang seemed to be in a mental conversation by their facial expressions between each other. It was frustrating for me to watch and wonder if they would complete the story or leave us hungry for more.

"What else is it you would like to know?" Francois took over.

"Well, for one thing," I jumped right in, "my lineage. Am I a direct descendent of one of those young Manchester boys?"

"You could not be. They were born before Winston Manchester became an Elder in the process. Until he travelled by the slide, he had nothing to pass on. After his journey, he fathered another son. It is that offspring that passed on the family bloodline through the generations."

"His wife became a Photographer?"

"No," Francois said. "When Manchester explained what had occurred, she believed it was the work of the devil and wanted nothing to do with it. Sara, his wife, was a devout Christian, and refused to go along with the process. Her husband, on the other hand, could not resist the adventure the process offered. He soon divorced Sara and she returned to England with the two boys. The third son was from his second marriage with the woman that did become his Photographer."

I checked my watch again. Time was nearly done. As much as I wanted to know everything, it also frightened me. What if this made it too intriguing to let go after the thirtieth match? The wheels in my head began to turn. With my Family Slide, perhaps I could travel to one of the original proprietors and ask questions. How receptive would they be to my queries?

"How were you able to live so long?" was the next thing on my mind.

"Ahhh, I wondered when you would get around to that, Mademoiselle. It is the effect of using the Family Slide for the first time, and never to be repeated. That is what we were told."

"It obviously didn't make you invincible since Manchester and Fortuno are dead. Paolo told me the last of the Manchester clan except my mother died in a fire. I'm assuming it was really Winston that died in the fire, along with his descendants."

"You are correct. As for Antonio Fortuno, he died by his own hand. Right after Paolo, Sr., was born, he could not bear the thought of watching another generation grow old and die before him."

"Then how have you two survived all these years?" I continued to prod.

"Sami, honey, it's time," Jimmy interrupted as he pointed at the clock on the wall. "We have two minutes left."

"We always seem to run out of time, Miss Manchester," Chang said.

"Please, Francois," I pleaded, "tell me how you've survived all these years."

The Frenchman smiled, as if he wasn't going to answer.

"It's okay, honey, it won't change anything for us," Jimmy said as he stood up and walked to my side of the table. "Come, my love." He extended his hand to me.

If I didn't take hold of his hands, I would return alone. A second trip would be required. We could have more time to get the full story from the two men calling themselves Elders.

Instead I stood up. The chair scraped against the linoleum as I pushed it away from the table and took Jimmy's hand. He took hold of my other.

"We won't be seeing you again, will we?" I asked.

Chang remained seated and shrugged.

Francois stood up with a big grin. "It has been a pleasure, Mademoiselle. You truly are a special lady. *Young* Jimmy is a lucky man. And in answer to your question, it is the result of many journeys through time. As I told you upon our first meeting, it erases years. With the benefit of being the first to use our Family Slide, the effects are multiplied ten-fold. As Moderators of the matches we were kept quite busy leaping."

"Moderators? What do you mean Moderators? Did you witness all the matches?"

"You miss nothing, Mademoiselle. As Moderators we..."

Jimmy and I stood holding hands in my studio. We didn't get to hear Francois' explanation of what function a Moderator performed.

"Did your Grandfather happen to mention anything about being a Moderator?"

"Not a peep. That old man has more secrets than you or I could ever imagine. And now that's what they must remain."

"But, Jimmy, we could go back. They can finish the story. Let's power up the Family Slide," I said starting to pull my hands free from his.

"Sweetie," Jimmy said, keeping a firm grip on me.

I stopped.

"It's finished—for you and me anyway."

"But, honey, we could..." My voice drifted off, as I saw a broad grin spread across his face. His eyes sparkled as he began to laugh.

I joined him. "Always the voice of reason. That's why I love you," I told him, placing a soft, lingering kiss on his lips. "We place Cecily with Doug Pendry in New York and it is completed."

"For us, yes. Are you okay with that?" He asked as he tilted his head sideways to accentuate the question.

I didn't answer right away. Was I okay with finishing our quota and moving on to living only for ourselves? "Time will tell," I said with a smirk.

"Then it will have to be good enough. Have you met Cecily yet?" He released my hands.

"No, she comes next week. I didn't want to set her first

journey too close to my going back to retrieving you, since I didn't know what to expect."

While being tempted, I chose not to activate the Family Slide once more. I was torn between wanting to know everything and being satisfied with the thought of a life for only Jimmy and me. Cecily would be the last. The traveling would be finished.

Jimmy took the following week off from work to continue healing from his wounds. We did go visit Paolo, since we knew he would be racked with guilt over Jimmy being trapped in time also.

Approaching his home in Laguna Beach, we wondered how the old man would receive us. Perhaps he too was ready to be done with everything. Pulling up to the gates Jimmy pushed the button. This time our ring was answered by a stranger.

"Who is it," a female voice demanded.

"Jimmy and Sami here to see Paolo. Is he in?" Jimmy asked.

"No. Was he expecting you?" asked the disembodied voice.

"No, but we were hoping to talk with him. When will he be home?"

"Sorry, he did not say. I will tell him you stopped by. Good day."

We were being dismissed by the help. Perhaps he would contact us once he heard it was both of us visiting. Jimmy backed the car out of the entryway and took us north towards home in the South Bay.

That evening after dinner we sat on the porch enjoying a glass of Merlot. Not a surprise, we saw a black town car pull up to the curb of my house. Paolo got out and approached.

"Hello, Paolo," I said. "Good to see you."

"And you as well," he said, "both of you actually. So, your retrieval worked?"

"Not exactly," I said. "We had some help, but both of us have returned. Would you like to join us in a glass of Merlot?"

"It would be a pleasure," Paolo replied. "Thank you." As he spoke, he came up onto the porch and seated himself in the first available wicker chair. The branches whispered around him as they took his weight.

Going into the house to retrieve another glass, I heard a conversation begin, as Paolo said, "Jimmy Chang, I am sorry for what happened. You see..." was all I heard as I went into the kitchen.

When I returned with the additional glass, they were already talking about the Mediators.

"No," Paolo said, "while I did know that my ancestor was an Elder and how he began, I did not know he was a Mediator, as you say. He took his life when I was a teenager."

"Did he tell you anything more about the process?" I asked.

"He did tell me how it all began. But he did not say anything about being a Mediator. This is the first I have heard of that term. Perhaps he felt there was no value in my knowing, so he chose to keep it to himself. Did your Grandfather enlighten you about that, Jimmy?"

"Unfortunately, we ran out of time. Like we always do," Jimmy said as he turned and winked at me.

"Perhaps," said Paolo, "some things are best left unsaid. You are close to finishing your quota, are you not?" He asked, then took a sip of wine.

"Yes," I said. "We can then be done with this whole mess."

"While the loss of my Paolo was hard, I still regret his not fulfilling his quota. His death meant the unhappiness of all his Suitors. It is so unfair that they should suffer for his rash actions. But here we are. With the lack of any additional offspring, yours will be the last quota to be fulfilled."

We all sat sipping our wine and watching the sun sink into the ocean. As many times as I'd witnessed this scene, it still left me in awe. There was always a higher power greater than our meager lives.

His glass drained, Paolo gently set it on the table beside him and stood. Like everything else in this past day, it seemed very final.

"Well then," Paolo said, "I guess this is good-bye. I wish you every happiness in your upcoming marriage. It is time to focus on yourselves."

"Paolo," I said.

The old man turned around.

"What will you do now?" I asked.

He stood quietly a moment, then shrugged.

I understood his ambivalence. *What was left to say*, I thought.

The man turned and walked off the porch, down the driveway

and got into his car. It hesitated a moment, before being shifting into gear and driving away.

Jimmy drained his glass and extended an arm my way as he stood up. Without a word I allowed him to lead me into the house. We walked to the kitchen and set our empty glasses by the sink. I allowed him to lead me upstairs.

Chapter 48

The following Wednesday, Dede arrived with her granddaughter, Cecily, in tow. She was a petite little blond with a mischievous sparkle in her eyes, like her grandmother.

"So, you're the famous Sami that Grandma has talked so fondly about. It truly is a pleasure," Cecily said, giving me a warm, genuine hug.

"Well," I said, "I wouldn't say famous, but I'm glad your grandma spoke kindly of me."

"It seems she didn't have a life before meeting Grandpa. There isn't anyone from the past that she's ever spoken about except you," she said, looking slyly at Dede.

"Well, isn't that a sneaky way to get the real scoop on me," Dede replied, giving Cecily's shoulder a soft caress. "You think I'm tight lipped, you've met your match with my friend, Sami, here."

We all laughed as I motioned for them to come inside. Life at the Freeman household must be quite lively and full of energy, if the banter between these two was an example of the strong bonds.

"I have tea laid out on the kitchen table, shall we wander in there?"

The two women nodded in unison and followed me down the hallway. If Cecily was a good match for Doug, it would be heartbreaking for Dede to let her go. Yet the thought of her granddaughter being placed in as happy a life as she had been, should be consolation enough. Despite her bright smile, I knew this was difficult for Dede.

"Earl Grey, my favorite tea," the older woman said as we sat around the table. "Those croissants look delicious. What a lovely surprise, thank you."

I could tell there was more to Dede's gratitude than her appreciation of the spread on the table.

Once everyone got settled with a steaming cup in their hands, I decided to get the ball rolling. If Cecily was anything like Dede, beating around the bush wasn't her style. Directness would have to be the way to win over her confidence and trust.

"So, Cecily, it truly is a pleasure to meet you. Tell me, how have I earned my famous rating with your grandmother?"

"Your photography, of course. She told me of your wonderful portraits, and how she'd met you out on the Strand. The photo sessions you offer with dressing up in different periods sound like fun."

"Like her grandfather," Dede added, "Cecily is an amazingly talented artist with a paint brush. So naturally, she's intrigued by most forms of art. Her younger sister acquired my love of clay and sculpting. It's a shame she couldn't join us on this trip, but her studies have taken her abroad to Italy right now."

"Well, that's exciting for all of you," I said. "What type of subjects do you like to paint?" I asked the young woman.

"Cityscapes mostly. Occasionally I take on sweeping landscapes, but I love the busy aspects of large buildings and packed streets. Hard to believe with my growing up in Albuquerque, isn't it?"

Obviously, this young woman had been led to me for my final match. Her passion slid her into a good fit with New York City where Doug lived. His skills and wealth as a financial consultant would afford her the life she craved. "It does seem quite a contrast, especially given the style both your grandparents have with their artwork. What do you dream of doing with your life?"

"Living in happiness," she said. It was blatantly obvious she had lived a hard couple of years. The expression on her face turned sullen and distant, as if she recalled a horrible memory.

"What do you think would bring you that?" I had to tread

carefully, so as not to alarm her.

Dede placed an arm around the young woman and pulled her in close. "It's okay, Cecily, I've told Sami about Lionel." As an afterthought, she looked at me and added, "Lionel is her ex-husband."

We all sat in silence. The scent of rain drifted through the open kitchen window. I always loved a good storm. Cecily seemed to be battling her own type of squall for the moment.

Sitting up straight, she looked her grandmother in the eye and asked, "Why are we really here, Grandma?" The melancholy look slid off her face and bright determination replaced it. Cecily wasn't the type to dwell on things for long. She bounced back and once again had a certainty about the way she set her jaw and focused her eyes.

"I never could fool you for very long, could I?" Dede asked.

The young woman looked from Dede to me. I thought it best we get up and walked. "Would you like to see my studio?" I offered.

Squinting her eyes in a puzzled look, she said, "I would love to."

Leaving our empty tea cups and plates on the table, the noise in the kitchen burst with activity as our chairs scraped back against the tiles. Cecily still looked a bit confused, since neither her grandmother nor I answered the question. She seemed resumed to the fact that the answers would come clear as the afternoon went on.

Leading the women to my studio, I threw open the door and gestured with my hand for the young woman to go in first. As she strolled through the doorway, I placed a reassuring hand on Dede's arm. With a quick smile and nod, she smiled back and entered behind her granddaughter.

Cecily slowly walked around the room taking in all the portraits. With an appreciative gleam in her eye, she examined each one. At the end of the first wall, she turned to the opposite side and spied the photo of her grandparents.

"Look how young you and grandpa are," she commented.

"We still are, dear!" Dede faked indignation.

"You know what I mean," she laughed. "When was this taken?"

Both of use took a moment before answering. Dede looked to me and nodded, as if encouraging me to move in with my pitch. No sugar-coating here, she seemed to transmit. Turning around, Cecily looked at her grandmother, then to me for an answer.

Taking a deep breath, I answered the woman honestly. "It was taken last month."

Cecily giggled. Obviously, she felt we were playing with her. "Grandma, I do believe Sami has a charming sense of humor. Really, when did you and Grandpa pose for that portrait?"

"Well," Dede replied, "truthfully, your grandfather posed for that picture in 1975. However, I joined him only a month ago."

The young woman whipped back around and stared at the portrait for several moments. I could only imagine what was going through her mind, as we really had laid it out plainly. Perhaps it was best to forge ahead before she lost her sense of humor and decided we were just toying with her.

"Tell me, Cecily," I began, "what would make you happiest in life?"

Without skipping a beat or turning around, she answered, "To be as happy as my grandparents. To have a man in my life that cherishes me the way Grandpa cherishes Grandma. Someone that will allow me the freedom to pursue my painting, and who feeds off my support of him and his work, no matter what he chooses to do in life. Do you think that's too tall of an order?" With that question, she turned and looked at me.

Quietly I walked across the carpet to the young woman and gently put my arm around her shoulders. "I want to show you another portrait, over here," I said as I led her over to Doug Pendry's photo. "What's different with this one?"

She stood in front of his portrait and pondered it silently—no need to look around at the others on the wall. She already knew the answer. "All the others are couples. He's solo."

"Yes. Do you think he's someone you might want to meet?"

At this point she pulled away from me and moved even closer, taking in every detail. She studied the young man in a navy-blue tailored suit. His dark hair and eyes were a contrast to her blond waves and fair complexion—the opposite of Dede and Milton. Her hand went up and traced the features of Doug's hand, just as her grandmother had done the first time she'd seen Milton's picture. I knew she was ready to hear more.

"Cecily, the portrait of your grandparents is exactly as Dede told you. Milton posed for it in 1975, when my Collector interviewed him. A month ago, in our current time, your grandmother came to me and I sent her back to meet him. She was 32 years old at the time."

Her hand dropped. Facing us again, she looked from Dede to me. We both knew what spun through her mind. The battle of wanting to believe yet knowing how fantastic it all sounded. This time, however, it wasn't a woman alone having to trust a stranger. Cecily stood here with someone she loved and admired. Hopefully, that added more weight to what I presented.

Returning her focus to the face in the portrait, she asked, "What's his name?"

I heard Dede expel air. She'd been holding her breath, literally from the sounds of it, waiting for Cecily to believe our story.

"Doug Pendry," I said. "He's a financial consultant in New York City, and it's the year 1952. Doug is 31 years old."

The facts hung in the air, taunting the young woman to embrace them. Not seeing her face, I still knew the emotions playing across it, having witnessed them many times before. I hoped, this would be the last time this scene played out before me.

Chapter 49

Dede walked over and stood beside me with a tight jaw and concern resting in her eyes. Here was the moment I knew she hoped for and feared—when her granddaughter would accept the idea and leave her forever.

"Cecily," she said, "this is how I really met your grandfather." Her voice was so quiet, I wondered if the young woman even heard her speak.

Just as quietly, Cecily stated, "So you lied to all of us."

"We had to. Not only because of this bizarre process, but to protect everyone involved in the time travel. If this weren't kept a secret, it might hinder Sami and her Collector being able to continue matching couples. Please tell me you understand?" Dede pleaded.

"Of course, I do. The part why you would kept it a secret. Why have you brought me here today?"

Dede was at a loss for words. I stepped in, "To keep you safe, while offering a life of love and happiness."

Still looking at her grandmother, Cecily said, "But if I go…back…as you say, I'll never see you again. Or any of my family." At this, tears began to trickle down her face.

"No, but you'll be happy. You'll also be safe and away from Lionel." Dede's face began to glisten with tears also, as she reached out and embraced her granddaughter.

"I'll leave you two alone for a few moments." Not sure if either of them heard me, I didn't wait for a response. Going straight to my office and opening the safe, I retrieved the first slide for Doug Pendry. There was no doubt it would get used.

When I returned to the studio, the two women were sitting on the couch quietly talking. Walking to the end of the studio, I placed the slide in the holder and hit the power button. In an hour it would be activated to send Cecily back for her first 24-hour period.

As I approached them, they looked up with dry, smiling faces. "Did you explain how it will work?" I asked.

"I believe that's your job. We were talking about when I first met Milton and he gave me this necklace," she said clutching the pendant around her neck. "Please join us," she gestured to the seat on the other side of Cecily. "You're on."

Cecily settled in, ready to listen. "Okay, so you already know you'll be going back in time. The process works by your posing in front of my sepia camera. When it flashes, you'll be transported to New York City in 1952. The first journey lasts 24-hours. Doug will be there to greet your arrival, then the day is yours to get to know each other. If you two decide this is a good fit, normally I would say you have a week to get your life wrapped up. Since your situation is more urgent, if you want to go back on a second trip, we can do it as soon as you're ready. It takes a couple days to put together some credentials, so you can have a plausible background. Nothing extensive, just a few basics that are easy to remember. Blending into the 1950's is easier without the modern-day internet."

"How many times do I go back?"

"Twice—the second trip is permanent. You won't be returning to the present. That's why you have to be absolutely sure this is right for you."

This was a different situation. All the other women placed, left nobody behind to come looking for them once they exited this decade. In Cecily's case, there would be a bit of clean up for those left behind to cover her disappearance. "Dede, are you prepared with a story of where she went off to? Who else will know?"

"Only Milton and I will know where *and when* she really went."

"Good. It's best that way. What will you tell her parents and sister?"

"He and I decided to say she went to live in Europe to escape Lionel. Between the two of us, we've been quite successful financially with our art. It would be feasible for us to send her abroad with plenty of money to live on. It was the best we could think of to hide her sudden disappearance. What do you think Cecily?"

"I think I should meet Doug first, then go from there."

"You're so much like your grandma," I said admiringly. This young woman had a wonderful inner strength. Hard to believe she allowed a man like Lionel into her life. Love must have blinded her.

"Why don't you go out to the car, dear, and get the outfit we brought for your *photo* session."

"Sure Grandma. Now I know why you brought that along." She said, giving Dede's shoulder a squeeze as she stood.

Once Cecily left us alone, I asked Dede, "How did you know I would match her with a man from the 1950's? I'm assuming that's an appropriate outfit for the era."

"Well, I do have a very good memory for details—even at my age." We both chuckled at this. "I remember looking at the portraits before journeying back to see Milton the first time. There were only two other single men. Honestly, I didn't know which one would be available, but knew if this was right, it would be the one from the city wearing the suit, which fit his era. She always was fascinated with big cities. You can definitely see that in her art."

"Being she'll go back to a time about twenty years prior to your meeting Milton, it's quite possible by now she might be...well...she might..."

"She might be dead by now," the sadness consumed her face as she cast her eyes toward the floor, but only for a moment. Then a smile returned, "But if it means she led a happy life, that's all that matters. I'm willing to give up my remaining years with her, to know she had the same chance at life I did."

"You've thought this out, haven't you?"

"Yes, and it's the best thing for her. As much as I love Cecily and want to continue being part of her life, safety and happiness are more important than my selfish needs. She'll make a wonderful mother. This is her chance to have that with a man who will support her art, while creating a stable family environment. It will also eliminate the fear of Lionel showing up at any given moment."

"I'd say you're ready to let go. She acts very much like you," I said, "so I've no doubt she'll embrace this opportunity and give it the consideration it deserves. Another half an hour and she'll be ready to go back for her first trip. Are you staying nearby?"

"Yes. We're at a hotel in Manhattan Beach."

"Good. Then you can come back for her return in 24 hours. Are *you* ready to do this?"

"Absolutely. I believe she is too."

"Yes, I am," said Cecily from the doorway, holding a canvas bag. "Is there somewhere I can change?"

Getting up I walked to her and said, "There's a half bath just past the kitchen doorway. You're welcome to go upstairs and use my bedroom too, if you'd prefer."

"The half bath is fine. Thank you, Sami." Her sandals slapped quietly on the wooden floor as she walked down the hall.

We sat waiting for the young woman to don her 1950's garb. I could sense Dede's nervousness by the way she kept ringing her hands and fussing with her finger nails. She probably didn't realize she was doing it.

Walking back into the studio a few minutes later, Cecily now wore a calf-length beige skirt and a light blue blouse. Sensible pumps completed the outfit with her hair pulled back in a simple ponytail. She truly was a beautiful woman that, I knew, would take Doug's breath away before even speaking a word of greeting to him.

"Can I ask a couple more questions?" Cecily asked.

"Of course, dear," I said.

"You mentioned your *Collector* interviewed the men. Who exactly is that?"

"You don't miss a beat, do you? My Collector's name is Jimmy. His task is to photograph and interview the preselected Suitors or men. He needs to get a sense of their personality, disposition, as well as hopes and desires for life. Once their picture is taken, it appears here in the present. The majority crave a wife and children, but as you can see from the different eras and styles of couples on the walls, each one is unique."

"Who preselects the men?"

"Honestly, that's part of the process we were never given. I can assure you, however, I've performed this task many times, and the personalities have always meshed."

"There's a healthy dose of trust involved on everyone's part, isn't there?" Cecily asked.

"Yes, you could say that's true. Not everything in regular life is ever explained," I said with a sly smile. "Why should this be any different?" I gave her a wink, and she laughed.

Dede joined in, "So are you done giving Sami the third degree, young lady?"

"I believe I am, Grandma." A little more nervously, she asked, "Is it time for me to go?" Checking my watch, I walked over to the slide and looked at the timer. Holding up two fingers, we all waited. Finally, the light activated, signaling the slide was completely powered up. "Yes, it's time."

The older woman went to her granddaughter and wrapped her in a warm embrace. Pulling back, she then removed her half-moon necklace and fastened it around Cecily's neck.

Grasping the silver and turquoise pendant, her granddaughter tried to protest, "Grandma, I can't. This is special between you and Grandpa."

"As are you. It helped keep me focused on what was important after my first journey back. May it bring you that same clarity." With a quick kiss on the cheek, Dede whispered, "Good luck, sweetie. I'll be here when you return."

"Good-bye, Grandma. I love you."

"Love you too!"

"Come have a seat on the bench here." I patted the cushion.

As Cecily walked over and sat down, she straightened her back and looked directly into the camera. I reached behind and depressed the thirty second timer on the slide holder. Despite not needing the farce anymore, I still stepped behind my camera and grasped the cushioned button. It helped give the Betrothed something to focus on while the seconds ticked down.

A flash came from behind her and the seat was empty. Releasing the button and turning around, tears streamed down Dede's face. Without a word, I wrapped my arms around her and gave a quick hug. "Would you like some more tea?"

She smiled and wiped at her cheeks with the back of one hand. "I think I'd like to go walk on the beach for a while. It was always my happy place when I lived here. See you at this time tomorrow?"

"I'll be here," I said. "We can greet Cecily together and see what she thinks."

Dede nodded as she preceded me out of the studio and through the entryway.

As I turned the knob and opened the front door for her, I said, "You did the right thing, Dede."

With a smile she said, "I know." Turning to walk out, she nearly bumped into a young man standing in her way. "Lionel!" she shrieked.

Chapter 50

Dede retreated a step, bumping into me.

"Where's my wife?" he demanded. "I saw Cecily come in here."

We were both speechless. The menace in his voice frightened me—it had a *very* familiar tone.

Not being a stranger to such anger, it didn't fluster me long. Stepping around Dede, I put my arm in front of her and gently pushed backwards, as if to shield the woman. I mustered as much authority into my voice as possible, "She's not here, young man."

"Don't lie to me," he shot back, taking a step forward.

"I'm not lying," I held my ground. "Your *ex*-wife is *not* in this house."

"She came inside carrying a bag, probably with clothes. Cecily is staying here, and I want to see her," he said. His anger began subsiding—probably shocked I stood up to him. Men like Lionel rarely take it well when a woman goes toe to toe with them.

"Lionel, why can't you leave her alone?" Dede spoke up, inching even with me in the entryway. "She divorced you. Move on." From the timber in her voice, I could tell she was very shaken at his appearance.

"Never! She *is* my wife, despite what the courts say about it. Cecily will always be mine and I won't stop until she's back living under my roof where she belongs."

"Once again," I said, "she isn't here. Please leave."

"Not until I search the house for myself." He put a hand on the door jam, ready to force his way inside. "Get out of my way."

"I believe the lady asked you to leave," Jimmy said, standing at the edge of the porch. We were so wrapped up in dealing with the young man, I hadn't heard his car pull up.

Turning to look at Jimmy, then back at us, Lionel obviously realized he was outnumbered. He stood there with his brow wrinkled, as if undecided how to proceed. Finally, he started to walk across the porch toward Jimmy.

I was afraid Lionel intended harm, but then simply walked past him. "I'll be back for my *wife*," he said stomping off the porch and down the driveway to his pick-up truck at the curb. The engine revved harder than it needed to as he stomped on the gas and drove away.

Dede slumped and I threw my arm around her shoulder. She leaned into me, garnering strength and support.

"As usual," I said to Jimmy, "your timing is impeccable."

"You just can't stay out of trouble when I leave you alone," he joked, trying to lighten the situation. Acknowledging the other woman, he added, "You must be Dede. I'm Jimmy. It's a pleasure to meet you," he said extending his hand. The floor boards creaked as he walked toward us.

Dede stood up straight and I released my hold. "Nice to meet you too," she said with more confidence. "And I second the motion—your timing is impeccable." Grasping his hand, she firmly shook it.

"Let's go back in the house," I said.

"Thank you, but I'm going to the hotel. If he followed me here, then he must know where we're staying and will probably be watching. I'll pack our things and change hotels."

"I have a better idea," Jimmy said. "Pack your things and come stay here in the guest room."

Beaming at my man, I nodded agreement.

"I don't want to put you out," she started to say. "With Cecily safe for today…"

Cutting her off, I jumped in, "You're not putting us out. No need to put yourself at further risk. Jimmy and I will go with you."

"Thank you, but I've been through this before. No need for

you to babysit me. Lionel will be so hot and bothered right now, that he'll go off and sulk. Probably find the nearest bar and throw a few down. That's his style. He swoops in and blusters but doesn't always follow through. I'll be fine, don't you worry." Despite the emotion of losing her granddaughter forever, she rose to the occasion.

"Good enough," said Jimmy. "So, I take it your granddaughter chose to take her first journey back?"

"Yes, she's there now," Dede replied.

"We have until 2:00 tomorrow afternoon," I added. "Dede, wait a minute please." Going back into the house, I ran to my office and grabbed a blank form. Returning to the porch, I handed it to the woman.

Looking at it she said, "Of course, the information sheet. I remember this before I went back."

"Fill it out as thoroughly as you can. This will speed things up when she returns tomorrow. We can get her credentials expedited. From the looks of the situation, the sooner the better."

"You're sure she'll take the final journey?" Jimmy asked.

"She will," both Dede and I answered in unison. This elicited a hearty laugh from all of us, more from a release of tension than humor.

Dede gave me a hug and said, "I'll be back tomorrow."

"See you then and be careful. If he shows up, please call me. Jimmy and I will be right there."

"I'll be okay. A pleasure to meet you, Jimmy."

"You too," he said.

Dede continued across the porch. Her steps on the boards made a much quieter whispering than the pounding Lionel's feet had. At the curb she got behind the wheel of a white Dodge Ram. It was quite a bit of truck for a woman of her stature, but she seemed to handle it like a pro as she maneuvered down the street.

"Do you think she'll be all right?" Jimmy asked me.

"From what I can tell, she's good at assessing a situation. If she thinks he'll leave her be for now, he will."

"All right then," he said as we walked into the house and back toward the kitchen. "Tell me about Cecily."

"She's very much like her grandmother. A spunky little thing, with an artistic flair. It's her grandfather's gift for painting that was passed on to her though. Her forte is cityscapes, which lends itself perfectly to New York City. Honey," I said as I began to pull things out of the refrigerator to prep dinner, "I believe we're about to complete our quota."

"Now don't get too hasty. Let's see what Cecily's thoughts are on the match, before we pop the champagne cork," he laughed.

"I know. But look at how perfectly it's all coming together. The process will be completed."

"Not totally," Jimmy said cautiously.

"What do you mean?" I put my ingredients on the counter and turned toward him. "We'll have finished all thirty."

"*Our* thirty," he said, putting a hand on the small of my back and pulling me close.

"Yes, and that's all we're responsible for," I said defensively. "It isn't our job to complete Paolo, Jr.'s matches." I placed my arms around his neck.

He tucked a stray lock of hair behind my ear and placed a hand on my check. "No, honey, it's not. But Grandfather did say we could assist."

"I still don't understand that. How do we get removed from the process, yet are expected to assist?"

"As usual, Grandfather's words are in need of deciphering. Best I can figure is that he wants us to place the slides with a couple that can handle the job."

"That appears to be what he hinted at. While we thought our selection was completely random, there's more to it. Either the Collector or Photographer, or both in our case, are related to one of the Four Families. There aren't any offspring to hand it off to though," I pointed out.

Kissing me on the cheek, he pulled away. "My thoughts exactly. It doesn't mean whoever gets to complete them *needs* to be of the right lineage. Look at April," he said, with a catch in his voice. At this he walked over to the table and sat down.

Gong to him I gently caressed his shoulder. "You have a point. While destined to be involved with the process, she came from an unrelated heritage."

"Yes, and the ability to make good matches showed in her compassion. Appropriate women still crossed her path, it's just she didn't have full access to the Suitors to make proper matches," he said, recovering from the moment of melancholy over his old friend. He placed his hand over mine.

"Do you think we should make one more trip back to speak with your grandfather or Francois?"

He mulled this over a minute before answering. "No. I got the feeling with the last visit that our time with them had finished. They were washing their hands of it all."

"Honestly, I did too." I kissed him on the forehead, then went back to the counter to continue putting together some stuffed peppers.

Jimmy got up and walked toward the hallway. "I'm going to change and do a little research online. There's a few ideas bouncing around my head that I want to follow up on."

I knew better than to push for details right now. When he began formulating things, I waited until he chose to share. "Okay," I said, "dinner will be ready at 5:00."

"Noted," he yelled as I heard him climb the stairs.

Chapter 51

The next day Jimmy thought it best to stick around for Cecily's return. He didn't want us to be alone in case Lionel came back. I got concerned when Dede didn't show up early as expected. Five minutes before arrival time, she still wasn't here.

Standing in my studio alone, I watched Cecily materialize. Her face absolutely beamed with joy, sporting an ear to ear grin. No question about it—Dede would be losing her granddaughter.

Her eyes focused on me. "Oh, Sami, I don't know how to thank you."

"No thanks needed. Good first date?" I said with a mischievous note.

"None can compare!" Her eyes scanned the room. "Where's Grandma?"

"Probably stuck in traffic. I'm sure she'll arrive soon." I hoped my concern didn't worm its way through my voice.

Putting her hands on her hips, she demanded, "What's happened?"

"You're not easily fooled, are you?"

"Not any more. Has something happened to Grandma?"

"I hope not." There was no reason to lie to this young woman. "Okay, Sami, spill."

It was as if I were talking to Dede. "Lionel showed up here."

"When?"

"Yesterday. Right after you left, Dede was heading out the front door."

"What happened?" she looked absolutely frightened by the widening of her eyes and the whitened pallor of her skin.

"We found Lionel on the porch. I don't know if he was waiting or about to ring the bell. He must have followed the two of you as he said he saw you come in here. Did you notice his truck when you went outside to get your clothes?"

"No. But I have to admit, I really didn't look around. I was so excited to meet Doug, that Lionel could have been standing in front of me and I wouldn't have noticed him."

"Speaking of Doug," trying to pull the conversation away from worry about her grandma, "what did you think?"

"What an amazing man for his time! While being a successful businessman, he was all about wanting a family. He couldn't wait to see my painting. The apartment he lives in is huge and looks out on Central Park," she started to babble. "He gave me a tour and told me the corner room, he currently uses for an office, could be my studio since it had great lighting."

I let her enjoy the moment. The young woman was lost in her own world and didn't need me to interject any thoughts.

Just as suddenly, her mood changed. "Have you called Grandma?"

Cecily's abruptness took me by surprise, yet I understood her worry after meeting Lionel. Despite Dede's confidence at his being harmless, it concerned me she wasn't here yet.

The doorbell rang and made us jump. We both hurried to the front door. Jimmy beat us to it.

As he opened the door, Dede came rushing in. "Is she back yet?"

"Grandma!" Cecily yelled and threw herself into the woman's arms.

"Oh, sweetie! How did it go?"

"Are you okay, Grandma? Sami told me Lionel showed up here yesterday."

"Sorry," I said. "I'm not a good liar, and she knew immediately something happened."

"That's my girl." Dede encompassed Cecily in a big hug. "I just got slowed down a bit—four slashed tires."

"Oh, Grandma…but…"

"Shush. It's fixed and I'm fine. Now tell me about Doug."

Damn, I thought, now that's a woman of strength and class. She doesn't let things drag her down for long. Once again, I wished Dede and I had more time to enjoy a friendship. Maybe now that she was *my age*, we could.

"Well," Cecily switched gears quickly, "I'm going to miss you something awful." That playful smile they both shared appeared.

"You liked him," Dede said.

"No, Grandma, I think I love him."

The two women stood there looking at each other for a moment. Then Dede reached into her purse and retrieved a paper. "I guess you'll be needing this," she said handing me the information sheet she'd filled out on her granddaughter.

"What's that?" asked Cecily.

"Your new life," I told her.

She tilted her head to one side with a puzzled look on her face. I handed her the sheet and then she understood. "What will you do with this?"

"We'll have credentials made that will slip you into the 1950's and Doug's life as seamlessly as possible," Jimmy said. Extending his hand, he added, "By the way, I'm Jimmy, Sami's Collector."

Cecily took the outstretched hand and warmly shook it. "A pleasure to meet you. What an interesting role you have."

"Yes, I truly enjoy it. It gives me the pleasure of interviewing the men we match with charming ladies such as yourself," he said.

"So, you've met Doug?" Cecily asked.

"Yes, though it's been some years. When Sami and I began this process thirty years ago, the first step was for me to meet all the men and provide as much information to my Photographer as I could. That enabled her to match appropriate Betrotheds, such as yourself."

"Wow, that's wonderful. You got to travel back to all those decades. What an amazing job! I envy you. Sami, did you get to journey through time also?"

"Yes. Not as much as Jimmy." Thoughts of my latest travels to retrieve Jimmy from Elba Island sent chills down my body. Most of my trips were not a pleasure. The journeys had more ominous connotations. Shaking it off, I knew there would be no more of those.

As we talked, I led the women into the living room where I'd set out a light lunch on the coffee table. "Please, sit down and help yourselves." I gestured to the couch. Picking up a steel carafe I offered, "Tea anyone?"

"I would love a cup," said Dede. "Earl Grey, of course?"

Nodding, I poured the brew into one of the cups. Its delicate aroma drifted through the room. "Now, enough about Jimmy and me. I believe your grandma is anxious to hear about *your* adventure."

Cecily recounted to Dede what she'd already shared with me. Wrapping up her comments, she added, "I'm sorry, Grandma, but we'll have to say good bye."

With misty eyes, Dede took it in stride. "It's the result I prayed for when I brought you here. You'll be terribly missed by all of us, but at least your Grandpa and I will know you're happy and living the life you deserve. How can that make us sad?"

"Oh, Grandma," Cecily said throwing her arms around Dede and giving a quick squeeze. Pulling back, she looked at me and asked, "So what's next?"

Jimmy had followed us into the living room as well. Sitting in the love seat at the end of the table, he remained quiet during our whole exchange. I noticed him intently watching Cecily, as if assessing her. That would have to be a private conversation for later.

He left me to field all of Cecily's questions. "The next step is to have your credentials made. We can have our friend, Daniel, rush them through. The earlier decades are a breeze to duplicate. He'll craft a brief, but believable background that's close to your current life. That makes it easier for you to remember if anyone should question how you came into Doug's life. As I told your grandma when she went back to Milton—less is more. Don't offer any more details than necessary. Pretty soon people will stop asking and just accept you as his wife."

"Wife," said Cecily, "I like the sound of that this time around." The bright smile on her face said everything.

"How soon can she go back?" asked Dede. While her voice remained steady, the creases in her brow gave away her concern.

"If we get the information over to our friend, Daniel, today,

I'd say by tomorrow morning, don't you think, Jimmy?"

"Yes, he should have them early tomorrow. I'll run the sheet over to Daniel's after lunch."

"Cecily, I laid your clothes out on the bed upstairs, if you'd like to change."

"Thank you. I'll do that now, so Grandma and I can get out of your hair," she said with a playful laugh. Standing up she walked out of the room. We could hear her light footsteps bouncing up the stairs.

"Okay, Dede," I started in immediately. "What really happened?"

"Like you, I'm a terrible liar," she said. "Lionel slipped into the hotel and came pounding on my door in the middle of the night."

"Did you change hotels?"

"No, I should have, but thought he would go off and sulk. He was definitely drunk, by the way he yelled, so I'm sure he spent the better part of yesterday afternoon and evening in a bar."

"You should've stayed here," I said.

"Then he would've been pounding on your door instead. No, it turned out okay. One of my neighbors must have called down to the front desk as security came up pretty quickly and hauled him away."

"Did they turn him over to the police?"

"No. After removing him from the hallway, one of the security guards came back up to the room to check on me. He said they offered him one chance to leave the premises and he took it. I don't know when he went to work on my tires, but that could've been earlier."

"The offer still stands for the two of you to stay here tonight," Jimmy offered.

"Thank you, but while I got my tires taken care of, I checked us out of the hotel. We'll stay at another one tonight. Once we leave here, I'll make sure he isn't following us, then high tail it over to the Hyatt in Redondo Beach. The security there is good, so he won't get past the front desk."

"You're talking about Lionel, aren't you?" Cecily stood in the doorway, back in her shorts and blue t-shirt she wore yesterday when they arrived.

"Yes. I'm not going to lie to you, sweetie."

"I appreciate that, Grandma. The sooner I exit this decade the better for all of us. I would hate for him to cause you any more harm."

"Oh, shush. I'll be fine. It's you I'm concerned about," Dede said standing up. "Thank you for lunch and everything else," she added turning my way.

Standing up to escort them out, we walked to the front door. I could hear the clink of the tea cups and lunch plates as Jimmy remained behind cleaning up the meal. As expected, Dede gave me a big hug at the front door, followed by Cecily holding me in a warm embrace as well.

Looking back toward the living room, the women must have noticed Jimmy hadn't followed us. Dede gave me another hug. "This one is for your man," she said. "What time should we return tomorrow?"

"I'd say we'll have everything together by 10:00 in the morning."

"Perfect," said Dede. "See you then!"

The two women looked cautiously outside before venturing through the door. I followed them as far as the porch, and thankfully the street remained vacant of Lionel's truck. As they drove away, I watched and hoped there wouldn't be any more attempts by Cecily's ex-husband to find her.

Back in the house, I made a bee-line for the kitchen, where I heard the faucet in the sink running. "Okay," I said, walking into the room and seeing Jimmy washing the dishes, "they're gone. Now, what's going through your head?"

He turned, and a sly grin spread across his face. "I haven't worked out all the details yet. Give me some time."

Chapter 52

The next morning Jimmy left early to retrieve Cecily's new credentials. Daniel understood the urgency of the situation and said they would be ready by 8:00. With the work traffic in full swing, I knew it would take Jimmy about an hour and a half to return.

Just before 9:00 I retrieved the blue-framed slide for Doug Pendry and the holder from my office. Closing the safe door, I used a little too much force and it slammed with an ominous finality that echoed through the room.

I carried the items to the small table at the end of my studio and depressed the button on the holder for the last time. This second trip back for Cecily, would be the completion of our quota. Its significance weighed heavily on me—more than I ever expected.

As anxious as Jimmy and I were to fulfill our obligation, I felt a tinge of sadness. It would be finished forever. Despite all the tragedy connected to this process, the thought of placing several couples successfully filled me with joy.

Hesitant to leave the studio just yet, I walked around the cushioned bench and sat down. Viewing all the portraits that lined the walls, I felt tears trickling down my cheeks. So much had happened over the last thirty years. Now here I sat, ready to complete our final match.

Wrenched out of my reverie by the front doorbell, time had slipped away quicker than I realized. Giving my face a quick swipe with both hands to dry the moisture, I ran for the entryway, anxious to greet Dede and Cecily.

Swinging the door open, my happiness turned to horror. Lionel shoved me out of the way, knocking me to the ground. Stunned by the blow, I sat there a moment as he stepped over my body into the house.

"Cecily," he yelled. "Where the hell are you?" Without waiting for an answer, he ran into the living room. His footsteps could be heard stomping their way to the kitchen.

Regaining my senses, I pushed myself up off the floor and tried to remember where I left my phone. I had it in my hand while getting coffee earlier. It must still be on the counter.

As I ran for the kitchen, Lionel came out the door.

"Where is she, old woman?"

I cringed and braced myself for another blow as his body came full force at me. Instead he stopped and brought his face close to mine. "I know she's here. Tell me where she is before I get angry." His voice seethed with sheer malice.

I stood firm and said, "She isn't here. I told you that yesterday. Get out of my house!"

Pushing me aside as he went past, I slammed into the wall. My elbow took the brunt of it with my shoulder following. A piercing pain raced up my arm. Somehow, I stayed on my feet. Holding my sore elbow, I continued into the kitchen. My phone sat on the counter. I swiped it up and hit the speed dial for Jimmy.

His phone rang several times. *Pick up* I mentally transmitted. Thundering footsteps barreled down the stairs. As I was about to dash to the dining room, Lionel came in and snatched the phone from my hand.

"Who are you calling, old woman? Trying to warn that meddling grandmother of hers?"

Jimmy yelled my name through the phone, just before Lionel threw it across the room. It smashed against the wall with a crackle of breaking glass. Dragging me by my uninjured arm, he pulled me into the hallway.

"Lionel, let her go!" Cecily screeched from the open doorway.

Once again, he shoved me into the wall, as if discarding my

usefulness. He took a step toward her.

"Stop right there!" Dede stood beside her granddaughter with a .38 Special in her hand. The hammer was cocked and ready to fire. "You know I'll use this, you son-of-a-bitch, so don't test me." Her stance was rock solid. Even I believed she would lay him dead where he stood if he didn't obey her commands.

"Don't play with me, foolish woman," Lionel said to Dede, taking a step toward her. "I know you won't shoot."

The gun went off and now it was Lionel's turn to hold an injured arm. From the hole in the wall behind him, I knew he'd only been grazed.

"Need any more *proof?*" Dede's hand never wavered as she cocked the gun for a second shot. Shifting her eyes my way she added, "Sorry, Sami, I'll pay for the damage."

Blood seeped out between the fingers Lionel clasped on his arm. His eyes were wide and face a bit pale. "You'll pay for this too," he said to Dede.

"I don't think so, Lionel. With a witness saying you broke into her house, and the bruises I see forming on Sami's arm, I'd say it would be ruled self-defense. Don't turn this into a situation where they'll need a coroner instead of an ambulance."

As Dede talked, I quietly edged along the wall until I stood beside the two women. Recovering my voice, I said, "Don't worry about the mess, Dede, that can be easily cleaned." Turning to look at my abuser, he appeared to grasp the situation by the way his face struggled for composure. The color had returned, but his eyes were still wide.

"Why can't you just leave me alone," Cecily said. "Our marriage and life together is over."

"No. You belong to me. You always will."

"You never understood," she continued quietly, "I'm not a possession. You don't *own* me."

"I love you, Cecily."

"That's not love, Lionel."

"Sami," Dede cut in, "is it time?"

I looked down at the watch strapped to my wrist. The timer would have reached full power five minutes ago. "Yes, but Jimmy isn't back yet with her...," I hesitated, not wanting to say too much in front of her ex-son-in-law. "He's not back from Daniel's."

"That can't be helped. My baby is resourceful," Dede said, still aiming the gun firmly at her target, "they'll have to make due."

"Grandma, not like this. We should wait." Cecily's eyes began to tear up.

"It'll be alright. I don't like long good-byes anyway."

"Cecily, what is she talking about? Where are you going?" Lionel demanded.

The young woman turned toward her grandmother. Wiping away tears, she put on a brave smile. "I know, Grandma. I love you very much."

"Then make me proud and be happy," Dede gave a quick smile and glance before shifting her gaze back toward Lionel.

Wrapping her arms around the older woman's waist, Cecily gave a firm squeeze. Dede wrapped her free arm around her granddaughter and returned the hug.

"Now go, sweetie. It's time."

Pulling back, Cecily gave her a quick kiss on the cheek and I heard her whisper one more time, "I love you, Grandma." Looking past Dede to me, she said, "I'm ready, Sami."

Noticing Cecily carried the same bag as yesterday containing her period clothes, she also had a small back pack. I assumed it contained the few possessions she chose to take with her.

"Go ahead into the studio. I'll give you a few minutes to prepare," I said nodding toward the bag of clothing.

"All right." Going toward the open doorway, she went through without a second glance at Lionel, closing the door behind her.

"Cecily!" Lionel yelled taking a step toward the studio.

"Stop there," Dede said, with enough force to get his attention.

He halted but continued to yell. "Cecily, what are you doing? You get back out here." Not getting the result he expected, he called again louder. "Cecily. Cecily! If you know what's good for you, you'll get out here now. Cecily!!"

It was almost comical watching this man get flustered as his face reddened with anger. I could tell he wasn't used to being denied anything he demanded.

"Ok, Sami, go do your thing," Dede said after a couple minutes. "I'll just babysit out here until it's done."

Lionel snapped his head back in our direction as he seethed,

"You'll pay for this, old woman. Both of you."

"Oh, I don't think so," Dede remained calm and in charge. "Go on, Sami. Lock the door behind you, please. Just in case."

I nodded and walked behind Dede so as not to block her line of sight. At the studio door I opened it just enough to slip inside then closed and locked it. Cecily stood in front of her grandparents' portrait, already dressed in her 1950's garb and her backpack slung over one shoulder. She didn't turn around when I entered.

"It's time, dear," I said.

Answering me while still looking at the picture, she said, "I'm ready." With that she turned around with a sweet smile across her face. "I just wanted to burn that picture into my memory. They look so happy together, as I'm sure Doug and I will be in our life as husband and wife."

"Yes, I believe you will," I said with confidence. "I'm sorry Jimmy isn't back in time with your credentials."

"No worries, Sami. Like Grandma said, we'll make due. Now I believe it's my turn to travel." Walking over to the cushioned bench, she waited for me to join her.

Before stepping behind Cecily to depress the button, I gave her one last tight squeeze. "This is from your grandma," I whispered into her ear. "And me," I added, "be happy."

I felt her nod against my shoulder as she returned the hug. We released, and she took her seat. Stepping around the bench to the table, I activated the 30-second timer, then retreated to my spot behind the camera.

We waited in silence. With a burst of light from behind the young woman, the bench was empty. To my surprise, the fireworks weren't over. A second burst of light from the holder blinded me for a moment. When I could see clearly again, the used slide lay flat on the table amongst a scattering of ashes. The holder had incinerated.

Holding my breath, for fear something had gone wrong, I swung my gaze over to Doug's portrait. Letting out a sigh of relief, it now contained an image of both Cecily and Doug holding hands and staring into each other's eyes.

A shot rang out in the hallway. Barely a moment later, someone banged on the door and rattled the knob.

Chapter 53

"Open this door!" Yelled Lionel. "Open the door, you damn bitch."

I heard scuffling in the hallway. The noise stopped, then I heard a renewed assault on the door. With a splintering of wood, it was forced open as Lionel fell to the carpet, the latch torn from the frame.

Jumping up he said, "Cecily, now you…" He stopped dead in his tracks as he looked around the room. "Where is she? I saw her come in here." Spinning around, he took in the long studio with confusion on his wrinkled brow. "Where's the other door?"

Worry for Dede concerned me, until I saw both her and Jimmy standing in the doorway. The gun remained in Dede's hand, which hung down by her side. With her granddaughter gone, there was no more threat.

"What are you talking about, Lionel, Cecily isn't here," Dede said calmly.

Looking in her direction, he said, "What are *you* talking about. I saw her come into this room."

"You're crazy. I'm here visiting my friend, Sami. Cecily is in Europe."

"Don't even try that, old woman. I watched her go through that door," he said pointing at the shredded entry.

"Well," Dede continued, with so much composure she could have been an actress, "do you see her now? There's only one door into here and no windows. So, unless Cecily just," she hesitated, giving me a sly grin, "*vanished* into thin air, she's not here."

Lionel continued turning around looking at every corner of the room. Spying the newly formed couple in the portrait, he ran over to their picture. Pointing at it he said, "She was here at some point. How else could you have her picture. Who is that man?"

Taking up the pretense, I asked, "Don't they make a cute couple?"

Glaring at me with narrowed eyes, he took a step in my direction.

"I don't think so," Jimmy said. "It's time for you to leave. Your *ex*-wife isn't here. Go now and I won't call the police and have you arrested for trespassing."

"Prove it," Lionel said menacingly.

"That broken door is proof enough. Now do you need an escort, or will you go quietly?"

Lionel's hands balled up into fists, then relaxed. Taking one more look around the room, he stormed out of the studio. Moving toward the doorway myself, I saw him leave. Footsteps echoed across the boards on the porch as he stomped away like a spoiled child having a tantrum.

"Sami, Jimmy, I can't tell you how sorry I am about all this…and how eternally grateful both Milton and I are," she said throwing her arms around me.

"You're most welcome. Can you put the gun away now?"

She released me as we all laughed. "Sorry, almost forgot I still had it out. About the bullet hole, well, now there's two…"

"Not another word about it," Jimmy chimed in. "Besides, I feel responsible for the second one as I startled you."

"Is that what spurred Lionel to action?" I asked.

"Yes. I got distracted and he lunged. The gun went off and I was knocked off balance. Your man here, caught me from going over."

"What do you think he'll do now?" I asked her.

"Honestly, I'm not sure. What could he possibly say? He saw Cecily go into a locked room and never come out?" She grinned.

"People will think he's crazy," Jimmy said, "which doesn't

appear to be far from the truth."

Dede slipped the gun back into her purse, and walked over to her granddaughter's portrait. She looked up at the couple. "See how happy they are?"

"Yes, their match is a success, like yours," I added walking up behind her.

Without turning around, Dede said, "I just want to burn this image into my memory."

Taken aback, I told her, "That's exactly what Cecily said as she gazed at yours and Milton's portrait."

"She's always been my favorite," she said turning to me. "Don't get me wrong, I love all my children and grandchildren. But there was always something special about Cecily that set her apart."

"Maybe because you saw so much of yourself in her?"

"I'd have to agree. I'm almost a bit jealous that she's just beginning her time with Doug. Which reminds me—it's time I get back to my wonderful man in New Mexico."

"You're welcome to stay the night."

"Yes," Jimmy added, "we have plenty of room."

"Thank you both, but it's time I take my leave. You two have gone over the top to keep my Cecily safe. It's time you get back to focusing on your own lives. Besides, you've got a wedding to plan!"

"We do," I said as we walked toward the still open front door. "You're sure Lionel won't bother you?"

"Oh, he'll be back. We'll still hear from him in Albuquerque, but I don't think he'll come around here anymore. He'll assume she went home to be with her parents. Probably watch their house for a while."

"That's creepy," I said with a shiver running down my back. It made me think of how Carney watched our house from his tower on the hill.

"He'll give up eventually when he sees he's been beaten. Probably even believe the whole gone off to Europe story," Dede said. "I better hit the road. It's a twelve-hour drive."

"You aren't driving straight through, are you?" We could hear the concern in Jimmy's voice.

"Not to worry," she said. "I'll get in a good five or six hours, then stop for the night."

"It's been so good to see you," I said, embracing the woman.

"Maybe we could see one another again?"

"You and Milton just may get a wedding invite one of these days," I said. "How would that be?"

"We'd love it. You could meet Milton too!" I heard the excitement in her voice. She turned to Jimmy and gave him a warm hug as well. "Now you take care of this special lady."

"I always do," Jimmy said, glancing my way. "Safe travels home. Let us know when you get there."

"Thank you, will do. Well, I hate long good-byes, and this one has gotten quite lengthy. So I'm off." She strode across the porch with a little bounce in her step. I knew a giant weight had been lifted off her shoulders by getting Cecily to a safe and happy life away from Lionel.

Throwing my arms around Jimmy's neck, I planted a firm kiss on his lips. "I want to show you something."

Leading him back into the studio, I took him to the far end behind the cushioned bench. "Look," I said, pointing to the pile of ashes.

"What's that?"

"The frame holder. It incinerated after Cecily's final journey."

"The process knew it was our thirtieth match," Jimmy said.

"Yes. I guess that's what happens after the quota has been met. Now what? Are we finally done?" I asked him.

"I believe we have one more chore to attend to before we call it quits," he said with a mischievous grin.

"Should I be frightened or elated over this last *chore*?"

"You can decide for yourself. Part of it took place on my errand this morning. I added an extra stop on my way back from Daniel's."

Squinting my eyes and turning my head sideways, I knew he was dragging this out just to tease me. "Don't make me guess. What's going on?"

"Wait. I left them in the car."

"What did you leave in the car?"

Jimmy went out the front door and I followed him as far as the porch. The fresh scent of ocean air surrounded me. I took a seat on the nearest wicker chair. It whispered the familiar sound of crackling twigs.

Jimmy returned from his car in the driveway carrying a wooden box. I knew it could only be from one person. "You went to Paolo's," I said. "Those are Junior's slides, aren't they?"

"Yes," he said. "I have an idea what to do with these final thirty matches."

Chapter 54

Jimmy sat the box on the table between our chairs. Neither of us spoke. Noises from the surrounding community filled the air. Waves crashed on the beach below. The screeching of seagulls blended with the squealing of children playing.

Not able to stand the suspense anymore, I broke the silence. "You hinted at this, as well as your grandfather. Something about helping to complete this task, but not actually doing it ourselves."

"Yes. We place the slides with another couple willing to continue the process."

His solution was simple, yet brilliant. "Do you have anyone in mind?"

"Our thirtieth match."

I thought about this a moment. They'd be perfect! At least Cecily would as a Photographer. I didn't know Doug, but Jimmy had met him during the initial interview of his becoming a Suitor. "I know Cecily would dive in with both feet."

"Doug was very intuitive," he said. "I believe he'd be the perfect match in this process."

"Paolo said his son completed all the interviews. That means all the Collector's slides are spent. They'd have to depend on Junior's biographies of the Suitors. Do you think it's possible for them to make good matches simply based on someone else's notes?"

"There you go making sense again," he said with a light chuckle.

"Well, we can't just set them adrift. Maybe we should sift through the bios before making a final decision."

"You're right, sweetie. Maybe it's a good thing Lionel crashed the party. I was ready to hand this box over to Cecily along with her credentials."

"The process always interjects itself, doesn't it? There's more than simple magic at work here. Perhaps destiny?" I said, resting a hand on the rough wooden box.

"I don't know," Jimmy said, "but it seems to happen that way. Let's take this stuff into the house and sort through what we have." Wrapping his arms around the slides, he hoisted them off the table.

"Do you think we should tell Dede what we're up too? She knows her granddaughter better than anyone."

"No," he said. "It needs to be up to Cecily and Doug. No outside influence."

"I guess you're right, honey."

With that I stood and walked to the front door. Holding it open, Jimmy preceded me into the house carrying the slides and info sheets. I followed him down the hall to the kitchen, where he placed his load on the table.

"Coffee?" I asked.

"Love some," he said, pulling the bios out of the back of the box.

We spent the next few hours poring over the information sheets compiled by a young man long dead. I could tell by Jimmy's demeanor he was torn over this process. "It still bothers you that April was supposed to be the Photographer for all these matches, doesn't it?"

"How could you know?" His eyes were wide with surprise.

"Seriously? After thirty years, there isn't much I don't know about you." I reached over and stroked his cheek.

"You're not jealous, are you?" He grasped my hand.

"What?"

"It's just, well, you know April and I were very close. On some level, I did love her."

"Yes," I said, returning the squeeze on his hand, "I could tell."

"We truly were just friends. I loved her, but not in a romantic way. I always sensed there would be someone else. Then I met you," he said gazing into my eyes.

"For the second time," I smiled.

"Well, you were pretty hot when you walked into Grandfather's shop," he said bursting into a hearty laugh. "Honestly, when I met you a couple years later and realized you were the older woman that came into the Jade Pagoda, I was excited. Even then I felt drawn to you."

We stopped to enjoy the silent understanding between us. "So," I said after a few moments, "have you noticed how all the Suitors reside in years prior to the 1950's?"

"Yes, I have," Jimmy said. "This is the right thing to do."

"How does this happen?"

"I don't know. Look at the story Francois and Grandfather told us about how they were pulled into the process originally. There isn't any logical explanation to any of this. You just accept it or walk away. From the lives we've led, I'd say you accepted it quite well," he smirked.

"What did Paolo think about us placing the slides with our final match?"

"He was grateful. After we turned him down the first time he asked, Paolo feared they would never be completed. With no heirs left, he had no other options."

"Well," I said, "neither Cecily nor Doug are descendants."

"Yes, but they're not naïve to the process. With first-hand experience in time traveling, at least on Cecily's part, and being matched up, they have an insight some descendants don't have to draw from."

"Doug won't have the opportunity to journey through time unless the emergency slides are needed. I'm sure Cecily can fill him in on what it's like." As we spoke, I gathered up the bios and tucked them back into the box. "The only decision now is, when do you think we should take this to them?"

Jimmy's chair creaked a bit as he leaned back looking pensive. "It's best to give them time to get to know each other. If we show up too soon after their meeting, they may be a bit apprehensive taking this on right away."

Standing up, my chair scraped gently across the tiles. I walked over to the window, placing my hands on the counter as I leaned closer to the glass panes. It wouldn't be fair to interrupt their intimacy too soon. "Why don't we set the Family Slide for one year after their meeting? Besides, even if they agree to take this on, it doesn't have to start immediately."

"Yes and no," Jimmy said.

Turning to face him, I tipped my head a bit sideways. "What do you mean?"

"Well, you know how the process won't be denied. If they take it on, there's no knowing when the first Betrothed will come across their path. There isn't any planning on the part of the Photographer and the Collector. It just happens. Look at the matches we made?"

"Our matches?"

"Yes. While the first ten took almost fifteen years, the rest happened rather quickly—especially the last five."

Leaning back against the counter, I thought about what Jimmy was saying. It rang true. Even when I thought about abandoning the process, Betrotheds still managed to find me. "You're right," I said. "I think a year is enough. If they're willing to take this on, we'll have our answer. Let's get a good night's sleep and plan to go tomorrow."

"Agreed. Now, are you hungry?"

"Famished," I realized.

"Good. Let's head over to Redondo Beach to our favorite little hideaway for some clam chowder and local crab. What do you say?"

"I'm in!"

"Good. I'll lock these in the safe and we can head out."

"Works for me," I said, grabbing our coffee cups and setting them in the sink. "I could use an afternoon off."

"Me too," Jimmy said as he carried the slides out to the hallway.

Walking toward the front door, I veered off into my studio. Hard to believe we were finally done. A bit of melancholy took me. As anxious as I had been to complete our quota, I knew the process would be sorely missed. The joy all the women expressed over the men we introduced them to was overwhelming. It helped to blot out those that weren't able to complete happy unions.

I felt a pair of strong arms slide around my waist, pulling me in close. Lips brushed my neck. A voice whispered in my ear, "You didn't think I'd just give up and go away, did you bitch?"

Chapter 55

"Where's my wife?" The voice in my ear took on a harsh tone.

I struggled against the arms gripping me, but they wouldn't loosen. Doing the only thing I could think of, I slammed my head backward into his face. My assaulter's surprise was enough to stun him. He released me, and I stumbled forward, catching my balance before going all the way to the floor. Spinning around I saw Lionel holding the bridge of his nose.

Glaring at me, he repeated his menacing query, "Where...is...my...wife?" He spoke as if out of breath from the unexpected blow. I'm sure he wasn't prepared for me to fight back.

Movement by the door caught my eye. Too late to mask my gasp of surprise, Lionel looked behind him and saw Jimmy coming through the door. With his hand on the side of his head, I could see blood trickling through his fingers. Lionel must have attacked him first, thinking he'd be out of the way.

"Jimmy," I called. "Are you all right?"

"I'm fine," he assured me. "Stay back."

"You're tougher than you look, old man. That blow should have put you out for a while, yet here you are."

"Your *ex*-wife isn't here. It's time you accepted that and moved on," Jimmy said.

"I know you're hiding her. She's mine, and I deserve to know where she is. Tell me or *your* wife will not escape this room without injury."

Backing away while Lionel's focus was on Jimmy, I got over to the table behind the Betrotheds' bench. Grabbing a vase from its perch on the surface, I sidled back toward the man, hiding it with my body. Catching the movement, he looked my way.

"What are you up to?"

"Lionel," I said trying to reason with him while raising my free hand for a distraction, "Cecily isn't here. I guarantee, she isn't even in California."

"Then where is she?" he yelled.

"Like Dede said, she's gone abroad. She only stopped here briefly before leaving."

"That meddling woman will get hers. Don't you worry," he said with a manic gleam in his eyes. "First I will find my wife. Now, where is she?" He accented this with a wave of the pistol he retrieved from his pocket.

"Lionel," I said, continuing to wave my free hand as if in surrender, "there's no reason for violence. I understand you love Cecily, but she's moved on. Believe me, we can't help you."

"You're lying," he said. "Stay where you are!" With this he whipped around to aim the weapon at Jimmy, who had inched closer.

"Tell me, Lionel, what would you do if you found her? It's obvious she doesn't want to be with you anymore. Do you really think you can force her to love you?" Jimmy asked.

"What do you mean force? Cecily loves me. She stood up in front of our families and God and said so."

"Lionel," I chimed in, hoping the peppering from both Jimmy and I might throw him off balance, "she doesn't love you anymore. Why can't you move on?"

"Move on? I promised to love and cherish her until death do us part. And so did she!"

"Sometimes," I said, in a calm voice, "that doesn't always remain the same. Things change. People change. She wasn't the right match for you." I didn't know if I was getting through to him, but I had to keep talking as he seemed to physically relax. His grip on the gun loosened. Lionel may not see reason, but I needed to keep him from firing. That was my whole focus right now.

Jimmy picked up on my line of thought. "Lionel, speaking

man to man, you can't *own* the woman you love. She must come to you freely, not forcibly."

"She came to me freely. I asked for her hand in marriage and she jumped at the chance to be my wife." He looked from me to Jimmy. The constant switching of focus started making me nervous. Maybe coming at him from both sides wasn't a good idea. He might panic at being surrounded and start shooting. We had to find a way to diffuse the situation so we all survived.

As if reading my mind about being attacked, Lionel said, "Stop trying to confuse me. You," he said pointing the gun at Jimmy, "go sit on that couch." He motioned toward the far side of the room.

Jimmy complied and walked over to the couch. Slowly he sank down onto the cushions.

"Now you," he said aiming in my direction. "Go sit next to him. I want both of you in full view."

I slowly moved toward Jimmy while hiding the vase behind me. Hoping he didn't notice, we might be able to use it as a weapon, or at least a distraction. I was wrong.

"And drop that vase. Don't think I didn't see you holding it, old woman."

Freezing at having been found out, I wasn't sure what to do. "Drop it!"

With that I simply released the vase and it slipped to the floor with a dull thud. I expected there to be pieces scattered over the carpet about my feet, but it remained intact.

As I eased down to a perch on the edge of the cushions, Jimmy put his arm around me. Pulling me close, he kissed my cheek and whispered, "Stall."

Turning to look at him, his eyes widened for a second, then he turned back toward Lionel. "Now what?"

Lionel narrowed his eyes and said, "We're going to stay here until you tell me exactly where my wife is."

Both Jimmy and I were silent for a moment. I wasn't sure exactly what Jimmy had in mind, but whatever it was, we needed time. If my guess was right, we needed to keep him occupied for another forty minutes or so. Unless he had simply called the police, in which case I expected to hear sirens any moment.

"Dede told you," I said, "she went abroad."

"What do you mean, abroad? I saw her go into this room. You're hiding her in this house."

"No," I continued calmly, "we aren't."

"That's impossible! I saw her go into this room. No matter how many times you tell me otherwise, I know she's around here somewhere. Show me the secret passageway she used to get out of here. All these old houses have hidden doorways."

"Lionel, the only way in and out of this room is through that door," I pointed. "I've lived in this house for thirty years. I assure you, there are no hidden passageways."

Lionel looked toward the only entry. Next, he scanned the room with narrowed eyes.

"You're lying!" His hand wavered with anger as he continued to point the gun in our direction.

"Okay, we lied," Jimmy said.

"I knew it! Where is she?"

"We made her disappear."

This answer made him shake his head in confusion. "Come again, old man?"

"You heard me."

"Say it again."

"All right," Jimmy said. "We made her disappear. We sent her to another place and time."

I turned toward him, my face taut with fear. While I didn't say a word, I'm sure Jimmy understood my meaning—*what are you doing?* My wide eyes conveyed the question.

Barely visible, Jimmy shook his head once.

"You're talking nonsense, old man."

"Am I? Are you really that sure she escaped from a locked room? Look around. Do you see any other doors or windows?"

Lionel panned the area with glassy paranoia in his eyes. It appeared he started to doubt what he knew to be true. Cecily had entered this room, and not come out.

"How could you have sent her to another time and place? That's impossible."

"Is it?" Jimmy toyed with him, a slight grin spreading across his face.

It scared me he was revealing the process to this lunatic. There had to be a plan formulating in my man's head allowing him such

281

liberties. I wish I knew what he intended.

"Take a look around this room," Jimmy continued. "What do you see?"

"You're trying to trick me," Lionel said.

"Why would we do that? You obviously love Cecily and want the best for her."

"Of course, I do. The best life she can have is with me. Why won't you tell me where she is?"

"I would rather show you," Jimmy said.

I looked intently at Jimmy. He was about to endanger Cecily and Doug. Why would he do that? Surely not to save our lives. Ours weren't worth any more than our Suitor and Betrothed's.

Jimmy saw the scared look on my face as he glanced my way and gave me a wink.

This helped me believe he had a plan that would work. I had to trust him to get us both out of this safely.

Chapter 56

"Allow me to give you a tour of our studio," Jimmy offered.

"Why would I do that?" Lionel squinted.

"Because it will help you understand what happens here…in this room."

"You're trying to confuse me. There's nothing special that goes on here. All I know is you're keeping Cecily from me."

"Lionel," I said, keeping my voice calm, "give us a chance to explain. You're a smart man. Cecily wouldn't have fallen in love with you otherwise." Flattery seemed the only thing he responded to favorably. From his arrogant actions, I could tell his ego was too great to accept anything less.

"All right, but don't try anything or one of you gets shot," he waved the gun again. "I don't need both of you to tell me where she's hiding."

"Yes," Jimmy said, "we understand. Now, will you let me show you our studio?"

"Fine. Show me."

"May I get up? I can't do it from here."

Lionel took a few steps backward. I'm sure it wasn't in fear. He surveilled the area around Jimmy and me, taking in the whole scene.

"Okay, but no sudden movements."

Jimmy stood up while applying a bit of pressure on my

shoulder with his hand. The gesture told me to stay seated. Lionel wouldn't hear of it.

"Oh no, you stick together. I see what you're trying to do, and it won't work," Lionel said. "Get moving—both of you!"

Jimmy nodded his head in my direction and I rose. Wrapping his arm around my waist, he held me close while walking over to the row of portraits on the far wall. "Let's start over here," he gestured towards the first portrait.

Lionel stood firm until we walked past him and came to a halt in front of the picture of Judy and Willis—the first couple we matched. Willis sported a blue t-shirt and white dress pants. Judy wore a red polka dot dress with matching sandals. They stood hand in hand on a dock in front of a large sail boat.

"Lionel, let me introduce you to Judy and Willis. They were our first."

Lionel scowled at him. "What do you mean, your *first*?"

"They were the very first couple Sami and I brought together. That was thirty years ago."

"Brought together? You're talking gibberish. Exactly what did you do for those people in the portrait?"

"We introduced them to each other," Jimmy said.

"So, they took a picture together. Big deal. You match up people to have their photo shoots together?"

"Not exactly, Lionel," I said. "You see, we're matchmakers. Every one of these portraits are of people that we've introduced to each other. All of them chose to stay together, get married, and share a life."

"Sounds like a glorified escort agency to me. Are all these women whores?" Lionel asked, as he looked around the room. His gaze stopped on the portrait of Cecily and Doug.

I could only see the profile of his face, but the expression changed and hardened. With his jaw firmly set, he turned back to us and said, "Are you trying to tell me Cecily is involved in an affair with *that* man?" He used his gun to point at the picture and accentuate his question.

"What do you think?" Jimmy asked.

He hesitated, then chose not to answer. Instead he asked, "Why are they all dressed funny in the portraits. Those aren't normal clothes. They must be costumes."

"Ah, you really are a bright one," Jimmy played up to him. "You see, for the men, those aren't costumes. Those are the clothes for their...era."

I cringed. It was only a matter of time before Lionel realized Jimmy was really talking down to him.

"Old man, if you don't get to your point soon, I may lose my patience. Speak plainly!"

"Okay, okay. What I mean is, all those men are dressed for the period they live in. The women have been sent *back* to be with them."

Lionel's face began to redden in frustration.

Jimmy held up his hand in a gesture for him to calm down. "The short version, Lionel, is that we send women back in time to meet the man of their dreams." He let that sink in for a few moments.

"You're joking. That's impossible."

"Is it? What makes you so sure?"

"For one thing, Cecily wouldn't do that. She loves me and wouldn't leave me."

I clutched at Jimmy's arm, afraid Lionel would get tired of this and become violent.

"Cecily chose the life she wanted. It's the life she felt drawn too. Maybe...," Jimmy hesitated, "just maybe, we could help you too?"

"Help me? Help me do what? All I want is my Cecily. Can you help me do that?"

"Maybe we can."

Jimmy couldn't possibly be thinking of sending Lionel back to the 1950's where Cecily now lived. He looked my way and gestured with his hand for me to calm down. In a quick motion, he glanced at his watch, then mouthed the words, "Ten minutes."

There was no doubt in my mind he had activated the Family Slide. Where would he send Lionel, if the chance presented itself?

Slowly Jimmy walked to the next picture. "Now here's Madge and Jerome. Don't they look happy?" He stood in front of a couple both dressed in bell-bottomed jeans and tie-dyed t-shirts. The era was distinct. These two resided in the early 1970's.

"Enough of this! Tell me about the man in the picture with Cecily. Who is he?"

There was no distracting this angry young man. He had a singular purpose in mind. Lionel wanted his ex-wife back and would not be deterred from that goal. We needed to do something soon or we would all lose. It was time for Jimmy to put the final step of his plan in action. I hoped it would be a location far from Cecily and Doug.

"Lionel, think about what I've been telling you. What does it suggest?"

"It suggests you're crazy!"

"Is that all you've gotten out of this tour? You can do better. Think about it. Dig deeper. What have I been saying?"

Lionel glared at Jimmy, with pure hatred. I wasn't sure he was capable of any serious thought, given the anger simmering inside. The reddening of his face told me he was trying desperately to hold it together until we gave him the information he craved.

"Tell me, Lionel, what am I really saying about these couples?"

The young man stood there looking intent. His response surprised the hell out of me.

"Send me back to her." He whispered, but I heard it clearly.

Jimmy took a deep breath—his sales pitch worked. Now what?

"I need a couple tools from the office down the hall. May I get them?"

"We'll all go. I want both of you in my sight."

As Jimmy turned toward the door with his arm still around me, Lionel added, "Uh uh, she's with me."

We both turned to look at him, and he waggled the gun at me in a come here motion. Looking into Jimmy's eyes, he gave my waist a reassuring squeeze, then released me.

Stepping toward Lionel, he grabbed my sore arm and nudged the gun into my side. "You know how this plays out if you try anything."

I winced with pain at the pressure on my bruise.

"No need for violence, young man. I'll send you back to Cecily. How you two decide to work things out, is a personal matter."

Lionel nodded as we all walked into the hallway toward the office, with Jimmy in the lead. Once there I saw the Family Slide sitting on the desk. The indicator light showed it had reached full power. I couldn't see all the settings Jimmy selected, but hoped it was somewhere far away from New York City in the year 1952. Looking closer, I saw it did say New York City. Fear washed over me thinking Jimmy was giving up Cecily to save me. That wasn't an acceptable trade off.

"We need to take this back into the studio for it to work properly," Jimmy said picking up the slide.

"What do you mean it needs to be *there* to work properly?" Lionel's agitation increased.

"Hear me out. You sit on the bench, and I place this device behind you. Once I press that button," he said, pointing at the slide, "it counts down from 30 seconds. When the flash goes off, you'll be transported to New York City in the year 1952. The exact time and place Cecily travelled to. Do you understand?"

Lionel took a deep breath and set his jaw. I wasn't sure if he bought all this or was deciding what to do once he arrived in 1952.

I opened my mouth to speak, but Jimmy shook his head. It was a subtle expression with barely any movement involved, but I understood and kept quiet. We needed Lionel to absorb all this and believe it.

Holding my breath, I waited for him to agree.

Chapter 57

Lionel kept the gun tucked up against my rib cage. The tension grew until I was ready to scream. Someone needed to say something.

"Okay, move," Lionel said. "Bring that thing into the studio."

Jimmy picked up the Family Slide and walked back into the hallway ahead of us. Lionel and I followed a few steps behind. Not stopping at the door, Jimmy went to the end of the room and placed the device on the table behind the bench.

"What now?" Lionel demanded.

"You sit on the bench," Jimmy said, "by yourself."

Lionel narrowed his eyes. I figured he contemplated the odds of what Jimmy told him being true. Hopefully he believed and would agree to sit alone on the bench. It still scared me we were sending him back to the same time and place as Cecily. It didn't seem fair, so I hoped Jimmy had more up his sleeve.

Releasing his grip, Lionel shoved me away. Slowly sitting on the bench facing the device, he waved the gun at Jimmy. Holding my bruised arm, I backed away, out of his direct line of sight. Trusting in Jimmy's plan, I kept silent.

"Now what?" Lionel demanded.

"Just sit there. I'll press this button, and in 30 seconds there will be a flash and you'll go back in time."

With narrowed eyes and a furrowed brow, he asked, "How

will I bring her back here?"

"Ah, I see your concern," Jimmy said. "I've set the timer for 24 hours. When that time span is up, you will both hold hands, and travel back together. Mind you, the timing is exact, so keep track."

Nodding his head, Lionel sat there looking intently at the slide. "How do I know you've set it properly?"

"It's obvious you and Cecily have true love. We're matchmakers—there's no reason for us to stand in your way any longer. You've proven your love for her. I commend you!"

Lionel grinned from ear to ear, as if he'd just won the Nobel prize. "She deserves a man like me. I'm glad you see it my way."

His smugness continued to make me nervous. We weren't out of danger yet. Lionel still held a loaded gun aimed at Jimmy.

He broke out of his complacency. "What are you waiting for old man, press the button!"

Jimmy reached over to press the button, then backed away. He aligned himself between me and Lionel, as if trying to shield me from Lionel's view.

Finally, his viciousness surfaced. "Sorry, but I can't take the chance you'll try something once I return with my Cecily." Lionel raised the gun and took aim at Jimmy.

The flash went off before he could pull the trigger. The bench was empty.

"How did it go off so fast? And how could you send him to New York City. Cecily deserved a chance. Jimmy, how could you?" With my voice getting out of control, I moved to his side.

"Sweetie, would I really put others at risk?" Jimmy asked with a sly grin, as he pulled me close. "Especially you?"

I opened my mouth to respond. Then closed it again, with an exasperated gasp. Of course, there was more to this. It embarrassed me to think I doubted him.

Wrapping my arms around his waist, I nuzzled my face into his shoulder and let out a quiet sob. The pressure had taken its toll on me. Remembering the location, I pulled back and asked, "What about Cecily and Doug? And how did you get it to go off before the 30 seconds was up?"

"I pressed the timer when I set it down, hoping my body blocked the action. Obviously, it did since Lionel didn't suspect anything. Now, as far as his ex-wife and the right man she's now with, they'll live happily ever after."

"But he could find them."

"Doubtful," Jimmy said. "While I sent him to New York City, he'll be 100 years too early."

"What?"

"Honey," he put a hand on my cheek, "I sent him to New York City, but the year was 1852, not 1952. Luckily, he didn't look closely at the settings."

"What do we do when he returns?"

"Unfortunately, we won't be around anymore. Most likely, he'll have lived out his life as well."

"You didn't set it for 24 hours, did you?"

"I set it for a bit longer than that." He slid his hand down my sore arm and rubbed it gently.

I looked at him with a tilt of my head, waiting for the punch line.

Finally, he admitted, "It was set for 99 years. I'd say we have some time to prepare for his return—if it should ever happen."

"Have I told you how much I love you?"

"Not in the last day," he said, placing a soft kiss on my lips.

Releasing me, Jimmy scooped up my Family Slide from the table, and we walked together to the office. Locking it securely in the safe, he turned and said, "We're not going anywhere outside of our own time frame for at least a week. It's time we celebrate completing our thirtieth match."

"What have you got in mind?"

"Shhhh…no more questions. Go pack a bag for a long weekend. You'll want casual clothes, and one nice evening outfit. That's all you need to know. We leave tomorrow morning. If you don't mind, I'll need a few minutes alone on your computer."

Studying his face, he wasn't giving any other clues away. I had no idea what Jimmy had in mind, and I didn't care. The thought of moving on to a normal life that only involved our happiness, excited me. Turning on my heel, I went upstairs to get out my travel bag and do as he told me.

The next morning, we hopped in his car and drove north on Pacific Coast Highway. Working our way up the freeways to Santa Barbara, we aimed inland. Jimmy had a three-night stay booked at a little boutique hotel in the middle of Solvang, California. We spent the next three days touring intimate little wineries scattered about the Santa Ynez Valley.

We spoke of nothing but cabernets, syrahs and anything else wine related. Not one word was mentioned about the process or slides. It was sheer ecstasy. We even delved into wedding plans. While touring, we came across a small chapel that appealed to us both. Nuptials would probably take place right there in the not too distant future.

Once back home, I broached the subject of placing the final 30 slides with Cecily and Doug. After celebrating our fulfillment of our quota, we knew the time had come to finalize plans for Paolo, Jr.'s couples. The end to the process at last.

"Still feel this is the thing to do?" I asked Jimmy.

"No doubt in my mind. You?"

"It feels right. When do we go?"

"Tomorrow morning. We'll travel together. I think it would be best if you spoke with Cecily while I filled Doug in on his role. Despite the Suitor interviews being completed, Cecily will need guidance and insight. They have to do this together or not at all."

"I agree." Secretly I hoped this would be our last journey through time. Its appeal had waned, and I was finally ready to be done with the whole thing. I only hoped the process was finished with us.

The next morning, we enjoyed coffee on the porch as usual. Breathing in the fresh ocean air, I counted myself lucky to live in such a beautiful place full of life and happy activity. At 9:55 I retrieved my Family Slide from the safe and set the device for New York City in 1953—one year after Cecily had arrived on her final journey to begin life with Doug. Our arrival time would be noon. We decided 24 hours would be sufficient.

Standing in the studio, Jimmy and I faced each other holding hands. The box of slides hung awkwardly off his back in a large ruck sack. The smaller backpack hanging from my shoulders contained a few overnight things.

"Ready for one last blast through time?" I asked, squeezing his hands

"So long as it's with you," he winked. "Time to complete our roles."

As the thirty seconds counted down, we gazed into each

other's eyes. Having travelled a couple times together, I harbored no fears about our safety.

We arrived in a deserted alleyway between two high rise buildings. I wore a simple beige skirt and white blouse, while Jimmy had on tan khaki pants and a blue, short sleeved shirt. We decided to limit intimate contact while in public. Interracial couples were not widely accepted yet, but at least being in a large city, we could probably skate by without too much animosity.

Our arrival was next to Doug's apartment building. He resided in the penthouse, so we expected there to be some security. A bored looking guard sat at a desk, and barely looked up as we approached.

"Can I help you?" he asked, though his slouching demeanor transmitted that he really didn't want to.

"Yes," I spoke up. "We're here to see Doug Pendry. May we go up?"

"I'll have to ring him. Your names?"

"Sami Manchester and Jimmy Chang."

As I mentioned Jimmy's name, he took a good look. With vacant eyes and a bit of reddening in the face, he turned. I knew what he was thinking. What was a white woman doing with a Chinese man? While these were simpler times, they were also filled with small-mindedness.

Picking up the handset from a rotary telephone attached to the wall, he dialed a number. After only seconds, he spoke into the phone. "Yes, Mr. Pendry? You have visitors. A woman named Sami Manchester, and a Chinese man."

I grasped Jimmy's arm, attempting to quell my anger. Jimmy put his hand over mine, and gently rubbed. I knew he was telling me to calm down.

Out of the corner of his mouth he whispered, "This simpleton isn't worth it."

Taking a deep breath, I shook off my contempt as the guard hung up the phone and gestured toward the elevator. "You may go up, Miss Manchester."

He didn't even acknowledge Jimmy at all. Once again, his hand brushed against mine as I gripped his arm, and allowed him to lead me to the elevator. Neither one of us bothered to thank the guard.

Once in the elevator I said, "I really wasn't prepared for people's reaction."

"No worries, honey. The good thing is we won't be staying long."

I smiled and nodded. The elevator crawled upward to the twelfth floor, dinging as it passed each level. Finally arriving at the top, the doors slid apart. Before they'd completely opened, Cecily flung herself at me in an encompassing hug.

"Oh, Sami, it's so good to see you! Is Grandmother with you?"

Returning the hug, I said, "No, she's not."

Pulling back with fear in her eyes, she asked, "Is she all right?"

It never occurred to me she might leap to that conclusion. "Everything is fine. It's actually only one week after you left. Well, for us, anyway," I smiled.

Breathing a sigh of relief, she turned to Jimmy. "Don't think you get to escape my greeting." With that she threw her arms around his neck and pulled him into a warm hug. Jimmy returned the embrace. Pulling back Cecily asked indicating the back pack, "What's that you're toting?"

"Well, I guess you could call it a wedding gift for you and your...*husband?*" Jimmy asked.

Cecily stepped back and looked at him with narrowed eyes. Obviously, her curiosity was peaked.

Chapter 58

"Well," Cecily said, "you've got my attention. And yes, Doug and I tied the knot six months ago."

The elevator doors started to close, and Jimmy's hand shot out to stop them. We all laughed. "Perhaps," Jimmy said, we could come in?"

"Of course, sorry, didn't mean to way lay you in the elevator. Doug is in the studio, admiring my latest painting. I told him I wanted to be the one to greet you. He indulged me—as he always does," she said with a sly grin.

It gave my heart joy to see the happiness and love in this woman's eyes. Dede would be beside herself, if she could see the radiance her granddaughter exuded.

Entering their home, it hardly did justice calling it an apartment. The massive entryway had a vaulted ceiling spanning what should be two floors of the building. Artfully decorated with beautiful paintings of various cityscapes, I was sure Cecily had created them. Our footsteps echoed off the marble-tiled floor.

Doug came from a hallway off to the left. Despite having seen his portrait for years, it didn't prepare me for his finely chiseled features and good looks. Walking directly up to me, without a word, I was engulfed in a hug. After a moment, he pulled back. "Forgive me for my forwardness, but it truly is a pleasure to meet you, Sami. I can't thank you enough for sending this absolute treasure my way," he said looking lovingly at his bride.

Turning to Jimmy, he extended both his hands and warmly wrapped them around Jimmy's hand. "You, I've already met, but let me extend my thanks a second time to you, sir."

"It was our pleasure," Jimmy said. "Seeing the two of you beaming with joy, fills our hearts."

"They've brought us a wedding present too!" Cecily gushed.

Removing the bulky bag from his shoulders, Jimmy asked, "Is there someplace we can sit and talk?"

Cecily and Doug looked at each other, then back at us. "Of course," Doug said, "this way."

We walked into their living room. If I thought the entryway impressive, this room was even more incredible. It ran the length of half the building with huge picture windows looking out on Central Park. The furniture was clustered in a few intimate sitting areas. Doug gestured to a gold colored, overstuffed couch, while the two of them sat on the opposite sofa made of green and gold fibers.

"It isn't exactly a wedding present, but we hope it's a gift you will accept," I said.

"I'm sure whatever you've brought us is wonderful and..."

"Cecily, honey," Doug said putting his hand on her knee, "perhaps we should let them talk. While we're both excited to see them, there seems to be a serious tone to their visit."

Wow, I thought, he truly is intuitive. We'd barely had moments together, yet Doug picked up on the seriousness of our visit. More and more I believed we'd made the right decision.

"All right dear," Cecily said placing her hand over his.

They both turned to us with eyes wide. I could tell they were anxious to hear more.

"You see," I continued, "you two are very special. Not just in the way you were brought together, but to us as well. In this business, we're required to fulfill a quota of thirty couples. Your union completed our thirtieth match."

We all remained quiet a moment. Cecily broke the silence. "So, you two can essentially retire. Is that what you're saying?"

"Yes, I guess you could put it that way," Jimmy said.

"So, forgive me if I sound rude, but then why are you here?" Doug asked. "Not that we aren't happy to see you, but I can't imagine you're visiting all of your successful matches."

"Yes," Cecily added, "it's great to see the two of you. You're always welcome here."

"Ok, we'll cut to the chase," Jimmy said. "We've brought more than just a gift. We would like to present you with an opportunity. The same one we had that lasted thirty years."

I grasped his hand, he squeezed back. "You see," I said, "in this bag," I gestured toward the backpack Jimmy placed on the coffee table, "is a set of thirty slides. The slides of a Collector, who was murdered before he could complete his task."

Cecily grabbed onto Doug's arm. Both must have had an inkling of what we were getting at with this conversation.

"You want us to complete his matches," Cecily stated with excitement in her voice.

"Yes, we want you to complete his matches," I agreed, with relief. In that moment, I knew Paolo's dream of his son's job being completed would be fulfilled.

"How exactly do we do that?" Doug asked. "Would that mean I go back and interview all thirty Suitors?"

"Normally," Jimmy answered, "you would. But the interviews were completed before the man died. So, the slides used to do that are spent. You need to depend on the biographies he filled out on each Suitor, as well as your instincts, to complete each match. Is that something you two would be interested in?"

Cecily, bubbled with excitement. I could tell she wanted to take this on. Doug was a bit harder to read. If they chose to do this, he would be the voice of reason.

"This is quite a *gift* you're presenting us with," said Doug. Turning to his wife he continued, "and I suspect it isn't a task we should take on lightly. We'll need time to discuss it. How long are you here for?"

"I can see why you're a successful businessman. You grasp the concept quickly and give it careful consideration," Jimmy said. "We're here for 24 hours. Why don't you give us each a bit of time to talk to you about your individual roles? That way you'll be armed with all the particulars, and can decide if this life is right for the two of you. You also need to be aware of a few rules."

"Seems fair," Doug said with a nod of his head. "Tell me, why isn't his Photographer completing the matches? If the interviews were completed, she should have everything she needs."

"He never met his Photographer," I said. Jimmy and I agreed to not delve into the drama caused by Carney. It was best to leave it as the meeting never took place. "Besides, even though the Suitor interviews are done, it doesn't end the Collector's involvement. While the Photographer will be finding and qualifying the Betrotheds, she'll still need support and input from her Collector. It's always been a team effort, best handled by a compatible couple."

"Makes sense. I can't imagine it's a solo job. Well, Cecily, why don't you and Sami retreat to your studio. Jimmy and I can sit in here and talk."

"Ok, love," she said with a light kiss to his cheek. "Come on, Sami, I can show off my work too. I've got a show opening at a gallery on 5th Avenue next month. They like to highlight local artists, and hopefully launch their careers."

"Sounds wonderful," I said.

"Care for a brandy?" I heard Doug ask Jimmy as we left the room.

"Yes, thank you," Jimmy answered.

Cecily led me back through the entryway and down the hall Doug had greeted us from when we arrived. Her *studio* was more like a huge workshop. Twice the size of my photo studio, large picture windows lined the outside walls. I could see why it was the perfect place for her to craft her paintings.

The inner walls were filled with intricate cityscapes, that were obviously from all around the five Boroughs of New York. She also had some wonderful scenery paintings full of grapevines and farmscapes. Obviously, she had ventured out with her easel and oil paints to some of the surrounding areas.

Cecily noticed me admiring these last ones. "Those were inspired by our tour of the Long Island wineries."

"They're beautiful, as are all of your scenes. Now what are those over there? It looks like your subject is a child."

"I'm trying to branch out and vary my work. Those started as a gift for our neighbors on the third floor. That's their little boy, Todd. His mother heard I was a painter and asked if she could commission me to do a three-piece series of her son."

"What a wonderful idea. Will you use those in your show as

well?"

"I'm on the fence. The ones hanging in here are mine to keep. I've already delivered the ones our neighbor wanted. Painting a live subject was so exciting that I created several, and let her choose the three she liked best. I felt it was the least I could do, after she almost lost him."

Chapter 59

"Lost him? Was he sick?"

"No, the most amazing thing happened...the way we met, that is. Doug was coming home from work—his usual walk from the subway. Actually, it was two months ago today. He heard a child crying and looked up. The little boy hung from their balcony on the third floor. He must have climbed over the rail."

"Oh, my goodness, what happened?"

"He fell. Doug caught him and saved his life."

"Wow, what a hero."

"Yes, he is," she said beaming. "We've been friends with the family ever since. The mother is very sweet."

We fell into a comfortable silence. Finally, she spoke up about what was foremost on her mind. "So, Grandma made it back to New Mexico okay?"

"Honestly," I said turning toward her, "I haven't spoken to her since she left. I'm sure everything is fine, otherwise Milton would have contacted me."

Cecily nodded in agreement. "What happened with Lionel when I wasn't there anymore?"

"Dede was amazing. She went on and on convincing him he was crazy and that you'd already left for Europe. The man was so confused, he finally left in a huff."

"He just believed her?"

"What choice did he have? You were gone, and I was alone in my studio. Now, enough of that nonsense." I thought it best to leave out his final visit to my house. No need to worry her further. "Time to talk about the *process*, as we like to call it. It's no guess that you're interested. You do need to know all the details before making a final decision, however."

"Doug is more sensible than I am," she admitted. "I like to dive into things. Not always the best plan. He's got his hands full with me," she laughed.

"He seems quite all right with that."

"I guess you could say we complement each other. As I'm sure you've picked up, I'm ready to take this on, but Doug wants details. He's absolutely right. We do need all the specifics before making a final decision. I would like to know," she said hesitantly, "what happened to the Collector. How was he murdered?"

I pinched my lips together, wondering just how much I should share with her. Jimmy and I agreed it wasn't information they would need, but I also didn't anticipate her asking.

"That distresses you, doesn't it? Was he a close friend?"

"No, we'd never met. He was the son of a man we've gotten acquainted with accidentally. Paolo, the man we met, had been a Collector in his own time. Passing the torch on to his son, the young man wasn't able to complete the task. He'd witnessed the murder of a shop keeper, and the assailants chased and stabbed him as well." I felt guilty leaving out all the details, but again, that information wouldn't have any bearing on their decision to become part of the process.

"How awful!"

"Yes. His father asked Jimmy and I to complete the matches, but we're ready to bow out of this life. We did agree to help place the slides with another couple willing to carry on his son's work. It was actually Jimmy that suggested the two of you."

"There's symmetry in that, isn't there?

"Yes, I believe so. I always felt your grandmother would have made a great Photographer. Seeing so much of her in you, I thought this would be a good fit."

Smiling, Cecily clutched the necklace her grandmother had given her, then walked over to a small couch in the corner and gestured to the seat next to her. "Then you'd best fill me in on what I need to know about the...*process*."

We sat and talked for almost two hours. I filled her in on the details of how the Betrotheds will naturally cross her path. There wouldn't be much searching, as she would have thought. The magic of the slides would take over. I warned her about the use of the emergency slides, and the danger of repeating a location in time. It was also important to stress the fact that they were not to be used for personal gain, nor would their task be complete until all 30 couples were matched.

Before we knew it, the late afternoon sun shone through the windows, as the men knocked on the door of the studio.

"You girls about done?" Doug asked as he opened the door.

I looked at Cecily and she smiled. "Yes," I called, "I believe we are. How about the two of you?"

"Discussed enough to be dangerous," Jimmy said with a laugh.

"Then, it's time we took our leave and left these two to discuss the prospects," I suggested.

"Oh, won't you stay for dinner?" Cecily asked.

"Thank you," Jimmy said, "but I think we'll head off on our own. We'll be back in the morning."

"It won't be a bother," Doug said. "We're already expecting our neighbors, the Merchants, from the third floor for dinner. Two more won't be an issue."

"Thanks, I said, but we....wait, who are you expecting?" I asked.

"The family of the little boy I told you about—Todd Merchant and his parents," Cecily said, getting concerned as she looked at me. "Sami, are you all right?"

The color drained from my face as I reached down to steady myself on the arm of the couch. The room began to spin. Realizing I needed to sit down, my body collapsed onto the cushions. I leaned forward and held my head in my hands.

Jimmy rushed over and sat beside me. His arm reached around and pulled me close. "Sami, are you okay?"

"Does she need some water?" Cecily asked.

"No, no, she'll be all right," Jimmy said. "I think she needs some fresh air."

I looked up into his eyes. "Yes, fresh air is a good idea," I said, starting to recover. The reality of this way of life came full circle and slammed into me.

Jimmy helped me to my feet. "Don't worry, our lives have been so hectic lately. It's no wonder all this is catching up to her," he said, helping to support my weight with his strong arm. Whispering into my ear, he added, "Don't say anything."

"Well, if you're sure she's okay," Doug said.

"Yes," Jimmy assured him as he led me out of the studio and down the hall to the entryway. "I think we all need some time on our own. You two discuss what you've learned, and decide how you want to proceed. How about we return tomorrow at 9:00?"

"Sounds good," Cecily said, still concerned. "Sami, you'll be okay?"

"Oh, yes," I stuttered, starting to recover. "I'll be fine. I think the whirlwind of the last few days, and especially today, is catching up to me. We'll see you tomorrow."

Cecily hugged both Jimmy then me before we boarded the elevator. Doug waved, then wrapped his arm around his wife.

Once the doors closed, I nearly crumpled to the floor, but Jimmy managed to keep me on my feet.

At ground level we exited the elevator, ignoring the security guard's offer to hail a cab for us. It was a different man on duty than when we entered, obviously one that was open-minded and disregarded any racial opinions.

Walking out to the sidewalk, Jimmy flagged down a cab. I noticed he had grabbed my backpack and carried it over one shoulder. He told the driver to take us to the Plaza Hotel on 5th Avenue and Central Park South.

"Are you okay," Jimmy asked during our cab ride.

"Yes, but did you hear the name they said? Their neighbors are Carney and his parents. How does this happen?"

Jimmy sat there holding me. "It'll be okay. Just relax, sweetie. Our goal is to get Paolo, Jr.'s, slides delivered. I believe we'll accomplish that."

I leaned back taking deep breaths.

Chapter 60

Once checked into the hotel and up in our room, Jimmy ordered a light meal and bottle of wine from room service. All thoughts of enjoying the city and having a nice dinner out were erased.

"I thought you told me Carney grew up in San Francisco, close to your neighborhood?"

"He did mention moving there as a small boy. The family must have started here in New York City. I never questioned him much about his upbringing," Jimmy said.

I sat in the window looking out at the streets below. As much as I wanted to block out this new information, I couldn't help but view this as an opportunity. It wasn't a coincidence, the way everything happened. What to do about it though?

Turning away from the window, I shared with Jimmy the story Cecily told me of how Doug saved toddler Carney from falling to his death.

As he digested the story, there was a knock on the door. We froze.

Laughing to lighten the mood, Jimmy said, "I forgot I ordered room service. Back in a minute."

I breathed out, releasing some tension. Focusing back on the city below, I heard Jimmy letting in the bellman. The wheels of the delivery cart squeaked as he eased it into the room.

"Thank you, sir," a young male voice said—Jimmy must have tipped him. "Will there be anything else?"

"No thanks, we're good."

Alone again, Jimmy came over and grabbed my hand. He raised it to his lips and kissed the back.

"You're my hero, you know."

"Just keep reminding me," he said with a laugh.

"How did things go with Doug. Do you think he's interested?"

"He was a little hard to read. I believe he'll agree to it, more so to indulge his young bride. He truly is head over heels for Cecily."

"If his heart isn't in the process, it won't work," I pointed out.

"True enough. He doesn't strike me as someone that takes on a responsibility lightly. If he decides to do this, he'll be all in with no hesitation. You have a good feeling about Cecily, don't you?"

"Yes. No doubt in my mind she wants to take on those thirty matches and will devote her soul to making sure they're all a good fit."

Jimmy stood up and led me by the hand to the small dining table by the service cart. "Now, my dear, no more thoughts of the process for at least an hour. We have a wonderful bottle of Cabernet, accompanied by lobster bisque, a house salad with broiled chicken, and I even indulged in dessert."

"You ordered tiramisu, didn't you?" My excitement was clear. "I did indeed."

"I love you," I said kissing him before sitting down.

For the next hour and a half, we enjoyed a delicious meal with a wine no longer available in our current time. While dinner out on the town would have be fun, this was really what we both needed—an intimate evening together with no interruptions from outsiders. We were in our own bubble of time. It didn't matter what year we were in, this was *our* time.

Once finished with the meal and the cart pushed into the hallway, we decided to venture out for a walk down Fifth Avenue. New York City in the 1950's was a wonderful place to stroll on clean streets.

That night I slept like a stone and awoke refreshed at 6:00, finding Jimmy already up with a hot carafe of coffee waiting for me. There was a small bottle of Irish Cream to accompany our brew.

Enjoying our spiked coffee with a view of the city, it was the perfect morning. The sun shone as the bustle of rush hour took place on the streets below. After showering and getting dressed, we lounged around until it was time to head back to Doug and Cecily's apartment.

The same guard that worked last night when we arrived, monitored the podium. "Visiting the Pendry's?" he asked.

"Yes," Jimmy said.

After announcing our arrival, he gestured toward the elevator. "Sir, Ma'am, please go on up." He acknowledged both Jimmy and me with equal respect this time. I wondered about his change of heart, but not enough to inquire.

Both Cecily and Doug greeted us as the elevator doors slid open. This encouraged me that they were anxious to accept the opportunity presented to them.

"Please, come in," Doug said, as he led us into the living room. We sat in the same cozy seating area as yesterday. The box of slides resided on the coffee table between us. The couple must have been looking through them, as they were no longer inside the backpack.

"So," Jimmy began, "what do you think?"

Doug glanced at Cecily, who nodded at him with a smile. Looking back at us, he said, "We accept." With that he broke out into a big grin himself.

I jumped up and walked around the coffee table to hug Cecily. "I knew you would," I said, engulfing her in a warm embrace. She returned the squeeze with just as much zeal.

"You're both in agreement?" Jimmy asked.

"We are!" stated Cecily.

"Well then," Jimmy said, "I guess our work here is done. Do you have any more questions?"

The two of them sat there. Doug spoke up, "I think you've answered everything. Will we see you again?"

"No," Jimmy said. "The only connection I can offer you is a local proprietor that originally gave me my slides. Despite going there in the mid-1970's, Mr. Lin began his shop in the 1940's. It's in Chinatown called the Purple Lotus. Only go there if you run into a situation for which you need guidance. He should be able to answer any questions."

"We understand," said Doug.

We spent the remainder of the morning chatting. When we entered Cecily's studio to admire her artwork one more time, we all had another surprise. Lining the walls, amongst her own handy work, were thirty portraits of men in different eras before the 1950's.

"Where did those come from?" Cecily asked in awe.

"My guess," answered Jimmy, "was they appeared when you accepted the slides. You see, once I met Sami and she agreed to be my Photographer, the portraits appeared in the room she now uses as her studio. Since the two of you agreed to take on this task, they must have followed the slides here."

"Amazing," said Doug. "I guess if we had any doubts about this being the right decision, our affirmation is before us."

It never occurred to me we would need to have the portraits brought here for potential Betrotheds to see. This was truly spectacular.

While moving on to Cecily's paintings, I did my best to ignore the grouping of Carney's portrait as a child. Unfortunately, I felt myself drawn to the display. The morality struggled within me thinking how easy it would be to arrive two months earlier, and distract Doug long enough on his walk home from work.

Staring at the paintings, I felt Jimmy's hands on my shoulders. He had to know what was going through my mind. Giving me a squeeze, he turned me away from Carney's array.

The morning slipped away before we knew it, and the clock read 11:55. Our departure was at hand. Going back to the sitting area, Jimmy scooped up our small overnight backpack and slipped it on his shoulders.

"I guess this is it, then?" Doug asked.

"Yes, you're on your own. I believe you two will make a fabulous pair of matchmakers," I said.

"No doubt," Jimmy added. "Ready, sweetie?" he asked.

Giving both Cecily and Doug a hug, I turned to Jimmy. "I am now."

"Good luck you two. It really is a rewarding life," Jimmy said with a wave.

"I believe you're right. My love to Grandma and Grandpa."

"It will be conveyed," I said as Jimmy took both my hands in his.

We gazed into each other's eyes, until we stood back in my studio in Palos Verdes. I felt good about the final placement of Paolo's slides. I knew they would be well attended to. We felt it wouldn't be fair to Paolo, Sr., to keep him in suspense.

Hopping into Jimmy's car, we drove south to Laguna Beach. Paolo granted us entrance immediately and waited at the front door. His grin conveyed that he already knew the good news.

"The portraits are gone. I take it they accepted the task?" There was no doubt in his voice.

"Yes, Paolo, they did," I responded, as I walked up and threw my arms around his waist. He returned the embrace, while extending a hand to Jimmy.

"Please," he said, "come enjoy a glass of sparkling wine in celebration and honor of Junior."

"Of course," Jimmy said as he threw his arm around my shoulders. "We'd be honored."

After toasting what could only be described as victory, we returned home.

Our final chapter had closed.

Or had it?

Back at the house in Palo Verdes, we popped open a bottle of our favorite Merlot. Enjoying the wine out on the porch overlooking the South Bay, Jimmy grasped my free hand. "You're still thinking about Carney as a child, aren't you?"

"How can I not? We have the opportunity to stop him before it begins."

"By killing him?" Jimmy asked.

"Maybe that's how things were supposed to have played out. Carney should have fallen to his death as a child."

"Neither one of us is a murderer."

"It wouldn't be murder."

"Wouldn't it be?" Jimmy asked.

Setting my glass on the table I stood up and walked to the end of the porch. My steps echoed across the boards. He was right. Whether it's by my own hand or through diversion, it would still be murder.

"Think about it, sweetie, what if some actions in his life resulted in good? Those would be wiped out too. How can we be the judge of that?"

"He took lives. How many innocents died at his hands?" Turning to face him, I asked, "What about April?"

"What about her? It isn't our place to decide who lives or dies," Jimmy stated getting agitated.

"Yet he's allowed the choice? How does that work?" My tone escalated.

"Honey, come sit back down." He extended his hand to me, his voice softened. "This should be our time to contemplate retirement. The process is complete. It's time to walk away and focus on our own lives."

Returning to my seat and picking up the wine glass, I reeled my emotions in. "You're right—time to move on," I said staring out to the ocean.

Chapter 61

Standing on the street across from the Pendry's building, I watched the toddler playing on the balcony. By the way he looked up into the apartment every once in a while, someone obviously spoke to him through the open door. Probably a parent or nanny warning him to be careful.

All the furniture was placed at least a couple feet away from the wrought iron railing encircling the area. It was quite a large platform—one only found in an upscale city neighborhood. The boy brushed his blond hair out of his eyes as he crawled between the rail and the back of a wicker couch, pushing a toy car.

Finally, a young woman walked out onto the balcony and the boy dutifully went over to her as she bent down giving him a kiss and hug. Patting him on the head, she went back inside and he resumed focus on his little car and its travels.

A few minutes later I noticed her walking across the intersection nearest the front entryway to the building. Returning my focus to the balcony, a man stood in front of the boy. With his back to me, even from this distance, he looked too old to be the boy's father. He sported a full head of gray hair. The tyke looked up at him, smiled, then went about his game.

The gentleman pushed the wicker chair on the side up against the railing. I noticed the couch sat in a new position, backed up against the wrought iron as well. He even carried the small glass topped coffee table over and set it in the corner.

What was he doing? I wondered.

After completing his rearrangement of the furniture, the man gazed down at the child still playing. Shaking his head, he turned and looked directly at me. I recognized him immediately— Francois. He nodded his head once in acknowledgement.

Unable to move for a moment, the shock overwhelmed me. With his gaze still focused on my face, Francois disappeared.

Quickly looking back at the child, I saw him swiveling his head, probably wondering where his grandfather had gone. Abandoning his toy, the boy got up and spun around once taking in the whole balcony. Jumping up onto the couch, Carney leaned over the back. Placing his little foot on the arm, he pushed further up over the top and toward the rail.

Recovering my wits, I looked at my watch and realized I stayed here watching too long. Hurrying down the sidewalk at a brisk pace, I rounded the corner. There were other pedestrians, but not so dense that I couldn't get through.

Scanning the sparse crowd for Doug, I spied him strolling along with his briefcase in one hand. My thoughts suddenly went blank, not sure what I should say to delay his trek. Being so intent on getting here, it never occurred to me to have a valid reason planned out.

He was still half a block away. The scene from the balcony played out in my mind—the child brushing hair from his eyes, a young mother kissing her son good-by, Francois enabling the boy to climb over the rail. It all swirled out of control. Did I have the right to take that woman's child away? Francois had been ready and knew I was here to help. Would it be considered right or wrong to allow the boy to live, knowing the man he would become?

Standing motionless on the sidewalk, the people passing me became blurred. The only one I could focus on was Doug, as he drew closer. Now in front of me, he had to step a little to the side to get around. With a brief smile, he nodded in my direction and kept walking. I let him.

People continued to swarm past me until I stepped aside to lean against the nearest wall. My breath came in gasps, then finally sobs.

Behind me a male voice asked, "Are you all right, ma'am? Can I help you with anything?"

Standing up straight, I felt the plush carpet underneath my feet. With tears streaming down my cheeks, I stood in front of the bench facing the table where the Family Slide should have been. It was gone. Turning slowly around, the portraits looked the same as they had before I left. They were filled with happy couples smiling at each other. Instead of the thirty I'd hoped for upon taking this journey, there remained only twenty-six.

Wandering out into the hall, I heard noises in the kitchen. As I walked through the doorway, Jimmy turned around from where he stood by the stove cooking dinner. Setting a spatula on the counter, he walked toward me with his arms open. I fell into them and buried my face in his chest.

"You couldn't do it, could you?"

Shaking my head back and forth, still pressed to his body, he squeezed me tighter. Jimmy knew I wouldn't go through with it in the end. That's probably why he didn't stop me from going. He left for work this morning, without mentioning a word of how I shouldn't take the journey.

Releasing his hold, while keeping one arm around me, Jimmy led us to the living room. Sitting down on the couch, the tears finally stopped. I wiped the remaining moisture away with the backs of my hands.

"Do you want to tell me what happened?"

"Some other time. It doesn't matter now. I failed and didn't save those women."

"They weren't yours to save. If you had, it would make you no better than Carney."

Gazing into Jimmy's sparkling blue eyes, I said, "The process is over. Doug and Cecily would have placed all of their matches by now."

"Yes," he said, "and now it's time for us to focus on the rest of our lives together. It's our time."

"Believe it or not, I'm ready for that to happen."

"Good. We'll start after dinner with a roaring blaze in the fireplace," he nodded toward the other side of the room.

Looking over at the hearth, I saw a stack of logs ready to be lit. Atop the pile, sat my Family Slide.

ABOUT THE AUTHOR

Terry Segan currently calls the state of Nevada home. Most weekends she can be found riding backseat on a red Victory Cross Country Tour, heading for the beach, mountains or anywhere else her gypsy soul cares to wander. Exploring new places, be it cities or backroads, is a passion she shares with her boyfriend, who indulges these travel cravings every chance he gets. The musings conjured by her imagination while riding on the back of the bike can be found throughout the pages of her writing.

Look for her next book, Precious Treasure, publishing in 2019—a thriller with a paranormal twist. A grieving widow must discover the connection between her missing husband and the journal of a long-dead Confederate soldier. As this mystery unfolds and her life unravels, Janie discovers things about the man she thought she knew, while experiencing other-worldly encounters.

Made in the USA
San Bernardino, CA
22 December 2018